BROKEN TRUST

BROKEN TRUST

Una-Mary Parker

First published in 1999 by Headline Book Publishing

Compass Press Large Print Book Series; an imprint of
ISIS Publishing Ltd, Great Britain, and Bolinda Press, Australia
Published in Large Print 2000 by ISIS Publishing Ltd,
7 Centremead, Osney Mead, Oxford OX2 0ES,
and Bolinda Publishing Pty. Ltd,
17 Mohr Street, Tullamarine, Victoria 3043
by arrangement with Headline Book Publishing Ltd

British Library Cataloguing in Publication Data

Parker, Una-Mary
Broken trust. – Large print ed.
1. Large type books
I. Title
823.9'14 [F]

Australian Cataloguing in Publication Data

Broken Trust/Una-Mary Parker
– (Compass Press large book series)
1. Large print books.
2. Domestic fiction.
I. Title
823.914

ISBN 1–74030–136–6 (hb) 1–74030–137–4 (pb)
(Bolinda Publishing Pty. Ltd)
ISBN 0–7531–6282–2 (hb) 0–7531–6285–7 (pb)
(ISIS Publishing Ltd)

Printed and bound by Antony Rowe, Chippenham and Reading

This is for all
the family
with lots of love

CHAPTER ONE

"I can't believe he's getting married again." Elizabeth looked at the others, stunned. They were all in a state of shock.

"Well, at least we know now why he invited us all up here for the weekend," her brother Giles replied sadly. "I had a nasty feeling he was up to something." He stood by the tall windows of the library, gazing disconsolately at the russet-gold of the autumnal trees edging the River Avon as it wound its way through their land. This time last year their mother Rosalind had died "bravely after a long illness", according to the announcement in *The Times*, but in reality in great pain and with a loss of dignity that was heart-rending to witness. And now their father was remarrying.

Margaret, who'd been married to Giles for the past three years, shifted anxiously on the sofa, already sensing that her position as the wife of Nick Driver's eldest son and heir was about to be threatened, if not usurped. Ever since her mother-in-law's death she'd assumed the role of mistress-in-waiting of Wingfield Court when she and Giles came to stay. But now, in spite of his devastation at Rosalind's death, here was Nick, at fifty-eight, proudly announcing he intended getting married again to someone called Philippa Sykes who, it had transpired on closer questioning, was only thirty-one.

"Frankly, I'm appalled," Margaret said forcefully, adding hurriedly, "it's so hurtful for all of you."

She glanced at Elizabeth, the eldest of the family, and at Giles, already going bald at twenty-seven. Then there were the younger two, Jonathan, who was already a successful artist at twenty-three, and Cathy, in her first year at university; the four offspring of Nick and Rosalind. She tried to gauge their inner feelings at this moment of crisis and wondered what they were thinking. They'd all been so close to their mother and seemed so deeply shocked now she doubted if the realization that Nick was to share his future years with another woman had really sunk in.

Jonathan, tall and lanky and looking much younger than his age, with his fair hair flopping over his eyes and his skin pale and unblemished, lay sprawled in an armchair. When he was working in his London studio he was full of energy, a dynamic figure who thought nothing of standing at his easel for hours, oblivious of time, forgetting to eat and living on his nerves. But the minute he stopped it was as if he'd switched off completely.

He turned to look at his sister-in-law Margaret, sitting on the sofa on the opposite side of the library fireplace, seeing her through the eyes of an artist. She was very plump, with ginger hair and a sharp-nosed face covered in freckles, and he couldn't help being reminded of an inquisitive Buff Orpington hen.

"Well, I suppose as long as he's happy, it's OK," he replied lazily, "but I don't see how anyone can take Ma's place and I hope she doesn't try."

No one had so far actually said their future stepmother's name, as if that would be the final betrayal.

Instead they sank into silence again, contemplating this unwelcome intrusion into their family circle. The weather had turned crisply cold during the last couple of days, after a long languid Indian summer, and the chill in the atmosphere seemed to echo the cold sense of dread they were feeling.

Each of them was recalling the events of the previous evening when they'd all arrived for the weekend in happy ignorance. It was like watching a complex play whose meaning eluded them.

Their presence had of course been requested by their father who at times still treated them like children.

"Arrive by seven o'clock," he'd instructed them, not bothering to ask if they were free or if it was convenient for them to travel to Wiltshire on a Friday evening.

"That will give us time for a drink before dinner at eight," he'd continued, and then added mysteriously, "I have a surprise for you all."

They'd each secretly hoped the surprise would be something which they could enjoy together as a family. Some time ago Nick had talked about them all spending Christmas in St Lucia: "Anything to get away from turkey and stuffing and the ghastliness of it all here," he'd said. But Jonathan couldn't help praying his father had bought a boat, while Elizabeth fantasized that Nick would say he'd taken a chalet in Switzerland so they could all go skiing next March.

Last night's surprise had not been at all what they'd expected. Elizabeth and her husband, Laurence Vickers, had been the first to arrive, driving over in the Range Rover from their farm house in Northamptonshire. They'd left their three small children behind on this occasion because they were all recovering from measles, but Laurence's mother and the current au pairs were looking after them and, as Elizabeth said to her husband, probably spoiling them to death so they'd be quite unmanageable for the rest of the week.

Cathy arrived soon after, tired and stressed from having driven all the way down from Edinburgh University where she was reading English but excited as always to be home again. Then Jonathan appeared with Giles and Margaret who also lived in London and had given him a lift. They had had to drop off a table at Margaret's mother's on the way and Jonathan had been squashed into the back of their car with it for almost the entire journey.

"It was hell on horseback," he cried, stretching his long limbs as he climbed out.

"Jonno, you're such an old queen." Cathy laughed fondly as he dropped his baggage in the middle of the hall and slumped dramatically onto a carved chest which held picnic rugs.

"Less of the 'old', my dear!" he retorted. Jonathan never minded his siblings teasing him about being gay, but he could be touchy with outsiders.

"For God's sake, Jonno, count yourself lucky you didn't have to catch the train," said Giles.

The two brothers had never been close. While Jonathan was immersed in the arts and had his own circle of friends, Giles had recently been made a director of Bartwell's, the biggest philately company in Britain with branches all over the country. He worked in the London head office.

As soon as they'd all entered the hall of Wingfield Court they'd realized something was up. Elizabeth immediately noticed that vases had been filled with flowers, something Rosalind had always insisted on but which their father had not kept up in the past year. There were fires lit in every room and all the lights had been turned on, filling the house with cheerful warmth and the scent of lilies.

Nick Driver, with his handsome face tanned as usual and his dark hair combed smoothly back from his forehead, came to greet them, dark eyes alight with eagerness. He was grinning delightedly and full of bonhomie.

None of them could remember when they'd last seen him look so happy. Or so young and buoyant. Dressed in cream moleskin trousers and a sky blue shirt open at the neck, he'd exuded an energy and joyfulness that had been lacking in him since Rosalind's death.

"Come in, darlings! Lovely to see you. Come and get warm and we'll have drinks," he'd exclaimed when they'd arrived. He grabbed cases and coats and kissed and hugged them as he led them through the large hall which was furnished with dark red velvet sofas, Jacobean tables and chests, its walls hung with tapestries. In the deep brick fireplace apple wood burned brightly and filled the air with its evocative aroma. The chill of a purple twilight which was closing in over the surrounding hills and valleys was forgotten as they gathered around the comforting warmth of the library fire, greeting each other affectionately and catching up on the family news.

It had been Jonathan, who had never been intimidated by his father as Giles was still inclined to be, who had finally asked why they'd all been asked for the weekend.

"So what gives, Dad? Have you won the lottery or what?"

But Nick had kept them in suspense, enjoying his moment of power.

"Let's have a drink, get you settled in your rooms and have dinner first. Then I'll tell you my surprise," he'd replied teasingly.

"And when it came it was more of a bloody shock than a surprise," Giles had whispered as they'd all finally gone up to bed after what seemed like a very long and emotional evening.

When their father had announced, brandy glass in hand, standing with his back to the ornate fireplace in the drawing room after dinner, that he was getting married again, there was a collective gasp of horror. It was the last thing any of them had expected.

"Well, aren't you going to congratulate me?" he asked with forced joviality as his family sat looking at him in stunned silence. Cathy could see his eyes were filling with disappointment at their reaction and his tanned face became gaunt, the skin stretched over his cheek bones.

She tried to smile at him but as the news sank in felt sick with misery at the thought that he was bringing someone into the family who might try to take their mother's place — not in their life, perhaps, but certainly in his. In his house . . . and in his bed. And would this step-mother want to do things differently?

Cathy thought of all their little family traditions at Christmas, at Easter, and if they were home for their birthdays; customs that their mother had insisted on, and which had made these annual events so special. Would that all change? Would their father let it change? She heard Elizabeth give a strangled sob and knew that somehow she must put on a show of being pleased, for her father's sake.

"Congratulations, Daddy," she said hastily, jumping up from the sofa and running to kiss him. "That's wonderful news. I hope you'll be terribly happy." Don't cry, she told herself fiercely. You're not a baby. You're nineteen. You *have* a life and Dad hasn't had one for the past year. Of course you miss Mummy, you'll always miss her, but she'd have wanted Dad to be happy. Be glad for him. Stop being a selfish brat . . .

But, oh, it was going to be so hard! Digging her nails into the palms of her hands, she struggled for composure, hearing the others mutter something about hoping he'd be happy. But nobody was fooled.

"It's going to be all right," Nick told them confidently, pretending not to notice their stunned reaction. "You've nothing to worry about. In fact, you'll all love Philippa. She's incredibly sweet and kind and when we met we were instantly attracted to each other."

"Isn't this all rather sudden, Dad?" Giles asked uneasily. His father had been lonely since their mother had died, that he could understand. And because he was lonely he was vulnerable. It was also a well-known fact that Nick Driver was very rich, as they would all be one day, thanks to the trust fund that had been set up by their grandfather. But it was a truism that there was no fool like an old fool, and how many gold diggers had gone after rich widowers in the history of mankind? It was a hideously clichéd situation which could threaten not only his father's future happiness but the comfort and stability of the whole family.

"No, it's not a sudden decision at all," Nick replied smoothly, as if he'd been expecting one of them to put forward that argument. "When something is right, you know it. And when that's the case, there's no point in hanging around. Her name is Philippa Sykes and she's the daughter of Sir Archie and Lady Sykes. She's never been married before . . ." And that was when he told them she was thirty-one.

". . . and she works in Christie's silver department," he continued, but they weren't listening. The figure thirty-one had obliterated everything else from their minds, mesmerizing them with its potential significance.

"That means she's only two years older than me," Elizabeth blurted out before she could stop herself.

"Thirty-one?" Jonathan echoed, suddenly sitting upright. "Dad, you're doing a bit of cradle snatching, aren't you? She's young enough to be your daughter."

"That's a year younger than *me*!" Margaret exclaimed. Then she had a horrifying thought. At thirty-one this woman would probably want to have a baby. Start a family even. In a few years Wingfield Court could be crawling with masses of new little Drivers. The very thought of it set Margaret's heart pounding with frustration. She was desperate to have a baby herself, to give Giles an heir and Nick a grandchild to dangle on his knee . . . she managed to stifle a sigh but felt sick with longing.

But Giles was not thinking of babies at this moment. He was racking his brains to think of a way his father could be deflected from a disastrous liaison. How could this young woman make him happy for a start? Nick was a sophisticated, much-travelled man, a director of several public companies and former chairman of an investment company. Dad's worldly and experienced, Giles reflected. Philippa's going to need to be quite something to keep up with him.

"When were you thinking of getting married?" he asked cautiously.

Nick's smile broadened, showing expensively capped teeth, white against his tanned skin.

"Before Christmas," he replied, immediately. "Philippa's handed in her notice at Christie's and she'll be moving up here in about a month's time."

Laurence, who had been sitting in silence beside Elizabeth, suddenly spoke up.

"And when are we going to have the pleasure of meeting your intended?"

Nick raised his chin. "Philippa's arriving in time for lunch tomorrow. She's so looking forward to meeting you all."

Cathy climbed wearily into bed. It was the only place she'd feel safe and able to cope with this new family drama. For all her efforts at appearing delighted at her father's news, she felt sad and confused; wanting him to be happy yet wishing a new woman in his life wasn't the answer. By this time tomorrow she'd have met her future step-mother — it was a frightening thought.

If only her mother was still alive, she reflected, snuggling down under the duvet. Then life would have been perfect. She loved being at university and was absorbed in her English studies. Her boyfriend, Jack Hamilton, who was also nineteen, was reading politics. He shared a house with four other men while Cathy's rented house in India Street was shared by three other girls. She and Jack spent every moment they could together, though, and had become very close, closer than she'd ever been with anyone. She had told him all her secrets and shared with him the pain of her mother's death. In return he'd praised her for being strong and promised her she'd never be alone again.

Strong, she thought, as she curled up on her side. That was a joke! Jack wouldn't think her strong if he saw her now, quivering at the thought of the future, wondering if this Philippa Sykes would be one of those brassy blondes, over-friendly, over-dressed, and obviously going for gold.

Still awake at one in the morning, Cathy had by then persuaded herself that Philippa would want to tart up the house with flash furnishings, invite all her ghastly friends to stay, and whistle through Dad's money like a dose of salts.

God! Tomorrow's going to be hell, she reflected, trying to find a comfortable position. Giles will be grumpy and Margaret resentful. Elizabeth will weep and Laurence will pretend nothing's happening. And Jonathan? He'll be flippant and jokey, to cover up his real feelings. And all the while Daddy will be trying to put a good face on the situation in front of the young woman he has promised to marry.

Cathy, who would do anything short of downright lying in order to avoid confrontations or rows, clambered out of bed, unable to sleep for worrying, wondering if she should try to appear happy in order to please her father.

Looking out of her bedroom window which overlooked the stables, now a place for parking motor mowers, golf buggies, motor-scooters and bikes but once the home of the family's ponies, she fell into a nostalgic mood.

When she'd been small she'd loved hearing the comforting sounds of the horses shuffling around in their stalls when she'd awakened on summer mornings . . . and why, in one's childhood memories, was it always summer? There'd be the clop of hoofs on cobbles, the swish of hay being tugged gently from the mangers and an occasional contented snort or whinny, as if they were beckoning her to come riding. She sighed. Those days had been untouched by adult knowledge or understanding. Life had been so simple then and she'd been sure things were going to stay as they were forever.

They no longer kept ponies. Going away to boarding school and university had brought fresh interests into their lives, and then Elizabeth and Giles had left home to get married and soon after Jonathan had hit the flesh pots of London, so Nick had sold Paddy, White Socks, Dainty and Taffy, and the smell of diesel and petrol soon replaced the earthy scent of hay and manure, and thus their equestrian interests had come to an end, signalling also the end of their childhood.

In the darkness the stables stood silent and deserted now, and Cathy mourned the loss of her childhood and the end of an era. Tomorrow even greater changes would befall Wingfield Court and she felt a deep sense of foreboding at the prospect.

Along the corridor, in what had originally been a large spare room but which Elizabeth had been promoted to since her marriage, she sat up in bed, reading, while Laurence lay silent and inert, his face turned away from her.

Elizabeth's one luxury was getting into bed at night with a good book. It was the moment she looked forward to all day and relished when it was realized. With a large rambling farm house to look after, three children under the age of six, four dogs, two cats, three rabbits and a goat called Geraldine, she had her hands more than full, in spite of the help of a couple of Austrian au pairs whom she had thought would be two girls when she'd booked them through an agency but had turned out to be an engaged couple, Herta and Gerhard. Then there was her mother-in-law, Laura Vickers, who lived in a cottage in the grounds but who seemed to spend all her time at the farm, poking her nose into everything they did and ruining the children's teeth by sneaking them bags of sweets when no one was looking.

Elizabeth snuggled deliciously deeper under the duvet and started chapter four of *A Woman with a Past*. Delving into the tempting pages of lust-filled fiction was her only respite from unrelenting domesticity, her one indulgence and temporary escape from the long journey through marriage and motherhood.

But tonight she couldn't concentrate. All she could think about was how hurt Mummy would have been to know she was being replaced so quickly. Of course she was aware Rosalind had wanted Nick to marry again, knowing that he was a man who needed a woman in his life . . . but surely not so soon? And not to someone they'd never even met; someone only two years older than herself.

Elizabeth put down the book and tried to imagine what this would mean. Philippa Sykes sitting in Mummy's chair at the opposite end of the table from Dad. Philippa Sykes running Wingfield Court as if she owned the place. Philippa Sykes sleeping with their father . . .

Laurence only turned to look at her when he heard her sobbing.

"There's nothing you can do about it," he observed quietly.

"Maybe not, but that doesn't mean I have to like it," Elizabeth wept.

"It won't affect you, though. This isn't your home any longer. If you don't like her, just don't come back here. It's as simple as that."

She stopped crying to turn and stare at him as if she couldn't believe what she was hearing.

"Of course it's my home!" she protested. "It's where I was born. I love coming to stay, and so do the children."

Laurence stared at the ceiling, his expression pained. "I'm aware Willow Farm probably seems like a dump to you after this place, but it's our home now."

"That's not what I mean and you know it," she replied crossly, reaching for the box of tissues on the bedside table.

"Well, then." But he wasn't mollified. He moved his long thin limbs restlessly and ruffled his dark hair in a nervous gesture. "Why don't you let your father get on with his life while we get on with ours? What he does has nothing to do with us. Stop interfering."

"I'm not interfering, but we don't know anything about this woman so how can we just welcome her with open arms? You seem to forget Mummy only died last September. And if you've got over her death, *I* haven't." She started weeping again, great tears running down the sides of her face into the pillow, a tissue held to her mouth.

Laurence remained silent for a few minutes, staring ahead, wondering if Elizabeth would be equally upset if anything happened to him. She'd seemed to love him when they'd first got married eight years ago and had thrown herself into life at Willow Farm, apparently delighted to have a place of her own. But that devotion had gradually seemed to shift away from him when the children were born. It was she, with her private income, who had been the one who could afford to have help in the house, put in extra bathrooms, enlarge the kitchen —

and of course buy expensive toys for the children. There were even moments when he felt he was only there as a token figure, the necessary other half of a marriage.

"Nothing will ever be the same again," Elizabeth said, breaking into his thoughts.

It hasn't been the same for a long time, Laurence thought unhappily as he turned off his bedside light and rolled away from her.

"That you, Pip?" Jonathan asked, holding his mobile phone to his ear as he sat on the loo in what had originally been the nursery bathroom on the top floor of the house but which had become his quarters when Cathy went away to boarding school. The night nursery was now his bedroom, and the day nursery a games room with television and video. Otherwise little had changed. The toy cupboard still stood in one corner, and the comfortable old sofa they used to clamber all over was still placed in front of the fireplace. Even the safety bars remained fixed to the windows, and a lampshade emulating a drum hung from the centre of the ceiling. But vividly coloured posters had replaced framed pictures of Peter Rabbit and Pooh Bear, and one weekend Jonathan had painted the walls a deep sapphire blue, thinking all the while with amusement how their old dragon of a nanny would have hated it.

"Are you there, Pip?" he called, through a series of buzzing noises.

Pip, with whom he shared a flat in London, sounded very far away, almost on another planet. "It's me. Ring me back," Jonathan shouted, switching off.

A minute later his mobile rang. This time the line was clearer.

"What's up?" Pip asked. "Why are you calling at this hour?"

"Where have you been? I've been trying to ring you all evening. Been on the town, have you, in the old sling-backs?"

Pip laughed. "What else does one do on a Friday night?"

"Any luck? Where did you go?"

"Bliss, of course. It's the only decent club at the moment, and no, I didn't have any luck tonight. There was no talent around worth talking about. So what's your news? Don't tell me there's a rave-up in Malmesbury."

Jonathan chuckled. "That would be something! No, I rang because my dad's shocked us all to death tonight. He's getting married again!"

Pip made loud mock yawning sounds. "God, how boring. I thought you had something riveting to tell me."

"It's a bit of a family crisis," Jonathan pointed out, knowing that while he could be flippant himself, Pip was unlikely to treat any subject seriously. "She's young enough to be his daughter . . ."

"Glad to hear the old boy can still get it up, or is his coffee laced with Viagra these days?"

"Fuck off, Pip. It's causing a big upset here. Elizabeth's been crying her eyes out all evening, and Cathy's been doing her let's-be-brave-in-spite-of-our-broken-hearts performance. It's no laughing matter," Jonathan said heatedly.

"OK, OK, I'm sorry. But what's it to you? You don't live at home any more. You needn't go within a hundred miles of your pa if you don't want to. Live and let live, old thing."

Jonathan felt unreasonably upset. He'd phoned Pip because he'd thought he'd be sympathetic, instead of which he was treating the whole thing as a joke.

"If that's all you've got to say, up yours!" he shouted, switching off the mobile furiously. He realized he was having a major sense of humour failure but nobody knew, beneath his banter, how much he actually missed his mother.

Rosalind had been the one who had shown him instant and unconditional love and understanding when he'd gone to her, at the age of seventeen, to confess he was gay. He'd supposed, in his early teens, that mucking about with other boys at public school was a phase most teenage males went through. Everyone seemed to be at it at Newton College, having races wanking under their desks during class to see who could come the quickest without being detected by the teacher, messing around in the showers, and the final bliss at fourteen of rutting like rabbits after lights out.

He'd imagined it was just a way of experimenting with sex, until the glorious day arrived when girls would be the object of desire; a wet run, so to speak, to get in a bit of practice. But that day never came, and when he fell deeply and hopelessly in love with a boy he met at a party during the Christmas holidays, just after his seventeenth birthday, he knew he was drawn exclusively towards his own sex. It had put an end to all his expectations of getting married, and particularly of becoming a father. That hurt a lot. He loved children and had always presumed he'd have a family of his own one day.

Without fear of rejection, knowing instinctively his mother would understand, he'd told her everything as they walked through the grounds of Wingfield Court one sharp wet day in April when the wind flung the rain into their faces and their feet sank into the mud.

Rosalind had listened with quiet attentiveness and then she had turned and hugged him, her cheek pressed to his. When she spoke it was with sympathy and love.

"I've always suspected this was the way things would be with you, my darling," she'd told him, "and the most important thing in life is that you should be true to yourself." Then she'd linked her arm into his and they'd strode on in their wet mackintoshes, she with a battered old felt hat crammed on her head and water trickling down her cheeks. He wasn't sure whether it was tears or rain.

"That way you'll never go wrong, and you'll never hurt anyone else," she continued. "Thank God this isn't the fifties or sixties. No problems with the law nowadays and people have a much greater understanding. It's nothing to be ashamed of." Then she'd stopped and looked at him tenderly.

"I do hope you find happiness, you deserve that," she'd said softly. "It won't always be as easy for you as it will for the others, but remember, I'll always be here for you if you want to talk about it."

That had been five years ago. Now she was no longer here with her words of support and comfort and her reassuring presence. Jonathan crawled into bed without bothering to have a bath. He felt cold and tired and deeply wretched. The news his father had imparted had reopened the wounds of last year and exposed the depth of his grief.

Margaret bathed with care, having liberally splashed her favourite Gardenia bath oil into the steaming water. Her body, plump and peachy, broke the cloudy surface with its undulating curves as she soaped herself slowly and languorously, knowing it was the right time of the month to get pregnant and even fantasizing about how wonderful it would be if she and Giles were to conceive a baby here, in Wingfield Court, where he himself had been conceived.

Her desire for a child was like a gnawing pain that wouldn't go away. How long had they been trying? They'd been married for nearly four years and never in that time had . . . Oh, God, let it be tonight, she thought desperately. Dominating her thoughts was this new fear, too. If Philippa Sykes got pregnant before her it would be galling in the extreme. It would be an admission of failure and everyone would look at her pityingly and whisper behind her back that she must be barren.

Giles, having had his bath first, was already in bed when she re-entered their room. He was absorbed in a newspaper article and didn't look up as she seated herself at the dressing table, wrapped only in a semi-transparent negligee she'd bought at Harrods, it having been suggested to her by the assistant that it was "beautifully seductive". Was *she* beautifully seductive?

She wished she wasn't speckled all over with freckles, which only added to the reddish tinge of her skin. She wished her hair wasn't quite so stridently ginger. And she wished she had one of those willowy figures that could drape itself across sofas with languid elegance. Instead she was rather more like a tightly stuffed upright bolster, but what could she do about that? Dieting had never worked.

Dabbing perfume behind her ears, between her breasts and on her wrists, she slipped off her negligee and, naked, got into bed beside Giles, who smiled at her uncertainly.

"I want you, darling," she whispered, pressing her hot body against his. The newspaper slipped from his fingers and without demur he put his arms around her and lay by her side.

Skilfully, because she'd been sexually experienced before she met Giles, she kissed him, biting his bottom lip gently, flicking her tongue around his open mouth while her hands stroked his chest, working their way slowly around his ribs, waist and hips, and then up and down his spine until she squeezed his buttocks. She sucked the lobe of his ear and ran her tongue down his neck, knowing all his erogenous zones as if she was following the route of a well-studied map. Then she slid down the bed and took his flaccid penis in her mouth, coaxing it to become stiff and strong, willing it to become erect, while all the time her hands deftly stroked and probed and squeezed in an effort to stimulate him.

Giles responded but he had not studied the female body in the same way nor did he have her experience; he sucked gently at her large nipples, and vaguely stroked between her legs, but remained largely inactive by comparison while she worked until her jaws ached and her hands grew tired. At last, he was stiff enough to penetrate her.

"Oh, yes!" she whispered excitedly, shifting position to kneel astride him and hold him so he could enter her. At last, at last, she thought jubilantly. Thirty minutes of dedicated stimulation had worked. She started to plunge down on him, desperate to feel him inside her, desperate for his seed to impregnate her ripe and willing body — but at that moment his erection died on him, shrivelling away in a second like a deflating balloon and he was once again as flaccid as a new-born baby.

Margaret slumped, filled with despair. This was what always happened. Every bloody time they attempted sex, Giles was unable to maintain an erection.

"I'm sorry." He swore, in frustration. "Let me have a go." He started to jerk his penis roughly and angrily while Margaret lay back, exhausted. She let him get on with it, making no further effort to arouse him. There was nothing she could do. Over the years she'd read every book on the subject and had tried every recommended method of bringing an impotent man to erection and ejaculation, but nothing worked with Giles. And the worst part of it all was he was in complete denial about his condition. He wouldn't go to a doctor or a sex therapist; wouldn't even talk to *her* about it. It was as if they had a perfectly normal sex life. Whenever she mentioned wanting a baby, he'd smile and say reassuringly, "It'll happen one day."

"No, it's no use," she heard him say eventually. "Are you going to read for a bit?"

Read? She felt so maddened with anger and frustration that she could have hit him. No, she didn't want to read. What she wanted was to be fucked rigid, have multiple orgasms and be made pregnant. She'd had such hopes for tonight, too, though now she wondered why. Because Giles was in his old home? Because talk of Nick remarrying might just have made him feel a bit randy? Because he hadn't had too much to drink?

Margaret got into her nightdress and lay down on the farthest edge of the bed, weeping silently with frustrated rage, her body tormented by its lack of fulfilment. She curled up in a foetal position, her hand pressed to her mouth. After a while she pretended she'd gone to sleep. Giles read for a bit and then turned out the light and settled himself on his side of the bed.

She lay listening to his breathing and as soon as it became even, surreptitiously gave herself the only pleasure she knew these days.

Nick Driver stayed up late, wanting to cheek that everything was right for tomorrow because it was a momentous day for his entire family and he felt as nervous and excited as a twenty year old.

Philippa had already stayed at Wingfield Court. In fact he'd invited her for a weekend shortly after they'd met, wanting to impress her with the stately home his father, Henry Driver, had bought from the Earl of Drysdale during the 1930 depression. Having inherited a vast fortune in steel from Nick's grandfather, George Driver,

Henry had wanted to provide his descendants with a grand setting, and so the beautiful building, built in 1410, had become theirs, along with many of the Drysdale family portraits and a magnificent library of four thousand books, which Nick had inherited in 1955.

Philippa, who came from the ranks of the upper classes herself hadn't said much, but he was sure she couldn't have failed to love the exquisitely proportioned rooms which Rosalind had decorated with great taste and the furnishings they'd bought in the early years of their marriage.

As Nick went from room to room he realized there wasn't a single thing that didn't remind him of Rosalind. Maybe these memories would become overlaid with new ones, he thought. But it was with a heightened awareness that he glanced around, haunted by the shadows of that shared and loving past.

There was the French gilt clock on the drawing-room mantelpiece which Rosalind had picked up in a Devon junk shop for three pounds in 1965. It still ticked as gently as ever. Soon it would be Philippa's ears that would hear the tinkling chimes. The pair of Rockingham parrots Rosalind had given him for their tenth anniversary still looked handsome as they stood on one of the dining-room window sills, but it would be Philippa who would see them every day in future. And the Italian silk curtains he and Rosalind had chosen together on holiday in Rome still hung in the library, as wonderful a shade of jade green shot with gold as on the day they'd bought them. With a tiny stab of pain he wondered if Philippa would want to change them? But would it really matter if she did? She'd brought him back to life, filling his heart and his head and his bed with a happiness he'd never thought he'd know again. Life moved on, he told himself. Rosalind wouldn't have wanted him to dwell nostalgically in the past. The future was going to be so wonderful but nevertheless everything he saw and touched and smelled brought his wife back to mind so vividly . . . her lovely laughing face, perfectly heart-shaped, her artistic hands, slender body . . . Cathy was her mother all over again and in the days immediately after Rosalind's death had stirred such poignant recollections in him that it was like a beautiful torture.

Nick sighed deeply, as if by exhaling he could blow away those silken ties that tried to bind him to the past. Tonight he knew he was saying goodbye to those memories, preserving them out of sight while he got on with the rest of his life.

After helping himself to a brandy, he went and sat at his desk in the library so he could take a final look at the weekend menus which had been prepared for him by Morton, the major-domo he'd employed for eleven years. But it was hard to concentrate. It was like an emotional tug-of-war, his thoughts clinging to what had been while sexual desire clamoured for what was and would be.

From the moment he'd set eyes on Philippa he'd been besotted with her. He'd kept it from his children until he was sure she felt the same way, and that hadn't been difficult. They were all so busy with their own lives he sometimes felt they hardly noticed what he was doing.

Their reaction tonight had really startled him, in fact. Why couldn't they be happy for him?

The hostility they'd shown towards a woman they'd never met had been both hurtful and disturbing. Nick turned off the lights and made his way up to bed. In twelve hours' time Philippa would be here, his own wonderful darling love who'd given him back his youth, his enthusiasm for life, and who wanted him as much as he wanted her. He'd been given a second chance of happiness, another bite at the cherry, and vowed to cherish her for the rest of his life. The past was the past. Rest in peace, dear Rosalind, and thank you for all you gave me. Welcome, Philippa, and the future you're prepared to give me.

Nick's gratitude was so heartfelt at that moment that he made up his mind his new wife could have anything she wanted when they were married. She had only to ask and it would be hers.

By mid-morning the next day Nick's children had all gravitated to the library, proprietorial feelings towards their home bonding them as they had not been since they were small.

"What if she starts making changes to the house?" Elizabeth said tearfully. She hadn't slept, so upset was she at the thought of their father's future wife becoming mistress of Wingfield Court. She had puffy bulges under her eyes, and never one for wearing smart clothes and make-up, had scraped her long fair hair back into a ponytail and put on an old pair of jeans and the baggy red sweater she'd worn throughout her three pregnancies.

"She'd better not try," Margaret agreed vehemently. In contrast to Elizabeth she'd spent an hour getting ready for lunch. Clothes were her armour, make-up gave her confidence. She wore her favourite shade of tan in the form of a tweed suit, with shoes to match and a quantity of gold jewellery. And although she'd tried to mask her freckles with heavy foundation, to her dismay they still showed.

"But we must be pleasant to her for Daddy's sake," Cathy protested, anxious to avoid a confrontation. "He's had a grotty year and I think we should at least try to be happy for him."

"Listen to Miss Goody Two-shoes," Jonathan mocked, all cocky bravado this morning after a night during which he'd wept like a young boy on his first night at boarding school. "Are you going to lead the welcome delegation when she arrives?"

Cathy flushed. Pushing back her long dark hair, she scooped it up at the back, clipping it in place with a large blue butterfly slide. However far she went with her style of up-market grunge dressing which consisted of long ethnic-patterned wraparound skirts, high platform sandals and layers of tops and cardigans and shawls, some of them tied around her slender hips, she still managed to look gleamingly clean, hair shining and skin tanned a rich golden brown. Silver rings adorned her slender hands and bangles clinked on her wrists alongside several brightly coloured friendship bracelets. She was a gypsy version of her mother; the wild rose in the hedgerow where Rosalind had been the exotic orchid in the greenhouse.

"Don't be silly, Jonno," Cathy retorted, eyes like melted chocolate looking at her brother reprovingly. "We've got to be polite or we'll let ourselves down and look like a bunch of spoiled brats."

"Of course we must be polite, but we needn't be warm," Margaret pointed out.

Giles spoke up. "Let's just try and be gracious," he said, avoiding eye contact with his wife.

"I could do with a drink," Jonathan remarked, getting up and prowling around the room. His long legs in black jeans seemed to dangle from his lean body like a puppet's. "Christ! Is it only eleven o'clock? I'm going to get myself a Bloody Mary. She's not due for hours."

"You can get me one, too," said Giles.

"You mustn't start drinking yet," Margaret reproved.

Jonathan raised his eyebrows. "Watch us," he replied languidly, sauntering out of the room. A minute later they heard the clink of glasses in the drinks pantry off the hall.

"Why not?" Elizabeth said indulgently. "Jonno!" She raised her voice. "Get me a glass of wine, will you, love? White, please. I could do with fortifying in view of the coming ordeal."

"OK!" he shouted back. "Anyone else want anything?"

"Actually I'll have some wine, too, please," Cathy called out, not because she wanted it but to show loyalty to the others. "Where's Daddy?"

"Gone out," Giles replied. "Said he had to go into Malmesbury for something."

Elizabeth pulled down her jersey and looked alarmed. "My God, I hope he gets back before she arrives."

Jonathan, coming back into the room, handed Elizabeth her drink. "Take a chill pill, sis! It's not the Queen coming to lunch," he bantered. "Where's Laurence, by the way? Skulking out in the garden?"

"Laurence doesn't skulk," Elizabeth protested, giggling.

Jonathan guffawed. "Of course he skulks. He's always skulking. Creeping stealthily around the place without saying a word. I bet he was a fox in a previous life."

"Well . . . he's a bit shy," she agreed.

Jonathan lowered himself into a chair and remarked, deadpan, "Isn't this jolly?"

They all laughed nervously, except for Margaret who was making it obvious that her first encounter with Philippa was going to be a competitive confrontation rather than a welcoming reception for a newcomer to the family.

"I think we should . . ." she began, when the sudden crunch of gravel as a car swept up the drive made them all jump in panic.

"Shit, she's here!" Giles exclaimed, turning white.

"Oh, God! Where's Dad?" Elizabeth croaked. Her hand shook as she put her glass down on a side table, and her heart pounded in her ears.

Giles looked frantic. "Christ! I don't know. How bloody like him to go off just when he's needed . . ."

Jonathan looked at them all as if they'd gone mad. Suddenly he was Mr Cool, determined to be unfazed by the arrival of this unknown woman.

"I'll go and greet her," he said calmly, adding jokingly, "I don't know why the fuck you're all acting like blue-arsed flies in a colander."

At that moment Nick walked briskly into the room.

"Hello," he said, brimming with bonhomie. He had a package tucked under his arm. He glanced at Jonathan. "Drinking already?"

Elizabeth, Cathy and Jonathan looked embarrassed, like children caught doing something naughty. Elizabeth sank back on to the sofa in relief.

"Dad, where have you been? We thought we heard her arriving . . ."

"*Her*?" Nick frowned. "Philippa does have a name, you know, Elizabeth. It was probably me you heard. I've been into Malmesbury to get a box of mint chocolates. And if you insist on drinking before noon, for goodness' sake open some decent champagne," he added, as he turned to leave the room. A minute later they heard a phone ring and Nick picked it up in the hall.

"Hello? Oh, darling! Where are you?" His voice was filled with sudden enthusiasm. "That's great. OK. 'Bye."

Then he came bounding into the library again. "That was Philippa. She's turned into Colwall Lane. She'll be here in five minutes," he announced jubilantly.

CHAPTER TWO

"There's nothing we can do to stop this marriage," Sir Archie Sykes pointed out. "You know what Philippa's like. She's made up her mind to marry this man, and that's that."

He was sitting at the round central table in their small but cosy kitchen, sipping a weak whisky and soda, his first of the day, while he watched his wife peel some potatoes for lunch. Sliding gently into middle-aged spread, she stooped over the sink, her short straight hair failing forward as she peered, frowning, at a large King Edward. Over her baggy tweed skirt and peach-coloured blouse she wore an apron which did little to prevent her front from getting splashed by the running tap. Her ringless hands, plump and red, worked the knife clumsily, betraying her culinary inexperience.

After a moment she said hesitantly, without looking up, "You don't suppose she's doing it for us, do you?"

"Us, Honor?" He pretended not to understand.

"Yes. Us. You know." Honor Sykes scooped up the peelings with both hands and tipped them into the trash can. "She does worry about us. Wonders how we're managing."

There was a long painful pause while Sir Archie gazed into the depths of his whisky, gently swilling the ice cube around until it looked like a sliver of glass. He was short and stocky, like his wife. He looked so typically ex-army, with his bristling white moustache, keen blue eyes and clipped way of talking, that there was nothing else he could have been. Lieutenant General Sir Archibald Sykes, KCMG, DSO, MC, Retired. Still one of the old school, he liked to think. Patriotic. Gave his youth and the best part of his life for Queen and Country. Wished he'd had a son to carry on the Sykes tradition in the Gunners. Never mind, Philippa was a good girl. He was proud of her.

He looked across at Honor and said a trifle anxiously, "But she wouldn't be marrying for that reason, would she?"

Honor shrugged and dropped the cut up pieces of potato, one by one, into a saucepan of boiling salted water.

"I hope to God not," she replied, "but you never know."

Sir Archie shook his head. "No, of course she wouldn't," he replied dismissively. His eyes glinted. "Unless, . . . you haven't been saying anything, have you? Telling her we're having financial difficulties?"

"I never mention money," his wife replied emphatically. Her lined face, square-jawed and with deep-set dark eyes, looked tired as she sank onto a wooden chair opposite him. "But Philippa's not a fool, Archie. When we were wiped out by the collapse of

Belgar she was terribly concerned. She always said she wished there was something she could do to help. It's a miracle we've survived as well as we have. At least we've got this cottage . . ."

"Because we were forced to sell Merryfields and everything we owned," he said regretfully. Naively, perhaps even stupidly, when he'd retired from the army he'd invested every penny they had in a new electronics firm started by an old friend of theirs which made secret components for certain parts of nuclear warheads. It was a big operation, shrouded in secrecy for security reasons, and their biggest client was the Ministry of Defence. At first everything seemed fine. He and Honor had been looking forward to living off the proceeds of their investment, perhaps even becoming rich, when disaster struck. The Ministry cancelled their contract, forcing Belgar Electronics into voluntary liquidation. The firm owed hundreds of thousands of pounds in debts incurred by their expansion which had only been carried out in the first place in order to fulfil the Ministry contract.

The family silver had to be sold, then his mother's jewellery which Honor had enjoyed wearing, and finally the antique furniture his father had left him, along with Merryfields, their lovely house in Hertfordshire.

Not even Hitler, as Sir Archie told everyone, had forced him into such an untenable position. He was unable to do anything but surrender to the demands of his creditors, reducing himself and his family to a state of miserable poverty compared to what they'd once known.

"Philippa is thirty-one, Honor," he pointed out. "One presumes she knows her own mind and she did seem very happy the other evening, didn't she?" Philippa had invited them up to London the previous week, to tell them she'd got engaged and to introduce them to Nick Driver. He'd taken them all to dinner at the Ritz, champagne had been drunk and toasts proposed, and Philippa had showed them her large solitaire diamond ring. It was an evening of much jollity and celebration and Honor had been glad she'd put on her best dress for the occasion. But on the way home, as the effects of the wine wore off, she'd expressed concern about the whole thing.

"I didn't think he'd be so old," she'd told Archie as they sat facing each other on the train taking them back to Ashford in Kent. The carriage was almost empty at this late hour, and the train, swaying in the darkness like a drunken caterpillar as it careered through the sleeping countryside, seemed to enclose them in a capsule of intimacy where they could talk without risk of being overheard.

"He doesn't act old, though," Archie replied, admiring the shine on his old black shoes which he'd polished vigorously before they'd set off for London. "I think he'll look after her. They seem very happy."

Honor was silent, a sure sign she had something to say but wasn't sure whether she should air her opinions or not.

"Don't you agree, m'dear?" he continued encouragingly.

Her dark eyes looked straight into his. "The trouble is, I don't trust him," she said defiantly.

Archie blinked, perplexed. "Don't trust him?" he repeated. "What's wrong with the feller?"

Honor hesitated, uncertain about putting her thoughts into words yet knowing she must follow her instincts.

"It's just . . . well, I'm not exactly sure what . . ."

Archie raised his eyebrows. They sprouted thick fawn hair that looked like arched prawns hovering over his eyes. "I received the impression of a pleasant, kind man who is obviously besotted with Philippa and wants to look after her and give her everything he can."

Honor spoke drily. "That's one very good way of being controlling. You do realize he's insisting she gives up her good job at Christie's? I have a strong suspicion he intends her to dance attendance on *him* for the rest of her life."

"Isn't that a bit strong, dearest?" Archie asked mildly.

But Honor wasn't listening. "And what about all his children?" she asked, gaining in confidence now she'd started. "How are they going to feel about her? Children can make a step-mother's life hell."

"But they're grown-up, Honor. Nick said two of them are married and he has three grandchildren! It sounds as if they've all got lives of their own — they're not going to be a problem to Philippa."

Honor lapsed into thoughtful silence for the rest of the journey. In spite of what her husband said, she couldn't help being filled with misgivings. Philippa was her only child, her beloved daughter whom she adored. And whatever happened to her affected Honor deeply.

Philippa Sykes gripped the steering wheel tightly, her feelings of apprehension mounting as she approached the now familiar road that led to Wingfield Court. When

Nick had asked her to marry him, the last time she'd stayed, she remembered saying to him: "It will take me time to get used to living in this big house." She hadn't mentioned his four children. As if he knew what she was thinking he'd said, "The family are going to love you."

Somehow she rather doubted it, under the circumstances. Surely four grown-up sons and daughters were going to resent her being brought into the family so soon after their mother's death? She couldn't even begin to imagine how they'd be feeling; to lose a parent was the thing she most dreaded. But to have a surviving parent marry someone else, within twelve months, was beyond anything she could imagine. And yet Nick needed her, had told her repeatedly how lonely and wretched he'd been since Rosalind had died.

"My children all have their own lives so I'm very much on my own," he'd added.

She'd met him at a dinner party given by mutual friends and the attraction had been instant. Philippa believed in fate and her first meeting with him had seemed to confirm that belief. She felt a magnetic force pulling them towards each other, and when she'd looked up into his lean tanned face and blue eyes, she'd thought: This man is for me. I'm going to marry him.

Never before had she had such a strong premonition. It was suddenly terribly important that they were seated next to each other at dinner and that they talked. By the end of the evening Nick had asked her out and, quite calmly, because she knew that it was going to happen, she'd accepted. From then on, as if they were following a course that was preordained, they saw each other constantly and the most wonderful part was that neither of them was surprised by what was happening. When he asked her to marry him she accepted at once, because that was her destiny, and from then on it seemed to be the most natural thing in the world that they should make love, sleep together, get up in the morning and have breakfast together, and plan the rest of their lives with the assurance of a couple planning a mere holiday.

She'd reached the end of Colwall Lane now and there it stood, Wingfield Court, visible through the high wrought-iron gates, glowing like a jewel in the autumn sunshine. Part Tudor, with its small pink bricks and wooden beams darkened by the elements of six centuries, and part eighteenth-century, it had square leaded window panes overlooking the forecourt, in the centre of which stood a formal pond and fountain. From here she could see the imposing entrance with the coat of arms of the Earls of Drysdale carved in stone above the doorway. As a light breeze riffled through the clumps of pampas grass that waved on the edge of the lawn it all looked infinitely welcoming. Her future home where Nick was awaiting her. With his four children.

Philippa took a deep breath and turned her car into the drive. I'm here, she thought. This is it. There is no turning back now.

The first thing Margaret noticed as Philippa entered the hall was that her leather boots were beautifully polished. She had short, light brown hair and its blonde highlights must have cost a fortune at a top London stylist. Elizabeth, on the other hand, suddenly felt frumpish and fat as she took in Philippa's slim figure which was set off by well-cut grey trousers and a white polo neck sweater. Cathy was struck by her attractive face with its warm smile and kind hazel eyes which right now looked scared as she glanced around the hall and saw them all grouped in a semi-circle, waiting to meet her.

"This is Giles," Nick was saying, pushing her gently forward. Philippa extended a hand that was visibly shaking and Giles stared straight into her eyes with a fixed smile.

"How d'you do?" he said stiffly.

"Hello." She grinned disarmingly, showing lovely even teeth. Jonathan moved forward next, looking down on her from his great height, summing her up quizzically.

"Hi! I'm Jonathan," he announced. "The cutest and the best," he added, as if determined to take control of this first introduction.

Philippa's eyes suddenly lit up and she laughed with genuine amusement. "Really? And do the rest of the family agree with you?"

He smiled lazily. "I'm the favourite, believe me."

"I don't think I do, but it's very nice to meet you," she replied, smiling.

The others looked at Jonathan. He was breaking ranks, currying favour, and they didn't approve. Nick, on the other hand, looked delighted. Holding Philippa by the elbow, he steered her gently in the direction of the drawing room, after he'd introduced the others.

"Let's have a drink before lunch," he said. A tray with champagne and glasses had been set up on a table in the window. "Giles, will you be barman?"

The three women of the family went and stood in front of the crackling log fire, as if unconsciously forming a guard to keep their future step-mother away from its warmth. Laurence, who'd acknowledged Philippa with the briefest of handshakes and a formal inclination of the head, helped Giles hand the champagne round while Jonathan propped himself against a bookcase and continued to engage Philippa in conversation.

"So where you do live in London? Have you got a flat or something?"

"I've got a shoe-box in Chelsea," she replied, relaxing a little as she sipped her drink.

"Whereabouts in Chelsea?"

"Chelsea Cloisters."

"Handy for wining and dining," Jonathan agreed, "if you like that sort of thing. I prefer Regent's Park. Earls Court has a depressingly tacky gay scene, but there are some great joints in the West End where I can take my pick . . . if you know what I mean?" He gave a suggestive laugh.

He's seeing if he can shock her, Cathy thought, overhearing. It was his way of testing people, finding out if they could accept him and his lifestyle or not. Covertly, Cathy watched Philippa out of the corner of her eye. Unshockable, she realized with surprise. Most people, when Jonathan thrust his private life under their noses, looked embarrassed and brushed his remarks aside as if refusing to acknowledge what he was saying. Or else were over-anxious to appear understanding. Not so Philippa. She's not some silly bimbo, Cathy realized, and for some reason found this discouraging; it looked as if her father's fiancee knew exactly what she was doing.

After a few minutes Philippa moved towards the group of women; the wary look had returned to her eyes but she was obviously doing her best to mingle. Instinctively Nick came and stood close to her and as she faced his daughters slid an arm around her waist.

"I hear you have three adorable children," said Philippa, smiling at Elizabeth.

She nodded, wanting not to like her but with no real reason so far not to. At the same time she hated her for coming to take Rosalind's place. Proud of becoming a grandmother, Rosalind had adored Dominic and Tamsin, and had lived just long enough to see Jasper when he'd been born . . . but now this other woman, this stranger in their midst, was going to be around to enjoy the children and it seemed so terribly unfair. To her fury she felt her eyes brim and her throat contract; she looked down at her feet, not replying.

Spotting the upsurge of emotion, Philippa turned quickly to Cathy.

"And I gather you're at Edinburgh," she said conversationally. "I wish I'd gone to university. It must be great."

Cathy's tone was politely measured. "I'm only in my first year but I love it." She glanced at her father who was watching her anxiously. So far, two out of four of his children were being stand-offish and he was worried that Philippa would be hurt by their obvious rejection.

At that moment Margaret spotted the large solitaire diamond ring on Philippa's finger.

"Is that stone big enough for you?" she demanded rudely.

Everyone stopped drinking and talking and looked at Philippa's left hand. Elizabeth at least felt grateful it wasn't one of their mother's rings. Jonathan gave a long low whistle. "Wow! A diamond as big as the Ritz!" he remarked breezily.

Giles regarded it sullenly, reckoning it must have cost at least forty thousand pounds.

"Very pretty," Cathy said peaceably, thinking it was horribly vulgar and not the sort of ring she'd have expected Philippa to choose. It didn't seem to go with her personality.

A moment later all was explained.

"I bought it as a surprise," Nick announced proudly. He turned to gaze tenderly into Philippa's eyes. "You'd no idea what sort of engagement ring you were getting, did you, darling."

"None," she said, smiling back at him, basking in the warmth of his obvious love. "I nearly died when I saw it, it's so big!"

"I don't wish to hear about your private life," Jonathan mocked with camp humour.

Philippa blushed but Nick chortled with delight like an elderly teenager. "At least you acknowledge it's big!"

"Did you ever hear anything so disgusting in your life?" Elizabeth remarked as she and Margaret went for a walk after lunch. "I mean, Daddy's fifty-eight . . . and indulging in all that schoolboy humour. It's one thing

Jonno making a double entendre, but when Daddy joins in, it's so undignified."

"And she didn't seem to mind," Margaret pointed out triumphantly, as if that said a lot more about Philippa than it did about Nick.

They tramped on up the side of a muddy field, wrapped up in Barbours and with green wellington boots, sisters for the first time since Margaret had married Giles as they expressed their misgivings about their future step-mother. They shared a common bond now.

Elizabeth didn't want anyone to take her mother's place, and Margaret didn't want anyone depriving her of what she considered to be hers by right.

"And as for that ring!" she continued rancorously. *Her* engagement ring had belonged to Giles's grandmother. It was a rather ordinary ruby surrounded by tiny diamonds. It looked like a trinket from a Christmas cracker compared to that of the next Mrs Nick Driver.

"I think she's a conniving bitch," she announced suddenly, kicking a stone vigorously out of her path.

"I agree she's probably out for all she can get," Elizabeth agreed. "I mean, it's obvious Dad's a rich man and he's a very good catch for her."

"But she may not realize she can't get her hands on the capital," Margaret pointed out with satisfaction. "What with the family trust set up by your grandfather, and Wingfield Court belonging to a limited company of which we're all directors, all she can actually gain is the privilege of living in the house and enjoying the interest from the trust like the rest of us."

Elizabeth was always amused by that royal "we". In fact, Nick had discretionary rights to manage the family trust of which the beneficiaries were himself and his four children. He was likewise chairman of Wingland Estate Ltd, a company set up by the late Henry Driver, which owned the house and the surrounding land which included nineteen cottages and the Home Farm. Giles, Jonathan, Cathy and herself were its only directors. Laurence didn't make a fuss about not being on the same financial footing as Elizabeth but it really got to Margaret who hated to be excluded from anything.

"Actually . . ." Elizabeth stopped in her tracks and gazed thoughtfully at the golden landscape, bathed now in the muted rays of an autumn sun. She stuck her hands deeper into the pockets of her Barbour. "I wonder if Philippa knows that both the house and the money are all tied up in a trust and a limited company? And that Daddy can't do anything without our sanction?"

"She'll find out soon enough," Margaret retorted, cheering up considerably at the prospect.

"Darling, it's so wonderful to have you here," Nick said softly, taking Philippa's hand as they strolled across the lawn after lunch. "Is it beginning to feel like home?"

"I still can't get used to what an enormous house it is," she laughed, "but it's certainly beautiful."

On her first visit he had taken her over every inch of the place, from the attics, through all the bedrooms, to the magnificent ground-floor drawing room, the dining room, library, morning room and estate office. He'd even taken her down to the cellars where thousands of bottles of wine lay under a lacy tangle of cobwebs.

"But you'll be happy here?" he persisted. "If you want anything changed . . ."

Philippa hesitated and he looked at her anxiously.

"What is it, sweetheart?"

"Do you think your children will get to like me?" she asked in a small voice.

He put his arms around her and pulled her close. The breeze was whipping tendrils of hair across her forehead and he raised his hand to push them tenderly away.

"They'll come to love you as much as I do," he assured her warmly.

"They didn't seem very . . . apart from Jonathan . . ."

Nick looked deep into her eyes. "You've got to remember they lost their mother only a year ago. It's going to take them a while to get over her death, but when they do I can see you becoming their best friend. You're too young to be their step-mother, rather a perfect friend for them all."

"I do hope so," she said, leaning against him, feeling so lucky to have met him just when, after a string of failed relationships, she'd thought she'd never find the right person. But of course their meeting had been meant. She was sure her destiny had been carved in stone from the minute of her birth and that Nick had been waiting for her all this time.

Then it struck her that if he was her destiny, so was everything else that came with him. She hadn't thought of it like that until today. Before she'd met his children she'd looked upon them as mere appendages who would not affect her very much because they were grown-up. Seeing them in the flesh had been a shock, especially as she'd sensed the hostility hidden beneath a veil of politeness, with the exception of Nick's daughter-in-law who had been openly rude. And then there was Wingfield Court; magnificent to look at and wonderful to visit . . . but could it ever be her home? Suddenly the enormity of what she was letting herself in for became plain.

Gently, she pulled away from Nick. Keeping her expression calm so as not to upset him, she looked around at the formal box parterre, the neat gravel paths and stone urns and statues, and then the house itself, standing as it had stood for nearly six hundred years, as much a part of the surrounding countryside as the distant blue hills. And in that instant she knew this place was wrong for her. Nick was right but the house was wrong. It was Rosalind's house, every stick and stone and inch of it. Her presence was imprinted on the atmosphere as if she'd just left the room for a few minutes. Her perfume seemed to linger in the air. The children were hers, the house was hers, every single thing in it was hers, and Philippa suddenly wondered if her love for Nick was strong enough to help her cope in the face of such ghostly possession.

"Come and see the swimming pool in the walled garden," he suggested, breaking into her thoughts as he linked his arm through hers. "It's a beautiful setting, very secluded."

"Lovely," she replied automatically.

"Are you all right, darling?" He looked at her quizzically, almost teasingly, as if he didn't really want to know if anything was wrong.

"I'm fine," Philippa replied, resting her head against his shoulder for a moment. "It's just that everything is so new and strange after my tiny flat in London."

Nick took her face in his hands and kissed her, tenderly and thoughtfully, his lips sweetly gentle on hers. Philippa felt herself melt with desire as she responded to his kisses. She loved him more than anyone else on earth and with him to look after her, everything was going to be all right. Of course it was. She was being silly and fanciful, what her grandmother would have called fey.

"I love you," she whispered.

"And I love you, more than you'll ever know," he replied, softly, gazing deep into her eyes. "We're going to be wonderfully happy, my darling."

Nick's libido had rocketed after the death of Rosalind. He'd always been highly sexed but during her illness had hardly thought about it. He had experienced absolutely no feelings of desire as he'd tried to juggle the work of running the estate as well as looking after the family trust while also endeavouring to be at his wife's bedside as much as possible. At the time his lack of interest had vaguely surprised him. Here was the woman he'd loved and desired for thirty-one years, and whose body was as familiar to him as his own, and yet sex was no longer a part of the equation. As he watched Rosalind shrink until she was no more that a fragile husk, the last thing on his mind was making love. Yet no sooner was she buried than, almost as a part of his grieving, he wanted to find a way of expressing what it meant to be still alive, still able to enjoy life to the full, still able to sow the seeds of a new life. Suddenly he found himself obsessed, driven by his basic urges all the time, erections plaguing him at inconvenient moments during the day, and at night causing him to wake up, ejaculating from erotic dreams.

When he first met Philippa he was bowled over. Her long white neck and softly rounded breasts, lean thighs and flat stomach, drove him crazy. He wanted nothing more than to make love to her, but something made him hesitate, realizing instinctively that if he moved in on her too soon he'd scare her away. This was a woman who needed wooing. There was something serenely dignified about her, something that kept him at arm's length but at the same time enticed him to come closer. She was intelligent and well educated but most important of all, so far as Nick was concerned, she was a sympathetic listener and as he found himself pouring out his heart to her, he saw she was also compassionate.

This heady mixture of head and heart sent him into a spin. Realizing Philippa was an old-fashioned type of young woman who expected no less than to have a formal relationship with him, he asked her to marry him.

For Nick she was a ripe peach which he'd been lucky enough to pluck from the bough at exactly the right moment. He reckoned she'd got to the age when she most probably wanted to settle down and he was cynical enough to see that, with impoverished parents and a job that produced only an average salary, classy though it was, she'd find it a welcome change to become a rich man's wife.

And she loved sex. Oh, God, how she loved sex. From the moment she'd realized Nick was serious and really did want to spend the rest of his life with her, she made herself available to his urgent and passionate needs with a responsiveness that shook him. What she lacked in experience he discovered she made up for in ardour, thrilling him with her adventurousness. The cool maiden had metamorphosized into a hot sex queen; the calm surface quickly revealed hidden fire below and Nick's mind was utterly and absolutely blown. Consequently nothing was too good for Philippa. And this was only the beginning, he thought, as they went to join the family for tea. The clichéd saying "Today is the first day of the rest of your life" rang through his head like a joyous clarion call of trumpets. He couldn't remember when he'd last felt so young or so happy.

Tea in the formal drawing room was a strained occasion, with Nick and Philippa trying to keep a bright conversation going in the face of his unhappy looking family. Elizabeth had remained up in her room and the others, apart from Cathy, seemed monosyllabic.

Morton had produced a Ritz Hotel-style afternoon tea at Nick's request, with tiny sandwiches, homemade scones with raspberry jam and Cornish cream, and a rich fruit cake. But no one seemed to have any appetite for it.

“Where’s Elizabeth?” Laurence asked. He’d been out for a solitary walk and was the last to join the group around the blazing fire.

“She has a bit of a headache,” Cathy said quickly.

Her father gave her a sidelong look, making it obvious he didn’t believe her.

“I’ll go and see how she is,” Laurence remarked lugubriously. “She doesn’t usually get headaches.”

“Why don’t you let her sleep?” Jonathan observed. The way Laurence trailed after his sister, like an insecure child, always irritated him. Why couldn’t he leave her alone for a while? It was not, he reflected, as if Elizabeth was a racy, red nail-varnished type of woman who’d sneak off for a quickie while Laurence made a phone call, was it? Hardly the sort who would slip into Janet Reger scanties and carry on a *liaison dangereuse* while loading the dishwasher with one hand and feeding one of the children with the other! And yet Laurence persisted in shadowing her, his face filled with angst, his purpose in life ill defined. And all the while dear old Elizabeth, plump and not caring how she looked, plodded on being the dutiful wife and mother, living in a warm but chaotic old farm house, giving him no cause whatever for jealous speculation.

Laurence hovered in the doorway. “She might like a cup of tea. And a scone.”

Margaret, who had lain in wait for Morton so she could take charge of the teapot, saying “Shall I be mother?” rather too firmly, now poured a cup for Elizabeth and handed it to Laurence together with a cucumber sandwich on a small plate.

"There you go," she said gaily, happy because she was in charge. "Tell her there are some aspirins on the dressing table in my room."

"Thanks."

"Giles will open the door for you," she added kindly.

"Thanks."

Giles threw Margaret a filthy look as he lumbered to his feet.

"This is going to be a very long weekend," Jonathan murmured sotto voce to Cathy.

"You can say that again," she whispered back, casting her eyes to heaven in mock despair. A moment later she realized Philippa was watching her and smiling. Blushing, Cathy smiled back, a great wide cheesy grin, suddenly feeling her future step-mother might not be so bad after all.

"I love your silver jewellery," Philippa remarked conversationally. "Did you buy it in this country or abroad?"

Cathy recognized banal small-talk when she heard it but she responded nevertheless. "All over the place, actually. My boyfriend Jack gave me a lot of it and I bought some in Portobello Road market. I like little pieces of jewellery," she added, thinking: My God, this is like a game of verbal tennis. Philippa serves, I return the shot with a backhander. In a minute she'll serve again and we might have a bit of a rally . . .

"I prefer small pieces of jewellery, too," Margaret cut in, joining the game. "Rather more tasteful."

Nick was frowning.

Who's going to make it a foursome? Cathy wondered. Then she heard her father speak, his voice cold.

"It takes style to carry off important jewellery."

"One all," Jonathan murmured, smiling wickedly at Cathy and she blushed again, realizing they were now being rude and her father was angry.

Giles, overhearing, asked stupidly, "One all . . . what?"

Philippa's eyes were dancing with amusement and for a stricken second Cathy was reminded of her mother. Rosalind was always laughing, her eyes sparkling, her sense of humour like a young girl's.

"One for all . . . and all for one," Philippa explained smoothly. "It's a good old family motto. My mother and father swear by it," she added, grinning conspiratorially.

Giles lay awake, more tormented by what was happening in the family than he admitted. Margaret, sleeping heavily by his side, was no help either. Her rejection of Philippa was caused by jealousy, of course, even he could see that, but it was making the situation worse. It was galling for him, too, that his father had managed to secure for himself a woman who was better looking, slimmer, smarter and sexier than Margaret, but he didn't see any point in being bitchy about it. Not that he trusted Philippa or had any intention of befriending her. He feared that once she was married to his father, that light-hearted, smiling façade would vanish. Then they'd all see her in her true light. He'd actually caught her looking speculatively around the hall earlier in the day. Was she planning a make-over of Wingfield Court?

Giles rolled on to his back and gazed into the darkness. The trouble was, his father had always expected too much from him. He'd been made aware that he was the eldest son and heir ever since he could remember. That meant he had to do well at school, get into university, take his place in society, marry someone suitable, and then produce a string of little Drivers to carry on the family tradition, which was mainly to be successful in business like his father and grandfather who was constantly held up as an example of perfect manhood. It was as if he'd been fed into a great machine; as if as a baby he'd been popped in at one end and expected to come out the other good-looking, clever, amusing and charming. With a bevy of beautiful girls forever chasing him, of course, so that he could take his pick. Things, Giles had to admit, had turned out rather differently. He didn't have his father's looks or charisma, for a start, and the few romantic encounters he'd experienced had been unsatisfactory, although at least he'd been able to consummate them which was something. Then, rather than do the picking, he'd found himself picked by Margaret who'd swept him up the aisle before he knew what was happening.

Restlessly, Giles shifted to his side. He wished he could have a fuck. He wished he could get to sleep. He didn't even have a good book to read and Margaret was snoring now in a light wheezy way. His mind jangled with worries about his future step-mother, who was only four years older than him, and the new catalogue they were printing at Bartwell's, featuring thousands of stamps which he was responsible for captioning.

At last, in desperation, he clambered out of bed and made his way quietly downstairs to the kitchen where he heated up some milk and made himself a cup of Ovaltine. Rosalind had always given him this when he'd been a child and it invariably sent him to sleep.

Ten minutes later, steaming mug in hand, he crossed the first-floor landing to go back to bed. Then he heard a low moan. He stopped dead, frowning. Then he heard it again: louder, deeper, more frantic, more ecstatic . . . And then he heard his father crying out: "Oh, God! I'm coming . . . Oh, yes, darling! Yes . . . Oh, God!"

Giles spilt his Ovaltine, scalding his hand and wetting the front of his dressing gown as he stumbled back to his room.

Even more humiliating than the fact that his father's future wife was young and beautiful was the realization that at fifty-eight Nick was having a marvellous sex life, while he, a mere twenty-seven, was unable to perform the simple act of coupling.

CHAPTER THREE

As soon as Elizabeth saw the thick, white, expensive-looking envelope she knew what it contained and a hollow feeling yawned in her stomach.

On legs that felt suddenly weak, she slumped into a chair, oblivious to her surroundings. Plum, one of the four spaniels, pattered across the comfortable, cluttered farm house kitchen and nuzzled her hand, sensing something was wrong. The others raised their heads from where they lay sprawled on an old duvet, and a couple of even older blankets, to look questioningly at her.

With shaking hands, Elizabeth slit the envelope. Although she knew what the folded card would say, the words when she saw them printed in elegant Palace script nevertheless sent darts of pain through her heart.

Lieutenant General Sir Archie and Lady Sykes request the pleasure of your company at the marriage of their daughter, Philippa Clare, to Mr Nicholas George Driver on Wednesday 15th October . . .

The invitation made them sound like a young couple, getting married for the first time, leaving the parental nest to embark on a new life together. Not a future that included the bridegroom having four grown-up children and three grandchildren; not a marriage over-shadowed by a deceased wife and a life already lived to the full. She wondered what Sir Archie and Lady Sykes were like, and what they thought of this marriage.

As Elizabeth forced herself to read on, knowing it was sheer masochism, like listening to a piece of sad music that would inevitably produce tears, she realized her father had gone ahead with the original plan he'd told her about when he'd asked if Dominic and Tamsin would like to be the page and bridesmaid.

The marriage *was* to take place in St Mark's, the Norman church in the village. Where Rosalind had been buried the previous year. And the reception was to be held afterwards at Wingfield Court.

Elizabeth pressed her hand to her mouth in an effort to stifle her sobs, and Plum licked her other hand and looked up at her with anxious eyes. She wouldn't go, of course. It would be too painful. But she'd have to reply or the Sykeses would think her rude.

On the other hand, "Mr and Mrs Laurence Vickers regret they are unable to attend . . ." sounded even ruder. It would seem like a snub to them personally, making her look like a spoiled child.

"Oh, shit!" She threw the stiff folded card down on to the kitchen table amidst a muddle of dirty breakfast dishes and wiped her eyes with a tea towel which had been slung over the back of her chair. Cathy would go, of course, because she always tried to please everyone, and so would Jonathan who already seemed to like Philippa. Margaret would definitely be there rather than miss out on something, and she'd drag Giles along with her.

If only she could turn to Laurence for understanding, thought Elizabeth, wondering where the sweet, lovable young man she'd married had gone. In fact it seemed as if that man had vanished on their honeymoon seven years before, leaving behind instead a sullen doppelgänger, always walking in her shadow like a dark image himself.

Dominic came hurtling into the kitchen at that moment, looking like a miniature commando in his camouflage combat trousers and "army" shirt, which he insisted on wearing every day and which she had to sneak from his room to wash overnight or it would be standing up by itself with dirt and mud by now. His thatch of pale gold hair looked so silky she longed to stroke it, but any attempt at such soppiness would have brought a sharp head-tossing rebuke from him, even though he was only six.

"Mum," he said breathlessly, "I'm digging a trench . . ."

"Where?" Elizabeth tried to sound casual. Dominic's digging had been known to reduce sections of the garden to something resembling a war zone.

"At the bottom . . . you know, by the wood. By the hedge where we found that dead rat." As he spoke he helped himself to a cherry from a bowl on the table and, opening his mouth, held it expertly between his teeth while he pulled the stalk away.

"But I need a bigger spade," he concluded, munching.

"What's wrong with the spade you've got?"

"Mum!" It was a slightly petulant wail, expressing exasperated patience at his mother's stupidity. "It's a spade for the beach. For little children to play with in the sand. I need a proper spade if I'm going to dig a real trench."

"Why are you digging a ditch in the first place?" Elizabeth was playing for time, though she'd no idea why. What was she going to gain by obstructing her eldest child from doing what he wanted? He'd get his own way in the end.

"Because . . . because . . ." The huffing and puffing began again, as he jammed another cherry into his mouth and struggled to find words adequate to describe his important mission. "If I don't . . . if I don't make a proper trench, Tamsin's going to get into the barracks and mess everything up," he finished fiercely.

"Your barracks happen to be her Wendy house," Elizabeth pointed out as she started to clear the table. By accident the invitation got knocked over and fell to the ground. Dominic pounced on it.

"What's this?"

"An invitation to Grandpa's wedding." Her mouth tightened as she loaded the crockery into the dishwasher. "But we're not going."

"Why not?"

"Because . . ." For a moment she reminded herself of Dominic, struggling to find words . . . or were they excuses?

"Because we're not," she said firmly.

"But . . ."

Laurence loomed tall and rangy in the doorway, his presence casting a darkness over the room. "What's going on? Why aren't you playing in the garden, Dominic? Look at the mess your feet are making on the floor."

He looked up at his father; he was all golden light and innocence by comparison. Elizabeth had a great longing to sweep her son up in her arms and hug him to death.

"Daddy, Mummy says we're not going to Grandpa's wedding," he announced importantly.

Laurence's spirit detached itself from hers; she could feel the cold wrench as he ignored her, the cut-off as he turned his back on her, no longer linking himself to her in any way.

He looked down at his son. "Well, that's up to Mummy, isn't it? She's the boss around here."

Elizabeth busied herself loading the dish washer, not wanting them to see how hurt she felt by those words.

Laurence Vickers had lived at Willow Farm, near Honeybourne in Northamptonshire, all his life. When Elizabeth had first seen it she'd delighted in the old stone building with its stabling and outhouses, and the cottage at the end of the garden where her future mother-in-law, widowed Laura Vickers, had gone to live, to "make way for Laurence's bride", as she put it.

Although the property had originally been part of a large farm, Laurence had sold most of the land and at the age of forty decided to retire because all the jobs suggested to him "weren't worth taking", he'd explained, meaning in monetary terms.

"I don't know what he expects," Elizabeth had once confided anxiously to Cathy. "He seems to think that unless he's offered a hundred thousand pounds a year or more, it's not worth it! He says that by the time he'd paid tax, there'd be no point."

Cathy had looked at her with anxious eyes, knowing how much her sister received annually from the trust. It could only mean one thing. Laurence didn't intend to work again. He'd obviously made up his mind to cruise through the rest of his life being financially supported by Elizabeth, in a house he hadn't even had to buy for himself.

And so he spent his days getting up late in the mornings, long after Elizabeth, who with the help of Herta and Gerhard had by then given the children breakfast and got the older two off to the local nursery school while Jasper was put in his pram. Later, much later, Laurence would descend for a leisurely breakfast at the kitchen table, surrounded by the aroma of shepherd's pie or roast chicken, rhubarb fool or apple crumble, for Elizabeth was an enthusiastic if messy cook, and there was always something steaming or bubbling or grilling as she prepared lunch for them all. Then he went off to his "den" with the newspapers and wasn't seen for an hour or so. In the afternoon he pottered across the lawn to visit his mother and have a little chat and perhaps a cup of tea with her. Afterwards he'd have a word with the part-time gardener then take a stroll around the three acres, which was all he had left by way of land, with the air of a man who owns a botanical showpiece on the lines of Kew.

After tea, for which Elizabeth invariably made drop scones, sponge cakes, jam tarts and flapjacks, with all of them sitting in what was by now a chaotically untidy kitchen, Laurence would suddenly seem to realize the day was nearly over and that he had nothing to show for it. Full of importance then, saying he had so much work to do, he would hurry off to the den and proceed to "work". This meant tapping away furiously at an old electric IBM golfball typewriter, composing lengthy letters to the local council, the gas board, the electricity board, the post office, the bank, their local MP, Sainsbury's, and any other organization or individual he could think of, in order to bore them to death with trivial complaints/suggestions for improvements or vague threats of further action he might take if they didn't pull their socks up.

As soon as Elizabeth heard the familiar tap-tap of the old machine she'd close the kitchen door and throw herself into a frenzy of cooking, stocking up the fridge and freezer as if a famine was nigh. That sound drove her mad.

"Daddy's writing letters," she'd say with forced cheerfulness. "Come along. Let's stay in the kitchen and let him have some peace."

Privately, she thought the "peace" he already had in his life was not dissimilar to that of the graveyard.

"Giles?" The day after she'd received the invitation Elizabeth phoned her brother at his office, desperate to know what he thought of it.

"Hello. How are you?" he asked.

"Did you get it?"

"You mean the thingy to Dad's wedding? Yes, I did. Sounds as if he intends to make a big splash."

"I've no intention of going."

"Don't you think you should? Margaret says we must go to show a united front."

"Who to, for God's sake?"

"Sir Archie and Lady Sykes, of course. We don't want them to think we're a family divided against itself."

"As far as I'm concerned we're not! We're united in hating the idea of Daddy marrying this woman. That's different."

"It's a view you can hardly expect her parents to appreciate, though," Giles retorted drily. "Anyway, Margaret says that as the eventual heir to Wingfield, I should certainly be there and she should sort of be . . . well, sort of act as hostess."

Elizabeth nearly laughed outright. Of course Margaret would want to make her presence felt under these circumstances. No doubt she'd splash out on an amazing outfit, too, in order to try and steal the show.

"How nice for her," she remarked with amusement.

"Don't start getting at Margaret," Giles said defensively. "Remember, Dad's not *her* father; she's not as involved in all this as we are . . ."

"As the future chatelaine of Wingfield I'd have thought she'd feel very involved. Anyway, that's beside the point. None of us is going and that's that."

"Well, it's up to you but I think you're making a mistake."

"Giles, I can't do it. It will be too painful, can't you see that? I can't sit and watch Daddy marry someone else when he should still be with Mummy . . ." Her voice broke and she couldn't continue.

"I know." Giles sounded sympathetic for him. "But we're going to have to block that out of our mind on the day."

In a terraced house in the centre of Edinburgh, which Cathy shared with Venetia, Jessica and Flora, all students like herself, she too looked at the wedding invitation in her trembling hand, knowing she must attend. It wasn't just going to be an emotional time for them, it would surely be a bittersweet occasion for her father, too. If Rosalind had been their mother, she'd also been Nick's wife and Cathy refused to believe he wouldn't feel a pang on his wedding day, just like the rest of them.

She had read somewhere that women were better able to cope on their own when their partner died; men left by themselves found it very hard and nearly always got married again. But how could he, and so soon? she asked herself for the umpteenth time, wrapping her thin brown arms around her stomach as if it ached. She'd have to go to the wedding, of course, because he'd want her there; his "nut brown maiden," as he always fondly called her.

As she was about to leave the house for her first lecture of the day, Venetia appeared from her bedroom, blonde hair ruffled, bright blue eyes wide and immediately curious when she saw the invitation propped up on the mantelpiece.

"What's this?" she asked. She was still in her pyjamas, feet bare and toenails painted a bright iridescent blue. "Ooooh, cool! Your father's wedding invitation."

Cathy had told her all about the weekend when Nick had sprung a future step-mother on them and Venetia was intrigued.

"Bit of a nightmare, actually," Cathy commented, nodding in the direction of the invitation. "I shall have to go but it's bound to be hellish."

"Why aren't they going somewhere on their own for a romantic private ceremony? The cool thing nowadays is to get married on some beach in the Caribbean then none of you would be expected to go."

Cathy couldn't help grinning as a vision of her father standing in his morning suit, barefoot at the edge of the ocean, came to her.

"Not quite his style, 'Netia," she joked. "Dad loves being the lord of the manor and all that crap. I fear he intends making quite a splash."

"Gross!" Venetia groaned. "Poor you. What are you going to wear?"

"Shit, that's the last thing on my mind. Listen, I'd better go or I'll be late. See you tonight. Let's get a take away then go to the pub."

"Cool. I'll tell the others. See you tonight, babe."

Ten minutes later the phone rang but they'd all left the house except for Venetia who was in the bath and didn't hear it.

"Damn!" said Jonathan, finally hanging up. He was still in bed, a mug of coffee balanced precariously on a pile of books by his side, and the phone on his chest.

"Who are you trying to call?" asked a male voice from the adjoining bathroom.

"My sister."

"A likely story! I bet you're fixing yourself up for

tonight as I've got to go away." The tone was teasing, as though it didn't matter.

"I am not," Jonathan retorted defensively. "I actually want to talk to my sister about something important."

"What's she like, your sister?"

"Why do you want to know?"

A tall young man with a golden tan emerged from the bathroom, drying his dark hair with a towel. He stood, feet wide apart, framed in the doorway. "I just wondered. Is she like you?"

Jonathan sat upright, and rearranged the pillows behind his head. "What are you, Francis, bi?"

Francis laughed. Throwing the towel on the floor, he started to get dressed. "Depends how the mood takes me," he replied lightly. "A female version of you might be amusing."

"Then you're definitely *not* meeting her."

Jonathan realized Francis was gathering up his things, ready to leave. "You're off then?" he said, trying not to mind. They'd only known each other for a few weeks, having originally met in a bar, but Francis was secretive about where he lived and what he did and who he knew.

"Yup. I'll be away for a coupla weeks. I'll give you a bell when I get back." He bent to kiss Jonathan swiftly on the mouth and without a backward glance was gone, slamming the door of the flat behind him.

The way he'd left and the empty silence afterwards made Jonathan realize he'd probably never see him again. It was always that way. He was twenty-three and still hadn't had a lasting relationship. This one didn't look like it was going to turn into one either. What was wrong with him? He was quite good-looking in a gangling sort of way, and he was amusing or at least made people laugh. Sadly, though, and for no reason he could fathom, he wasn't that attractive to other gays. In fact it was girls who chased him with embarrassing ardour, refusing to believe he couldn't be seduced into being straight. And so, apart from his platonic friendship with his flatmate Pip, he remained basically alone, except for the occasional one night stand and Francis, and he'd only actually seen *him* half a dozen times since they'd met.

"You're too needy," one lover had informed him after a long weekend together. "It's a pity you're gay. You'd do much better with women because they love to be needed by a man. It brings out their maternal instincts. But with me it's a turn-off. It reeks of commitment and that's the last thing on my agenda." And with that he too had left.

Jonathan looked dispiritedly at the phone, wanting to talk to someone to relieve his loneliness. What a shame Cathy was out, he reflected. He wanted to talk to her about this wedding of Dad's, and discuss the arrangements. Were they supposed to spend the weekend at Wingfield? Or just turn up for the church and the reception, like the guests?

On impulse he dialled Elizabeth's number. She answered almost immediately

"It's me," Jonathan told her.

"Oh . . . Jonno! How are you?"

It was obvious she was making an effort to sound affable.

"Better than you by the sound of it," he replied. "What's up?"

"Nothing, really."

"I suppose you've had the invitation?"

"I have indeed. Not that we're going."

"Jesus! Aren't you? What will Dad say if you don't go?"

"That's his problem, Jonno. He should have considered *our* feelings before he embarked on this ludicrous marriage. Giles and Margaret will be there so you won't be on your own."

"Have you heard from Cathy? Is she going?"

"That's up to her," Elizabeth said brusquely. "Jonno, I've got to go. Jasper is bawling his head off and I'm in the middle of making a casserole."

"OK, sis. Keep in touch. 'Bye." Disconsolately, he replaced the receiver then put the phone on the floor and pulled the duvet up over his head. What damn fool had ever utilized the word "gay" to describe someone who was lonely, unloved and bored witless?

"Are you sure they're happy about all the arrangements?" Philippa asked, as she looked at Nick over the rim of her wine glass.

He'd taken her to dinner at Pasha, a Moroccan-style restaurant in Kensington with lanterns and an ornamental pond with a fountain, brilliantly patterned floor tiles and Arab drapes, which made her feel she was in a kasbah. They'd been seated in an alcove with a cushioned banquette around three walls and a round table in the middle, out of sight of the other diners.

"Of course they're happy, darling," Nick assured her expansively. "Elizabeth and Laurence will probably stay for the weekend so the children are rested. I'm hoping Dominic will be a page and Tamsin a bridesmaid. Are you sure there's no one you want as bridesmaids?" His tanned hand with its well-kept nails reached across the table, covering hers. "After all, it's your day, sweetheart."

Philippa laughed. "My friends are far too old to want to be bridesmaids, and not old enough to have small children who might fit the bill. Who's going to be your best man?"

"My old friend Adrian Hopkins. I was his a few years ago."

"You're not having Giles?" She sounded surprised; as Nick's eldest son, she'd have thought he'd be first choice.

"I thought of having him as chief usher as he'll know everyone. At least," Nick added hurriedly, "everyone on my side. Who would you like to be chief usher for your side, darling?"

"I hadn't really thought about it." With a faint twinge of dismay Philippa realized she hadn't really thought about any of the details. Nick had arranged to have the invitations printed, he'd asked her parents for their list and his secretary was in the middle of mailing them all. He'd also booked the church and made all the catering and florist's arrangements for the reception.

"It'll save your parents a lot of hassle if we have it at Wingfield," he'd said casually, almost *en passant*, which she knew was his diplomatic way of saying he'd be saving them thousands of pounds, which they couldn't afford, by holding the whole thing at his home.

Now, faced with decisions about the arrangements, she realized that she and her parents were, in both financial and social terms, in a very different league from Nick. If, socially speaking, they'd once been in the fast lane, now they were parked firmly on the hard shoulder. There is nothing more embarrassing, her father had once told her, than trying to keep up with friends who have a lot more money than you do.

Philippa now had her own circle of friends, mostly contemporaries who were in the same income bracket as herself and were teasing her now about "doing very well for herself", but none were high flyers; there'd be no captains of industry, company chairmen or Members of Parliament on her list which, combined with her parents', numbered around fifty guests.

Nick, she knew, had invited over two hundred; all from the A-list, of course.

"What are you thinking about, my darling?" He squeezed her hand more tightly.

Philippa blinked, coming out of her reverie. "Everything's happening so fast," she replied, smiling, but in the candle light her eyes had a vulnerable look.

"But not too fast, surely?" He held her gaze, defying her to look away.

"I feel I've lost control . . ."

Nick raised his chin and looked amused. "You *have* lost control. I'm in control now," he said softly.

She felt a sexual thrill, basic and primitive, at the very thought of being possessed; the weak female in the power of the male. The idea of surrendering herself, of allowing herself to be taken, was suddenly exciting. She felt hot and knew her face was flushed. With an effort she tore her gaze away from his.

"Shall we skip the coffee?" he whispered.

Philippa nodded. "This alcove should have curtains. Then we could . . ."

"Oh, I don't know." There was a pause. Nick's eyes were glittering as if he had a fever. Then she gasped as she felt his bare foot slide between her legs under the table.

A moment later his toes, gently curling and uncurling, set to work with tenderness.

"What do you mean . . . you're not coming to the wedding?" Nick demanded.

Elizabeth braced herself. "Daddy, I've told you. Please don't go on about it. We're not coming and that's the end of it."

"Not so far as I'm concerned, it isn't," he retorted, upset. "How do you think it will look? What will people say? How am I going to explain your absence to Philippa without her being hurt?"

"I'm sure she'll understand."

He wasn't listening. "And what, in God's name, will Archie and Honor Sykes say? You're my eldest. How can you possibly stay away on what will be the happiest day of my life?"

"Daddy!" Surely the happiest day of his life had been when he'd married Mummy? Or the day she and the others had been born? And if it hadn't been so, at least he might have lied to spare her feelings, instead of implying he'd been miserable up to now and it was only Philippa who could make him happy.

"I *hate* you, Daddy!" she sobbed with the ferocity of an abandoned ten year old. "I don't know how you can do this to us. I never want to see you again!" Then she slammed the phone down, trembling all over.

"Do you really hate your daddy?" a small voice piped up, just beside her. Elizabeth looked down and found Tamsin standing there, in muddy dungarees, clutching her favourite doll to her chest. Violet-blue eyes gazed up earnestly at Elizabeth from a small heart-shaped face framed in a wild tangle of blonde curls.

Elizabeth gathered up her four-year-old daughter and carried her into the garden where she sank on to a wooden bench which stood under a shady old apple tree.

"No, I don't hate my daddy," she said, wiping away her tears on the tail of one of Laurence's old shirts which she liked wearing around the house with her comfortable baggy jeans. "I'm just angry with him but of course I didn't mean it." Didn't she? she wondered. At this moment she wasn't so sure.

"Why, Mummy? Why are you angry?"

"Because . . ." Elizabeth hesitated, not knowing how to answer. "Because grown-ups often get angry with each other, but it's nothing to worry about."

"Like you and Daddy? When you keep telling him what to do and you shout?" Tamsin said, small fingers carefully smoothing the skirt of her doll's dress.

"I don't shout at Daddy."

"Yes, you do. Dominic says he's never going to get married because he doesn't want to be shouted at."

"Tamsin!" For the second time that morning, Elizabeth felt hurt. First her father had shattered her illusions, and now her small daughter was portraying her as a nagging shrew.

"I love your daddy, like I love you and Dominic and Jasper. If I shout it's only because I want to be heard above the din," she said, placatingly. She cuddled Tamsin closer, burying her face in the warm baby smell of her hair, relishing the petal softness of her little brown arms.

Only one thing scared her now. What was she going to do when the children grew up and left home? The thought of being alone with Laurence struck a chill in her heart and a sense of dark foreboding in her mind. What would they say to each other? What would they do to fill the long hours and the empty house?

Suddenly she jumped to her feet, refusing to think about it yet. Setting Tamsin on the ground, she forced a note of gaiety into her voice.

"How about making a cake for tea, sweetheart?"

"Can we make a chocolate cake?"

"If you like."

"Because it's Daddy's favourite."

It might have been Elizabeth talking, twenty-five years ago. Were all little girls Daddy's girls until they grew up?

"OK. Let's make a chocolate cake for Daddy, darling," she replied, putting on her butcher's striped apron.

Another month had passed and Margaret knew another opportunity to get pregnant had been and gone and her desperation was mounting. On the surface life continued as if everything was fine; she and Giles had given the usual dinner parties, gone to friends' and clients' drinks parties, shopped on Saturdays in Kensington High Street, watered their formal back garden every evening and done the hundred and one other activities of any well-to-do couple, but the one thing she hoped for, and the thing most couples took for granted, hadn't happened.

When they attempted to have sex, Giles remained unable to perform and so once again, after three years and eight months of marriage, she'd been left high and dry, dissatisfied and frustrated, feeling like a plant waiting for a friendly bee to come along and fertilize her — or didn't some gardeners transfer the pollen from the stamen to the female plant with a feather?

She was going to need more than a feather, she reflected grimly, if she was ever going to have a decent sex life and get pregnant. Reading books and talking to her gynaecologist had made her feel she'd become part-therapist, part-seductress, and she was beginning to lose sight of the fact that sex was supposed to be fun. Fun? Some nights Giles simply fell asleep, having given her a perfunctory peck on the cheek, while on other nights they both worked feverishly at getting a little stiffness into his nether regions, only to be met with zero response.

Giles would huff and puff and get in a state, groaning that he didn't know why things weren't working, and she'd try out all the techniques suggested in the *Remedies for Impotence* handbook, but to no avail. Eventually they would give up, exhausted and disappointed.

"Don't worry about it, darling," Margaret had said at the beginning, in what she hoped was an encouraging voice. "Shore up his ego," the handbook said. "Don't let him feel it's his fault." Now, after this long time she'd begun to feel like a virgin again. And she couldn't help feeling the pressure was on to get pregnant now that Nick Driver was about to marry a much younger woman.

Today she was going to buy her outfit for the wedding, something smart which would set off her gingery hair but bring cooling tones to her skin, which was inclined to look ruddy when she got hot. An outfit, most importantly, to make her look dignified, as befitted wife of Nick's eldest son and heir.

Philippa Sykes might be tall, slim and attractive, but Margaret intended to bring a regal air to the occasion; she would ask Giles if he would get his father to lend her Rosalind's pearl choker with the diamond clasp. That should show her future step-mother-in-law that Margaret had been part of the Driver family for a long time and that one day everything would be hers. And Giles's, too, of course.

Also shopping for something to wear at her daughter's wedding, but in her local branch of Marks & Spencer rather than a smart boutique, Honor Sykes headed for a rail of navy blue woollen skirts and matching cardigan jackets, which had cream collar and cuffs and, she thought, looked neat and tidy. And not expensive. She already had a pair of navy blue shoes that would do, and a handbag, so all she needed now was a hat.

It had all been so different a few years ago when she'd been able to go up to London and think nothing of buying an outfit costing several hundred pounds. But she didn't really care. She'd never been a beauty, never turned a head in the street or received compliments, so what did it matter? So long as she didn't let Philippa down in front of her future husband and his family whom she had yet to meet.

In a nearby shop she spotted a navy blue hat that would do perfectly. It had a small brim and plain petersham ribbon around the crown. Archie would approve. He hated frills and things that were showy. Then she took the bus back to Ashford, relieved to have completed her shopping but more apprehensive than ever about the wedding. Now that she'd bought an outfit the occasion seemed to have taken on an air of reality. While it was a great relief that she and Archie had not been expected to fork out thousands of pounds, she couldn't help feeling a deep pang of sadness that the whole thing had been taken out of her hands, along with Philippa herself, making her feel like just another guest at her own daughter's wedding.

Neither she nor Archie had been consulted on a single point; she didn't even know what Philippa was wearing.

"Nick's giving me my dress," her daughter had explained when Honor asked about it. "It's been specially designed for me by a top couturier."

"That's lovely, darling," Honor had responded, wishing she'd been rich enough to provide the wedding dress at least. "What's it like?"

"It's a surprise, Mummy," Philippa teased, high with happiness and so far above everyone else's feelings that she did not realize she was being hurtful. "You'll have to wait and see it like everyone else!"

And, like everyone else, Honor reflected, clutching her shopping bags on her knee as the bus rumbled along the country lanes, I'll just have to stand and watch the whole thing, an outsider, while Nick Driver runs the show.

"Get kitted out all right, m'dear?" Archie greeted her when she arrived home.

"Yes, thank you. What have you been doing?" She smiled at him, not wanting him to see how depressed she was feeling.

"Nick phoned."

"And?"

Sir Archie looked in very good spirits. He was holding a tumbler of whisky and soda, from which he kept sipping, and Honor could tell it wasn't his first drink of the day.

"He's invited us to stay there the night before the wedding. He's giving a huge dinner party for all his family and some friends and said we'd be most welcome. Nice of him, isn't it? I must say, he's being exceedingly generous. It's going to be quite a weekend."

"I'm sure it is," Honor said quietly.

"One has to admit Philippa's doing very well for herself."

Honor paused in her customary fashion before stating an opinion. Then she spoke.

"Money doesn't always bring happiness."

Sir Archie took several swigs of whisky. "Poverty definitely causes unhappiness, though," he affirmed, looking serious. "She seems to love this feller so why should she be unhappy? She'll never want for anything again."

"I know." Honor's voice was almost a whisper, "but I wish I didn't feel so guilty."

He dabbed his moustache, dewy with whisky, and his voice was filled with understanding. "It's not our fault, m'dear."

Honor's faded eyes shone with tears as she lowered herself unsteadily on to the sitting-room sofa. "But I'd always planned, ever since she was a little girl, that we'd be able to give her a wonderful wedding one day. I know I'm being selfish in resenting Nick's being able to do it all but I feel dreadful that we haven't been able to do anything. I'm not even able to give her a little piece of jewellery . . ." She pressed her hand to her mouth in an effort to hold back the sobs. "I feel we're letting her down, Archie."

He went and sat down beside her, patting her arm clumsily. "Don't get in a state, dearest. Philippa understands. She knows what we've been through. She's not expecting us to contribute."

"But isn't it awful that we can't?" Honor cut in furiously. "Isn't it awful that at this time in our lives, when we should be nicely set up, we're poorer than we were when we started out?"

"No one ever said life was fair." He blamed himself, of course, although he found it hard to admit it. The money side of their marriage had been his responsibility and he was aware he'd been naive. At least, thank God, Philippa was getting out of the poverty rut by marrying Nick Driver. And if it crossed Archie's mind she might be doing it for that very reason, he quenched the thought immediately because it only added to his own feelings of guilt.

CHAPTER FOUR

After the small Chelsea flat Philippa had shared with her best friend, Natasha Maxwell, Nick's Eaton Square apartment seemed gloriously spacious and extravagantly elegant.

"You could fit the whole of my old flat into the main bedroom, here," Philippa laughingly told her mother over the phone. "You and Daddy must come and stay. We have an enormous drawing room with a dining room leading off it through an archway. There are three bedrooms and two bathrooms — and wait until you see the state-of-the-art kitchen! There's only one snag . . ."

"What's that?" Honor asked.

Philippa giggled happily. "I'm going to have to learn how to cook, aren't I? Natasha and I never bothered. If we were in we opened a few tins or got a takeaway."

"I don't think that will do for Nick," Honor agreed. "Anyway won't you be spending most of your time in the country?"

Philippa didn't answer, remembering the strange reservations she'd felt about Wingfield Court that weekend when she'd met Nick's children there. Instead she said, "Probably. Look, Mummy, I'm sorry but I've got to go. We're going out this evening and I haven't even changed yet."

When Nick got back from his business meeting, discussing the acquisition of some old warehouses in the docklands area, she'd just stepped out of the bath. Her skin was warm and scented with jasmine. She was glowing.

"I've missed you," he said immediately, putting his arms around her.

"You'll get all wet," she laughed, reaching for a towel.

"Perhaps I want to." He held her close, kissing her on the mouth, stroking her back, running his hands down over her hips. She raised her arms, slipping them around his neck. Then he slowly swivelled her round until she was facing the steamed-up mirror and he was standing behind her.

"You're so beautiful," he whispered, aroused by the reflection of her slim body and rounded breasts in the looking glass. He cupped them in his hands, squeezing them gently, watching the large nipples stiffen. Then his hands strayed lower and with a tender touch he explored the warmth of her secret parts — stroking, probing, gently round and round — until she suddenly convulsed, gasping as if she could hardly breathe.

"Oh . . . Nick." Her voice was husky, her hands were finding him, there . . . there . . . and there. In moments he'd stripped off his clothes and pulled her down until they were kneeling, face to face, body to body, tongue to tongue, the heat of passion making him tremble, making her weak, so that her voice was a faint whisper.

"Nick, I want you . . . I want you."

With swift care he rolled her and himself on to the thick carpet and took her with a plunge that made her cry out as if she were in pain. She arched her back, feeling the heat rise, feeling his strength and his hardness and his excitement as he rode her, bringing them both to a climax, his breath rasping, and then the final unbelievable sensation exploding between them. Her mind seemed to be away into the stratosphere and she opened her eyes and saw that his were glazed, blind-looking, as if his life depended on his sense of touch alone.

Later, after they'd dressed and he'd poured them both a glass of champagne, they went down to where his car, with driver, was waiting to take them to meet friends in the foyer of Wyndham's Theatre to see a comedy called *Adult Games*.

Philippa, holding Nick's hand, spoke tentatively.

"How much time are we going to be spending up at Malmesbury when we're married?"

He looked surprised. "We'll be based there, darling. Isn't that what you want? I only have to be down here for two or three days each week, if that. I thought we'd make Wingfield our main home. You won't need to come down to London at all if you don't want to."

"Oh, but I love London," she said with more enthusiasm than she'd intended. "We are keeping on the flat, aren't we?"

"Yes. Why? What's wrong? I thought you were a country girl at heart." He looked at her closely, but her expression was serene and her hazel eyes untroubled as she looked back at him.

"I am a country girl."

Nick's mouth twitched. "Not that you look it," he pointed out, eyes sweeping over her slim-fitting black dress, which she was wearing with black silk tights and stilettos. The street lights caught the blonde streaks in her fashionably short hair and made the diamond stud earrings he'd given her flash with fire.

"You look like a top model, my darling. You don't know how proud I am of you," he whispered.

Nick had made sure it would be an unforgettable winter wedding. He was starting a new life with the most fabulous creature, who'd given him a reason to live again, and he didn't care what it cost. It was going to be spectacular.

Every eventuality had been covered. In case it rained, as was quite probable in late October, the four-hundred-yard route from St Mark's church to the house was to be turned into a canopied and carpeted walkway. If it was bitterly cold, braziers were to be placed in the drive by the front door so guests could warm their hands as they waited in line to enter the house.

Florists had been ordered to decorate the church and house with a profusion of white flowers only, mixed with greenery. And caterers had been instructed to provide original and exquisite canapés, to include several kilos of Beluga caviar and a three-tiered cake embellished with white royal icing.

Nick's final order to the catering staff was that he didn't want to see an empty glass in a guest's hand throughout the reception.

"Keep the champagne flowing," he commanded, wanting to impress everyone by having the most stylish wedding of the year. Although it wasn't his first, and he was aware of the criticism behind his back, it was the first time for Philippa, and he was determined she would have all the trimmings. She might not have money but she had class. By God! she had class, he reflected. Rosalind had been classy too, and Nick valued that special attribute, feeling it had less to do with social rank and more to do with innate stylishness. He hoped he had it too, acquired along the way through education and money. He was the third generation of Drivers, and they said it took three generations to leave your origins behind. Well, he'd made it. Or, to be absolutely honest, his grandfather and father had made it and he was reaping the benefits. It had been a gigantic leap from his grandfather, George Driver, who had started out as a foreman in a steel works in 1900, to himself today, owner of Wingfield Court and managing trustee of a discretionary ten-million-pound family trust set up by his father Henry. He stifled the knowledge that the fund was no longer actually worth ten million. In fact it was now worth quite a bit less due to unwise investments and the 1991 recession, but he saw no reason to mention this to his children. So long as their income remained much the same, because he was running a bank overdraft to make up the balance, there was no reason to alarm them. At least, not for the time being. And who knows? he thought. One of his new schemes might prove to be wildly successful and then he could build up the trust fund again without the family being any the wiser.

As for Philippa, if it cost him everything he still had, he was determined to make sure she had whatever she wanted. And that included a fabulous wedding, a honeymoon in the West Indies, and all the clothes and jewels a woman could desire.

It had been arranged that Sir Archie and Lady Sykes, with Philippa, should stay the night before the wedding at the Grand Hotel in Malmesbury, following the age-old tradition of the bride and groom not seeing each other on the day until they came together in the church. They were to stay there as Nick's guests and he'd given instructions they were to be well looked after.

But first there was the big dinner party the night before to which he'd invited forty-two guests.

Giles, Margaret, Jonathan and Cathy had arrived during the day, but Elizabeth had remained adamant in her refusal to attend. The whole thing was too painful to her and she told Laurence she simply couldn't face it.

"I know I'm being childish," she said, "but I feel betrayed and I can't help it. By marrying Philippa I feel Daddy's deserting all of us, not to mention the memory of Mummy. If I attended I'd cry and be a real wet blanket, so it's far better I stay away."

He had patted her shoulder sympathetically but said little because he didn't know how to comfort her. Her anguish was outside his experience.

"Cathy! What the hell have you come as? Bo-Peep?" Jonathan chortled, glancing up the stairs as his sister came down, ready for dinner.

"Oh, God, do I really look that awful?" she sighed. She'd borrowed a cocktail dress from a friend at university because Nick had said she must make an effort to try and look more conventional. It was a pink taffeta confection with a big swirly skirt and lots of frills.

"Darling, you do *not* suit Little-Fuckable-Me frocks," he scolded with mock severity. "Take it off, for God's sake. It's not you."

"But, Jonno, I haven't got anything else. Daddy told me I must wear something smart this weekend. He hates all my clothes. He says I look like I'm wearing the stuff Oxfam throw out."

"But they're you, Cathy. I love all your things and your silver jewellery. It's stylish, and nobody else will be dressed like that at the wedding."

"That's what Daddy's afraid of! Oh, Jonno, what shall I do?"

"Let's have a look upstairs," he said, grabbing her hand. "Quick, before anyone sees you in that hysterical pink blancmange. What sort of a girl would buy a frock like that in the first place?"

Giggling now, they sped up to Cathy's room where Jonathan, with his quick eye for style and colour, decided she should wear a long deep blue and white batik sarong as a wraparound ankle-length skirt, with a skimpy blue top which had narrow shoulder straps, and over it a cream linen jacket she'd bought in a second-hand clothes shop.

"And these shoes," he commanded, producing from the back of her cupboard a pair of sandals she'd bought on holiday in Greece when she'd been fifteen. "They go beautifully," he assured her as he sifted through the contents of a chocolate box in which she kept her silver chains and bangles, rings and extravagant earrings.

Fifteen minutes later Cathy emerged from her room with Jonathan holding her arm. He pushed her along the corridor where there was a full-length mirror.

"*Now* have a look at yourself! Don't you look great? Like a sort of royal gipsy. Never borrow anything from one of your friends again, darling. You've got your own look, you don't need anyone else's."

"But Bryony has good taste," Cathy protested. "I could have borrowed some lovely things from her but the trouble is she's smaller than me. I couldn't get into anything."

"What is she, anorexic? You're slim but you've got womanly curves. You've got a sort of ripe look."

"You make me sound like a piece of Brie." She turned this way and that, studying her reflection. "If you want to describe me as anything, I'd rather it was as an Indian princess."

"Or Daddy's nut brown maiden," he teased. "Come on, let's go. We're missing valuable drinking time."

"I wish Elizabeth was here. This is the first time any of us has been missing from a family get-together."

Jonathan nodded, understanding.

"It's going to take time before she'll accept Philippa."

"It's going to take us all time to get used to the situation but at least we can make the best of it and be happy for Daddy," Cathy said stoutly. "She's got to face the fact he's marrying again, whether she likes it or not."

"D'you know something? I'm the only person in the family now who hasn't got a partner of any sort," he said with a touch of sadness. "You've got Jack, and although he couldn't get away to be here today, at least you've got a love life. So has Elizabeth, and Giles." He clutched her hand as they went down the stairs. "You know, I can't help feeling very alone, Cathy, especially at a time like this."

"Oh, Jonno, darling!" She paused and turned to fling her arms around him, pressing her cheek against his. "I'm sure you'll find someone soon. You deserve to be loved, more than anyone I know."

He hugged her back gratefully. Although she was four years younger she'd become very maternal towards him since Rosalind's death and he was touched by her compassion.

"The gay scene isn't known for its love of fidelity," he remarked drily.

"Jonno?" She looked up into his face, her eyes suddenly anxious. "You are careful, aren't you? I mean . . . you do use condoms?"

"My dear, I drape myself in yards of plastic sheeting!" he retorted with a wicked smile. "No balloons, no party."

Cathy shrieked with laughter and guests gathered in the hall below looked up to see her clinging to her brother with mirth, and thought to themselves what a jolly pair they made.

Good old Jonno, he reflected, as he led Cathy down the stairs. Always cracking flippant one-liners which made other people laugh and managed to hide the pain he felt below the surface of his seemingly pleasant life.

"Come on, Cathy, let's get stuck into the shampoo before the dinner gong." Then he stopped suddenly and drew her attention to an elderly couple. They stood to either side of Philippa, who looked very elegant and composed in a silvery grey silk trouser suit. She was introducing them to some friends of Nick's.

"Her parents?" Cathy whispered.

"Must be. They look OK actually," he observed in surprise.

"Oh, well." She gave a little sigh. "Come on, Jonno. This is where the weekend starts."

With grim determination Margaret had established herself in the drawing room long before the first guest was even due to arrive. Forcing Giles to join her, she reckoned this would be the last time she could play hostess because by tomorrow Wingfield Court would have a new mistress.

Damn you, Philippa Sykes, she reflected bitterly, as she sat by the fire and smoothed the skirt of her green and gold brocade dinner dress. Damn you for coming here, for marrying Nick, for becoming the future chatelaine, for being attractive, young and smart. Damn you for usurping my place. And damn you forever if you have a baby before I do.

"Stand in front of the fireplace, Giles," she snapped irritably. "What's the matter with you? Assert yourself, for God's sake."

"I'm fine here," he replied, from where he sat, remote and far away from her on the window seat. It was dark outside. The room was reflected dimly in the glass. So were they, unreal and ghostly figures, sitting apart from each other like Chekhovian characters.

Giles was thinking about the cost of this wedding and what a waste of money it was. He'd been doing some mental arithmetic that afternoon and had come to a conclusion that staggered him. One way or another his father must have spent over two hundred thousand pounds in the past two months, if you threw in the engagement ring and the honeymoon in the West Indies.

He and Margaret believed in living within their means. Giles simply couldn't understand why people called him "tight". He was merely careful. He, his father and his siblings all received the same amount each year from the family trust, as his grandfather had stipulated, but he believed in looking after his share. It was only sensible. If Jonathan wanted to waste his on going to theatres, clubs and dining in expensive restaurants, then that was his affair. If Elizabeth chose to support a husband who wouldn't work that was her business. And if Cathy wanted to "live for the moment", as she was always saying, spreading her money generously among her friends, why should he care?

Giles was a man who preferred to let his nest egg grow. His policy was to spend only on those things which would advance his career, and that meant a house in the "right" area, a smart car to impress clients, and entertaining those who might be useful and interested in dealing in stamps. Friends got in the way. His time was valuable. He was one of the most knowledgeable philatelists in the country and determined to end up as Chairman of Bartwell's eventually.

"Do you think I should go and check that everything's under control in the kitchen?" Margaret asked, breaking into his thoughts.

"I wouldn't bother. Dad's only gone and hired one of the most expensive catering companies to do tonight's dinner as well as the reception tomorrow. I'd let them get on with it," he told her sourly. "Morgan doesn't seem to care so why should you?"

But Margaret was restless, longing to do something that would make her feel she was in charge. Suddenly she wished she was back in her own home where she ruled supreme and had no doubts about her abilities. Anxiety had tied a tight knot in her stomach, her teeth were clamped together until her jaw ached, and she wondered if this was the beginning of a nervous breakdown. Could one go mad from apprehension and the realization that one is about to be permanently upstaged?

By the time guests started to arrive she was in a frenzy of self-importance, introducing herself to everyone and anyone as "Nick's daughter-in-law" as she asserted herself as the hostess.

"We love giving parties and the house does lend itself to entertaining, doesn't it?" she crooned to anyone who would listen. To Margaret's great disappointment, Philippa didn't seem to mind. She made no effort to compete but instead clung to Nick's side, starry-eyed and beaming with all the radiance of a first-time bride.

Deflated, Margaret nevertheless continued to work the room, taking it upon herself to invite certain friends of Nick's whom she'd met before to: "Come and stay for a weekend in the spring. The garden looks so wonderful then."

"Steady on," Giles admonished her when he overheard her attempts at largesse. "I think we should be more careful until we know which way the wind's blowing."

"What do you mean?" she asked aggressively.

"Well . . . we want to get on the right side of Philippa before we show our muscle, don't we? We mustn't antagonize her. Let's go easy for a while. Then we can do as we like."

Margaret shook her head. "No, Giles, we must start as we mean to go on. After all, this is going to be our house in due course. But while your father is living here, looking after your inheritance, we must establish ourselves so that Philippa doesn't get any ideas."

Giles frowned. "We've got to be subtle, though. Rush in like a bull at a gate and you'll only put everyone's back up," he warned.

She flushed unbecomingly. There was a deadly chill in her eyes as she looked across the room at Philippa.

"It's important she gets the message she's only going to be around while Nick's alive," Margaret pointed out.

Dinner was announced and the guests were ushered into the long dining room where a U-shaped table, seating forty-four people, had been set up. Nick, with his exacting placement, had divided Margaret, Giles, Jonathan and Cathy amongst the guests, putting them next to people who needed looking after, either because of their great age or the fact that they didn't know anyone else. Giles himself had to look after Honor Sykes whom he proceeded to question closely until he'd ascertained that, as he'd suspected, they were an impoverished family. At which point he turned to the attractive woman on his left and, finding out her husband was a rich industrialist, proceeded to talk to her for the rest of the evening.

Cathy, struck by the realization that this was the first party that had been held at Wingfield Court since her mother's death — and how strange it was to see so many people laughing and joking as if nothing had ever happened — found herself sitting next to Sir Archie Sykes.

"Oh, you're Philippa's father!" she exclaimed with unaffected warmth. "How very nice to meet you. I'm Cathy."

Old Archie Sykes was bowled over. His blue eyes instantly twinkled as he gazed at her, enchanted by her dark gipsy looks and unusual but distinctive way of dressing.

"I've heard all about you from Philippa," he responded, with equal warmth.

"Oh, dear, have you? That doesn't sound very promising," she joked. "Are you happy about your daughter marrying my father?"

He blinked, taken aback by her candour. Cathy was watching him with her big dark eyes and there was a teasing smile on her lips.

"I'm sure he'll make her very happy," Archie replied with careful diplomacy. "He seems like a very nice feller."

"He *is* nice," Cathy said, but he heard a note of what sounded like regret in her voice.

"This must be very hard for you and your brothers and sister," he said astutely. "She isn't here tonight, is she? Philippa told me she wasn't coming to the wedding."

Cathy nodded sadly. "That's right. She couldn't face it . . . Oh! That sounds rude." Her cheeks were suddenly red.

His smile was sympathetic. "No, it's not rude, my dear, it's quite understandable. I gather your mother died last year. You must not only miss her but also resent anyone coming into the family who might try to fill her shoes."

Cathy's eyes widened and were over-bright as she tried to control her emotions. "It *is* hard," she agreed with devastating honesty. "We've all had a struggle to come to terms with it and Elizabeth hasn't quite got there yet. But, really, I'm grateful if Philippa can make Daddy happy again. He suffered so much when Mummy was ill and . . . dying," she finished in a low voice.

"I'm sure, my dear. I'm sure." Archie sounded genuinely sorrowful. "It must have been a truly terrible time for you all and I'm so sorry. I can only assure you of one thing. Philippa wants to be a friend to you all. Not someone who will try to take your mother's place, not even a step-mother, but a real friend."

Cathy's smile was shaky but her slim brown hand, bedecked with several silver rings, reached out and closed over his.

"Thank you," she said simply. "I'm sure in time everything will work out. Not that any of us ever had anything personal against Philippa . . ."

"I'm sure. It's what she might represent that's so hurtful, isn't it?"

"Exactly." Cathy gazed at him, delighted by his understanding. "Oh, I do wish we'd met you sooner," she added impulsively. "Five minutes with you and even Elizabeth would be persuaded everything's going to be all right."

Archie threw back his head and laughed at her outspoken frankness. "So tell me about yourself, my dear? I hear you're at university."

From then on, as Cathy told the others afterwards, she had a wonderful evening. Sir Archie seemed to show a genuine interest in them all, asking her about Giles's career as a philatelist, and Jonathan's painting, and of course Elizabeth and her children.

"He's the tops!" she assured them as they went to bed that night. "I honestly don't think we've got anything to worry about. If Philippa turns out to be half as nice as her father, everything's going to be OK."

The next day dawned blue and gold, a perfect October day with warmth in the sun's rays and a sky as clear as an azure glass dome.

Nick had booked two suites for Philippa and her parents at the Grand and they breakfasted together in their own private sitting room.

"How are you feeling, darling?" Honor asked her daughter, watching as Philippa sipped her *café filtré* but refused to eat anything.

She gave a shaky laugh. "Nervous, I suppose. But excited."

"It's going to be a beautiful day." Honor felt shaky herself and very emotional. How was she going to get through the marriage service without having a little weep, she wondered. Especially when it came to Archie's giving Philippa away?

He, on the other hand was up-beat, greatly reassured about his daughter's future after last night's dinner. He'd told them about his conversation with Cathy and her honesty, and it had reassured Philippa to learn that there was no personal animus in the attitude of Nick's children.

"I've never had a problem with Jonathan," she remarked, "and I had a feeling that Cathy would come round in time, but I'm not sure about the others. Elizabeth really hates me and so does Margaret. Giles? Well, I don't think he actually dislikes me but I'm sure Margaret is working on him. I think she's afraid I'm going to take something away from her."

"All you need is time, darling," Archie assured her. "They'll all come round when they get to know you better."

Philippa suddenly leaned forward and spoke urgently.

"You will come and stay for Christmas, won't you? Nick suggested it last night. All his children and the grandchildren will be coming, and I couldn't bear it without both of you."

Honor looked pleased but surprised. "Are you sure, darling? We don't want to be in the way and this will be your first Christmas with Nick . . ." Her voice drifted, croaking dangerously. She was going to miss Philippa terribly if they didn't see her over the festive season, but she really hadn't counted on being included in Nick's family circle.

"Mummy, I'll *need* you," Philippa exclaimed, sounding like a little girl again. "And Daddy can woo Elizabeth and Margaret like he did Cathy last night, and it will make a huge difference to the atmosphere. Oh, you've got to come."

Archie chuckled. "I don't think we really need any persuading, do we, Honor? Christmas wouldn't be Christmas without our girl, would it? It sounds great fun."

"Then that's settled." Philippa leaned back, relieved.

The rest of the morning passed slowly; the wedding wasn't taking place until three o'clock, and so they relaxed in the luxury of the Grand, with room service sending up smoked salmon sandwiches and champagne at lunchtime. Then the hairdresser arrived in their suite, ordered by Nick to attend to both the bride and her mother, and from then on it was a flurry of getting ready, of Philippa applying her makeup carefully and Honor being persuaded that a little blusher and pink lipstick would "give her a bit of colour". Of Archie getting into his morning suit, which he proudly announced he'd had for forty years and could still fit into, and of Honor dressing in her new navy blue outfit and being pronounced "very smart and elegant-looking" by her daughter. And then Philippa, helped by the hairdresser, stepped into her wedding dress, a wonderfully draped white silk gown with long sleeves and a train, which clung to her shapely figure so that she reminded Honor of an arum lily.

Finally a tiara of white orchids and a long filmy veil, which floated around her and covered the train, was fixed to her fair hair. And then she stood looking into a long mirror, unable to believe it was really her own reflection she saw.

"You look fantastic, m'dear," Archie crowed. "Doesn't she look pukka, Honor?"

"Absolutely beautiful," she agreed proudly. "Don't forget your bouquet, darling." She reached into the florist's box to lift out the spray of white orchids, gardenias and stephanotis. Then she paused, her hand hovering, her expression perplexed.

"What's this?"

"What?" Philippa turned to look and there, tucked under the flowers, was a white leather case. "I don't believe it!" She lifted the case out of the box and opened it. Lying on a bed of white velvet was a diamond necklace, the stones blazing in their platinum setting, the design a series of lover's knots linked by drop pearls.

"Oh . . . my . . . God," she said slowly. There was a note too, tucked under the clasp, in Nick's handwriting.

My only darling love,

It seems I have been waiting for today for a very long time. You are making me the happiest of men by becoming my wife. With my deepest love forever,

Nick

Philippa's eyes brimmed with unshed tears as she took the necklace out of its case.

"Let me help you, darling," said Honor gently as she placed the jewels around her daughter's neck and fastened the dazzling clasp.

St Mark's glowed like a jewel inside, its mellow stone columns, oak pews and gold mosaic altar embellished on this day by banks of white flowers and candles. The organ music of Handel and Bach filled the air.

Giles, as chief usher, was concerned when he realized the bridegroom's side of the church was packed while the bride's side was half empty. It looked bad. People might think his father was marrying a nobody. He consulted the other ushers and it was decided newcomers should be invited to sit on the bride's side, whether they knew Philippa or not.

Meanwhile only Margaret, Jonathan and Cathy were seated in the front pew. A final call to Elizabeth by Nick that morning had merely been responded to by a peevish Laurence who informed him that Elizabeth had taken the children out for the day and he didn't know when they'd be back.

"Could they be on their way to the wedding?" Nick had asked hopefully.

"With rugs, a picnic basket and the dogs?" Laurence had retorted.

However, by the time Philippa glided up the aisle with her father, to the strains of "Lead Us, Heavenly Father, Lead Us", the balance on both sides was just about right, and Nick was standing waiting for her with his best man by his side.

Honor glanced at him, this man who was about to become her son-in-law and who was almost exactly the same age as her, and saw on his perhaps too smoothly handsome face an expression of triumph as his eyes swept over the congregation. He seemed to be saying: Look how successful I am. Rich, powerful and about to marry a beautiful young woman. How many of you could do that?

Honor caught the look and felt deeply shaken by this insight into the soul of Nick Driver. Then, in a flash, he was smiling tenderly at Philippa as she approached him and when he turned to look at the vicar who was about to join them in holy matrimony, his expression, Honor thought, could almost have been taken for one of humility.

On the opposite side of the aisle, Cathy found herself clutching Jonathan's hand and gazing at Philippa in awe. She really did look beautiful: serene, quietly confident and very, very happy. For the first time Cathy could see why her father wanted to marry her. Philippa would be a source of comfort to him as he grew older, a gentle nurturing presence who would pander willingly to his needs.

Giles, sitting with Margaret, looked flushed and grumpy, fidgeting with his service sheet and hardly concentrating at all. He's probably too busy costing everything, Cathy reflected with amusement.

". . . with this ring I thee wed . . ." Nick's voice was steady and filled with loving sincerity.

Suddenly, Cathy bit her lip and started counting the number of stones in the nave's archway to stop herself from crying.

". . . with my body I thee worship . . ."

Giles silently ground his teeth and cursed his father for his virility ". . . and with all my worldly goods I thee endow."

Like hell! Margaret reflected furiously.

But it was Jonathan who thought, How lucky Dad is to have someone to love and share his life with. He squeezed Cathy's hand tighter and at that moment they both knew what the other was thinking: If only Mummy hadn't died, and if only she were still here, none of this would be happening.

Ninety miles away Elizabeth sat on the grass making a daisy chain for Tamsin. They'd had a picnic lunch with all the children's favourite things like potato crisps, sausage rolls, chocolate biscuits and ice cream, and now Jasper lay on the rug waving his fat little legs in the air and gazed unseeingly at the fluffy clouds overhead. Dominic, meanwhile, was engaged on a secret mission which seemed to involve discovering an "enemy camp" behind some bushes.

For the past three hours Elizabeth had enjoyed a special kind of freedom on this golden day, away from the farm and gloomy Laurence, the brisk Teutonic manners of Herta and Gerhard and nosy interference of Laura. Just her and the three children, answerable to no one, enjoying the peace of the countryside, refusing to acknowledge what was happening in the rest of the world.

"There you are, Tamsin," she said, holding out the delicate strand of daisies. "Shall I put it round your neck?"

Tamsin got to her feet, still carrying her doll, from which she refused to be parted.

"No. On Eckit," she said, looking lovingly into the painted face. Eckit, who for some unknown reason had originally been called Erica which was too difficult for Tamsin to pronounce, was thrust forward.

"Like a cwown," Tamsin added importantly.

"Like a crown? Is she a princess?"

Tamsin nodded. "There you are, my darling." With great care, Elizabeth placed the flowers in a circle on the doll's head.

"There you are, my darling," Tamsin echoed, gazing adoringly into the blue glass eyes.

Elizabeth lay back on the rug beside Jasper, smiling with contentment. If every day could be like this, she'd ask for nothing more in life.

She had no idea what made her suddenly look at her wrist watch but when she did her heart contracted with physical pain as if it had been squeezed by a strong fist. At this very moment her father was getting married to Philippa.

Cathy clutched at her straw beach hat. To smarten it up for the wedding she'd bought a mass of pink ostrich feathers in a street market and stitched them to the brim but now a stiff breeze was whipping across the graveyard of St Marks, stirring the fallen leaves and raking the grass with icy fingers.

The wedding ceremony had ended and grouped outside the church for the formal photographs. Nick and Philippa stood, surrounded by his children and Sir

Archie and Lady Sykes, all of them stiffly in a line and being told to "say cheese".

Suddenly the wind caught Philippa's veil and scooped it high above her head so she looked as if she'd just flown down to earth and landed in their midst.

"What a wind!" Cathy heard someone remark and couldn't help glancing over to her mother's grave on the far side of the burial ground, with its inscribed headstone. It looked so painfully new and clean beside all the others tinged green with moss and yellow lichen.

Then, as the wind strengthened, gusting up the path and whirling Philippa's veil into an uncontrollable tangle of tulle, she saw that her new step-mother was shivering.

Cathy turned to Jonathan. "It's an omen, isn't it?" she whispered.

He nodded, as always on the same wavelength as her.

"The Ides of March also take place on the fifteenth of May, July and October, unlike all the other months when it's on the thirteenth," he whispered back.

She looked startled. "I didn't know that."

Her brother nodded again and glanced at their father who was smiling into the camera. "Someone will pay for this," he muttered with foreboding.

CHAPTER FIVE

"My God! She didn't waste any time, did she? What does Dad say?" Cathy asked, mobile phone held to one ear, fingers pressed to the other in order to deaden the background noise of the busy Edinburgh cafe.

Jack Hamilton, her boyfriend, was sitting opposite her, sipping his frothy cappuccino and watching her expression which had suddenly become alert. Listening to her side of the conversation, it seemed something had happened in the Driver family.

Over three hundred miles away Elizabeth was sitting on the edge of the kitchen table, feet resting on a chair, full of gossip and all of it negative.

"Oh, Dad's delighted," she replied dully. "Over the moon. Says he doesn't want to know whether it's a boy or a girl so long as it's healthy. What a cliché!"

"Imagine! A new baby for him." Cathy rolled her eyes at Jack, whispering in an aside: "Philippa's preggers." Aloud she continued, "How is she? Having morning sickness and all that?"

Elizabeth responded by shrugging her shoulders as if she and her sister were face to face. "How should I know? I never speak to her. It was Daddy who phoned. He told Laurence, actually. I was out with the children."

"I suppose I'd better call and congratulate him. Do the others know?"

"Dad said he'd told Giles but hadn't been able to get hold of Jonathan. Margaret's furious, of course," Elizabeth added. "She was on the phone to me within seconds, saying she'd always known this would happen and wasn't it disgusting for a man of Dad's age to be having a baby?"

"He's not *that* old. I mean, he's not seventy or something. Lots of men start a second family in their fifties."

"Yes, but you know Margaret. She's desperate for a baby herself, and besides that she's the sort of person who gets jealous if someone has one more lump of sugar in their coffee than her. She's also so damn anxious to get everything she can when Giles inherits, it's pathetic."

"But you've got to admit it must be pretty galling for her that Philippa's pregnant," Cathy pointed out. "That's why she's such a driven piece, as Jonno would say."

"I suppose so."

"Anyway," Cathy continued peaceably, "Jack and I are driving down next week, for Easter, before we go skiing. Will we be seeing you?"

"Where are you staying?"

"Where do you think we're staying? We're going home, of course. Do you realize, I haven't seen you since last September?"

There was a pause before Elizabeth spoke. "We're staying here for Easter."

"Aren't you all coming for the weekend, like you always do? Oh, come on! You wouldn't come to Dad's wedding, and you wouldn't stay for Christmas . . . but surely you can come for Easter? You must have got used to the idea of Dad's being married to Philippa by now? Mummy wouldn't have wanted you to go on grieving and resenting Dad for being happy. And when am I ever going to see Dominic, Tamsin and Jasper again?" Cathy's voice rose to a plaintive wail and Jack looked at her sympathetically.

"You don't understand . . ." Elizabeth's voice broke. She could hear the children playing in the garden outside the kitchen window, their young voices alive with innocent enthusiasm and laughter, and she felt so filled with a pain she hardly understood herself that she was unable to continue.

"I do understand," she heard Cathy say against a background of buzz and clatter. But how could her sister possibly understand? She was just twenty. She had her whole life before her and wasn't responsible for the happiness of three little children who asked only to be loved and looked after in a secure family home. Something Elizabeth was finding it increasingly difficult to give them. "You don't understand Cathy," she burst out angrily.

During the months following Rosalind's death she'd been so numbed with grief, only managing to get through one day at a time by cruising along on automatic pilot, that the full impact of her loss had only really registered when her father had said he was bringing Philippa into the family as his new wife. And that had been a second body blow, a second cause of intense shock and sorrow, and the opening of the original wound all over again. The one thing that kept going round and round in her mind was how little her father must have cared for her mother, and for all of them too, in the first place.

Elizabeth wiped her tears with an already damp tea towel.

"You don't understand," she repeated sadly. "It's just that I can't bear being without Mummy. I *need* her. I can't bear to go home and for her not to be there. And it makes it worse that someone else is."

"I feel the same," Cathy replied, slightly impatiently. "But Dad's married to Philippa and there's nothing we can do about it. And we can't stay away from home forever."

"We can, love. Oh, yes, we can."

"But you can't change anything now, why waste your energy resenting her for the rest of your life?"

"It's not only that," Elizabeth replied. "You don't know how difficult it is for a family to get away. There are so many animals to look after and it's such a performance packing all the things the children need. We shall be definitely be spending Easter on the farm."

"She's just making excuses," Cathy told Jack sadly as they strolled along Princes Street. "I wish she'd try and accept the situation."

"I expect it'll take time," he replied, putting his arm around her shoulders and pulling her close to his side. Much taller than her, and strongly built with broad shoulders, he was very protective towards her and aware how sensitive she was to other people's feelings.

"They'd been together for nearly a year now and she was his first love as he was hers. What the future held neither of them had the slightest idea, so, like all their friends, they lived for today and let tomorrow take care of itself. Meanwhile they were inseparable, although Cathy was aware other girls were always throwing themselves at him. She couldn't blame them. Jack had aquamarine blue eyes that were slightly slanting, a strong profile and a wide generous mouth. She beamed with pride when people turned to look at him in the street, which happened all the time since he'd cut his hair very short and then, with an old toothbrush, applied peroxide to the upstanding tips so that now they sprang up like platinum feathers all over his head, giving him the look of an ancient Greek god on a coin.

"Hey, cool!" Cathy had said approvingly when she saw what he'd done. Inspired, she'd then had peacock blue and red extensions fixed to the front of her dark hair. Walking down the street now, dressed in their baggy clothes and with matching silver ear studs, they drew amused looks from the residents of Edinburgh.

When Cathy had first told Jack about Philippa, he'd said: "She doesn't sound like someone who's going to upset the apple cart."

Now she wasn't so sure. If Elizabeth was refusing to go to Wingfield Court again, that meant neither were Dominic, Tamsin or Jasper so her step-mother's presence *was* making waves within the family.

Philippa sank back on to her pillows, feeling weak and exhausted. It was the sixth time she'd been sick that morning and she wondered, after seven weeks of being pregnant, how long this was going to last. No one had warned her that expecting a baby was so awful. She felt tired all the time, she was sick every morning, and at night she had stomach cramps.

"None of my friends has suffered like this," she told Nick worriedly. "They've all continued working and at the most felt a little tired in the evenings. I feel ill, can't get out of bed until nearly lunchtime because I'm so tired, and by the evening I feel like collapsing."

He held her tenderly in his arms and tried to reassure her. "You'll soon feel better, darling. Remember, you're not ill, just pregnant. Within a few weeks you'll be fine again and feeling wonderful."

Somehow she doubted it. She didn't like to ask him how Rosalind had managed with her four pregnancies. Four! It didn't bear thinking about. If she hadn't been so happy she'd have felt like dying with misery.

At least, she thought, opening her eyes and looking around with pleasure, they had turned the largest spare bedroom, the one previously used by Elizabeth and Laurence, into the master bedroom, freshly redecorated and furnished to her choice. She'd insisted on everything being new, too. The king-size bed, the dressing table and mirrors, curtains and furnishings made from an exquisite French fabric, and a Victorian chaise-longue which was placed in the bay window overlooking the garden and covered with a white cashmere throw. She'd even had the adjoining bathroom refitted and redecorated and so, in this particular part of the house, had managed to erase every trace of Rosalind.

The problem, which she was sure partly caused her continual angst and feeling of illness, was that the rest of the place, including the garden, still spoke of her predecessor. Rosalind was everywhere. In the polished surfaces of the furniture that seemed to reflect her shadow and the lingering scent of the bowls of pot pourri. In the rustle of the silk drawing-room curtains, which seemed to sway although there was no breeze, and in the creaks in the night as if someone was coming up the wide oak staircase.

The bedroom Rosalind had shared with Nick for over thirty years had also been redecorated and refurbished and made into a guest room, with all her brushes and trinkets and personal possessions carefully packed away, ready for when Elizabeth and Cathy wanted them. But the room still contained the essence of its previous owner. Even the new carpet, a stretch of pale blue to go with the new blue and white curtains, seemed to bear the imprint of her feet, and her perfume . . . was it Jolie Madame? . . . lingered in the air like a soft breath. Philippa never went into that room now. If she could, she'd have locked the door and hidden the key, pretending it wasn't there.

And all the time she had to appear happy with her new home and her suggestions for change had to be made diplomatically for fear of offending not only Nick but Giles and Margaret, who kept proposing themselves for weekend visits as if they didn't have a home of their own. Not that she didn't understand how much they'd loved Rosalind and how much they still missed her, but Wingfield Court was *her* home now and Philippa knew she could never be truly happy for as long as its atmosphere remained filled with the presence of its former mistress.

Nick breezed into the bedroom about noon, looking as always as if he'd just bathed and changed, brushed his hair and dabbed himself with aftershave. Gleamingly clean and polished, his tanned face breaking into a smile as he approached the bed, he sat down and took Philippa's hand.

"Feeling better, sweetheart?" he asked, that aura of deep intimacy that was his trademark, and which Philippa found so arousingly attractive, exuding from him like a powerful aroma.

She nodded and smiled weakly. "I'm sorry to be such a bore, darling. I can't wait to feel normal again."

"Would you like some tea and toast?"

"Some dry toast would be lovely."

"Good. I'll get Morton to bring it up to you. Meanwhile, are you feeling up to talking about Easter?"

"Easter?" She sounded appalled. "What about it?"

He moved closer, seductively stroking her breasts through the thin silk of her nightdress with the lightness of touch of a blind man reading braille.

"Easter Sunday is in ten days' time. I wondered if you'd like your parents to come for the weekend? Giles and Margaret will be here, and Cathy's driving down from Edinburgh bringing Jack with her. Jonathan has said he'll come too so I thought we'd have a nice family weekend." His expression bland, he was smiling reassuringly.

"What about Elizabeth and Laurence and the children?" she asked.

The grey eyes became veiled but Nick's smile did not falter.

"They can't get away from the farm apparently. That's the trouble with having so many animals."

Philippa knew he was lying but smiled understandingly.

"What a shame. You should drive over and visit them, Nick, if they can't come here."

His hand slid gently down to her stomach, stroking it tenderly as he leaned forward to kiss her on the lips.

"We'll soon be busy with a baby of our own," he whispered tenderly. Leaning closer, he put his arms around her and she knew he was aroused. It was weeks since they'd made love because she'd been feeling so unwell. She pulled him closer, knowing how he must be missing having sex.

"I love you. You know that, don't you?" she said softly, stroking the hair back from his temple.

"Not as much as I love you." He buried his face in her neck, pressing himself tightly against her. He found it agony these days to be in bed beside her, night after night, his body yearning for hers so that he was unable to sleep, his skin hot and feverish in his need, while she lay, fast asleep, her breasts rising and falling gently, one hand resting on her as yet flat stomach. How desperately he wanted her. How he longed to fill her with his love and make her his, again and again. And how the memories of those nights together when they'd first fallen in love came back to torture him with exquisite longing. Never before in his life had he reached such heights of bliss while making love to a woman; not in his youth when he'd played the field with dozens of gorgeous girls; not even with Rosalind in the years when she'd been young and strong and full of life.

"I love you in a way I never thought possible," he told his wife now, looking into her eyes. "I never thought life could be as wonderful as this."

"You're so good to me," Philippa murmured gratefully.

"My darling, I want you to be happy. I want you to have everything you've ever wanted. You only have to ask and it will be yours . . . and the baby's," he added, in a reckless burst of generosity, prompted by memories of past sexual gratification and the thought of resuming their love life again as soon as she felt better. "Is there anything you want? Anything at all?"

That morning he'd received a strong letter from his personal banker's, cautioning him that his overdraft had now reached three million pounds and if he didn't start reducing this figure they might be forced to foreclose on his account. During the next hour he locked himself in the estate office and made several urgent phone calls, wanting to find out how various investments were doing, wondering how he could raise a large capital sum to pay off his overdraft without dipping any further into the family trust, finally coming to the conclusion that his scheme for redevelopment in London's dock area would probably reap large profits . . . one day. Meanwhile to hell with money worries. He had other things to think about. Like enjoying every moment of his life with Philippa. Having her was the most important thing to him. His hand reached out to touch her and she caught it and held it between her own hands, kissing his finger tips gently. Then she sighed and no longer looked serene.

"What is it? Tell me," Nick urged. "You know you can ask for anything, my darling."

Philippa looked into his eyes, trying to gauge the depths of his sincerity. At last she spoke.

"I know it's probably not possible, but it would be lovely to sell this house, and have a place that was really ours, wouldn't it? Where you and I and the baby could make a fresh start."

"Is that what you'd like?" he asked, surprised. "I thought you loved it here?"

"It's not that, sweetheart. Of course this is a beautiful house. It's just that . . ." She hesitated, not wanting to offend him or hurt his feelings. "It's your family home and there's nothing wrong with that. But it doesn't feel as if it belongs to *us*, you, me and the baby, does it?"

Nick's eyes widened as he saw an opportunity opening up before him, a chance to raise a capital sum with which to pay off some of the money he owed the bank. It would have to be handled carefully so far as his children were concerned but it might just be the answer to his financial problem.

"OK, darling," he said slowly. "We'll move. But let's keep it to ourselves for the moment."

Philippa cupped his face in her hands, her eyes blazing with delight. "Really, Nick? You mean it? Oh, darling . . . I love you. You're so good to me." She covered his face in kisses, her breath warm on his cheek.

He instantly became aroused, again folding her in his arms and holding her close. It was as if he were drowning in hot sweet honey while his head spun dizzily and his longing for her became a tortuous ache.

"Sweet Jesus, you drive me crazy," he murmured. brushing her nipples with his lips. "Oh, darling . . . Oh, Christ, darling . . ."

Philippa had slid down the bed and was pleasuring him in a way that always drove him demented with ecstasy. As far as he was concerned, nothing in the world mattered as long as she didn't stop.

"Will you just shut the fuck up?" Jonathan stormed, red in the face with fury.

The thin young man with the dissolute mouth and louche appearance remained lounging on a chair in Jonathan's sitting room, staring up at him with eyes that spelled danger.

"Who the fuck do you think you are?" he sneered. "You wanted it. Now pay for it."

"I've never paid for it in my life and I don't intend to start now." Jonathan tried to sound arrogant, as if he were in control of the situation, but knew he wasn't. He must have been mad, or more probably very drunk last night, to have picked up this young man who was now refusing to leave unless he was given fifty pounds.

Jonathan had dropped into a famous gay bar in Shaftesbury Avenue for a beer at around eleven o'clock before going home and immediately spotted this young man, standing by the bar and looking both interesting and interested. There was something about him that was sordidly sexy and deeply attractive. Jonathan could just imagine . . .

"Like to come back to my place?" he'd asked with studied casualness.

"Where d'you live?" The voice was uneducated but not unpleasant.

"Near Regent's Park." Jonathan knew Pip was away for a few days so didn't mention him. "I've got a flat."

The pale blue eyes quickened and looked sharp. "OK," he replied laconically. "What's your name, by the way?"

"Jonathan. What's yours?"

"Chris."

"Let's go then."

Up to that point everything had gone according to form so far as Jonathan was concerned. It was the old routine. Pick someone up in a club or a pub then back to his own place which made him feel more secure than trailing out to some godforsaken seedy room in Clapham or Crouch End or wherever. Then it was a couple of drinks and down to business. Mostly, they left after a couple of hours and Jonathan was glad. To wake up facing last night's indiscretion was not the best way to start the day. Occasionally they stayed all night but left early to get to work, leaving him to have a leisurely breakfast before going off to his studio.

Either scenario suited him fine if all he wanted was sex. A quick fuck. See you around some time. 'Bye.

It was only when he longed for a proper loving relationship that the whole thing was heartbreaking.

But a relationship with Chris was the last thing he'd had on his mind when he'd turned the key in his front door and led him into the flat. Everything went swimmingly at first, and when Chris finally fell asleep, Jonathan thought, Oh, well. I'm tired too. He'll leave in the morning.

But he had been woken at dawn by a rustling sound and, opening his eyes, saw Chris going through his chest of drawers.

"What the hell . . . ?"

Chris spun round, startled. Then he dropped his hands to his sides and looked sulky.

"I was looking for a fag."

"You said you didn't smoke last night."

"So?" He shrugged and dug his hands into his pockets.

"Are you off, then?" Jonathan asked.

"When I've had m'breakfast."

Jonathan began to feel uneasy. He gave a false laugh.

"This isn't a five-star hotel, you know," he pointed out, getting out of bed and pulling on some clothes. Usually laid back and relaxed, he now felt alert and suspicious, anxious to get rid of Chris as quickly as possible. What had seemed seductive the previous night now seemed distinctly threatening. When Chris strolled out of the bedroom and into the living room, Jonathan followed him closely.

"I've got to get to work, actually," he remarked. "So if you'll excuse me . . ."

"You fucking little snotty toe rag . . . *actually*," Chris snapped back, flopping into an armchair. "Got a rich family, I suppose? Nice flat. Nice furniture. Mummy spoils her little boy, does she?"

"Get out."

"I'll go when I'm ready. You haven't paid me yet."

"Paid you? Like hell! You never said you wanted money when you came back here last night. Suddenly turned into a rent boy, have you? Just because you've seen this flat?"

Chris narrowed his eyes and something in his expression made Jonathan think of the gay murders he'd heard of, the victims left stabbed to death, their bodies sometimes not discovered for days. He remembered Pip was away. Wouldn't be back until Thursday and this was Tuesday morning. A cold frisson crawled down his spine.

"Give me a hundred pounds now and I'll go," Chris was saying in a soft quiet voice. "Otherwise I'll come back this evening. And I'll bring some friends with me. Get my meaning?"

"I don't keep cash in the house." Jonathan was determined not to give way. "This is a try on and you know it. Now fuck off or I'll call the police."

"Oh, yeah?" said Chris. The pale eyes bored into his sardonically and Jonathan suddenly felt absurdly young and foolish. Then he heard a click and a moment later Chris had sprung from the chair and was pointing a flick knife inches from his face.

"I'll be back this evening with my friends, you pathetic little queen. Have the money ready. Make it five hundred now, for all the trouble you've caused me, and don't think about running back to Mummy because if you do we'll torch your fucking precious flat."

Jonathan stood impassively, trying to control the beating of his heart, cursing himself for his choice of partner the previous night.

At that moment the phone began to ring. It rang several times as they stared at one other, the shrill notes echoing in the silence. Then Chris snatched up his leather coat and, turning, crashed swiftly out of the front door.

Shaken, Jonathan sank on to the sofa and picked up the phone.

"Hello?"

"Jonno? It's me, Cathy."

"Hi, babe."

"What's the matter? You sound odd."

"I'm fine. Absolutely fine. I was just . . ."

"You don't sound fine," she said, concerned. "Did I wake you up?"

He took a deep breath, making an effort to pull himself together. "Sort of. I was just getting up," he lied. "How's everything with you? I suppose you've heard we're about to have a step-brother or sister?"

"Yes." She sounded doubtful, not quite believing him. "I rang to check that you're coming home for Easter?"

"I suppose so. Dad's already been on the phone, full of himself as usual. I dare say I'll try and get a lift from Giles on Thursday evening."

"Not until then? Jack and I are driving down today. We're leaving in a few minutes and I suddenly thought it would be lovely if you were to arrive tonight as well. Elizabeth and the family aren't coming, you know. She's absolutely refused . . ."

"I can't make it by tonight, Cathy," he cut in. "I've got a lot of work on at the moment. A commission to finish, for one thing."

"Oh, Jonno! How dreadfully disappointing. It'll be so boring without you." She sounded genuinely sad. "I haven't seen you since Christmas and I was hoping we could have nearly a week together before I go skiing. Can't you possibly come sooner?"

He hesitated. He was going to have to deal with this Chris business. Maybe he'd enlist the help of some of *his* friends, frighten the rotten little faggot off, but the one thing he couldn't do was risk having his flat set alight.

"Listen, I'll come up as soon as I can, I promise."

"Are you sure nothing's wrong?" she asked again. "You would tell me if there was, wouldn't you?"

"I'm fine. Stop fussing. See you Thursday or Friday. 'Bye, honey child." He hung up before she could probe any further.

The trouble was, Cathy could read him like an open book and this was a story he didn't want her to know about because it was so abysmally sordid he'd feel ashamed.

"I suppose she'll be doing up the old nurseries," Margaret commented bitterly as she did the packing in the bedroom of their Holland Park house. Giles knew exactly what she was talking about because she talked of nothing else these days.

"That's what people usually do when they're having a baby," he retorted shortly.

Margaret straightened up from folding her sweaters.

"We've got to do something about having one, Giles. We can't go on like this." There was desperation in her voice, as if she no longer cared whether she annoyed him or not.

"We've got plenty of time," he replied, not looking at her.

"That's just what we *haven't* got. I'm thirty-two, and if we're going to have to resort to artificial insemination or in vitro fertilization we've got to get on with it." A tear splashed on to her best rust-coloured sweater and she brushed it away swiftly.

"We're not going to get into any of that business," Giles retorted coldly. "We'll have children one day." He had his back to her, getting his shoes out of the cupboard, placing them carefully at the bottom of his holdall. It was as if a thick glass wall had risen between them in the last few moments so that if either of them spoke now the other would not hear.

"But we have a problem, you've got to face that," Margaret burst out with reckless anguish, prepared to hammer at the wall until she smashed it.

Giles continued to ignore her, smiling pleasantly as if she hadn't spoken. Then without another word he turned and walked out of the bedroom. She stared at his receding back, unable to speak for anger and frustration.

It was always the same. He absolutely refused to discuss the matter; worse, as far as he was concerned, there didn't seem to be anything to discuss. He was in complete denial and it drove her mad. Made her want to hit him over the head with something. Kick him in his useless balls. Tell him that if *he* couldn't make her pregnant, she'd find someone who could.

Everything she'd feared was coming true and Margaret slumped on the bed, beside her half-packed suitcase, and wept with sheer misery. Meanwhile she had to get through five days of hell without even Elizabeth to talk to, watching Philippa swan around

Wingfield Court as lady of the manor as she'd done at Christmas — highly organized, with the house running smoothly and even Morton full of her praises.

Nick had spent most of the morning on the phone, cursing the fact that everyone seemed to go away over Easter, leaving a few dogsbodies in charge. However, and most importantly, he managed to get hold of his stockbroker, Andrew Kingsley, and his accountant, Ernest Lomax, both of whom worked with him on the Driver Family Trust as well as Wingland Estate Ltd, and managed to set up meetings with them in London early the following week.

Meanwhile, he was seeing his lawyer, Norman Sheridan, on Tuesday morning. Both Lomax and Sheridan were heads of small local firms, two-man bands, a joke beside the big firms in the city. But they were both valuable to Nick. They did as they was told.

Elizabeth scrubbed the hall wall with feverish haste, for Laurence would be back in a few minutes and would go ballistic if he saw Tamsin's crayon "draw-rings" on the newly painted pale yellow emulsion.

"You mustn't draw on the walls again," she scolded, but Tamsin just stood and watched, wide-eyed and unrepentant, knowing her mother wasn't really angry.

Exhausted, Elizabeth gave the wall a final swipe and, although it wasn't perfect, prayed Laurence wouldn't notice.

It had been one of those days. She'd been glad he'd been out, driving his mother over to Coventry to see her sister. Tai-Tai, one of the cats, had been sick on their bedroom carpet; the second spaniel, Muffet, had succumbed to diarrhoea behind the drawing-room sofa after stealing and guzzling a large bar of chocolate; and Jasper had thrown his bowl of cereal across the kitchen with gladiatorial force. Finally Herta had broken the new vacuum cleaner and Gerhard had dropped Laurence's favourite mug, smashing it to bits as it hit the terracotta floor tiles.

When Elizabeth had first married she'd tried to keep the rooms of Willow Farm looking neat and tidy in a countrified style, with simple bright colour schemes and practical furnishings, hooks by the back door for coats and racks for shoes and wellies, plenty of shelves for depositing the detritus of busy lives and cupboards for storing what wasn't in daily use.

But after a while the novelty of picking things up and putting them somewhere else began to pall. Unwilling to have domestic help at this stage and happy to live in cosy confusion, she found that if you left a chore long enough, it rarely needed doing. Things had an odd way of settling themselves where you left them and she had better things to do with her time, like curling up with a book in front of a comfortingly crackling log fire or listening to music as she cooked, obsessively, in the kitchen.

But when Jasper was on the way Laurence said he couldn't stand the mess any more. He'd stood in the kitchen doorway one day, while she was cooking and the children had all their toys strewn around, and shouted: "I need a JCB to get in here. This is absurd. We've *got* to have live-in help."

"I can manage," Elizabeth pleaded, hating the thought of their privacy being invaded.

But Laurence insisted. There was no shortage of money, he reminded her. Not that she needed reminding because the money was all hers anyway.

Their first au pair was a German girl called Elfreda which, Elizabeth saw in a book of baby names, meant "wise counsellor". It seemed like a good omen. Elfreda scrubbed and polished, tidied and rearranged the entire contents of Willow Farm with such Teutonic efficiency Elizabeth spent most of her time looking for things.

"I can't stand this," she'd said at last, fed up with being reluctant to sit down in case she flattened the cushions.

And so, when Jasper was eight months old, Elfreda departed and Herta and Gerhard arrived; not quite "the couple" they'd had in mind but Gerhard could no doubt chop logs and wash the car and do the heavy stuff around the place, while Herta helped with the housework and the children.

It wasn't long before Laurence suggested that Gerhard should redecorate Willow Farm and Elizabeth had agreed. Seven years of humans, animals and children blundering around had left their mark in more ways than one. Primary colours were chosen, and now at least the place looked fresh and clean, if not exactly tidy. But Laurence had suddenly become house-proud, and besides his staccato stints at the Olivetti had taken to prowling around the rooms looking for new signs of damage to the paintwork.

Herta came through to the hall from the kitchen.

"Their supper's ready," she announced in her heavy Bavarian accent. "I make them macaroni cheese like you tell me."

She always seemed to be on the defensive, Elizabeth reflected, as she carried Jasper into the kitchen and strapped him into his high chair.

Herta was small and dark and surly, unlike Gerhard who was big and blond and amiable. She seemed to live in permanent fear of being ticked off, and when she was, flew into a rage telling Elizabeth she didn't know how lucky she was. Gerhard, on the other hand, was relaxed and lazy, and laughed with amusement when Laurence informed him he was pulling up the plants in the garden instead of the weeds.

Settled around the kitchen table, the children started on their ritual complaining.

"I don't like marconi," Tamsin wailed, waving her spoon in the air.

"Macaroni," Elizabeth corrected her, adding in a coaxing voice, "and you'll love it."

Tamsin immediately started to howl, saying she'd wanted cheesy-toast, whereupon Dominic, overtired because he'd spent the whole afternoon on his bike, said he wanted cheesy-toast, too.

"I *hate* macaroni!" he yelled, red in the face. "We want cheesy-toast. Cheesy-toast! Cheesy-toast!"

Just then Jasper knocked over his beaker of milk and it streamed on to the floor, frightening Muffet who leaped up barking, and at that moment Laurence walked into the kitchen.

“What the hell’s going on?” he demanded, looking accusingly at Elizabeth as if the whole thing was her fault.

“What do you think’s going on?” she snapped. “It’s what normally goes on in family life. Dogs shit, cats throw up, children have tantrums and throw their food around . . .”

Dominic and Tamsin started to laugh uproariously, rolling around in their chairs and clapping their hands.

“Dogs shit, cats throw up!” Dominic chortled in a sing-song voice.

Herta was not going to be left out. “I make the children nice supper and they don’t like it,” she complained angrily.

Laurence looked at his children with distaste. “You’ll eat what you’re given without any fuss,” he told them coldly. “You can’t waste good food when there are people starving in the world.”

“You don’t know how lucky you are,” Herta rejoined, back on her usual theme. “When I was a child in Bavaria . . .”

“Oh, for God’s sake! What a fuss over nothing,” Elizabeth exclaimed, reaching for a roll of kitchen paper.

Laurence remained sulky and silent for the rest of the evening, ignoring his wife as they ate dinner together after the children had gone to bed and then studiously going off to his den with a mug of tea. A few minutes later she heard the familiar tap-tap-tap as he settled down for a martyred late night’s “work”.

After her bath Elizabeth decided she couldn't stand this cold war that he waged any more. When he was like this he took offence at the least thing, brooding resentfully over every imagined slight and sleeping on the farthest edge of the bed, barely even bidding her good morning or good night.

Unless she could coax him out of this latest decline, she and the children would suffer for the next two months from his moodiness. And all because she had snapped at him in the kitchen earlier.

"Would you like some more tea, darling?" she asked him sweetly, entering the den.

He was stooping over the now silent typewriter but at the sound of her voice started tapping the keys again with rapt concentration as if working on state papers.

"No, thank you," he replied with vague politeness.

"Or some hot chocolate? I was thinking of making some for myself, actually."

"No, thank you." He didn't pause in his typing.

"You're working so hard, sweetheart."

He didn't answer but she sensed a lightening of his black mood. "I was thinking about your letter to the local council about erecting more road signs, and of course you're absolutely right. This area is so badly signposted people are always getting lost," she pressed on.

Laurence didn't reply but at least he'd stopped typing.

Elizabeth continued, "That's why they're always careering up our drive and asking for directions, isn't it?" Her tone was chatty as if everything between them was all right.

He nodded and turned to look at her. She was making headway.

"Why don't you get up a petition, darling? Lobby our neighbours. You could draw up a plan, based on an Ordnance Survey map, showing where you suggest road signs should be put. You've got more clout than anyone else around here and they'd listen to you," she added.

He raised his dark brows. He was definitely unbending.

"Do you think that would work?"

Elizabeth beamed encouragingly. "Of course it would."

There was a pause. "I might do it then," he said at last.

"It would make a real difference to the traffic around here," she agreed. She pulled her dressing-gown cord tighter around her waist. "I'm going to make that hot chocolate now. Shall I make you a cup, darling?"

"Yes. That would be very nice."

"We might as well have it in bed, as it's getting late."

"OK. I'll be up in a minute. I'll just finish this letter."

As she left the den, Laurence was removing the sheet of paper from his typewriter, his pride mollified. Peace had been restored. By pretending to be the Little Woman, she'd coaxed him into a better frame of mind. But as she went into the kitchen she couldn't help feeling sorry for him. It was the same feeling she had towards Dominic if he made a fool of himself in front of his friends.

To avoid his frail male ego being constantly battered, Laurence should really have married a Little Woman type who genuinely looked up to him, but it was too late now. She was who she was; strong, resolute, and through no fault of her own, rich.

Elizabeth knew she'd have to tread carefully if her marriage were to survive but it was going to be like walking on bubbles; too heavy a tread and they'd burst and vanish.

For a moment she wished they were going to Wingfield Court for Easter. Laurence wasn't so proud that he didn't relish the extravagant luxury of her old home.

Before her mother became ill, Easter had been as special an occasion as Christmas. There had been an Easter egg hunt in the garden for the children after they'd all been to church, and simnel cake for tea. Branches of blossom and freshly cut daffodils had been arranged in large vases, and tiny carved rabbits and chickens placed in the centre of the dining-room table.

Rosalind and Nick had basked in the presence of their four children and the first of their grandchildren. It had seemed then that nothing would ever change.

Last Easter, six months after their mother's death, they'd all gathered together once again to carry out the old traditions and reassure each other that Rosalind's presence could still, and always would, be felt. The children had shrieked with triumph when they found the eggs to fill their little baskets and Elizabeth had been greatly comforted by the closeness of her brothers and Cathy, hoping that each year from now on would see lessening of the pain they all felt, a gradual acceptance of that terrible vacant spot their mother had left. They would all keep on coming back, they promised each other, bringing their children with them in the years to come. And remembering Rosalind and how much they'd loved her.

But now there was Philippa and in due course it would be *her* children who would hunt for chocolate eggs and ask for more simnel cake. Everything had changed. Even Nick was different. He had become besotted with his new wife and the prospect of a new baby. It seemed Rosalind had been forgotten. And for that reason Elizabeth knew she couldn't go back, not for this Easter or any other.

Like guests checking into a five-star hotel, as Honor Sykes described it, everyone started arriving at Wingfield Court on Thursday afternoon. The drive was filled with cars and luggage and the sound of laughter. Philippa, looking radiant in beige cashmere and feeling much better, was running around greeting each new arrival, much to Margaret's annoyance. She didn't like being treated as a guest and felt that if anyone should be acting as the hostess it ought to be her.

Nick, by Philippa's side, was oozing bonhomie in his usual charming way, greeting Adrian Hopkins, who'd been his best man, and his actress wife, Ondine Marley. Then old friends Freddie and Andrea Perry, who'd flown over from Ireland, and a few minutes later Cathy whom he welcomed rapturously, hugging and kissing her before turning to be introduced to Jack whom he'd never met before. There were still more guests to come. Philippa's ex-flatmate, Natasha Maxwell, and her boyfriend Mortimer Elliott had been invited, and so had her godmother, Freya Trevelyan-West.

It was going to be a bit of a squash, even for Wingfield Court, but Philippa had decided that as it was the last time they'd have people to stay before they moved, they might as well ask as many friends as possible and make it a memorable weekend. She'd hired extra staff, ordered caterers to provide a lot of the food to ease Morton's burden, and got a woman from the village to do the flowers.

"But don't tell anyone we're selling the Court, for God's sake, darling," Nick had warned her, alarmed. "I don't want this getting out. You've no idea how people gossip in a small village. And I don't want Giles and the others to know about it yet."

"Why don't you tell them, sweetheart? They've got to know sooner or later," she'd protested.

"Yes, but not yet." She'd never heard him speak so firmly. "We'll make this just like any other weekend. There's to be no mention of selling up and buying another house."

Philippa promised, touched by his wish to impart the news to his children himself. It was enough for her that he'd agreed to leave Wingfield Court. They'd even been going through the housing ads in *Country Life*, to see what was on the market, which was at least, a start. But she was bursting with the news because it was going to make such a enormous difference to her life and when she found herself alone with her mother, couldn't resist blurting it out.

"Can you keep a secret, Ma? Even from Daddy?"

Honor felt apprehensive. She'd never kept a secret from Archie in her life. "What is it?" she asked nervously.

Philippa laughed, plumping herself down on Honor's bed and grinning with delight. "Oh, it's all right. It's something wonderful. But it's got to be kept secret for the time being."

"Yes. All right," her mother agreed, only slightly reassured.

Philippa leaned towards her, although they were alone.

"We're going to sell this place, and buy another house," she whispered. "As soon as Easter's over, Nick's going to put this house on the market and we'll start looking for a place we can really call our own. Won't it be marvellous?"

Honor looked startled. "But this is their family home, isn't it?"

For a moment Philippa looked disconcerted. "Well . . . yes, but Nick thinks it's a good idea. Obviously if he hadn't been happy to sell, I wouldn't have said anything more." She moved closer to her mother. "I've never been really happy in this house, you know. Everything is linked to Rosalind. It's still her place and I've never been able to make it mine."

"But weren't all Nick's children born here?"

Philippa nodded. "But I don't think they care about the place so much, now that they've grown up. As he says, they've all got their own lives. Elizabeth hasn't even been here since that first weekend I met them."

Honor was more than aware of this. Elizabeth's absence had been very noticeable at the wedding and then again two months later at Christmas. She remembered the house had been fantastically decorated by Morton but the enormous tree in the hall, presents stacked underneath its glittering branches, had seemed rather *de trop* without the shining faces of small children to gaze at it in wonder.

"Anyway," Philippa continued, so elated she didn't notice her mother's look of consternation, "we're going to get another house big enough to have you and Daddy to stay, as well as all Nick's family, so that will keep everyone happy. But remember, Mummy, not a word to a living soul. Not even Daddy."

Honor nodded. The secret was safe with her as she certainly didn't want to be the one to rock the boat when word got out.

"This is my favourite room," Cathy explained to Jack as she led him by the hand into the library. Book-lined walls and oak panelling, deep buttoned leather sofas, a cluttered desk and a big coffee table in front of the fire, stacked with more books, magazines and a bowl of snowy white narcissi, gave the room a comfortable and peaceful atmosphere.

Jack immediately pulled her down beside him on one of the sofas.

"I can see why you love it," he agreed. "Has anyone ever read any of these books?"

Cathy burst out laughing. "You've summed up Dad very well, haven't you? I don't think he's read a book since he left school." She gazed up at the long lines of neatly arranged volumes, some quite valuable with leather bindings and gold tooling.

"I hate to admit it but my grandfather bought most of the books from the previous owner of the house, and then he bought some more by the yard."

Jack looked at her quizzically. "What do you mean, by the yard?"

She giggled. "One used to be able to buy books literally by the yard. Any old books so long as they were nicely bound and filled thirty-six inches of shelf space." Seeing his expression she added, "Well, it's better than buying wallpaper patterned with shelves of books."

"God, I'm shocked! Didn't your mother read?"

Cathy smiled. "Of course. Most of her books are upstairs in my room now."

"Thank God for that. For a moment I thought I was going out with a philistine."

"How dare you!" she yelped, grabbing him round the waist and tickling him. They were wrestling on the sofa, shrieking with laughter, when the library door opened and after a moment they became aware of a tall figure standing watching them.

"Jonno!" Cathy exclaimed, wriggling to get out from under Jack. Then she stopped dead, looking at her brother in horror.

"Shit! What have you done? What's happened to you?" she gasped, jumping up and running over to him.

His arm was in a sling, he had a black eye and a badly grazed cheek, and as he entered the room she noticed he was limping. He gave her a rather lopsided grin.

"I just got caught up in a bit of a bar-room brawl," he said lightly. "No great damage done." He sat down gingerly in one of leather chairs by the fire and winced with pain.

"My God, Jonno. What have you done to your arm?" She was on her knees beside him, taking his hand in hers, staring up into his face with concern. His left eye was a bloodshot slit, the surrounding skin black and swollen, and his cheek was deep purple.

"I've dislocated my shoulder, but it's nothing," he replied with an attempt at breeziness, "and my eye's OK. It'll clear up in a couple of days."

Aware that Jack was watching, Cathy turned to him. "This is my brother Jonathan. You two haven't met before, have you? This is Jack, Jonno."

"Hi," said Jonathan, peering at Jack with his good eye from under a lock of blond hair. "Sorry if I disturbed things just now."

Jack looked at him sympathetically. "Looks like you've done ten rounds with Mike Tyson."

Jonathan spoke drily. "Yeah. You wouldn't think a bunch of queens could inflict this much damage, would you?"

"And this was in a pub? Which pub?" Cathy asked anxiously.

"Oh, just a pub in the West End . . ." His voice trailed off, not wanting her to know the sordid saga of Chris, who hadn't turned up the same night with a bunch of his friends as he'd threatened but the following night, accompanied by three louts, when Jonathan was alone and unprepared and a sitting target for a rent boy's revenge.

After they'd beaten him up, leaving him unconscious, they'd trashed the flat, stealing everything they could lay hands on, including a gold watch he'd been given by his father for his twenty-first birthday, a camera and camcorder, television and video recorder, and a new suede coat belonging to Pip.

When Jonathan had regained consciousness shortly after they'd left, with a splitting headache, his shoulder twisted to an impossible angle, his legs kicked black and blue and his face running with blood, he'd managed to persuade a taxi driver to take him to the casualty department of St Mary's Hospital where he told them he'd been involved in a "domestic fight with his cousin", because he knew from previous experience that gays who'd been beaten up didn't seem to qualify for much sympathy.

"Shouldn't you be in bed?" Jack asked gently. "You must be suffering from shock apart from everything else."

Jonathan closed his eyes and sank lower into the chair, nursing the arm carefully across his chest.

"I don't want to be in bed, I just wanted to come home," he said quietly. He'd had bolts and a chain fixed to his front door that morning, but with Pip away with his parents over Easter, didn't fancy staying in the flat by himself.

"Oh, Jonno sweetheart," Cathy said sadly. She guessed he wasn't telling her everything, but he looked so battered and dispirited she didn't want to press him for an explanation. "Did Giles and Margaret give you a lift up here?"

"Yup. She was jolly kind. Settled me in the back of the car with pillows and a rug and fed me coffee from a thermos. She should have been a nurse. She even had Nurofen in her bag in case I was in pain."

"Does Daddy know you've arrived?" Cathy asked.

"Yup, but I haven't seen the expectant mum yet. How is she, by the way?"

"In great form," Cathy assured him. "I'll go and find her and tell her you're here."

"Can I get you anything?" Jack offered when he and Jonathan were on their own.

"No, thanks. It's just great to be back here, in the bosom of the family, as they say, which is probably the only bosom I'm ever likely to know," he added with a self-deprecating laugh.

"There's nowhere like home," Jack agreed. "My parents are living in Dubai at the moment so, I haven't got a real home to go to. Except wherever Cathy is — that's home to me."

Jonathan grinned lopsidedly, thinking he'd never seen anyone as good-looking and attractive as Jack with his magnificent bone structure and unusual eyes. "Cathy's the one I'm closest to," he said. "Elizabeth is six years older than me and Giles four years. When you're young that seems like a big gap."

"I suppose so. I'm an only child and sometimes wish I had a few siblings. It must be great."

"Most of the time it is."

There was a peaceful silence in the room as the two men sat and stared into the glowing log fire, watching for the occasional little spurts of blue flame that leaped from the wood as the sap exploded.

"D'you think you could put on another couple of logs?" Jonathan asked after a few minutes. "It's a bit cold in here, isn't it?"

"Yeah. Sure." It was actually very warm but Jonathan had sunk deeper into his chair and in spite of his thick sweater looked chilled.

After Jack had piled on more pieces of apple wood he returned to his place on the sofa, asking: "So . . . did the police get whoever started this fight?"

"In my position one doesn't involve the police unless one is forced to," Jonathan replied succinctly.

Philippa came hurrying into the room at that moment, followed by Cathy.

"My dear Jonathan," she exclaimed. "I was upstairs settling my mother in her room and didn't realize you'd arrived with Giles and Margaret. How are you feeling? Is there anything I can get you? That eye looks awfully painful. Shall I get Morton to bring you some raw steak to put on it?"

"I'm OK, Philippa, thanks all the same," he replied, struggling out of the chair and standing looking down at her, swaying slightly on his long legs. "How are you? You're looking blooming."

Philippa patted her stomach and grinned. "Junior here seems to be behaving himself. I feel great."

"Is it a boy?" Cathy exclaimed. "Do you know you're having a boy?"

Philippa laughed outright. "I've no idea. I'm just guessing. I don't mind what I have."

Nick came into the room, catching her last words. He slid one arm around her waist, and Jack, who'd never met him until today, was reminded of a middle-aged matinée idol, cosying up to his leading lady for the benefit of his audience.

"Isn't she looking fabulous?" Nick crowed and stroked her stomach. "Looking after my baby, are you?" he murmured in her ear.

Cathy turned away, a pained look in her eyes. Later, as she and Jack went for a walk in the grounds, he asked her why she was so quiet.

She tucked her arm under his.

"It's an awful thing to admit," she explained sadly, "but when Daddy was going on about the new baby, I actually felt jealous. I've been his baby since I was born, supposedly the last of his babies, and Mummy . . ." She couldn't continue, breaking away from him, half tearful, half angry. "Oh! How can I be so stupid?" she wailed. "I'm behaving so badly. Such a spoiled brat. Poor little baby, how can I be jealous of it?"

Jack regarded her fondly, his mouth twitching. "Cheer up, Bunny. It's bound to be a bit of a shock to realize you're going to be part of an extended family."

"It depends *how* extended," she replied, recovering. "I hope Dad isn't going to make a habit of this, although I suppose I'll get used to it."

As the weekend progressed through Good Friday, Saturday and Easter Sunday, the house party settled down, forming into various groups. And all the time Honor was observing Nick's family, wondering how they were going to take the news of the move. She longed to talk about it to Archie but she'd promised Philippa she wouldn't and so remained silent.

It was Margaret, unexpectedly, who found a sympathetic listener in Mortimer Elliott as she confided her resentment at having Philippa "foisted into our midst", as she put it.

"I know she was Natasha's flatmate and is probably an old friend of yours, too, but it has been difficult for us all to get used to her being here," she admitted in a burst of candour fuelled by a particularly good first-growth Latour at lunch.

"It must have been a shock," he agreed gently, "but I'm sure it's just a case of getting used to the situation, isn't it? And has she done much to change the place?"

Margaret considered this for a moment and conceded with surprise that apart from turning one of the spare rooms into a bedroom for herself and Nick, and redecorating Rosalind's room, Philippa hadn't changed much. The house looked exactly as it always had, even to the flower arrangements. Rosalind could walk through the door at any moment, once again mistress of Wingfield Court, and find almost everything exactly as she'd left it.

"No, Philippa hasn't made any real changes. Except perhaps to Nick," Margaret added perceptively.

While Philippa moved from group to group, the perfect hostess, making sure everyone was looked after, Cathy began to notice a shift in attitude amongst her siblings towards their new stepmother. Philippa was proving to be far more acceptable than they'd first feared. Her parents, always charming and courteous to everyone, were partly responsible for this, as were Natasha and Mortimer. Anyone who had such pleasant parents and friends couldn't be all bad. Nick's friends were also full of praise. Cathy reckoned that if all these nice people were right, then her father's new wife had to be OK. She said as much to Jonathan as he reclined on the library sofa watching television. The weekend was drawing to a close and they were all about to go their separate ways.

"I've always thought she was fine," he pointed out.

"Yes, but her being so much younger than Daddy did make us wonder what she was after," Cathy argued. "I mean, she couldn't have been short of boyfriends her own age. I think we were justified in being suspicious."

Jonathan cast his eyes to heaven in mock exasperation.

"Will you listen to yourself, Cathy? Wasn't it remotely possible she'd just fallen in love with him?"

"We know that now, but how could we have known before? Women of her age usually marry men in their thirties, not someone old enough to be their father. And let's face it, Dad was a single, eligible man when she met him. I bet even *her* friends wondered if she wasn't interested in his money. I'm just thankful, for all our sakes, that she's turned out to be really nice. And undemanding, too."

"'Bye, sweetheart . . . 'bye." It was time to go and as always Cathy hated it. She couldn't stop her nose stinging and her eyes brimming as they all hugged each other, ready to depart.

Jonathan put his good arm around her and held her close.

"Come and see me in London on your way back from skiing," he made her promise. "You and Jack can stay the night on the put-you-up sofa."

"That would be bliss." Cathy grinned sheepishly through her tears. Then she turned to kiss Giles goodbye. Dear old stodgy Giles, she thought, with his carefully planned social schedules and endless business networking. "Can we come and see you too?" she asked, as he returned her kiss with tidy decorum.

"Of course." He didn't sound as enthusiastic as Jonathan. Cathy knew it was because he hated the thought of luggage and skiing gear cluttering up his house.

"Be sure to let us know when you're coming," he observed in his organizing voice.

"Of course we will. We wouldn't dream of descending on you in case we interrupted one of your candle-lit dinners," Cathy rejoined wickedly.

"Must you really go, my darling?" Nick was asking her, his eyes sad.

"Oh, Daddy! It's been a really, really lovely weekend. Can Jack and I come back on our way up to Scotland? Before the summer term starts?" Cathy clung round his neck, pressing her cheek to his.

Before he could answer, Jonathan was thumping him gently on the shoulder. "I might come up with them, Dad. I'd like to spend a week or so up here. Get myself really fit and all that." He didn't add that he felt utterly sickened by his life in London after what had happened, and the thought of going back was a lonely prospect.

Margaret, coming down the stairs and fearing she was being left out of future arrangements, joined in with enthusiasm.

"Actually that's a good idea," she remarked, coming up to join them.

"And we'll jolly well get Elizabeth to bring the children over," Giles agreed. "It's ridiculous, her staying away like this. Life's far too short."

Nick smiled impassively but said nothing.

Sniffing loudly, Cathy looked around the hall for the last time. "I hate leaving here," she wailed.

"We all do," Margaret said sadly. "But for the time being one just has to be in London for Giles's career."

At that moment Philippa came hurrying back into the hall through the front door, having just seen her parents off.

"Are you all leaving?" she asked.

"Well, I don't think we're just arriving," Jonathan quipped. "Thanks for everything, Philippa." He kissed her lightly on the cheek.

How strange, Cathy thought, to be thanking someone for having you to stay in your own home.

"It's been lovely having you," Philippa was saying, kissing them all goodbye. "Thank goodness the weather's been fine," she kept adding, as if it had mattered.

Jonathan got carefully into the back of Giles's car, and Margaret arranged a pillow under his bad arm. Cathy gave Jack the keys so he could drive her. Dusk was gathering, folding the garden in melancholy violet dimness as Nick and Philippa stood on the front steps with their arms around each other, waving goodbye with a cheerfulness engendered by the knowledge they'd soon have the place to themselves again.

"It gets worse every time," Cathy wept as they set off down the drive. She turned to look through the rear window at the lovely old house. Lights glowed in the library and drawing room windows. Wisps of smoke trailed from the tall Tudor chimneys.

"I feel homesick already!" she said, blowing her nose. "I can't think what I'm doing in Edinburgh when I could be at home all the time."

Jack reached out to rest his hand on her knee. "It's OK, babe. You'll soon be back." He watched the road ahead as he drove with assurance. "It's hard for me to understand how you feel. My family's always been on the move. I think I'd like a settled home, though . . ."

"Oh, sweetheart." She grabbed his hand, as if to comfort him for the most awful deprivation. "My home is yours, too. We'll always regard Wingfield Court as home, even when we're old and grey and Margaret and Giles live there."

He smiled, touched by her generosity. "I don't know if I could ever get attached to bricks and mortar in that way," he said thoughtfully. "People are more important to me than places."

Cathy sat in silence, thinking about this for quite a while. At last she spoke. "I know what you mean, but when it comes to my home I look upon it like an old friend. Every nook and cranny means something to me, holds some memory going back to when I was a child." She looked at his profile with its straight nose, sculpted lips and strong jawline, and as always thought how wonderful it would look stamped on a coin.

"You'll come to love it as much as I do, in time."

"Is that because your mother loved it, do you suppose?" he asked gently, glancing at her quickly.

She shook her head. "No, I believe I love it for itself, because it's given me a feeling of security and continuity all my life, and of really belonging."

"And Giles feels the same, doesn't he?"

Cathy wrinkled her nose. "Yes." She drew out the word as if she doubted the truth of it. "But I think he and Margaret like it best because it's sort of grand and good for entertaining, and I suppose they feel it brings a lot of kudos to the family for owning it. But Jonno and I don't look upon it like that at all."

They'd joined the main road that led to the motorway and the mysterious beauty of the country lanes had given way to tarmac surfaces and crude fluorescent lighting. Cathy reached for a packet of chewing gum in the glove compartment.

"What Jonno and I are so pleased about is that apart from doing up a couple of bedrooms, Philippa hasn't changed much. We were all afraid she'd start redecorating and throwing out Mummy's stuff but everything's the same. I can't tell you how glad I am she's not going to alter anything else and we can all go on regarding Wingfield as our home."

CHAPTER SIX

Summer arrived suddenly that year in a flurry of instant flowering and warm breezes and a hot sun that promised to heat the cold damp earth for the next few months.

London seemed to blossom overnight into a riot of cheerful colour with bright awnings sprouting from cafes and restaurants, window boxes overflowing, red buses and taxis skimming along and women walking with confident ease in thin dresses, all under a dazzling blue sky. Margaret awoke early one morning, feeling in her bones that it was going to be a marvellous day. Sunshine glowed through their bedroom curtains. Then she remembered that tonight they were giving one of their dinner parties and she wanted to get to Waitrose really early.

"Time to get up, Giles," she said, pushing back the duvet. He grunted, turned over and pulled the bedding up again.

"Just five more minutes."

"There's a lot to do." Energized at the thought of a busy, socially active day ahead, Margaret bounded out of bed. She'd written out her list the night before. If she didn't hang around she could be back at the house by ten o'clock. Not that there was really a lot to do. Unlike

Elizabeth, who was obsessed with cooking, Margaret didn't so much cook as assemble food. Why spend hours getting hot and exhausted, she asked herself, cooking tricky dishes, when you could buy everything ready prepared, needing only to be popped into the oven and then put on serving dishes?

When she got back from the shops, having stopped on the way to buy the newspapers and magazines, she unloaded the car and decided to indulge herself by sitting down with a cup of coffee to have a quick look at *House & Garden* and *Country Life*. The former sometimes gave her wonderful decorating ideas and showed original table settings, and the latter helped her to keep up with the hunting, fishing and shooting news. Not that she was remotely interested in country pursuits but it was good to sound knowledgeable on such subjects. Many a lull in the conversation had been kick started with a remark like: "It's been a bad year for grouse, hasn't it?"

Kicking off her shoes, she settled herself on the drawing-room sofa and started turning the pages of *Country Life* with idle pleasure, glancing first at the fashion section, then some photographs of an exquisite garden, and on to a rather boring article on wild birds. She flipped the glossy pages with mild interest. There were some very nice country houses for sale.

Then she saw something that made her heart stop and the river of life freeze in her arteries with a terrible numbing sensation, as if she'd been dealt a savage physical blow. For a moment she thought she was going to faint and heard herself cry aloud: "No! Oh, no! It's not possible."

But it was true. Two-thirds of the page was filled with coloured photographs of Wingfield Court: the exterior, the hall, the library, the drawing room, and a section of the garden, showing the swimming pool. Under it were the words "Historic mansion set in magnificent mature formal gardens", and a list of all the rooms, including the wine cellars and stables. The bottom line said: "Freehold for sale. Price on application".

Beside herself with shock, Margaret reached for her mobile phone and with trembling fingers stabbed Giles's office number. This couldn't be happening. Wingfield Court was a part of Wingland Estate Ltd, of which Giles and the others were all directors. Not a single stick or stone could be sold without the permission of at least four of them at a properly convened meeting. This was a fact. This was the law.

When she got through she did her best not to sound as hysterical as she felt, but she had a terrible feeling that something precious, something she desperately wanted, was slipping through her fingers, and she didn't know how to stop it.

"Wingfield Court is up for sale," she blurted out. "It's advertised in *Country Life*. That bitch Philippa is behind this but she can't make your father sell, can she?" A long silence on the line prompted her to shriek again, "*Can* she? Giles, are you there?"

"Yes, I'm here," he replied faintly. Stunned, his mind refused to work. "It must be a mistake."

"It's not. It's here in black and white. 'Freehold for sale'," quoted Margaret. "'Price on application'."

"But he *can't* sell . . . the place belongs to all of us."

"That's what I mean." Margaret felt somewhat relieved to know she hadn't got that wrong. "Philippa must have put the house in the hands of agents without telling your father . . . but how could she? He was bound to find out. It doesn't make sense. God, I *knew* she was trouble from the start. And the way she was so sweet to us all at Easter! Get on to your father at once, Giles. Ask him what the hell's going on. Remind him the house is a part of the Wingland Estate and can't be touched."

"Yes. All right, all right." He hated Margaret telling him what to do.

"Get on to him *now*."

"I'm going to."

"And ring me back to tell me what he says."

"Yes, OK."

With reluctance, Margaret put down the phone, her mind in a turmoil. Sell Wingfield Court indeed! The family home. The place she and Giles were going to inherit. In that instant she saw all her dreams shatter and felt physically sick. But of course it couldn't be true. Giles, Elizabeth, Cathy and Jonathan had the law on their side. For a moment she felt a self-righteous satisfaction in the knowledge that she'd been right all along about their step-mother — but if there *was* a loophole in the Companies Act, being proved right would be poor consolation.

Margaret's hand hovered over the phone. She wanted to be first to impart this terrible news to the others. At last, unable to resist, she dialled Elizabeth's number. Hadn't they said to each other, right from the beginning, that Philippa was bad news?

"Is that you?" Margaret demanded as soon as she got through. Her speckled face was scarlet and she was breathless with eagerness to impart her news.

"Do you get *Country Life* by any chance?" she asked immediately, spinning out the suspense.

"No, never, actually," Elizabeth replied. She was in the middle of lining a bowl with slices of bread in preparation for making Summer Pudding and marvelled at Margaret's habitual bad sense of timing. Somehow she always managed to phone at the worst moments, like while Jasper's nappy was being changed or just as lunch was being dished up. Elizabeth tucked the phone into her shoulder. "What's so special about *Country Life*?"

Margaret delivered her bombshell with dramatic aplomb. "Wingfield Court is up for sale. I've been on to Giles and he's phoning your father now. It's obvious he can't know what's going on."

"I don't believe it!" Stunned, Elizabeth sank down on to a kitchen chair.

"Didn't I say we shouldn't trust Philippa? Right from the start? You felt that too, didn't you?"

"But it can't be sold." Elizabeth gazed in shock at the pudding she was making. The raspberries, black berries and redcurrants reminded her of rubies, bruised and bleeding, staining the white bread crimson.

"I know it can't. But imagine the nerve of her, trying. I'll get Giles to ring you, shall I? When he's spoken to Nick?"

"Yes, OK." But Elizabeth wasn't listening. She was thinking how her father had changed since he'd met Philippa. There was something reckless in his pursuit of a new life, an almost foolhardly heedlessness that had never showed in his character before. But then, she reflected, her mother had always had a calming effect on him; she'd been a cultured, highly educated woman and had managed to be a steadying influence on her sexually charged, fun-loving husband, satisfying his needs yet always mindful of the family as a whole. She'd been a serene presence, and without her that tranquillity had gone from his life.

Then Philippa had appeared on the scene, young, attractive, at the start of her own life. Elizabeth could see how Nick had been swept along, his wealth no doubt fuelling the passion for change. Slowly and methodically, she filled the bowl with more fruit, pressing it down with a large wooden spoon before adding a final slice of bread. Then she put a plate with a heavy weight on top and watched as the scarlet juices overflowed and ran down the outside of the bowl.

Sell Wingfield Court? It was unthinkable. Although she didn't go there any more, that was only because of Philippa's presence. She missed her old home deeply. Missed the weekends there with the children, missed the sweet familiarity of the house that had always been home to her. Missed showing Dominic and Tamsin the places where she'd played with Giles and the others.

Margaret must be mistaken. Her grandfather had ensured that the house could never be sold without the sanction of them all.

Shortly after she'd spoken to Elizabeth, Margaret phoned Cathy but there was no answer from the little terraced house in Edinburgh. Her mobile was also switched off which meant she must be in a tutorial. Disappointed, she tried to get hold of Jonathan and found him in his studio in Paddington.

He was in the middle of working on a new abstract painting. Her interruption couldn't have been more annoying. "I'm very busy . . ." he began, but Margaret was undeterred.

"I suppose you haven't heard?"

"Heard what?"

Jonathan's reaction when she told him was less stunned than the others, and consequently angrier.

"What the fuck . . . ?" he exploded. "Dad can't do that!"

"Giles is trying to get hold of him right now, but he's not at home nor is he in London. Morton's expecting them back later today, though. We'll let you know what's happening," Margaret added, deciding she would be the main line of communication between the siblings. "Of course Giles will put a stop to it. We've also got to inform the agents that the house is definitely not for sale."

"I think I love it already," Philippa exclaimed, laughing as she got out of the car and stood looking up at the house. It was utterly different from Wingfield Court. Built around the turn of the century, it was a white stuccoed building with a grey slate roof, built long and low and with only three storeys. A typical Edwardian verandah ran along one side, embellished by a fancy wrought-iron balcony festooned with a flowering wisteria. Well-kept lawns and pretty countryfied flower beds gave the house an air of comfort, informality and welcoming friendliness. It was called Woodlands.

"It doesn't look very large," Nick said, frowning. Neither did it have an air of grandeur, he thought.

Philippa consulted the agent's specifications. "Oh, I don't know, darling. It says, five reception rooms, nine bedrooms and seven bathrooms, a period coach house and a two-bedroomed detached cottage. And there are outhouses, garaging for three cars, and a tennis court. What more do we want? It sounds perfect to me, and it's only twenty miles from where we are now so we'll still be in the same county," she added persuasively.

Nick could detect the longing in her voice. "Let's have a look inside, darling," he said peaceably.

The owners of Woodlands were a charming middle-aged couple who wanted to move to a smaller place. On realizing Philippa and Nick were starting a family, they fell over themselves to describe the suitability of their home when it came to bringing up children. Philippa listened enraptured as they told tales of their children's playroom, in what was now the study, which led directly on to the walled garden where swings and a sand pit used to keep them safely occupied for hours. And how the room next to the master bedroom made a wonderful night nursery: "You can hear the children as soon as they wake up."

As soon as they got back into the car, Philippa turned to Nick, starry-eyed. "Oh, darling, isn't it perfect? It's absolutely right for us, isn't it? There's plenty of room and maybe we can do up the coach house so when Elizabeth and her children come to stay they've got their own place. And the garden is lovely and will be so easy to maintain. And isn't the house in a good state of repair? All we'll need to do is a bit of redecorating . . . Oh! And I liked the idea of having the baby in the room next to ours, didn't you? What I love about that house is it's so homely."

Nick opened his mouth to say that was exactly what he didn't like about it when he saw her radiant expression, the happiness glowing from her like a beacon, and in that instant saw this was more her sort of place. It had airy sunny rooms, simply and elegantly decorated in pastel shades. No tapestry-hung baronial hall; no high-ceilinged library housing four thousand books; no Tudor bedrooms or panelled dining rooms; no formally laid out grounds and neatly clipped parterres.

There was only one problem. When Wingfield Court was sold and he'd reduced his overdraft, he wasn't sure he could buy a new house immediately unless he dipped into the family trust again. In time, when the market improved and the docklands project was up and running, there'd be no problem, but right now he'd really wanted to rent a house for a couple of years. These were problems he was loath to share with Philippa for fear she'd be disappointed, especially as he'd promised her anything she wanted.

She, looking at him, took his doubtful expression to mean that he was having second thoughts about leaving Wingfield Court. She reached out and took his hand.

"Darling, I really don't mind if you decide you can't bear to sell up," she said softly. "I would never have suggested it if I thought it was going to upset you."

His expression changed instantly. “Of course I’m happy to sell Wingfield,” he assured her. “It’s becoming an impractical house to run for one thing. Once Morton and the others retire, I don’t know how we’re going to replace them. What I don’t want to do is to put in a firm offer for another house until Wingfield’s actually been sold.”

Philippa nodded understandingly, hiding her own disappointment. “I can see that.”

Nick kissed her firmly and sweetly on the lips. “Leave it with me, sweetheart. I’ll see what I can do.”

Trustingly, she smiled at him. “You’re so good to me,” she said softly.

Jack held Cathy’s hand, trying to calm her down. Because of his own nomadic family background, he was having a problem understanding how shattered she felt at the thought of Wingfield Court’s being sold.

“But you don’t understand,” she kept saying. “It’s not just bricks and mortar — it’s a lifetime’s memories. It’s my whole childhood. It’s our home and we love it. Daddy isn’t *allowed* to sell it and I can’t believe he’s trying to.” She shook her head, bewildered. “I can’t believe Philippa would do such a thing behind our backs either.”

“So Giles is going to let you know what your father says?”

She nodded. “Margaret said Daddy’s been out all day and they haven’t been able to get hold of him yet.”

“I suppose he wants to start his new life with a clean slate,” Jack said tentatively. He’d never seen Cathy so upset and it was unlike her to be so negative.

"He'll always have *us*," she said. "There's no such thing as a clean slate for a man with four children. He can't just wipe out the past thirty-two years."

Jack raised his eyebrows, one pierced by a silver stud, and his aquamarine eyes twinkled in an effort to cheer her up.

"Maybe he's going through a mid-life crisis or the male menopause? You know . . . the Last Chance Saloon and all that?" he suggested, grinning.

Cathy gave a watery smile. "More like senile dementia!"

Jack suddenly looked serious. "Would you like to drive down and see him, babe? I don't mind coming with you, if you'd like me to and you think it would help."

Cathy looked at him hopefully. "Would you really? You wouldn't mind? I shan't rest until I know first hand what's going on."

"Why don't you ring Giles and Elizabeth and Jonathan? Get everyone together for a family conference? Perhaps your father's just humouring Philippa. Maybe it's just a whim on her part. Pregnant women are supposed to get crazy ideas, aren't they? All part of the nesting syndrome?"

Cathy wasn't listening. "Are you sure you don't mind skipping lectures for the next few days? I really would like to have you with me."

Jack grabbed her and hugged her tight. "Count me in, babe."

Giles, in victory, was at his most pedantic. "It's exactly as I thought, Margaret," he told her over the phone later that day, having spent two hours with a client who was an avid stamp collector and also happened to be a lawyer. "Dad doesn't have the right to sell Wingfield Court. It's company property. It belongs to Wingland Estates Ltd, of which he and the four of us are directors. I don't know what the hell he thinks he's doing but the bottom line is, it's not his to sell."

Margaret clapped her hands, impressed. "Just what I thought. Oh, that's wonderful, Giles. Have you spoken to Nick?"

"I still haven't been able to get hold of him. He and Philippa seem to have gone off somewhere for the day. I thought we'd drive up to see him tomorrow and ask him what he thinks he's doing. Let's get the others to come, too, including Elizabeth and Laurence. She *must* come. This is a family crisis."

Margaret was quivering with delight at the thought of them all ganging up together on Philippa.

"I think we should do something else while we're there," Giles continued. "We should check the contents of the house. Everything belongs to the company, you know. If Dad can't sell Wingfield Court, he can't sell the contents either. We don't want to see bits of family . . . Oh, my God!" He stopped dead, hit by another thought.

"What is it?"

"I've just remembered that Philippa used to work in the silver department at Christie's!"

Nick was tight-lipped as he came out of the estate office that evening and met his wife coming down the stairs from their bedroom.

"What's wrong, sweetheart?" she asked instantly. She'd never seen him look like that before, eyes blazing, jaw working as he ground his teeth.

He immediately made an effort to pull himself together and managed a smile that didn't quite reach his eyes.

"The children are annoyed we're selling this place and moving," he said, trying to keep his voice even. "It's too ridiculous. They come here two or three times a year, use it like a hotel, then go back to their own homes again. Now they're acting like it's the only home they've got and if we sell they're all going to be without a roof."

Philippa looked strained, her face pale. "I thought you'd told them we were selling?"

He shrugged. "I haven't had time. It's that bloody advert in *Country Life*. Margaret, of all people, saw it this morning, and now of course she's got out the biggest wooden spoon she can find and is having a wonderful time, stirring it up amongst the others." He strode off across the hall in the direction of the library. Philippa followed him.

"Who were you talking to on the phone just now?"

"Giles." He lowered himself wearily, as if suddenly tired, on to one of the leather sofas.

"Oh, darling." Philippa sat down beside him and took one of his hands. "I'm so sorry. I feel this is all my fault."

His face softened as he looked at her. "Of course it's not your fault. You've as much right as anyone to decide where we should live. I want you to be happy. You've no idea how important that is to me."

Philippa smiled, touched by his words. "You're so sweet to me, Nick. But really, I mean it, if it's going to cause such an upset, don't sell the place. I can't bear to think of it causing trouble between you and your family. It's simply not worth it."

"But you'd like a place of our own, wouldn't you?" he insisted. "And I agree with you. Why should we change our plans because the children are having an attack of sentimentality?"

"Promise me you're not going to regret it?"

"I won't regret anything so long as you're by my side."

"But your family has lived here for over sixty years."

"If we were talking several hundred years I'd agree. It must have been a great wrench for the Drysdale family to sell up, seeing they'd been in the old part of the house since 1410, but we don't have that sort of heritage, darling. The steel works of the Midlands at the turn of the century is my background. Maybe Giles and the others should remember that. We're not a part of the old English aristocracy." There was a tinge of regret in his voice and, hearing it himself, he continued swiftly, "These old houses are a thing of the past anyway."

"So what are we going to do?" Philippa asked.

"I'm afraid tomorrow's not going to be much fun, my darling. You might prefer to absent yourself for a few hours while I do battle."

"What do you mean?"

"My family are arriving *en masse*, according to Giles. Morton will take care of everything, so don't worry."

"They're coming here?" she asked in surprise. "Wouldn't it have been easier if you'd met up in London?"

"This is nearer for Cathy."

"She's driving down from Scotland?" Philippa asked incredulously. "Why didn't she take the shuttle from Edinburgh to Heathrow? It only takes a couple of hours and she could have met you in London, too."

Nick looked uncomfortable, averting his gaze to glance out of the window. "She and Jack prefer to come by car."

"Jack? Is he coming too?"

"Yes, but don't worry about it, darling," he said hastily. Leaning forward, he wrapped his arms lovingly around her before starting to kiss her neck with a lingering tenderness that usually drove her crazy. "Would you like to get away for a couple of days of unadulterated spoiling at the Kingsdale health farm?" he whispered between kisses. "Think of it . . . massage, facials, manicures, aromatherapy. Then I can pick you up when the family's gone and we might go somewhere nice for the weekend. Paris, perhaps? Or, no, not Paris, let's go to Venice." His mouth found hers. Insistently he tried to slide his tongue into her mouth but she pushed him away.

"Nick, please, darling . . . Nick, no. We've got to talk about this . . ."

He stopped and looked into her eyes and the sheer magnetism of his sexuality made her catch her breath in spite of her reservations about his whole family descending on them.

"Don't you want to go to Venice?" he asked. "Think about it, beloved. We could be there in three hours, staying at the Cipriani, drinking Bellinis and listening to the water lapping below our bedroom window. What do you say?"

"It's not that." She straightened up, sitting back so that she could look at him directly. "I'm not going to run away. Why should I? If your family are upset about the sale of the house, we must explain the situation from our point of view."

Philippa saw a flicker of relief in Nick's eyes but pretended not to notice.

"OK, sweetheart," he replied. "I'll ask Morton to kill the fatted calf. And don't worry about a thing. This is just a storm in a tea cup. They'll see the sense of getting rid of this old place as soon as I've explained it to them."

It was all very different from Easter weekend. There were no merry greetings with everyone hugging and kissing as they arrived, no air of joyous celebration at all being together again. The atmosphere was serious and by six o'clock the whole family was gathered together under the very roof in dispute, with Elizabeth, Giles, Cathy and Jonathan, accompanied by their spouses, all presenting a united front to their father.

By unspoken agreement they'd gathered in the library, unconsciously deemed to be the room which would lend the most gravitas to the confrontation. While Nick stood defiantly with his back to the fireplace, they sat facing him, expressions serious.

Only Philippa made polite attempts to offer drinks, which were refused with equal politeness. No one had come for a party. Nick, tanned and smiling widely as usual, was the only one who didn't look as if there was a problem.

"It's lovely to see you all again," he said with studied casualness, as if addressing a charity committee, "but I'm not sure what this hullabaloo's all about."

No one spoke for a moment, then they all started talking at once.

"Why are you trying to sell the house . . ."

"You've gone behind out backs . . ."

"You've no right to . . ."

And from Giles: "What the hell are you playing at? This house is ours. It's part of the estate . . ."

Nick raised his hand for silence. "Are you going to give me a chance to explain?"

"I wish you would!" Jonathan retorted. "I'd like to hear this one."

"Jonathan!" Nick's voice boomed angrily. "Kindly allow me to speak."

A sullen silence, fuelled by suspicion, fell on the room. Philippa was aware they were all looking accusingly at her. She raised her chin and looked back at them. "Perhaps I am the one who should explain," she said quietly.

Nick turned sharply and laid a hand on her shoulder. He looked profoundly surprised. "You don't have to, darling," he said quickly.

"I think I do." She was without fear. They were not her children. It would be easier for her to explain the position to them, than it would for their father. And maybe, being a woman, she could do it more gently and diplomatically.

"As you know, I'm having a baby in October," she began, "and I want my child to be brought up in a relaxed homely atmosphere." She glanced at Elizabeth, who was watching her closely. "I'm sure you understand what I mean, having children yourself."

Elizabeth didn't respond and Margaret gave a loud sniff.

"I know this has been your home," Philippa continued, "and that this is where you were brought up by your mother and father, and I absolutely understand that Wingfield Court must mean a lot to you because you associate it with her. It was here you spent your youth with her, in an atmosphere she created for you all. I know how much you loved her. Everyone has told me she was a wonderful person and a very loving mother."

Elizabeth and Cathy started to weep quietly. Jack put his arm around Cathy's shoulders and wondered whether he ought to be here at this emotional family conference.

"Now I want to do the best for my baby and to give him or her the sort of happy loving atmosphere your mother gave you. You can understand that, can't you?" Philippa wasn't begging, just stating her point of view in measured tones. "And I'd like it to be a completely fresh start for both your father and me. That's why we want to move to a new house. Beautiful though Wingfield Court is, it will never be my home. I'll never feel comfortable here because it's still your mother's house. Sadly for you all that is an era that is over. Now we have to face the fact that life must go on, hard though it sounds.

"But there is a new life coming into the family, a half brother or sister for you all, and I asked your father if we could move to a new house where there are no memories of the past — a blank canvas, in fact, on which he and I can create new memories and our own atmosphere."

Elizabeth was the first to speak. "Why did you marry Dad in the first place if you didn't want to live here?" she asked quietly.

Philippa drew a deep breath before answering, not wanting to admit she'd had reservations about the house from the start. At first she'd been determined to get over her misgivings because she loved Nick, but over the months her unease had increased rather than diminished.

"I think my feelings only became focused when I knew I was pregnant," she explained carefully. "It was then that I suggested we leave here and buy a smaller, less formal house."

Margaret suddenly leaned forward, flushed and eager-looking. "I see your point exactly, Philippa," she exclaimed, causing the others to turn and look at her in astonishment.

"There is a perfect solution to all this," she enthused. "Why don't you and Nick find yourselves a nice little house somewhere? I think it's an excellent idea. Of course you don't want to live in the shadow of Rosalind for the rest of your life . . ."

"Wait a minute," Elizabeth cut in.

"No," Margaret countered swiftly. "The whole problem can be solved very easily. Giles will be taking over this place eventually, so why not now? That would leave Philippa and Nick free to go and live where they like. There's no need to sell this house. Just move out and get yourselves another one. Isn't that the best solution?" she added triumphantly.

There was stunned silence and Giles looked as if someone had hit him on the back of the head. He and Nick locked eyes, each as bemused as the other by Margaret's suggestion.

"Yes, why not?" Cathy exclaimed, brightening. If Giles and Margaret lived here things would stay the way they were. For all her social climbing, Margaret was at least a traditionalist and very proud of having married into their family. She wouldn't want to change a thing.

Jonathan had also warmed to the idea. He slapped Giles on the shoulder. "Go for it, bro! And if you're living here, wouldn't it save on death duties, or whatever they're called these days, when Dad pops his clogs?"

Nick's mouth suddenly tightened. "I must say, I had no idea my children were so eager to get rid of me," he remarked dryly.

"It's not like that, Daddy," Cathy burst out, genuinely distressed. "We want you to be happy. And Philippa *is* right, you probably do need a new start in a different place. This seems the perfect solution. Everyone gets what they want."

Giles came out of his shocked reverie with a start. "But I'd have to give up work. And what about our house in London?" Stricken, he turned to Margaret for guidance. He liked his life at present; he was climbing the ladder at Bartwell's, was in charge of cataloguing and had brought in new customers through their assiduous networking. Bartwell's thought highly of him and the steady routine of his days, dealing with small squares of valuable paper, gave him a feeling of security. With a flicker of panic he realized their neat, highly organized life could be disrupted forever if he was forced into becoming lord of the manor at this stage in his career.

"We can work it all out," Margaret replied airily. "The important thing is to keep this place in the family." She was smiling warmly at Philippa, and in return she felt grateful there was at least someone who understood how she felt.

"Might I be allowed to get a word in edgewise?" Nick asked cuttingly. Jack, the outsider, had been observing the family discussion as if he were watching a scene in a play and had noticed Nick growing steadily angrier while the others were talking. Philippa had reached for his hand as if to soothe him.

"I'm sorry, darling, I didn't mean to take over," she said contritely, hurt that he wasn't pleased by the way she'd handled his family.

Before Nick had time to say anything, Elizabeth spoke.

"Perhaps you didn't know, Philippa, that this is the family home? Our grandfather bought it in 1930 and planned that future generations of his family should live in it."

"That's right," Giles agreed. The others nodded.

Philippa looked taken aback. "Then if that's the case . . ." But Nick interrupted her, his face red with fury.

"You are the most greedy, grasping bunch of young people I've ever come across. Ungrateful, too," he stormed. "It's all take, take, take with you lot. You use this house like a hotel, coming here with your dirty washing and expecting to be fed whenever you feel like it. You seem to think this place is here for *your* benefit. Well, let me tell you, you're not the only pebbles on the beach! There is Philippa to consider, and the new baby . . ."

Jack, watching, was reminded of the needle on the Richter scale, registering the magnitude of an earthquake; any minute now it would fly beyond its bounds and shatter. Then it struck him, as he observed Nick's blazing eyes and his clenched fists, that there was more going on than Cathy or any of the others knew. Nick Driver had something to hide and selling Wingfield Court was only a part of it.

Giles, visibly wilting under his father's verbal onslaught, seemed to shrink inside his clothes, but Elizabeth looked stronger by the minute and when she spoke it was with conviction.

"We come back here because it's our home, you've always made us welcome and have never suggested to us we should act like guests. I always let you know when we're coming because with the children there are so many of us. Do you really expect the others to make formal arrangements? Ask if it would be convenient? Cathy and Jonathan still have their own rooms here, for God's sake, full of their things. And as Cathy's only renting a place in Edinburgh, where's she supposed to go in the holidays? You can't sell this place, Daddy, just like that, without even consulting us."

"Lizzie's right," Jonathan pointed out. "Leave here if you want to, but you can't sell anyway because . . ."

"I'll do as I bloody well like," Nick cut in swiftly. "Stop waiting for dead men's shoes, the lot of you."

Giles suddenly decided to square up to his father, but beside Nick he looked like an unkempt youth, hair ruffled and suit crumpled. "If I have to, I'll take you to court over this," he bleated.

"Take me to court?" his father scoffed. "Don't be so pathetic, Giles. You're not fit to run this place in any case. You're nothing but a loser."

"Stop talking to him like that," Jonathan exclaimed, shouting too. "You're nothing but a bully."

"I'm more of a man than *you'll* ever be."

Cathy's dark eyes sparked angrily. "That's really unfair, Dad. Don't talk to Jonno like that."

Elizabeth jumped to her feet, hands clamped over her ears. "Stop it! Stop it, all of you. What's happening to us? We used to be a happy family. Even after Mummy died we managed to stick together . . ."

"And then I came along," Philippa observed quietly.

Elizabeth looked at her defiantly and her voice was filled with bitterness. "Yes, and then you came along."

There was a moment's deadly silence then Nick sprang forward, eyes blazing. "Elizabeth, get out of this house at once. I will not have you talking to Philippa like that. She's done nothing to hurt any of you and you're behaving like a bunch of spoiled brats. Get out now, and take Laurence with you. If you can't be polite to my wife, I don't want to see you ever again."

Elizabeth stood staring at him, shocked, as if she couldn't believe what she was hearing. Her face, devoid of make-up and with her fair hair tied back in a ponytail, was that of a plump ungainly teenager with vulnerable eyes.

Suddenly Laurence came forward from his usual silent position in the background and put his arm around her waist in a surprisingly comforting gesture.

"Let's go back to the farm, Lizzie," he murmured softly. "That's a home you know will never be taken away from you."

Philippa ran sobbing from the room, shocked and appalled by the scene she'd just witnessed. For the first time since her marriage she was assailed by real doubts about her future. She'd seen a side of Nick she didn't know existed, a harsh, cruel side, causing him to say the most dreadful things to his children. And while it was obviously absurd of them to say Wingfield Court wasn't his to sell, today had nevertheless exposed a deep dissension within the family she hadn't known existed. It made her position intolerable. She would never be able to wipe from her mind the animosity and fury she'd just witnessed. And now they'd all blame her, were already blaming her for causing the trouble, for wanting to move house, for coming between them all.

Traumatized by what had happened, she went up to her bedroom and lay down on the bed, sobbing with sheer misery. Never before had she felt so isolated and alone, so stuck in an alien environment among a bunch of hostile in-laws who were reproaching her for the imminent loss of everything they held dear. Her friends were all in London, which felt as if it was a million miles away, and her parents even further in Kent. For a moment she thought wildly of running away, just she and the coming baby, from this house she'd come to hate and almost fear. But reason told her not to be so melodramatic. Family quarrels happened. Nick would sort it all out and once they'd moved, everything would be all right again. Just the two of them as they'd been at the beginning.

"Dad, how could you do that?" Jonathan had risen, languid elegance replaced by defiance as he stood facing Nick. "Grandpa must be turning in his grave, and what would Mum have said?"

"How are we going to resolve this situation?" Margaret asked in her practical manner.

Nick looked at her. "You can't wait to get your hands on this place, can you?"

"I don't know what you mean."

Giles spoke up. "We don't want to live here, Dad. Not for years yet." He looked drawn, worn out by the pressure Margaret was putting on him and the bullying manner of his father. If they only knew how much he liked his secure existence at Bartwell's and the routine of his days there, perhaps they'd leave him alone. "Can't we just leave things as they are?"

"Perhaps if you let Philippa do some redecorating it would help?" Cathy suggested tentatively. She'd been as shocked as the others by the way her father had treated Elizabeth, but it had made her see the depths of his devotion to her step-mother and that he was prepared to do anything to make her happy.

Nick's face softened. Cathy had always been his favourite child and now he knew why. She had a deep sense of fairness and compassion. If she knew the truth he was certain she'd be sympathetic; but if she were to know the full facts, so would everyone else, including Philippa, and he knew he couldn't face her disillusionment.

"I think we've got beyond that, Cathy," he said, smiling at her. "Philippa really wants a home of her own."

Margaret looked at him. "What do you mean . . . beyond that?"

"I've had a very good offer for this place. The agents phoned me this afternoon. An Arab sheikh saw the ad in *Country Life* and has offered more than the asking price. Under the circumstances, I'd be mad to refuse."

"But we, as directors of the Wingland Estate, don't want to sell, Dad," Jonathan pointed out, "and you can't accept the offer unless we vote on it."

"That's where you're all under a serious misapprehension," Nick replied, voice dangerously quiet now. "Wingland Estate Ltd owns seventy-five percent of the land, the nineteen tenanted cottages and the Home Farm, but I personally own this house and its contents and the surrounding garden. And I can do as I like with it."

CHAPTER SEVEN

Jonathan broke the frozen silence. "Let's get the hell out of here. I'm going to the pub."

A minute before, Nick had stalked out of the library, leaving them all sitting there, staring into space like victims of a mass-hypnosis stage show.

"I don't believe it," Margaret muttered, as if she hadn't heard Jonathan. "He's got to be bluffing."

"Who's coming with me? Cathy? Jack?" Jonathan asked.

Cathy nodded, dumb with shock, catching hold of Jack's hand.

"Are you coming?" she asked Giles and Margaret.

"No," her brother replied. "I'd rather stay here."

"So would I," Margaret added in hollow tones. "Morton will be announcing dinner in fifteen minutes."

"Fuck dinner," Jonathan retorted succinctly. "I need to get out of here."

They piled into Cathy's car and she drove the half mile into the village, where they parked in the forecourt of the Wag and Tail, a Tudor-style inn crammed full of brasses nailed to old beams, rustic furniture and dimly lit lanterns, the whole effect marred only by a pinball machine at the far end of the bar.

"So what happens now?" Jack asked, after they'd ordered a bottle of red wine and settled themselves in a corner.

"God knows," Jonathan replied as he drank deeply from his glass.

"But why is Daddy lying about owning the house?" Cathy asked. "He can't have purchased the main asset of the company without any of us knowing."

"To impress Philippa?"

"But if it's not his to sell, isn't it going a bit far to get an estate agent to put a whole page ad in *Country Life*?" Jack remarked. "I mean, if your father *is* only trying to impress, or more likely pacify your step-mother, surely he'd just go in for delaying tactics?"

"Dad's been bewitched by her," Jonathan said sadly.

Cathy looked at her brother in surprise. "You used to like her."

"I'm not saying I don't like her, I just said she's bewitched Dad. She's the one who wants to move."

"And it looks as if she wants to down-size! So that means she's certainly no gold digger," Jack remarked. "I know it's none of my business but I think she's feeling utterly overshadowed by the legacy of your mother and wants a fresh start with your father. She obviously feels very insecure at Wingfield Court."

Cathy smiled fondly at him and slid her hand into his. "You're very understanding, aren't you, babe?"

Jonathan was not so easily persuaded. "Nevertheless, there's something going on I don't understand. None of us knows anything about Philippa, but Elizabeth was right about one thing — ever since Dad brought her into the family there's been mayhem."

"What about this Arab sheikh? Does he really exist or was Daddy bluffing?" Cathy questioned.

"I've lost track of what the hell's going on," Jonathan admitted.

Jack leaned forward, topping up their glasses from the bottle. In the dim pub lighting, his hair looked to be tipped with silver and his eyes had darkened to a deep sea green. "Perhaps you two should have a quiet word with your father," he advised. "I have a feeling Margaret isn't exactly helping the situation."

Jonathan watched him closely, studying the finely sculpted lips and the strong line of his jaw, and suddenly a feeling of dread mixed with excitement shot through him. It was a dark sense of magic which had happened to him once before, irresistible and totally seductive. A wave of despair followed instantly. Trust him to fall for the most forbidden fruit of all: his sister's boyfriend.

"Poor old Giles," Cathy said sympathetically. "He's been pushed all his life by Daddy because he was the eldest son and heir. Now he's being pushed by Margaret."

Jonathan looked at his watch. "Are we going to have another drink or get back?"

Jack and Cathy looked at each other questioningly.

Jonathan rose. "Let's have another drink before we enter the bloody battlefield again," he announced, his voice determinedly jokey and his expression inscrutable.

Elizabeth sat quietly beside Laurence on the long drive back to Willow Farm. Darkness had fallen swiftly not long after they'd left Malmesbury and in the dim confines of their car a strangely companionable, almost cosy, silence pervaded the atmosphere, in contrast to the stormy, tearful departure from Wingfield Court. She stole a look at Laurence and saw his profile outlined by the lights of the dashboard, his nose strong and aquiline, eyes fixed on the road ahead, and for once his mouth surprisingly relaxed. Almost good-humoured, in fact. The sense of harmony between them was so peaceful at that moment she was afraid of saying the wrong thing in case it broke the spell.

It was Laurence who spoke first. "That was quite a scene with your father, wasn't it? I hope you're not too hurt, Liz?"

He hadn't called her Liz for years.

"Of course I'm hurt," she said in a small voice. "Daddy has never spoken to me like that in the whole of my life. Ordering me out of the house as if I were an interloper! Philippa has not only taken Mummy's place in his life, she's taken our place as well. All he thinks about now is her. I'm hurt for myself and hurt at what he's doing to the others."

"No doubt Philippa's put him up to it. I don't know how he thinks he can get away with it but Giles will sort it all out. He's the one it most directly affects. But it's sad for you because I know how much you love your old home."

Elizabeth remained silent, wanting to nurture this kindly mood for as long as possible.

He spoke again. "It would be nice if we made Willow Farm more of a family home, though, wouldn't it?"

She was grateful the darkness of the car hid her expression of astonishment.

"Yes," she replied tentatively.

"I mean," he continued, "if your father's going to move, set up a new home, and none of you have taken to Philippa, well . . . we could invite Cathy and your brothers for weekends, couldn't we? And Christmas, perhaps."

"You wouldn't mind?" she ventured. "All the chaos of a house full of people? Giles with Margaret? Cathy and her boyfriends? And Jonathan?"

There was a moment's silence while she held her breath, wondering if she'd burst the momentary golden bubble of goodwill.

"I think it would be good for Dominic and Tamsin to have all the family around from time to time," Laurence replied, and she knew he couldn't quite bring himself to admit he'd like them to have more to do with her family also. But on his terms, at his level of lifestyle, rather than always up at the grand house.

"Yes . . . well, it's a great idea," she agreed carefully, not wanting to appear over-eager.

They drove on in silence for a while and then he reached over to turn on the car radio. The soft darkness became filled with the melancholy strains of a Chopin nocturne and Elizabeth felt a fresh pang of sadness for all she'd lost in the past eighteen months.

Laurence was talking again. "I'd like you to feel about Willow Farm as you do about your old home, although I know you can't compare them. I suppose it takes time . . ."

She could tell he was making a great effort to be understanding, but she could also detect an undertone of hurt in his voice. She simply didn't know what to say.

It's not just the dilapidated old farm, Laurence, it's you. You're not the man I thought I'd married and life isn't much fun with you. Your mother always popping in drives me mad. If only you worked. Weren't so boring. Gave the day a sense of structure instead of always hanging around, moping.

She sighed inwardly. A dozen reasons why she didn't feel the same about Willow Farm flooded her mind but none of them actually had anything to do with the place itself.

"The farm is fine, and inviting family and friends to stay is a lovely idea," was all she said at last.

In the darkness she felt his hand rest briefly on her knee. God, he's trying so hard, she thought. It's up to me to meet him halfway, make an effort to improve the situation between us.

"Let's give some little dinner parties, too," she suggested. "It'll give me a chance to try out some new receipes."

"I'll make a list of people tomorrow."

Tap-tap on the typewriter, she thought, heart sinking, but he sounded much more cheerful.

In spite of Nick's pleading, Philippa did not come down to dinner, preferring some soup and toast which Morton took up on a tray.

"I simply can't face your family," she told Nick. "Why didn't you warn me they'd be so upset? And why did they seem to suggest the house wasn't yours to sell?"

He looked grim as he paced up and down their bedroom, hands dug deep into his pockets, deciding that Philippa would have to be told the truth, or at least part of it. There was no need to mention that most of his financial problems stemmed from shaky investments and schemes that had never quite got off the ground.

"They don't know what they're talking about. I bought it privately from the company when Rosalind was ill."

"Without their knowing? But why?"

He sighed in an exaggerated way, shrugging his shoulders as he did so. "Rosalind's medical expenses were exorbitant. For two years I'd been forking out hundreds of thousands of pounds to cover the cost of her treatment. We had the best specialists in the world flying in, the latest drugs . . . and in the final months we had to have night and day nurses." His voice trailed off despairingly. "I tried to keep from the children how ill she was until near the end. They had no idea what the costs were either, not that any of them would have begrudged a penny. Neither did I. But the doctors had to be paid, and I was having to borrow from the bank to meet the bills. In the end they wanted collateral to secure my ever-rising overdraft. It wasn't enough that I had a good income from the family trust and so could pay them back when . . . well, in time," he added lamely.

Philippa reached for his hand, held it in both of hers and looked at him sympathetically.

"It must have been awful for you," she said softly.

Nick nodded slowly. "I had no option but to borrow more money in order to buy this house from the Wingland Estate. That gave me the asset I needed. It's a common business practice, a matter of shifting things around on paper, but the children don't seem to understand that."

Philippa knew very little about private limited companies and family trusts and wasn't sure she herself understood all the ramifications of what he'd just told her.

"And have you paid off the bank loan?" she asked. "Can't you give this house back to the company — your children, that is? And then we could buy another one for ourselves with our own money?"

Nick smiled for the first time. Leaning forward, he took her in his arms and held her close.

"Everything's under control, darling," he murmured. "Just relax and don't worry. I promise you, everything's under control."

"Truly? You're not in any kind of financial trouble?"

He laughed easily. "Hardly, sweetheart. You and I and our baby are going to have the most marvellous life. Just you wait and see. Now have a rest, darling." He leaned forward and kissed her tenderly. "I'm planning to have an early night myself so maybe we could . . . ?"

"Oh, yes, sweetheart. Don't be too long." She gazed trustingly up at him, thinking herself the luckiest woman in the world.

* * *

Nick went quietly down the stairs and crossed the hall. There was still time before dinner to make a couple of urgent phone calls. Going into the estate office at the far end, he locked the door behind him, as was his practice, and sat down at his desk. The thought of Philippa's finding out all the details of what was going on filled him with alarm. If only Margaret hadn't spotted that damned advertisement, Wingfield Court could have been sold before his family were even aware he'd put it on the market.

Although it was late he'd phone Norman Sheridan at home. Not that Norman would mind. He was a good friend as well as Nick's lawyer, and right now he needed advice. Giles and the others were not going to let the matter drop and as directors of the Wingland Estate they had, unfortunately, every right to enquire about his actions.

Norman's wife answered the phone. Clarissa Sheridan was a bright little woman, perpetually cheerful and always sounding as if she'd just received good news.

"Hel-LO!" she shrieked in delight when she realized it was Nick. "How perfectly LOVE-ly to hear from you. How's Philippa? Is she well? Having a good pregnancy?"

It took Nick several moments to fend off her animated chatter and ask if he could speak to Norman.

"Of COURSE you can!" she gushed. "I'll get him right away."

If Clarissa was like a shining dart winging through the air at speed, Norman by contrast was a delightfully shambolic gung-ho figure, clothes perpetually dis-hevelled, hair standing on end, rosy-faced and vague-looking but with a razor sharp mind lurking beneath the deceptive exterior.

"Hello, old man," he greeted Nick.

"Sorry to call you at home but I need to talk to you. Can I see you tomorrow?" he asked tersely.

"Tomorrow's Saturday," Norman replied. He took a swig from his whisky and soda before continuing. "I thought I might get in a spot of fishing."

"How about first thing?"

"Can't you tell me what it's about now?"

"No, I need to see you. Shall I come to your house about nine-thirty? It won't take long. There are just a few details I want to check with you."

"Sure. No problem. How's everything going?"

"Badly," Nick replied. "The family have discovered I'm selling the house and all hell has broken loose."

Norman sounded unperturbed. "There's nothing they can do about it," he said airily.

"I hope you're right."

"Don't worry about it, Nick. It's all sorted."

"Giles is going to make trouble."

"Let him try. He won't get far."

Nick could hear the slurp of another mouthful of whisky going down. "I'm trying to keep Philippa out of the whole thing."

"Very wise," Norman agreed cheerfully. "Is that it, old boy? See you tomorrow then. G'bye."

Feeling calmer, Nick never the less immediately dialled the number of his accountant and thanked God he'd been wise enough ten years ago to move his financial and legal offers from the large London firms his late father had employed and given it instead to small local concerns like Norman's and Ernest's. This way he had immediate access not only to his two most important advisers and conspirators and what was going on with his business affairs, but because they all lived in such a relatively small community they did exactly as he asked. He was after all the most powerful person in the neighbourhood. He was also prepared to pay above the odds to get what he wanted in return for their expertise and discretion.

When Ernest Lomax answered his phone, Nick repeated to him what he'd just told Norman.

"You've absolutely nothing to worry about," the accountant assured him sycophantically. "It won't be worth Giles's while to contest the sale of Wingfield Court. That is . . . the sale of it to you six years ago."

"Are you certain?" Why was Nick suddenly filled with doubt? He'd told Philippa he'd bought the house during Rosalind's illness . . . but that probably didn't matter. She was unlikely to make a point of telling anyone. And then he realized he was more worried about her finding out what had been going on than he was his own children.

Ernest Lomax continued smoothly: "When has any of your family ever closely examined the accounts of either Wingland Estate Ltd or the trust fund? So long as all the taxes are paid and they get their dividends and nobody bothers them with boring details, they've always been quite happy to leave it to us, haven't they?"

He's right, Nick reflected, reassured. Elizabeth and Cathy barely understood the audited accounts and only glanced at them to be polite, Jonathan was completely uninterested and said so . . . and Giles trusted him.

"You can easily handle this," Ernest soothed him. "I can blind them with science but you, their father, should be able to assure them everything has been done for the best. Remember those medical fees?" he added, giving a little chuckle.

Nick froze, annoyed by this sudden over familiarity, the crossing of the delicate line between client and paid consultant.

"I might drop in and see you on Monday," he said coldly. "I'll ring you first."

"I'll look forward to that and meanwhile I'll go through all the files again so you can rest assured no loopholes were left," Ernest said obsequiously, knowing he'd overstepped the mark. "I'm at home all weekend so if you have any worries, please ring me at any time."

"Thanks, I will." Nick swiftly decided he couldn't afford to fall out with Ernest Lomax. He knew too much.

Giles and Margaret were waiting for him in the hall before they went into the dining room where Morton had laid the table for nine.

"As you can see there are just three of us," Nick told him tersely. "Take the other settings away, please. Mr and Mrs Vickers have already left and it seems the others prefer the charms of the local pub."

They sat in awkward silence, picking at their food and drinking a lot of wine.

"Philippa not coming down to join us?" Margaret asked.

Nick's silent look conveyed how stupid he thought her question was.

Giles asked his father, "So what happens now?" His voice sounded strained and wobbly.

"What do you think happens?" Nick asked. "I exchange contracts on the sale of this place, and Philippa and I move out. And there's not a damn thing you can do about it."

Margaret bristled aggressively. "You're not going to get away with this, Nick. You know as well as I do that the house is the main company asset. By law you have to hold a meeting and have a quorum of directors present before any valid business can be transacted. When did we last have such a meeting? Who was present? Giles certainly wasn't, and neither were the others."

Nick leaned back in his chair and looked at them as if he was terribly hurt by their lack of understanding.

"You've got to remember, Rosalind's illness put everything at sixes and sevens. Things like having annual general meetings, with agendas and minutes got forgotten during those long terrible months. Nobody knows how I suffered, seeing her fading away, day by day . . . how much we all suffered." He looked down as if he didn't want them to see the pain in his eyes. "Frankly, none of us bothered with things like company business, or business of any kind if it comes to that. It was a case of getting through each day as best we could. Maybe Ernest Lomax and Norman Sheridan should have reminded us, but they were anxious not to intrude on our grief. It's not as if the Wingland Estate is a public company, quoted on the Stock Exchange. My father set it up for tax reasons, and we get special dispensation because the company is registered as a farm. That was the only reason for forming a private limited company. Anyway, your mother was upstairs, dying inch by inch and suffering greatly . . . who cared about business at a time like that?" His voice faltered and he seemed steeped in grief at the memory. He sat with one hand resting around the stem of his wine glass, rubbing his eyes with the other.

Cathy, followed by Jonathan and Jack, came bursting into the dining room at that moment and stopped in her tracks, shocked to see him like that.

"Daddy!" She rushed forward and put her arms around his shoulders. "What's the matter?" She looked almost accusingly at Giles and Margaret. "What's going on?"

Nick recovered sufficiently to reach out and pat her hand reassuringly, but spoke with a poignancy that broke her heart.

"It's all right, darling," he said. "I was just explaining to Giles and Margaret that during Mummy's illness short cuts had to be taken in connection with the company. It's no good blaming me because we didn't do everything according to the book and have meetings with someone taking minutes and all that — I was in no state to cope, and frankly I don't think any of you were either."

Cathy hugged him tightly, remembering with painful clarity how he'd grieved the night their mother had died; he'd shut himself away in the estate office but his sobs were audible through the locked door.

The others hung back with silent embarrassment and Jack slipped out of the room, not wanting to encroach on their privacy any further.

"But the law's the law," Giles said, made braver by the presence of his siblings and the amount of wine he'd drunk. "Of course things got neglected during Mum's illness, but that was eighteen months ago. What have Norman Sheridan and Ernest Lomax been doing all this time, for God's sake? Ernest is company secretary. He must know this house can't be sold?"

Nick raised his eyebrows as if he thought Giles's remark profound. "I'll call them both first thing on Monday morning," he promised, nodding as if in agreement.

"Why don't you call tomorrow?" asked Jonathan. "And by the way, where's our dinner? I thought you were expecting us."

Nick was all suave urbanity. "Tomorrow's Saturday, Jonno. Both their offices will be closed. As for dinner, when you went out I wasn't sure when you were coming back so Morton is keeping yours hot for you. I'll get him to serve it right away." As he pushed back his chair he glanced at them all apologetically. "You'll forgive me if I go upstairs now to see how Philippa is? I was concerned about her earlier and it's been a very difficult day for her."

"Do you realize," Margaret pointed out later, as they all sat around the table toying with cheese and fruit, "that Nick hasn't actually told us anything? Given no explanations. All he's done is answer our questions like a politician."

"He's hiding something from us," Jonathan confirmed. "I don't know what's going on, but I don't like it."

"Giles, why don't you phone Norman and Ernest in the morning?" Margaret goaded him. "Ask them outright what gives your father the right to sell this house."

"But as he said, it's Saturday. They won't be in their offices."

"Ring them at home, for God's sake!" she exploded, not caring that the others saw how desperate she was about the whole situation. "Nick rings them at home whenever he wants to. Something he seems to have conveniently forgotten this evening."

Nick stayed upstairs with Philippa for the rest of the evening, but not before he'd slipped into the estate office to make a couple more phone calls. He rang Ernest and Norman again to tell them they were to be "unavailable" should any member of his family phone them over the weekend, and that as from Monday they were to be "in meetings" if any of his children tried to make contact.

Meanwhile, the others continued to sit around the dining-room table, drinking and talking, until Cathy finally said; "Come on, everyone, let's go to bed. We're getting nowhere and there's nothing we can do until tomorrow."

She rose, stretching her arms above her head, her silver bangles chinking, a silk shawl she'd draped over one shoulder slipping to the floor. Jack sat looking up at her, his sweet, funny, adorable love, so filled with compassion and kindness he knew she found it hard to see wrongdoing in anyone, especially her own father. Well, he thought, as he caught her hand and allowed her to pull him to his feet, he wasn't going to reveal to her his opinion of Nick. From the moment Jack had met him he'd taken a dislike to the smooth insincere manner of the man who acted as if he was a contemporary of theirs, with his young wife and baby on the way. There was something almost creepy in that turned-on charm. He personally wouldn't trust Nick Driver to post a letter, far less be in charge of the family fortune.

"Giles will ring the solicitor and the accountant in the morning," Margaret was assuring the others in a stage whisper as they said good night. "And he'll use the car phone so he can't be overheard," she added conspiratorially.

As Cathy and Jack trailed up the stairs, hand in hand, she was aware that Jonathan was watching them from the hall below, looking rather lost and forlorn. They'd always been so close, the two of them. They were the younger ones and had leaned heavily on each other when Rosalind had died. Jack hadn't been in her life then. He hadn't been in Jonathan's life either. She remembered now, with a feeling of foreboding, that she and Jonathan had always shared the same likes and dislikes when it came to people.

CHAPTER EIGHT

"Margaret and I want to get back to London. We're going to leave before lunch," Giles told the others. "Tomorrow's Monday and I want to hire a good lawyer of my own to find out what the hell's going on and act on our behalf."

Cathy looked worried. "It isn't necessarily sinister that you couldn't get hold of either Norman or Ernest," she told him as they all went into the garden, out of earshot of the house, after breakfast. "Did you really think you'd get hold of them over a weekend?"

"Yes, I did," Giles asserted. "They've always been available to discuss business with Dad or any of us on a Saturday or a Sunday in the past, because most of us are only here at weekends and they know that. If their wives hadn't been at home either, I'd have thought nothing of it, but for both Clarissa Sheridan *and* Jean Lomax to answer the phone and say their husbands were out and they'd no idea when they'd be back . . . well, it stinks."

"I suppose it is odd," Cathy agreed sadly. She sank to the ground and sat hugging her knees, with Jack beside her. "Oh dear, I do hate all this unpleasantness. I can't believe Daddy's done anything wrong. I don't agree with him, but I do understand why he and

Philippa would want to start their marriage with a clean slate."

"No one's stopping them," Margaret remarked tartly.

Jonathan lowered himself on to the wooden bench beside her with the slow elegance of someone tall and slender. He'd dressed with care that morning, in a blue shirt that brought out the colour of his eyes and cream linen trousers. He looked at Cathy and Jack.

"Are you going to London today, too? Or do you have to get back to Edinburgh?"

"I don't know," she replied hesitantly. She was hating this whole business of taking legal action against their father but then thought perhaps she should stay around, if only to see fair play.

He continued guilelessly: "Could give me a lift down? And stay with me? I don't get to see you enough, Cathy, and this would be a good opportunity."

She looked at him sharply, remembering his expression as he'd watched her and Jack go up stairs to bed the previous night. But he was staring innocently back at her as if his only interest lay in spending time with her, and she decided she'd been mistaken. It was too easy to imagine that all good-looking men were desirable to someone who was gay. Jonathan did not go around fancying every Dick, Tom and Harry, and she felt a pang of guilt for ever imagining he did. Before she could reply Margaret spoke.

"Cathy, wouldn't it be a good idea if you and Jack came and stayed with us for a few days? We should all stick together until we get this thing sorted out, and we've more room for you both than Jonathan."

"But we haven't even decided to go to London," she protested. "I've got some lectures this week."

She turned to look at Wingfield Court and saw her father through the dining-room window, helping himself to some fruit from the sideboard. He was stooping and because he didn't know he was being observed, the boastful arrogant stance he usually adopted had been replaced by an older, more weary posture. He looked like a man who knew he was about to be betrayed by his own children, Cathy reflected with guilty distress. Poor Daddy. As if he hadn't been through enough. Tender-heartedly, she wanted to run indoors and fling her arms around him and promise him they all really loved him, it was just that . . . just what?

Was it true they were waiting for dead men's shoes? Greedy for what was coming and scared they'd be done out of it? For a moment she felt quite ashamed, but then she remembered how much she loved her home, and how heartbroken she'd be if she had to leave it. It wasn't anything to do with money as far as she was concerned, it was to do with preserving the past and the continuity of her family home. One day she wanted to bring her children here; to have them play on these lawns, sleep upstairs in the nursery, slide down the banisters as she and Jonathan used to do. That was why they all had to rush back to London and hire a top lawyer, to find out if Nick could be stopped. But such knowledge was going to come at a terrible cost: their own gross disloyalty to a much-loved father.

She glanced up at the bedroom windows and saw that the curtains of the room he shared with Philippa were still drawn. That made her feel worse. While three of his four children were huddled in the garden, plotting against him as he was having breakfast alone, his wife was trustingly asleep upstairs.

Jack saw her expression of profound sadness. "Tough, eh, babe?"

She looked at him miserably. "It's awful, Jack." She turned to the others. "We must be able to sort this out another way. Daddy would never lie to us . . ."

"I don't think he's lying to us now," Giles argued. "I think he told us the truth when he said he now owns Wingfield Court. The question is . . . how can he unless he's done something highly illegal? Come on, Cathy, we've got to know the score. I bet it's all Philippa's fault. As Elizabeth said yesterday, everything was perfectly fine until she came along."

Margaret agreed loudly and Jonathan nodded.

Giles continued, "Let's all go to London and find out once and for all where we stand. I'm sure a few enquiries at Companies House will produce the facts we need about the Wingland Estate. And I'll talk to Andrew Kingsley, see if he knows anything."

"Who's Andrew Kingsley?" Jack asked Cathy, sotto voce.

"The family stockbroker."

"D'you want to go to London?" His tone was sympathetic.

"Can we get away for a few days? Haven't you any important lectures?" she asked.

He reached out to stroke her hair, which hung long and glossy down her back. "I can miss them. We come down next week anyway so what difference will a few extra days make? I want to be with you while you're going through this."

She shot him a grateful look.

"That's settled then," Margaret said with satisfaction. "But I suggest we don't say anything to Nick. We'll just tell him we have to get back to town for work tomorrow. He might try to cover his tracks if he knew we were about to make enquiries."

"You needn't make him sound like a criminal," Cathy protested, flushing.

"Oh, do shut up, Cathy," Giles snapped with brotherly candour. "You stand to lose as much as the rest of us if Dad's had his fingers in the till."

She jumped to her feet, eyes blazing. "How can you talk like that? You're so self-righteous. It would serve you right if you ended up with nothing." She stomped away across the lawn towards the house. Jack rose to follow but Jonathan stopped him.

"Let her cool down," he advised. "She's always been a bit of a Daddy's girl. Why don't we go for a walk? It's a lovely day and we needn't leave for London just yet, need we?"

"All right," Jack replied absently. His eyes were fixed on Cathy's receding back as, with a flourish of flowing skirts and long silk scarves, she disappeared into the house through the drawing room french windows.

"I really don't know how she can defend Nick," Margaret remarked. "He may be her father but from the moment he set eyes on Philippa he's been a different man." Then she turned to her husband. "Shall we get a move on? I don't want to hang around this place with everyone in such a bad mood. Let's get back to London."

Giles looked shaken by Cathy's attack. "All right." He sounded doubtful. "I suppose we're doing the right thing. Jonathan, are you coming with us?"

But he was already several yards away, walking across the lawn with Jack.

"I'll get a lift with Cathy and Jack," he called back over his shoulder.

Margaret and Giles found Nick in the hall. He was looking at the Sunday newspapers which had just been delivered.

"Had your breakfast?" he asked blandly.

"Yes, thank you," Margaret replied crisply. Giles said nothing.

"Philippa should be down in a few minutes." Nick handed her a copy of the *Mail On Sunday*. "Want a paper to read?"

"No, thanks. We've got to be on our way, Nick. Giles has a lot of work on tomorrow and you know what the traffic's like, getting back into London on a Sunday."

Nick looked from one to the other. They couldn't be sure whether it was a glint of astonishment or relief they saw in his eyes.

"You're going already? Surely you'll at least stay for lunch?"

"We ought to be getting back," Giles said, looking uncomfortable. "I have a lot to do."

"I see." Nick folded the paper he was holding with neat precision and put it back on the hall table. "Well, no hard feelings, I hope, old boy." A smile broke out on his tanned face. He was glad now he'd instructed Norman and Ernest to be "out" over the weekend, though they wouldn't be able to make themselves unavailable to his family indefinitely. "It's been lovely seeing you both again," he added sardonically.

"I'll just go and finish packing," Margaret announced and turned to go up the stairs. Her stairs one day. Her house. She felt more determined than ever that it should be kept in the family. She'd been looking forward to living here and having it as her home ever since she'd got engaged to Giles. She was damned if she was going to let this most glittering of all prizes slip through her fingers. To hell with Nick, she thought, clumping heavily up the stairs on her stocky legs, and to hell with his wife. She'd see them damned before she let Giles forfeit his inheritance.

Cathy, coming out of the library at that moment, from where she'd overheard the conversation, came face to face with her father.

"Good morning, sweetheart," he greeted her.

She flung her arms around his neck and hugged him, feeling her throat grow tight with unshed tears.

"Morning, Daddy. How are you?" She was sure he could see guilt at what they were about to do written all over her face.

"I'm fine, darling. You're not leaving right away, are you? Giles and Margaret are rushing off . . ."

"Of course we're not leaving right away," she retorted stoutly.

"Good. I think we're having rack of lamb for lunch, and you like lamb, don't you?"

She couldn't help noticing he was talking to her as if she were still a young child and for a moment it made her feel secure again.

"It's my favourite! Oh, Daddy, it's so good to be back here, you've no idea," she said impulsively. They walked slowly back into the library. Nick put his arm around her shoulders, and she looked up into his face; so dear, so familiar, a face she'd known all her life.

"Daddy," she said, tugging his arm to pull him down on to the sofa beside her, "we've got to talk."

"All right, what do you want to talk about?" he replied indulgently.

For a wild moment she felt like confessing what they were planning to do, but then she realized she couldn't do that without being disloyal to Elizabeth, Giles and Jonathan. She wanted no part of their investigation, already felt besmirched by being associated with it, and yet . . .

"Daddy, you can't sell this house," she pleaded. "You've no idea how much we love it. It's my home. When I finally come down from university, where will I live? We all regard this place as home. We all want to bring our children and our grandchildren here one day. It will break our hearts if you leave," she added earnestly. Surely, she thought, this was the way to go about persuading him not to sell? Not by being rude and aggressive but by making him see how desperately sad they were all feeling.

"It's not as simple as that, darling," Nick replied gently. "Philippa really isn't happy here. She says it's still your mother's house and it'll never be hers. You heard her yourself. She's adamant we should go. I fear for her health and that of the baby if we stay here."

"Why can't you buy a little house for yourselves, then?" Cathy implored. "You could surely afford to do that without selling Wingfield Court? A nice four-bedroomed house with a garden." Her eyes filled with tears. "Wouldn't that do? And then maybe, in time, after the baby's born, she'll feel confident enough to come back and live here once more. Especially if you let her do a little redecorating so she'd feel it was more her place?"

Cathy could see him hesitating, as if he wanted to say something, then he seemed to change his mind.

"If I thought that would work, I'd do it," he replied. "I had no intention of selling up when Philippa and I got married, and I don't think she knew at the time she wouldn't be happy here, either. But now there's no question of our staying. You see, darling, she genuinely wants to create a new home for us all."

Cathy sat looking at him, her face pale with misery.

"Do you think if I talked to her it would make any difference?"

He shook his head vehemently. "After last night, don't even mention it," he said firmly. "She thinks you're all against her and I really don't want her to get upset. The doctor says it gives her high blood pressure which is very dangerous at the moment."

"Oh, dear. What can we do then? Why don't you rent a nice house for a while, Daddy? Getting away from here for a bit might give her a new perspective on things. This is probably all caused by her hormones, you know. She might feel quite differently after she's had the baby, and then she could regret leaving here terribly." Cathy knew she was chattering on in a desperate bid to get Nick to change his mind but couldn't stop herself. To keep Wingfield Court in the family was paramount in her mind at this moment and she was prepared to go to any lengths to achieve it.

"It's no use, Cathy," he said decisively. "I shall be accepting the offer from this Arab chap tomorrow." He rose as if to bring the conversation to an end then strolled over towards the long windows and gazed into the garden. "Remember, sweetheart, that wherever we go, it will be your home, too. Philippa wants that, and so of course do I."

Making a home for Cathy was something that hadn't struck him until the previous evening. In settling into a new home he'd been thinking purely in terms of himself and Philippa and the new baby. But of course, while the others had their own houses or flats, Cathy had nothing except a share in a rented terraced house in India Street. Where was she to stay during her vacations except with him?

Jack strode through the long silky grass, hands in pockets, the breeze ruffling the platinum tips of his hair.

"So tell me about your painting," he asked Jonathan. "Cathy tells me you do portraits and abstract stuff."

"Abstract stuff?" Jonathan echoed, imitating an elderly dowager's voice. "Abstract stuff. Oh, the dear girl is a positive philistine, isn't she? What are we going to do with her?"

Jack threw back his head to laugh. That was the effect Jonathan had on everyone. He made life jolly, made people feel they'd suddenly become part of an instant party.

"Come and see my studio tomorrow," he continued. "I'm preparing for an exhibition in November at the Milestone Gallery."

Jack raised his eyebrows, impressed. "That must be a lot of work."

"Yes." Jonathan plucked a leaf from a low branch as they walked through the trees that grew alongside the Avon, which meandered through their land. The river shimmered, sparkling and restless today, and he felt that same restlessness in himself. The hollow ache had come back again, opening up the dark gulf of need in him, a need that was never truly or lastingly satisfied, a need that from time to time took over his life and shut him off from other people. He turned to look at Jack's back view as he stood and gazed into the depths of the glittering water and was painfully aware of his bronzed forearms, frosted with golden hairs, and the back of Jack's neck, a strong and muscular column as it rose out of his white shirt.

Jonathan turned abruptly away and started walking upstream, so Jack would not see the naked longing in his eyes. He mustn't even think of it. Mustn't fantasize. Nothing could ever happen between them. Jack was Cathy's . . . He blinked fiercely, banishing the over-brightness in his eyes that threatened to spill down his cheeks, gritting his teeth in the knowledge that he was most likely going to have to go through his whole life suffering from unrequited love, because that was the destiny of so many men like himself and he'd better get used to it.

"Do you ever take a boat on the river?" Jack asked, following behind. "I love being on the water . . . having a picnic with lots of wine."

"Oh, fuck that for a *chanson comique*," Jonathan mocked. "It sounds far too wet and messy for me. Come on, we'd better get back to the house before Margaret knifes Nick or something. You know what she's like, the dear little thing."

Elizabeth was putting the finishing touches to the succulent chickens she'd cooked for Sunday lunch when the phone rang. She grabbed it off the wall by the cooker and cradled it under her chin as she stirred the gravy.

"Lizzie?"

She recognized Giles's voice. "Hi, there! What's happening?"

"Margaret and I are on our way back to London."

"What . . . already? Has Dad kicked you out, too?" she joked. Laurence's concern for her the previous evening had put her in a good mood.

"Certainly not." Giles sounded offended. "We decided to leave because the atmosphere was so bad, and anyway I want to get on with finding a good lawyer first thing in the morning. Cathy and Jack, with Jonathan, are following later this afternoon and I'm hoping you and Laurence can come up to London tomorrow? Margaret and I thought that if we . . ."

"Not a chance, love," Elizabeth replied. "Herta and Gerhard have the day off, and why do you need us anyway? How many people does it take to hire a lawyer?"

Giles gave a dry laugh. "That's not the point. The important thing is that we form a group so we're all aware of what's going on. We must have a meeting as soon as possible so we can decide on a plan of action, based on our findings. Right now I'm not sure how we stand legally but when we do, we'll take the necessary steps to avert this disaster."

"OK, Giles," she said, and she deftly filled a gravy boat as she spoke. "You'll have to let us know what's happening. It's so difficult to get away from here because of the children and the animals . . ."

"But listen, Elizabeth. Dad may be trying to do us out of our inheritance," her brother interrupted, sounding fraught.

"I know that, but what can we do about it? I really don't feel we should take legal action. He is our father after all, and we simply can't wash our dirty linen in public . . ."

"Margaret says we must fight for our rights."

"Listen, Giles, the bread sauce is burning — I have to go. Keep me posted, will you, love?"

They said a brief goodbye and Elizabeth hung up. She was finding the whole situation so upsetting that in spite of her efforts to remain calm and cheerful, she simply couldn't help feeling prickly. Everything seemed to irritate her these days. Leaning down to open the oven door in order to take out the roast potatoes, a wave of hot air slapped her in the face like the blast from a furnace.

"Hell!" she exclaimed, stepping back. "Herta!"

At that moment the au pair walked slowly into the kitchen, a mutinous expression on her face.

"Did you call me?"

"Yes, I called you, Herta," Elizabeth retorted, flustered. "Where have you been? I need help with dishing up lunch. Will you please put the potatoes in that dish, and then can you drain the cauliflower? There's cheese sauce keeping warm on the hob, to pour over it. And please drain the runner beans. I still have to carve the chickens . . . where are the children, by the way? They'll need their hands and faces washed before they sit down."

"My mother's seeing to them now," said a calm voice behind her. Turning she saw Laurence holding out a glass of white wine.

"Oh, Laurence!" She looked at him, her face flushed, her hair escaping from the scrunchy at the nape of her neck, and wished she was one of those groomed-looking wives with lipstick and neat clothes. "Thank you."

His eyes were warm. "You're working far too hard. Why don't you sit down for five minutes and enjoy your drink? I'll carve the birds while Herta does the vegetables."

Elizabeth knew her mouth was falling open like an idiot's at this helpfulness on Laurence's part but she managed to close it with a quick grateful smile.

"Thank you," she repeated, dropping limply on to a kitchen chair. She watched as he carved the birds neatly and carefully, although he always professed to be hopeless at carving which was why she'd given up asking him to do it.

"The plates are warming in the oven," she reminded him.

But he was already getting them out while Herta laboriously drained the vegetables, as if she'd been asked to shift heavy sacks of coal. Elizabeth sipped her glass of beautifully chilled Chablis and the day took on an altogether pleasanter aspect.

"Here we are!" trilled Laura, carrying Jasper into the kitchen. He looked like a polished rosy apple, his face and hands scrubbed, dressed in tiny denim trousers and a striped T-shirt.

"Hello, sweetheart." Elizabeth held out her arms to him.

Dominic and Tamsin came hurtling into the kitchen next and in a few minutes everyone was sitting around the long pine table, with Laurence at one end, Elizabeth at the other, and the four spaniels and two cats perched around the room on seats and window sills as they regarded the pieces of chicken and chipolatas rolled in bacon with watchful eyes, ready to pounce on any fallen morsel.

Elizabeth didn't mention Giles's phone call to Laurence, and if she was forced to go to London to see a lawyer, was going to let him think she'd gone to do some shopping. It was obviously better that way. In the past twenty-four hours he had changed dramatically in his attitude towards her, in fact in his attitude towards life as a whole, and she wanted things to stay like this. She knew why, of course. He was glad because it looked as if her links with Wingfield Court might be severed, and that meant something else: in future her only home would be Willow Farm, old and ramshackle as it was, and she'd no longer be able to take refuge in the luxuries of a stately home. She'd have to make do with what she had, and that included him.

Elizabeth looked at him over the rim of her wine glass and felt quietly astonished he'd ever imagined she hankered for the magnificence of Wingfield Court. Of course she adored the place but not because it was grand. For her the important thing was its sentimental significance; it was where she'd been born, where she'd spent her childhood with her brothers and sister, and where she'd lived until she got married. It was also where her mother had died. It would be very sad to see the old place go but it hadn't been her home for a long time. She'd never realized until now how much Laurence had minded the notion that she might still see it that way.

"Why don't we all go for a walk after lunch?" she suggested, looking at him. He in turn looked at the children. "Would you all like to go for a walk?"

"When can we have a pony?" Dominic asked. "I'm fed up with always walking."

Tamsin's forget-me-not blue eyes widened. "A pony!" she echoed. She pushed back the tendrils of blonde hair from her forehead with tiny shrimp-like pink fingers. "Can I have a pony, too?"

"You'll have to ask Daddy," Elizabeth replied, thinking: I've always made these decisions in the past. Maybe I'm learning that Laurence is their parent, too, and must share in their upbringing.

"Can we, Daddy? Can we? Can we?" they chorused, and Jasper, determined not to be left out, banged his spoon and crowed loudly.

"Why don't you have a rest after lunch, Elizabeth?" Laura suggested. "Hansel and Gretel can surely take the children for a walk."

"Herta and Gerhard, Mother," Laurence corrected her.

"Well, whatever." Laura spoke dismissively. Renowned for her lack of diplomacy and for always speaking without thinking, she continued, looking at Elizabeth, "You look dreadfully tired, dear. Laurence says you're having a bad time with your family and that can be so exhausting. I'd go and put up your feet if I were you. Whatever are you paying these two for if it isn't to help with the children?"

Gerhard, big, blond and silent, having as Laura had once said nothing in his head but ivory from the teeth up, rose majestically and started loading the dish washer. "We can take them for walk," he said heavily.

"That's very kind," Laurence observed, "but I think Lizzie and I might like to take the children out ourselves today."

"Absolutely," she agreed robustly, although she'd privately rather have curled up on the swing seat in the garden with a good novel for a couple of hours.

Laura shrugged exaggeratedly. "Why pay dogs and bark yourself?" she demanded shrilly, and did not notice the looks of pure malice both Herta and Gerhard shot in her direction.

After Cathy and Jack had dropped Jonathan off at his studio, they drove on to Giles and Margaret's house in one of the quieter tree-lined streets of Holland Park, where they were staying for the next couple of nights.

Margaret had already fussed around the place, airing beds and taking things out of the deep freeze for dinner, patting the already fluffed up drawing-room cushions and sending Giles out to look for a shop that might be open on a Sunday where they sold flowers.

"It's only Cathy," he grumbled, "and she's here to discuss business, not be entertained."

"But Jack's never been here before," Margaret argued, straightening the invitations displayed on the mantelpiece.

"So who the hell's Jack? Some impoverished student she happens to be going out with."

"We don't know that he's impoverished. His parents are in Dubai."

"So?" Giles looked at her as if she was a stranger. But then his whole life felt as if it had been turned topsy-turvy in the past few days. From his earliest memory, his life had been planned for him; he'd always thought he knew where he was going. Nick had pushed him from an early age to do well at school, to pass his exams with high marks, to succeed in everything he did because he was the one who was going to take over one day. And at the end of the line, like a carrot dangling before his nose, had been Wingfield Court, his safety blanket if by any chance, he failed at everything else in his life. It had been his crutch; it was what had given him a sense of security. He could become a failed philatelist, go bankrupt, lose his Holland Park house, be struck down by illness, even get divorced, but Wingfield Court would always be there for him; a sheltering, welcoming, protective place where he could seek refuge until the day he died. But no longer. He felt as if the ground had been cut from under his feet.

Margaret had changed, too, in the past few days. Even his future with her no longer seemed assured. He was beginning to have the nasty nagging thought, buzzing around his mind like a tiresome fly, that perhaps she'd only married him because of Wingfield Court. Otherwise, why was she so obsessed with his inheritance? And would she still want him if they lost the family home? Especially as they had no children.

"I don't know where I'm going to find flowers on a Sunday," he complained.

"Then get a few nice house plants, there's bound to be a garden centre open — try Home Base. It's only down the road." Like a mother hen, she clucked him out of the house then went back to lay the table for dinner. They'd use the lace mats, she decided, and of course the silver candlesticks. Nothing like candle light to create a sophisticated ambience.

By the time Cathy and Jack arrived all was in readiness. Margaret had changed into a tan skirt and cream silk blouse, which made her look more big-breasted than ever, and welcomed them with the élan of a society hostess. They were ushered into the drawing room, plied with drinks as it was after six o'clock, then showed where they were sleeping.

"Separate rooms!" Cathy burst out before she could stop herself.

"You have separate rooms at Wingfield Court, don't you?" Margaret queried.

"This isn't Wingfield Court," Cathy giggled, "and Daddy only gives us separate rooms because of the servants. But don't worry, Margaret. Jack and I will be very happy bunking down in one bed."

She gave an affected laugh and thought how lucky they were to have a sex life that warranted the discomfort of sharing a single bed.

Meanwhile, downstairs in the drawing room, Giles was drinking heavily. By the time they sat down to dinner his eyes were glistening red and his speech had a top spin that made some of his words difficult to understand.

Margaret served up asparagus soup to start with, and then lobster Thermidor.

"How gorgeous, my favourite!" Cathy exclaimed, genuinely impressed. "How on earth did you manage to do all this? You only left home a few hours before us."

Margaret put her head on one side and looked roguish. "Ah! Pre-planning, a good deep freeze and a life-saving microwave," she confided. "I could do dinner for twenty in under an hour . . . without even having to go to the shops."

"Excep' for bloody f-f-flowers," Giles spluttered into his glass of Burgundy.

"That's cool," Jack observed, tactfully ignoring him.

"No, itch hot!" Giles declared, grinning. "Ha-ha! Itch hot. What do you say to that?" He rocked in his chair in a paroxysm of giggles. "Itch hot . . . ha-ha-ha!"

"It's not that funny, Giles," Cathy observed, but she was smiling. Her brother didn't often get drunk but when he did there was no stopping him.

Giles leaned confidentially towards Jack. "Do you know," he breathed heavily, "do you know the shim . . . shimal . . . similarity between lobster Thermi . . . what's it . . . Thermidor . . . and a blow job?"

Jack glanced quickly at Cathy, wondering how to field this one. She looked calmly back at Giles.

"What's the difference?"

He went into peals of laughter again. It was edged with a note of hysteria as if at any moment he might burst into tears.

"You don't get either at home. Ha-ha! Isn't that a good one? You don't get either at home . . ."

Next morning Giles was given an introduction through a colleague in Bartwell's to a solicitor who specialized in company law. His name was Sean Chapman and his offices were in Southampton Place, near High Holborn. He was supposedly young and sharp. Giles managed to arrange an appointment for them to see him early that afternoon, with the exception of Jack who said this was a family matter and he'd go shopping instead.

They arrived in good time and were ushered into a very bright waiting room, furnished with the traditional black leather sofas, a few magazines and a couple of token plants.

"I feel nervous," Cathy murmured, sitting next to Jonathan.

"But we've done nothing wrong," he assured her.

She looked uncertain. "It feels wrong . . . spying into what Daddy's been doing."

"With our property," Margaret reminded her.

"It has to be done," Giles pointed out.

"What if Dad has already exchanged contracts with this Arab?" Jonathan asked.

"But there hasn't been time," Cathy protested.

Margaret spoke anxiously, as if determined they were facing a crisis. "But do we know exactly when this Arab made his offer? It might actually have happened before I even saw *Country Life*, and Nick might be pretending he only heard about it a couple of days ago."

"This lawyer will find out all that for us, won't he?" Cathy asked in alarm. "I mean, it can't be a fait accompli already."

"I thought you had to have surveyor's reports and searches and everything," Jonathan pointed out.

Margaret looked shocked. "Oh my God! Supposing the house has already been sold?" The thought hadn't occurred to her until now. "And what about the contents?"

At that moment they were told they could see Sean Chapman. He turned out to be a short, thick-set man in his mid-thirties, brisk, matter-of-fact and cheerful. He looked a bit startled to see so many people troop into his minimalist office but wasted no time in getting down to business.

With occasional not very helpful interruptions from Margaret, Giles outlined the position. Sean Chapman made rapid notes from time to time and fired off short sharp questions, like the rat-a-tat-tat of a machine gun.

"You are all directors of the Wingland Estate?"

"That's right," Giles replied.

"And your father is Company Chairman?"

"Correct."

"And the estate consists of Wingfield Court, nineteen cottages with tenants, a thousand acres and the Home Farm? Are we talking arable or dairy farming?"

"Dairy. Four hundred head of Jersey cattle."

"Umm . . ." Sean Chapman made copious notes. "And you've had no Annual General Meeting for some time? You've passed no resolutions to make changes within the company?"

"None."

The interrogation continued. "You mentioned a family trust fund — is that separate from Wingland Estate Ltd?"

Giles nodded. "Quite separate," he confirmed. "My father is Managing Trustee with carte blanche to buy and sell shares, and to invest as he chooses, because it is a Discretionary Trust. I don't know why the estate is a limited company and not part of the trust but that's obviously the way my grandfather wanted it. We are all equal beneficiaries of the trust, including my father. Three times a year he is supposed to report back to us on the various investments he has made on our behalf."

"How much is the trust worth?"

"Ten million pounds."

There was a moment's silence and Cathy was glad Jack hadn't come with them. To be known to have a fifth share in such a fortune would be an embarrassment before one's peer group. Not that she could lay her hands on it just like that. It was all invested and re-invested for her, as she was only nineteen, and she only received a modest annual income.

Sean Chapman spoke briskly. "When did you last see the accounts for the trust, and hear from your father what he'd been doing?"

"Er . . . not recently." Giles sounded pitifully vague.

"Then you don't examine the annual audited figures in detail yourself. Or check the tax certificates? Or the list of investment of income pending distribution? Examine your R185E form at the end of the financial year? You leave that to an accountant or lawyer . . . do you?"

Silently Giles nodded, and then something hard and cold formed in the middle of his chest and spread like icy tendrils along his arteries. They all looked at each other and Margaret turned pale under her freckles.

"Oh . . . my . . . God!" Jonathan said slowly. "You don't think . . ."

"No!" Cathy spoke fiercely. "Never."

Sean Chapman spoke vigorously. "Give me all the details you can and I'll find out what's going on. It may take a few days but meanwhile we'll try and put a stop on the sale of Wingfield Court while I get all the records from Companies House."

They thanked him and left, shocked and silent, their heads reeling with a thousand dreadful suspicions. Once out in Southampton Place again, Jonathan hailed a passing cab, told the driver to go to Holland Park, and they all piled in.

Cathy was the first to break the spell.

"Daddy won't have done anything really wrong," she affirmed. "I think everyone is just jumping to conclusions because he's married someone much younger who wants them to start afresh together." Even as she spoke she knew she sounded naive. Nobody said anything but continued to gaze out of the taxi windows, deep in their own thoughts.

"What happens if he finds out we've been making these enquiries?" she continued. "He'll be so hurt. I don't want him to sell Wingfield Court any more then you do but to suggest he's been misusing the family trust . . . well, that's outrageous."

"No one has actually suggested that yet," Giles said.

She pushed back her hair impatiently, flipping it over her shoulder. "Oh, God, I hate all this."

"Its not much fun for anyone," Margaret reproached her. "Who's going to tell Elizabeth?"

"I will," Giles said.

"So there's no point in your coming up until later in the week," he told his sister on the phone that evening. "Sean Chapman isn't going to be able to tell us anything for at least a couple of days, and then we can meet and decide what to do."

"Thank heavens for that," she replied. "I've got a lot on here. But why is this solicitor looking into the trust fund? It's got nothing to do with the company."

"He thinks it's a good idea to go through everything," Giles replied evasively.

"Well, I suppose this chap knows what he's doing," she replied. "Maybe I won't need to go up to town at all. You can deal with it, can't you?"

"We must keep in close touch, though, Liz. The minute I have any news I'll ring. You should be involved in all this."

"You're worrying me now, Giles."

They talked for a few more minutes and then Elizabeth was aware that Laurence was standing in the doorway, listening to her side of the conversation. When she'd hung up she smiled up at him, saying briskly, "That was Giles, going on about the sale of Wingfield Court. Thank goodness I don't have to go up to London to see his lawyers."

"Don't you want to be there with the others, guarding your inheritance?"

She shrugged. "It's more Giles's inheritance than mine."

There was a long pause before he replied and then he said; "I thought . . . Wingfield Court . . . all that, meant everything to you?"

"No, not everything," she said quietly.

"Really?"

Elizabeth nodded. "The trust money's nice, of course. It gives us a comfortable standard of living . . ."

"Though I don't work."

She paused, refusing to be pressured into outright agreement on this point. "It's nice to be able to do things for the children. I loved my old home until Philippa came along and it's a great place to take the children, but all that's changed now. As I've said before, this is my real home now and I love it."

There was a painful silence and she knew Laurence was having difficulty finding the right words, but she didn't prompt him because it was important he searched his own mind to find what he wanted to say.

At last he spoke. "I've always feared this wasn't enough for you. You were brought up in such style. Only a millionaire could provide for you in the way your father did. And I have just enough money to get by in a very modest way."

"That's OK. I didn't marry you for your money."

"But do you think I married you for yours?" There was such naked pain in his eyes that Elizabeth felt a wave of pity sweep through her. He really did care.

She said honestly, "It's never crossed my mind that you married me for my money, Laurence. Not for a moment. But maybe my having it has prevented you from realizing your full potential."

He looked out of the window, his eyes unfocused, before replying, "You always seem able to provide everything. The money, the ability to make a home, everything the children need. There's seemed little point in exerting myself to provide anything extra."

"A family needs emotional input, not just financial."

Laurence sighed. "Of course you're right. It's just so difficult . . ."

"Why?" she asked softly. "Why is it difficult?"

"It's difficult when one feels overshadowed. Inferior."

Elizabeth looked shocked. "But I don't make you feel inferior, do I?"

He turned and gave her a wintry smile. "I don't think you can help yourself. You've got personality. You're capable. You manage everything so well."

Elizabeth tried not to show her hurt. "You make me sound like a factory foreman." She forced her voice to sound light.

"You know I don't mean that."

"I suppose so." Laurence wasn't the sort of person who flattered. He'd never once in all the years they'd been together referred to her as attractive, fun or sexy.

"I think we should do things that jolly us along," she suggested brightly. "For example, we never go away on holiday. Or take the children anywhere."

"Except to Wingfield Court."

"Yes . . . well, why don't we take them to a hotel by the sea? Cornwall is lovely."

"We never have time on our own either," Laurence continued.

Elizabeth could see he was trying to keep the bitterness out of his voice, but what he said was true. Since the children had been born they'd never been alone for more than an hour or so. It wasn't that she'd deliberately avoided being on her own with him, it was just that the children always seemed to need her, and they were so young and sweet, and were growing up so fast she could see a time when they'd be going to school and then there'd be only her and Laurence left and after that . . . She didn't want to think that far ahead, right now.

"Then let's take a trip on our own," she said firmly. "Maybe abroad."

"You wouldn't mind leaving the children?"

"Herta and Gerhard can look after them, and your mother's here. They'll be fine."

Laurence rose, energized, looking really pleased. "Right then." He rubbed his long thin hands together. "I'll write off for some brochures and we'll see what we can fix."

Elizabeth had visions of the old typewriter tapping away importantly for the next couple of hours. "Wouldn't it be better if you just went into Rugby tomorrow morning and got it fixed up on the spot? There are several good travel agents in the town."

He looked startled, as if this was an amazing idea, something akin to approaching NASA with a request to join the next space trip. "Go into Rugby and book it?" he echoed.

"Why not? Try and arrange it for the weekend after next. That'll give me time to fix it up with Herta and Gerhard, in case they're under the illusion they've got that weekend off."

"OK," he replied. And Elizabeth noticed he was smiling.

"Are you sure you're all right, darling?" Honor asked Philippa over the phone. They spoke to each other every few days and Honor was keenly attuned to her daughter's every mood.

"I'm fine, Ma, just a bit worried. We had Nick's children here for the weekend and it was dreadful. They seemed to be fighting all the time, and at one point he ordered Elizabeth to leave the house."

"Oh, my dear . . . was it about the sale of Wingfield Court?" Honor asked in concern.

"Yes. You were right, they're all terribly upset. They blame me too, I can see that."

"Then why go ahead? Can't you tell Nick you'd rather go on living in the house than cause all this trouble?"

"It's he who's desperate to move now, not me. He's found an Arab sheikh who wants it and there's no stopping him," Philippa explained. "Of course I'd rather stay than have them all at loggerheads with each other. It's terribly unpleasant."

"Isn't it rather strange?" Honor asked, perplexed. "I thought that house was Nick's pride and joy?"

"So did I, but now he's determined to leave."

"Have you found anywhere else?"

Philippa sounded dreamy. "Yes, the most beautiful house called Woodlands. It's light and airy and has such a friendly atmosphere. I hope we get it. It really is the house of my dreams."

CHAPTER NINE

Giles's hand was shaking as he gripped the phone. "Holy shit! No . . . oh, no! I don't believe it . . . Fuck, this is terrible!"

His colleagues at Bartwell's, sitting at their desks in the fusty old-fashioned office, stopped what they were doing and stared curiously as they heard his voice rise in anguish and saw his face turn a sickly shade of grey.

It was Thursday afternoon, in what had already been the longest week of his life, and what Sean Chapman had to say did nothing to calm his already strained nerves.

"I'm afraid," the lawyer told him, "that financially speaking you've had the rug pulled out from under your feet."

Giles found himself clinging to his desk like as if it was a life raft in a stormy sea. His whole world had spun adrift.

"But how?" he croaked. "Everything's tied up."

Those words, "tied up", were the ones he'd been repeating to himself like a mantra during the long dark nights when he couldn't sleep. Tied up. They assured him that everything was safe, secure, so carefully bound that nothing could break loose. Only now it looked as if everything might fast be coming unravelled and he felt a surge of panic.

Sean Chapman's reply was maddeningly calm.

"Why don't you come to my office and then we can go through everything? Plan what we're going to do."

"Do?" Giles parroted, unable to think clearly.

"Tomorrow morning? Ten o'clock here?"

Giles agreed hoarsely. It was only three-thirty but he decided to go home. "I've got a splitting headache," he explained to the others. "I'll be in late tomorrow, I've got an appointment."

"What did he actually say?" Margaret demanded when Giles arrived home and told her about the call. Cathy and Jack, who were still staying with them, were out shopping. They were alone in the house. Giles dropped into a chair and covered his face with his hands.

"There's nothing we can do about Wingfield Court."

"Why not?"

He raised his head and spoke in a dull flat voice. "Because my father bought it from the Wingland Estate for himself six years ago. He bought the freehold of the house and its contents, plus the garden, but not the surrounding land, farm or cottages." Giles sighed heavily. "He paid the company a knockdown price for it, too. About an eighth of what it was worth even then."

Margaret gave a thin little scream and threw herself on to the sofa. "How could he do that? It all belongs to the company, and the company belongs to us."

"He did it with the help of Norman Sheridan and Ernest Lomax who probably, though we can't prove it, received a back hander for organizing and then covering up what was going on. They must have forged papers, making it look as if we, the directors, had given our permission. The sale of the main assets must have affected the tax situation, too. And none of us suspected a thing."

"You mean they were involved?" Margaret asked, appalled.

"That's right."

"But, Giles . . . you were at all the meetings, weren't you? Why didn't you see what was happening?" Her voice was shrill and laden with accusation.

"It's my father we're talking about," he retorted hotly. "I obviously took a lot of things on trust because it's a family company. You don't expect this sort of thing to happen between the members of a family."

Her bird-bright eyes looked sharply into his. "You don't think the others are in on it, too, do you? Elizabeth has always resented the fact that even though she's the eldest . . ."

"Don't talk such rubbish. Elizabeth's not in the least materialistic. Neither are the others."

"But I don't understand." Margaret was trembling all over now and her eyes brimmed with tears. "I'm scared, Giles."

"*You're* scared!"

She looked at him in desperation. "You must sue Nick, Giles. You simply can't let him get away with this."

"Bad news, I'm afraid, darling," Nick announced, coming into the bedroom as Philippa sat in bed having breakfast on a tray.

"What is it?" She looked at him anxiously.

"The Arab sheikh doesn't want to buy the house after all. He's instructed the agents to find him something bigger and nearer London."

"Oh, sweetheart." She paused before continuing, "Maybe you should withdraw it from the market. Your children are so upset about selling . . . now perhaps you needn't?"

Nick plumped himself down on the bed and looked at her. "I thought you wanted to move?"

"Well, I did . . . but not if it's going to cause such trouble in the family. It simply isn't worth it, darling. If I'd realized they'd be so upset, I'd never have suggested it."

He grinned. "I think we should still move. Get away from here and all its unhappy memories and start afresh. Anyway, sweetheart, I've instructed the estate agent to find us another buyer. He said it shouldn't be difficult." He rose and wandered over to the window and looked down at the sweeping lawn and rose beds beyond.

He had to sell, though he didn't want Philippa to know that. He should have sold out as soon as he decently could after Rosalind's death, but there'd always been that hope at the back of his mind that one of his financial investments would be profitable and enable him to recoup the heavy losses he'd incurred and then his family would never need to find out the extent of his bad judgement. At least, not until after his death. And meanwhile he'd continued to spend with lavish abandon while pretending even to himself that everything would work out all right.

However, he'd had another letter from the bank this morning, urging him to bring down the loan. The day of reckoning was upon him.

"This delay won't mean we'll lose Woodlands, will it?" he heard Philippa ask. "I love that house so much."

He came back and bent over to kiss her tenderly on the mouth. "Don't worry about a thing, my darling. Just relax and keep that baby safe for me." He patted her stomach gently. "I've got everything under control."

Giles and Margaret had been invited to a party that evening and she insisted on going.

"I don't feel like socializing," Giles complained.

"It'll do you good. Take you out of yourself," she insisted. Nothing cheered her up so much as putting on her best dress and going out to drink champagne among people "who might be useful", which was another of her favourite sayings, and she presumed the same applied to Giles.

"Don't worry about us," Jonathan remarked from his position on the frilly chintz sofa where he was lying with his feet sticking over the end. One of his complaints about Giles and Margaret's house was that everything was so small and fiddly; little tables that were easy to knock over, ornaments and lamps placed hazardously at elbow level, books stacked so precariously the least thing sent them tumbling. The whole house was for effect and not practical use, he reflected, as he crossed his ankles and nearly sent a vase of flowers crashing to the ground.

"Careful!" warned Margaret nervously.

Jonathan ignored her and looked at Cathy and Jack. "Let's go to a restaurant for dinner as Giles and Margaret are going out. What about Japanese?"

"Oh, yes," Cathy said enthusiastically. "I love Japanese." She stroked Jack's arm. "You like it to, don't you, babe?"

He nodded. Anything to get away from Cathy's elder brother and sister-in-law, who kept going on and on about their father and the house and what he'd done or hadn't done. It made him quite thankful that he and his parents had always been on the move. Possessions had never become important. Roots had barely time to form before they were off again.

The Driver family's obsession with property struck him as a form of bondage, stifling of the spirit of adventure, a sense of stultifying priorities that had nothing to do with real living. All this tense speculation on whether or not they'd be able to keep Wingfield Court in the family was, in his opinion, a waste of time. Even Cathy seemed embroiled in the general air of intrigue.

"Yeah, let's go," he said, rising.

Jonathan looked up at him languidly. "You're in a hurry, aren't you?"

Cathy jumped to her feet. "We're starving," she said robustly.

"Don't you want a drink first?" Margaret asked. No matter how serious the situation, she never forgot her role as hostess.

"Let's get into the saki at the restaurant," Jonathan suggested. "Gallons of saki, with loads of shiake shioyki, sushi, sashimi and ebi tempura — that's my idea of a perfect dinner."

"And spring rolls and crispy seaweed," Cathy added, draping a long shaded chiffon scarf around her neck.

"That's Chinese not Japanese, fruitbat," he retorted with brotherly candour.

She waggled her head from side to side and spoke in a baby voice. "Japanese, Chinese, Thai, Vietnamese . . . what's the difference? They're *all* yummy."

"Stop doing ditsy!" he said with mock severity.

She grinned. "But I'm good at doing ditsy," she replied in her normal voice. "I'm getting through university doing ditsy. It enchants my tutors. I've got ancient professors eating out of the palm of my hand."

"It's not your ditsy they're after, dear heart." Jonathan's voice was a Noël Coward pastiche.

Jack, looking from one to the other, burst out laughing.

"Come on, you two. Let's go and eat. Are you taking your car, Cathy? Or shall we get a cab?"

"I want to do my share of drinking saki, we'll get a cab."

"Extraordinarily juvenile, aren't they?" Margaret observed after they'd gone. "I was never like that at their age."

"I don't suppose you were," her husband agreed.

"What do you mean by that?"

"Nothing," he replied, helping himself to a whisky and soda.

"I have as good a sense of humour as anyone."

"I think what they have is a sense of fun."

"Fun?" Margaret blinked her sandy eyelashes. "Who's got time for fun when we're facing a serious family crisis on top of everything else?"

There was a pause. He looked at her over the top of his drink. "On top of what else?"

Margaret looked uncomfortable, as if the embarrassment were hers. "You know . . ." she said in a low voice.

"I don't."

"Oh, for Christ's sake, Giles!" It was all going to come out in the open between them now, this dark secret that he denied existed and by which she was driven demented. It was going to explode in a great shattering burst of frustration and disappointment that had built up over the past three years. Why try to control the tide of resentment that was rising, threatening to sweep her away? What had she got to lose? She'd tried too hard and for too long to keep their unspoken pact of silence and denial.

"Your impotence, Giles. You are totally, absolutely and utterly impotent. You've *got* to go to a doctor. It's absurd the way you pretend everything's all right. It *isn't*! Why won't you admit it? Why pretend to me . . . *me!* . . . that everything's OK? Go to a doctor. Get it fixed. Lots of men are impotent. Why in God's name do you pretend you're not?"

Giles stood, rigid and almost to attention, like a small boy being chastised. He looked down into the depths of his glass and said nothing.

Margaret watched him, her rage abating now she'd given vent to it. "It needn't be a problem unless you make it one," she said more gently, but still he refused to look at her. "I want a baby, Giles. I desperately want a child. If only you'd cooperate, I could even have one by artificial insemination . . . with you as the father, of course."

There was a thud as he put his glass down on a side table.

"I'm going to go up and have a shower and get changed for this damn party," he said curtly, turning and walking out of the room.

Jonathan sat opposite Cathy and Jack as they took their seats in Hi, the Japanese restaurant in Soho where he often met friends for supper. After much discussion and poring over the menu they chose a delectable assortment of dishes from which they could all pick with their chopsticks, including Yaki-Tori, Una-Don, Zara-Soba, Hirane and Takobutsu.

"God, this is good," Jonathan said reverently as the dishes arrived, all in neat containers, kept hot by burning nightlights in little racks below. Soon they were absorbed in the exquisite food, exclaiming and comparing and recommending certain dishes to each other as the warm saki sent little rivers of fire down their throats to be instantly cooled by soothing glasses of beer. Cathy began to feel very relaxed, enjoying this evening with her two most favourite people in the world. Her worries about her father and Wingfield Court began dissolving. Let Giles and Margaret deal with it. If the house were sold, she could always live with Jack during the holidays. And anyway, as soon as she'd left university, she'd be getting a job and finding a place of her own.

"Don't you just love it here?" Jonathan asked, breaking into her thoughts.

"I love it, I do," she replied dreamily. "The food is absolute heaven." She reached out to take Jack's hand and then held it in both her own. "Do you like it, babe?" she asked, gazing into his eyes. Then she reached up and touched the platinum-tipped peaks of his hair. It was a delicate gesture, like laying her hand on a fine work of art.

"It's cool," he whispered. Then he fiddled with the silver rings on her brown fingers. "'Rings on her fingers and bells on her toes'," he quoted.

"'And she shall have music wherever she goes'," Jonathan finished the nursery rhyme for him.

Cathy and Jack both smiled. Neither of them noticed the pain in Jonathan's eyes.

After several more beers and another round of saki, of which Jonathan was the main imbiber by now, they took a taxi back to Holland Park.

"I'll get another cab to go on home," Jonathan announced as he stumbled out when they arrived.

"Why not take this taxi on?" Cathy asked.

"That's OK. I thought we could have another drink first."

Then he flung his arms wide and, standing on the pavement, swaying slightly, burst theatrically into song, his strong baritone echoing loudly along the quiet residential street.

"'You, and the night, and the music . . .'" he warbled.

"Hush! You'll wake up Giles and Margaret's neighbours," Cathy whispered, giggling.

But Jonathan was in full spate, grabbing her around the waist and waltzing her wildly in circles while he continued to sing.

"Jonno . . . will you stop?" she shrieked. "I'm getting giddy."

"'. . . You are my heart's desire . . .'" He was not to be stopped. His eyes glassy, his head thrown back, he twirled her faster as he sang all the louder. Watching them, Jack was laughing, too, amused by this madcap brother and sister who were not afraid of enjoying themselves.

At that moment a car drew up and an outraged Margaret stepped from its plush interior, hissing at them all to be quiet. "What time is it, for heaven's sake?"

"Who cares?" Jonathan asked, suddenly letting go of Cathy so she ricocheted into Giles. "'. . . You and the night and the music . . .'"

"Shut up!" Giles ordered, striding ahead to unlock the front door. "You're drunk."

"You're *so* observant, Giles," Cathy joked. "You're so sharp I'm surprised you don't cut yourself." She started giggling again.

"You're drunk, too, Cathy," Margaret pointed out. "Come in off the street before the neighbours complain, and have some strong black coffee."

Doubled up with laughter, Cathy, Jonathan and Jack tottered into the house, clinging to each other helplessly, the mixture of large quantities of saki and beer inducing a feeling of euphoria in them which bordered on the hysterical.

While Margaret went to the kitchen to make coffee, Giles sidled away, up to bed, saying he was tired.

"I'd better go and pacify Margaret," Cathy murmured, finally wiping the tears of laughter from her eyes, trying to pull herself together.

Waiting for the coffee, Jack slumped into a deep armchair, still laughing quietly to himself. It had been a great evening and he'd really enjoyed himself. He liked the way Cathy's family had accepted him, too, as one of them. With his parents so far away, and with no brothers and sisters of his own, it was good to feel a sense of belonging. Sleepily, he leaned back in the chair and closed his eyes. A moment later he sensed a shadow fall across his face and felt something pressing against his knees. When he opened his eyes he found Jonathan leaning over him, hands resting on the arms of the chair, face only inches away.

"You know, don't you . . . how I feel about you?" he asked thickly. His skin was glistening with sweat and his eyes looked dazed.

"Yeah, I guess I know," Jack replied, slowly and calmly, his voice as friendly as ever. "But you also know I'm straight, don't you? Sorry about that, Jonno, but you're a bit too hairy for me," he added, grinning, trying to keep it light, hoping this wasn't going to ruin everything between them in future.

Jonathan stood up abruptly. He looked dashed and his eyes suddenly brimmed with tears. "Of course. Sorry about that. I should never . . ." He stumbled from the room. A moment later the front door slammed and Jack heard him running down the front door steps.

Cathy rushed out of the kitchen and bumped into Jack who had run into the hall, his first instinct being to go after Jonathan to see if he was all right.

"Who was that?" she asked stupidly.

Jack sighed. "Jonathan. He ran off."

She looked stricken. "Oh, my God. Did he . . . ? Oh, I was afraid of this. I should never have let you two become friends. I *knew* he fancied you." She had sobered up instantly as she took in the situation.

"I'll go after him." Jack opened the front door, but she stopped him.

"Better not. He'll be OK . . . I mean, he'll get a cab all right, and he's going to be *so* embarrassed when he sobers up."

"But it's not really serious, is it? I mean . . ." Jack looked distressed. "I never encouraged anything. I had no idea. I'm sure it only happened because he was drunk."

Cathy nodded faintly. "Alcohol will have given him the courage to show his feelings. Poor Jonno. I do wish he'd find someone who's right for him."

"He won't . . . I mean . . . he'll have forgotten all about it in a few days, won't he?"

Cathy looked at him candidly. "Have you ever fallen in love, been rejected, suffered from unrequited passion and got over it in a couple of days?" she asked quietly. "No, well, I'm afraid he won't either. The last time it took him two years to get over someone."

"Oh, my God!" said Jack, appalled. "I'd no idea he . . ."

"I know you hadn't, babe. But I knew . . . in my heart I knew and now I'm kicking myself. I should have kept you apart, but at the same time I was so glad that you got on with each other. We've had such fun, the three of us, haven't we?" She was nearly in tears, so sad did she feel for her brother.

"We have had fun," he agreed, "but d'you know what? I'm going to head back to Edinburgh in the morning. You've got this big meeting with your lawyer, in any case, and I think it would be better if I wasn't around."

"But term is ending in a few days and we're going to France in a couple of weeks," she exclaimed. "Why go back to Scotland now? What will you do?"

"Tidy up some loose ends," he replied vaguely. He'd had it at the back of his mind that he and Cathy might stay at Wingfield Court until they went to France but that was out of the question now. "Honestly, babe, it would be better. I might go and stay with Alec and his family. Get in a bit of fishing." Alec Gordon was a friend of theirs who lived in Argyllshire. They'd often stayed with him in the past.

Cathy, with a woebegone expression, went and wrapped her arms around his neck. "I can't bear it," she said, her voice muffled against his shoulder. "A couple of hours ago we were all so happy and now Jonno's got a broken heart and you're off back to Edinburgh in the morning."

Jack held her very close, his blond head pressed against her dark one. "I don't like it much either but we've got to be sensible. And it's best for me to stay away from Jonathan for the time being."

Later, they squeezed into Cathy's single bed, but only to curl up side by side and hold hands. Out of an unspoken deference to what had happened, and an awareness of how Jonathan must be feeling, there was no lovemaking that night.

The family assembled in the waiting area of Sean Chapman's office at a quarter to ten the following morning. The previous afternoon Giles had phoned Elizabeth and persuaded her to come to the meeting too.

"Dad secretly bought Wingfield Court from the company six years ago," he told her, "so you've got to come. We've got to talk to the lawyer."

Elizabeth had arrived early, accompanied by Laurence who looked much more cheerful than usual. Elizabeth looked brighter, too, and had obviously taken trouble with her appearance, wearing a neat navy blue linen dress and smart shoes.

Jonathan also arrived on time and, having taken a quick look at Giles and Margaret, saw Cathy hadn't told them what had happened the previous night.

"Thanks, sis," he whispered gratefully.

"How are you?" She thought he looked dreadful, eyes swollen behind dark glasses, face pale and drawn.

"Alive," he replied succinctly.

"As good as that?" she quipped, squeezing his hand. "Before you ask, Jack's had to go back to Edinburgh to tie up some loose ends before the holidays start. He hopes, in time, you can be good friends."

Jonathan gave a brief nod, not daring to speak.

"Also," Cathy continued, trying to keep everything matter-of-fact for his sake in front of the rest of the family, "can I ask a favour?"

"Ask away." The usual zest was gone from his voice this morning.

She dropped her voice to a whisper. "Can I stay with you for the next few days? It's a bit heavy at Giles's. I'll sleep on the sofabed."

They both knew she was doing it as much because she felt he needed her as because staying with Margaret and Giles was exhausting.

Nevertheless Jonathan brightened. "Have Pip's bed, sweetheart. He's on another business trip. Have anything you like. Yes, come and stay. That would be wonderful."

"Come along, you two," Giles told them, "We can go in now."

Sean's secretary, Sarah Wells, was leading the way along the corridor to his office and Giles and Margaret barged ahead of the others, determined to play key roles in this family drama.

Sean greeted them and sat down behind a large desk. "So," he began, shuffling the papers in front of him importantly, "this is a far from straightforward situation. I've only unearthed the salient facts by doing a bit of detective work, coupled with asking favours of contacts who have access to certain areas of your family's finances that I do not, specializing as I do in company law."

"Right," said Giles, hoping the rest of the what Sean had to say was not going to be couched in similarly long-winded statements.

"So what's the bottom line?"

Sean raised his eyebrows. "There are several bottom lines. It depends which one you're referring to."

Giles started to waffle nervously. "You know, the house . . . Wingland Estate . . . whatever. You said we'd had the rug pulled out from beneath our feet. So how do we stand now?"

He was sweating, aware that Margaret was expecting him to be the spokesman.

"Let's take Wingfield Court first," Sean said, picking up one batch of papers.

"It seems my father-in-law has already done that," Margaret remarked tartly.

Sean continued as if she hadn't spoken. "You may want to begin proceedings against your father. If so, I would certainly be prepared to refer you to a solicitor specializing in criminal law."

It was Elizabeth who intervened then. "We certainly don't propose to sue our father. We're merely here to ascertain the facts. Can his purchase of the property be overturned or can we block the sale of Wingfield Court? And if that isn't possible, can we each claim a fifth of the profits from such a sale? After all, Wingfield Court and its contents, some of which are very valuable, formed the main assets of the company, so the four of us, as directors, should at least benefit if anything's sold."

Sean looked at her with renewed respect while Cathy and Jonathan nodded in agreement.

"But the whole lot was due to come to *us*," Margaret blurted out, her voice quavering.

Giles looked embarrassed. "My grandfather stipulated when he formed the company that my father's eldest son should inherit everything, for his lifetime, then it was to pass on to the next heir."

"Entailed is the legal term," Sean said, nodding. "Well, I have to tell you that unless you take your father to court and sue him for illegally obtaining the property in contravention of the rules of company law — which, by the way, will also mean charging his accountant and his solicitor with fraud — there's no way you can stop the sale of Wingfield Court."

A babble of incoherent and angry exclamations broke out.

"Giles . . . why did you let this happen?" Margaret wailed.

"It's hardly my fault," he snapped.

"Oh, my God," Cathy said sadly. "This can't be right. Daddy would never . . ."

"Why didn't he talk to us about it?" Elizabeth said, shocked.

Jonathan looked dazed. "Why did he do it? I mean, what was the point?"

Giles squared his shoulders defiantly. "We'll sue him, of course."

Elizabeth, Cathy and Jonathan turned on him, all speaking at once.

"We will not."

"No, we won't."

"Of course we can't."

"Why the hell not? He's swindled us," Margaret protested heatedly.

"But he's our father," Jonathan pointed out. "You don't sue your own father."

"You do if he's behaved like a common thief," she retorted. "He's done the most dreadful thing. Sold his children down the river . . ."

"For God's sake, stop being so dramatic, Margaret," Cathy told her. "This is Daddy you're talking about."

Sean Chapman looked from one to the other, noticing that Laurence was not joining in the general furore.

"What do you think?" he asked.

Before Laurence could reply, Margaret butted in, "He doesn't have a say in this. He's not family."

The others ignored her.

"There are many issues to be covered here," Sean continued smoothly. "I think you should look at the whole picture before coming to any conclusion and deciding what action to take."

Giles was a sickly shade of grey. His cheeks were hollow and his eyes held a haunted expression. "There's more, isn't there?"

Sean nodded. "Much more."

Elizabeth straightened up in her seat, looking alarmed. "What is it?"

There was a momentary lull that was heavy with foreboding. Sean took his time squaring up the papers on his desk before he began to speak.

"The trust set up by your grandfather was a discretionary one," he began. "He appointed his only son, your father, Nicholas Driver, as managing trustee." Then he looked up and surveyed them all before continuing in measured tones, "You are no doubt aware that a discretionary trust allows the managing trustee, on behalf of the beneficiaries — in this case the four of you but not your spouses — to invest the capital as he thinks fit. Providing, of course and this is the point, that the money is invested in such a way as to provide an income for you all. There are various ways of doing this." Sean leaned back in his black leather swivel chair, rather enjoying having a captive group gazing, attentively at him from the other side of his desk.

"A managing trustee may decide to invest the capital in various ways. He can take debentures in a commercial company or buy ordinary shares on the stock exchange; there are preference shares . . . or the money can be deposited in something as simple as a building society. There are also government index-linked certificates . . . treasury stock . . . National Development bonds."

He paused and decided to let them have it straight.

"Does any of you know how your father has been investing the money on your behalf?"

Six faces stared back at him.

Elizabeth was the first to find her voice. "I don't think any of us has the least idea."

"Why? What's happened?" Jonathan queried.

"I think you'll find the trust has been severely depleted, and I think your father may be personally in debt. From what I have been able to discover he's been investing the trust money foolishly and rashly for several years, and I'd guess the reason he illegally purchased your home from Wingland Estate Ltd is because his bank may have required collateral to cover his borrowings, which may in turn have gone to cover up losses incurred by his dealings as managing trustee. He wouldn't, for example, have wanted you to take a drop in annual dividends, because you'd have become suspicious wouldn't you?"

There was a silence in the room so profound that the ringing of a telephone in an outside office pierced the stillness like an alarm bell. The siblings didn't even look at each other they were so stunned, but continued to stare at Sean Chapman as if he were a curious talking machine.

"What do we do now?" Giles asked at last.

"I think you should go off and have a family conference," Sean advised. "You have the law on your side on all counts — your father's illegal purchase of the family home and the squandering or maybe even misuse of the family trust fund. Frankly, in a court of law your father wouldn't stand a chance. He'd be dead in the water."

CHAPTER TEN

"Before we do anything we've got to have it out with Daddy," Elizabeth insisted as they congregated in Margaret's spotless kitchen on their return from Sean's office. While the others made coffee she perched on a high stool, suddenly very much in charge.

"What's there to talk about?" Giles protested. "Once we're absolutely sure of all the facts, we sue him. That's all there is to it."

"Steady on," said Laurence. "I think you've got to listen to what he has to say before you start taking legal action."

Cathy nodded vigorously. "I absolutely agree. I mean, it wouldn't have been his fault if a few of the investments went pear-shaped, would it? It happens all the time. He was probably very badly advised and when things went wrong didn't want to worry us, so he didn't mention it. We must certainly hear what he has to say before we do anything."

"I bet Philippa's behind all this," Margaret snorted, plonking a plate of biscuits on the middle of the kitchen table.

"How can she be if Dad bought the house six . . . *six* . . . years ago? That was ages before Mum even became ill," Jonathan pointed out. He looked around the designer kitchen, all glowing maple cabinets, Mexican tiled worktops and terracotta flooring. "Haven't you anything stronger than coffee?"

Cathy could see that Jonathan, with great effort, was trying to hang on to his dignity as if it were a shroud with which to bind his broken heart but he badly needed something to get him through.

"You bet!" Giles said enthusiastically. "Let's get out the vodka."

"I'll get the ice," Cathy said with a grin.

"Isn't it rather early to start drinking?" Margaret remarked.

"Not under these circumstances," Cathy responded. "I think we're all in shock." Jonathan shot her a grateful look.

"I suggest we ask Daddy to come to London to meet us all," Elizabeth was saying. "It's ridiculous us trailing up to Malmesbury. Giles why don't you phone him and say we need to see him urgently? Try and get him to come up tomorrow, even if it is Saturday."

"He'll never come here at the weekend," Giles protested. "Anyway, I don't see why we have to see him. I think we should phone Sean this afternoon, say we've decided to sue Dad, and get him to introduce us to a criminal lawyer."

They all rounded on him, except for Margaret who sat at the kitchen table pecking at digestive biscuits and looking defiant.

"You're being utterly unfair, Giles," Elizabeth said, distressed. She hated all this dissertion. Until Philippa had come on the scene they'd been a close and loving family who never quarrelled. Now every relationship seemed dangerously unstable. It was as if Philippa was a catalyst, causing a violent reaction between them all while herself remaining a negative force. A shadowy figure who had set off a chain of events which was shattering the Driver family with its domino effect.

Jonathan, busy studying Giles, spoke with sudden insight. "You're scared of Dad, aren't you? You're too frightened to stand up to him and accuse him to his face of mishandling the trust and screwing the estate out of the house. You'd rather hide behind expensive lawyers who'd do your dirty work for you."

Giles looked pained. "That's the most absurd thing I've ever heard!"

Laurence put down his coffee cup and spoke in calm and sensible tones. "Elizabeth is right. You must talk to Nick first. After all, you've only got Sean's word for it that there's been a big loss from the trust fund in the first place. And you don't know exactly when, or how much, do you? Have bad investments lost you one million pounds? Two million? Five? I think in future, no matter what happens, it would be wise to examine the annual accounts carefully so that you know exactly what's going on," Laurence continued. "You father may simply have got himself into a mess and be worried about your finding out."

Elizabeth nodded sadly. "I'm sure Laurence is absolutely right. That's why it's vital we talk to Daddy before we do anything else." She smiled gratefully at him and he felt pleased by her reaction.

"Poor Daddy," Cathy said. "Maybe it's as big a wrench for him to leave Wingfield Court as it is for all of us."

"It's all very well for Laurence to talk," Giles grumbled, hanging on to his opinion like a dog with a bone. "It's not *his* father we're talking about. It's not *his* home he's losing."

"I'll ring him now, if you like," Elizabeth offered, sliding off the kitchen stool.

Margaret wasn't going to let anyone else take over. "If anyone's going to ring him, Giles should," she said firmly.

"I think it should be Cathy," Jonathan put in, helping himself to another vodka and tonic.

"Cathy?" Margaret exclaimed.

"Yes, Cathy," he repeated. "She can twist Dad around her little finger. I vote we make her spokesman. Sorry! Let's be politically correct . . . spokesperson."

Cathy looked aghast. "Oh, no, not me! I'll start crying and be utterly useless. You've no idea how much I hate even thinking he's done anything wrong."

Jonathan put his arm around her shoulders. He was already slightly drunk but in much better spirits.

"I have a plan. Cathy should ring Dad up now and invite him to London, saying we have to meet him to discuss the house and all that. Let's not make it sound too heavy at this stage. And then I'm going to take her back to stay with me at my flat," here he squeezed her hand surreptitiously, "and I'll draw up a list of all the questions she's to ask him. How about that?"

Giles and Margaret looked as if they were about to object but Laurence, sensing the closeness between the two youngest children, intervened.

"Great idea. Come on, everyone, let's leave Giles and Margaret in peace. There's nothing we can do until we see Nick, and I've a feeling that won't be until Monday."

Philippa couldn't help feeling uneasy. Why were Nick's children insisting on meeting him in London on Monday? They'd already aired their views on the subject of selling Wingfield Court. What more was there to say? Nick looked strained throughout the weekend, brushing aside her questions, shrugging when she pressed him for answers, telling her not to worry, everything was fine. He seemed distracted, though, spending most of his time locked in the estate office making phone calls, talking to Ernest Lomax and Norman Sheridan and hardly being with her at all.

On Sunday afternoon, as it was blisteringly hot, she took herself into the garden and went and sat in the shade of a beech tree that grew at the far end of the lawn.

She found it interesting to look back at the house from this perspective, as if she had stepped out of her self for a short while and was looking at the place through the eyes of a stranger. Certainly Wingfield Court looked beautiful, she reflected, its original brickwork rose pink in the sunlight, banded by the rich dark beams of ancient oak; it's Tudor windows winking brightly like the eyes of someone enjoying a private joke. If she'd been looking for a picture postcard, she'd have chosen this one. The great house looked as if it would be a safe and happy place to live in, its thick walls a protective shield against a cruel world, a haven of peace and cosiness and warmth in which to curl up and feel safe.

So why was she so crushingly unhappy here? Was it possible Rosalind's spirit was at work, making her feel unwanted and unwelcome? Was she the only one who felt an undercurrent of cold disapproval pervading every room of the place?

Oh, God, she thought, I do hope we can get away from this place soon.

Nick had reluctantly agreed they should all meet in his penthouse flat in Eaton Square.

"I shan't get up to town until lunchtime," he'd told Cathy with a degree of curtness she'd found chilling, "so why don't you and the others come to the flat at two-thirty? But I can't be long because I have to get home — we've people coming for drinks."

"How convenient," Margaret observed when she was told this. "How often do they have people to drinks on a Monday night, for God's sake?"

It was decided they should all meet for lunch at Santini at one o'clock, before going to see Nick.

"Then we can be sure of arriving on time and together," Giles pointed out pragmatically. "We don't want this meeting going off at half-cock. We must present a united front."

By the time Cathy and Jonathan arrived at the restaurant, where the others had already foregathered, she felt too nervous to eat.

"What's Daddy going to say?" she kept asking.

"I wouldn't worry about that," Jonathan reassured her. "When was Dad ever at a loss for words?" He seemed more cheerful today, although every now and then plunged back into a bout of depression.

"Now, do we know exactly what we're going to ask Nick?" Margaret asked in a businesslike way, her appetite not at all affected by the coming ordeal. She'd ordered linguine with crab to start with, followed by sea bass, and had assured the waiter she'd be ordering a pudding when the time came.

"Can't we keep this meeting informal?" Elizabeth queried. "I mean, this is Daddy we're seeing. Why can't we just ask him what's happening? In general terms."

Laurence, whom she'd insisted should come too, nodded in agreement. "It's probably best not to be too confrontational."

Margaret, whose life's breath was to be confrontational, scanned the others with beady eyes.

"If you're not careful," she warned them, "he'll soft soap you into accepting everthing's fine. I wish we'd brought Sean Chapman with us, you know. He'd have got the truth out of Nick."

Giles downed his glass of wine and reached for the bottle in the ice bucket to refill it. "But we don't want Dad to suspect we've hired a lawyer to go into the family finances. He'll cover his tracks if he realizes we're on to him."

Jonathan looked pained. "I don't like the idea of tricking him."

"Neither do I," Cathy agreed, looking upset. "Can't we do it tactfully?"

Margaret gave her a scathing look. "How do you ask someone tactfully if they've been cooking the books?"

"We don't know that!" Cathy exclaimed so loudly that people at nearby tables stopped talking and turned to look at them. "I will not have you referring to my father as if he was a criminal!"

"Now let's all calm down," Elizabeth said peaceably. "Laurence is right. We should approach Daddy in a friendly manner. The last thing any of us wants is a quarrel."

"I don't want a fight either," Giles agreed. "But if we've lost a large amount of capital I do think we have the right to know how it was lost. That's not asking too much, is it?"

There were murmurs and mumbles from the others and an uneasy feeling among them all that they were behaving like naughty children, about to rebel against a parent. And that was something you didn't do. It went against the Commandment to "Honour thy Father and Mother". Although they were all resolved to tackle Nick, the only person who was actually relishing the prospect was Margaret.

The young man from Rudd, Palmer and Wright, Estate Agents, sounded very enthusiastic on the phone.

"We have a client who's really interested in your property," he told Philippa. "I've let him think the Arab sheikh still wants it and has made an offer, and so of course he's keener than ever now. He'd really like to see Wingfield Court today, if that's possible?"

Philippa thought quickly. Nick was in London for the day but that didn't matter. She could show a prospective buyer around.

"That would be fine," she said swiftly. "What time shall I expect him?"

"He'll be coming in his own helicopter. Do you have a landing pad?"

"We've a big flat lawn that's been used for landing on before. I'll get the gardener to mark it with a white cross."

"Fine. He'll be with you in an hour." The agent was unable to keep the excitement out of his voice. "It's Matt Blade, actually."

Philippa drew in her breath sharply. Even she, at the decrepit age of thirty-one, had heard of Matt Blade, of the Young Blades, pop idol of every teenager in the country with his string of number one hits. Matt was not only the lead singer but composed all the group's songs as well.

"Wow!" she said. "I'm impressed."

"Yes, we all are," the agent admitted, laughing. "He'll go for the full asking price . . . but don't forget he thinks someone else is after it."

"Yeah, the sheikh who actually changed his mind."

"Right."

As soon as she came off the line she tried to get hold of Nick but he had his mobile switched off and there was no answer from the flat. She'd try later. Meanwhile she told Morton what was happening.

"No problem, madam," he replied. "I'll get the landing pad sorted out right away. And shall I serve coffee when Mr Blade arrives?"

"Yes, please."

Almost exactly an hour later, having dashed from room to room to make sure everything was looking perfect, Philippa heard the loud clatter of whirling blades and saw a very smart dark blue and white craft descend and land gently on the lawn. A minute later the door opened, steps were let down, and a tall dark young man came rocketing out of the helicopter as if he were in a great hurry.

She went forward to meet him. As soon as he saw her he grinned.

"Hi, there! I'm Matt Blade." He stretched out his hand to shake hers.

"Hello, I'm Philippa Driver." Vague memories of watching him perform on television conflicted with the appearance of the well-spoken young man who stood before her now in well-worn blue jeans and an open-necked shirt. He looked as conventional as one of Nick's sons. As if he knew just what she was thinking he suddenly laughed.

"Sorry to disappoint you but I'm in mufti today," he explained. "I saw pictures of your beautiful house in a magazine. It's exactly what I'm looking for — hence the rush."

"Well, come and have a look around," Philippa suggested, leading the way into the impressive hall. "We've actually already had an offer . . ."

He nodded. "I know. The agent told me. But if I like it, I'm prepared to make a higher bid. I've been searching the country for a really large house where I can set up my own recording company. And it needs to be in a remote area so I can get away from everyone."

Philippa looked at him more closely and could see what his thousands of young fans found attractive in him; a charming open face with a delightful smile, eyes warm with amusement, thick dark floppy hair and a lean physique. She liked his tanned hands, too, musician's hands, and the easy grace with which he moved.

They went all over the house and then she showed him the main part of the garden and finally the secluded swimming pool with its summer house and surrounding terrace. Then at last they made their way back to the drive, he stood, hands in pockets, looking up at the eaves.

"Why are you selling?" he asked abruptly.

"As you can see, I'm having a baby and I want a home that is really mine," she explained. "I'm Nick's second wife."

"I understand. Has he already got a family?"

"Yes, but they're all grown-up. Anyway, we've found a house I really want, not far from here, and we're hoping to move before the baby arrives."

She found Matt Blade sympathetic and responsive.

"Tell your husband when he gets back today that I want this house," he said decisively. "I'll up the offer on whatever this Sheikh is prepared to pay, and if that's known as gazumping then too bad!" He laughed easily "You'll be hearing from the agent later today."

Philippa found herself shaking his hand, feeling absurdly young and foolish at being bowled over by his charm like some fourteen-year-old fan, and hoping that he was serious and this wasn't all talk, an extravagant gesture he didn't mean.

Nick opened the door to the flat with a flourish. "Come in," he said briskly, refusing to reveal the dismay he felt as four children and two spouses trooped determinedly past him into his flat, like a delegation from some upmarket trades union.

"I'm afraid I haven't got anything to offer you unless you'd like some Perrier?"

Cathy's smile was tremulous. "That's OK, Daddy. We've just had lunch."

They stood around awkwardly in the sparkling white on white living room that had windows from floor to ceiling along one wall, overlooking the tree tops in the central garden of Eaton Square. The only colour in the sparkling room with its large mirrors and modern perspex furniture was an impressionist painting by Jonathan which, to his great pride, his father had actually bought from a gallery. As soon as he saw it again he felt acutely guilty. His father had supported him in his career from the beginning. Was coming here like this today any way to repay him?

"Well, come along, take a seat," Nick was saying. "Now, what's all this about?"

Momentarily confused, they looked at each other, wondering who was going to speak first. Giles seemed tongue-tied. Margaret edged forward on her chair, as if about to let fly a barrage of abuse.

"Daddy, we're all upset and worried," Cathy blurted out, her dark eyes over-bright. "We want to know how you've come to own Wingfield Court . . . and why the family trust seems to have lost money."

The room, all pure white and glittering perspex, seemed to fall still and silent around them. The only spot of colour and movement was Jonathan's canvas, its swirls of orange and crimson strangely shocking in the sterile atmosphere.

"Very well," said Nick, oleaginous as ever. "The facts are quite simple but I wanted to spare you the worry of dealing with financial difficulties because I thought you all had enough on your plate with Mummy's illness then her death."

"We are adults," Giles pointed out stiffly, "and don't need protecting. We want to know exactly what the position is."

Nick looked surprised at the notion that there was a "position" to discuss.

"I don't know why you're all so suspicious," he remarked lightly. "I've been the managing trustee ever since my father died and you've never before queried my handling of the trust, so what's your problem now? You have to remember that no matter how careful one is — and, believe me, we have the very best stockbroker in Andrew Kingsley — some investments turn out to be less successful than others. Shares drop in price all the time. The recession a few years ago forced certain companies into bankruptcy. On the other hand there was an up-swing with . . ."

"Dad, stop talking down to us as if we were a bunch of kids," Giles said angrily. He'd drunk rather a lot of wine at lunch in order to give himself Dutch courage and now it seemed to hit his bloodstream, surging into his brain in a burst of aggression. "The trust has lost money. Maybe millions. Now that's either the result of bloody bad management or else criminal activity."

His father looked at him coldly. “You’re only exposing your own blatant ignorance by talking like that, Giles. And I’d be interested to know where your information is coming from. It’s true we lost money on a few investments but we also made huge profits on others. It’s known as swings and roundabouts.”

“We’ll soon know exactly what’s been going on,” Giles countered rashly, “but in the meantime we’re giving you the opportunity to come clean.”

Nick’s face flamed. “How dare you talk to me like that!”

“Yes stop it, Giles,” Cathy implored. “I’d never have come today if I’d thought you were going to attack Daddy like this.”

“Neither would I,” Elizabeth agreed. “There’s no point in being abusive.”

“There’s no point in sitting back and doing nothing, either,” Margaret said, proud of Giles for once.

“You’re all being gutless,” he shouted, jumping to his feet and stamping around the room. “You’re prepared to talk behind Dad’s back about the trust and the sale of Wingfield Court, but the moment you have to face him you crumble to pieces.”

“That’s not true,” Jonathan protested, “but I thought we’d come here today to have a quiet discussion with Dad, not a head-on collision. For God’s sake, Giles, calm down. Let him explain.”

“What is there to explain?” Giles was beside himself with rage now, feeling the others had let him down. Why were they suddenly all on Nick’s side?

“If you’d listen, I’d be only too happy to explain the situation,” Nick said calmly. He was still completely in control of his emotions, coolly surveying his family from his armchair by the window.

"I've already told you that investments that were made both lost and made money. As for the sale of the house, your mother's medical bills were so astronomical I had to raise a large loan and the bank wanted collateral. They insisted they wanted it in something secure like bricks and mortar. I admit I should have consulted you all at the time but with Mummy so ill . . . and I knew you wouldn't begrudge her the best care it was possible to give her."

Elizabeth burst into tears. "That's emotional blackmail, Daddy. You know we'd have done anything to get her well."

"It's also a bloody lie," Giles shouted. "You bought Wingfield Court six years ago! Long before Mother was even ill. What you did was totally illegal. There should have been a quorum of four of us, as directors of Wingland Estate, before any business was transacted. That's company law."

"I do know the law," his father retorted.

"Well, you could have fooled me!" said Giles heatedly. "You bought the house and its contents for peanuts and now you intend selling it. *Our* house, *our* heritage . . ." He paused, throat clogged with bitterness and misery, arms spread wide as if trying to encompass all that he'd lost.

Nick jumped to his feet and stepped forward.

"Stop it!" Cathy shrieked. "Stop it, both of you!" She flung herself between them, but Giles wasn't going to fight his father anyway. He retreated a couple of steps, red and sweating, suddenly lost for words. Jonathan and Laurence had also jumped up, appalled at what was happening, but Nick was instantly in control of himself again. Wheeling round, he went and stood in the window, looking out at the fluttering leaves of the plane trees. When he spoke it was with icy calm.

"Will you leave, please, Giles? And take your wife with you. You have betrayed the family and everything you were brought up to believe in. Your mother would have been deeply shocked and upset if she'd lived to see this day."

Giles gulped. "Stop bringing Mum into this, it's got nothing whatever to do with her. It's *never* had anything to do with her. You're being completely unfair."

"And," Nick continued implacably, "from this day forth you are no longer a son of mine."

"I don't care, do you hear? I don't care. Who would want you as a father anyway?" With tears of wretchedness and anguish streaming from his eyes, Giles grabbed Margaret's hand and pulled her up roughly from her chair. In the doorway he turned for one parting shot at his father. "I'll see you in court or dead before I let you get away with this," he shouted.

Jonathan wavered, his loyalties suddenly torn. He couldn't agree with Giles's attitude towards their father and yet at the same time he felt his brother's pain, especially when Nick had tried to make Rosalind's illness an excuse for his obtaining the house personally.

"Let's go," he murmured to Cathy, grabbing her hand. Elizabeth had risen also and looked lost and confused.

"We'll come with you," Laurence said. "I think everyone needs to cool down."

Cathy broke away from Jonathan and ran over to Nick, tugging at his arm like a young child, tears running down her cheeks. "Giles didn't mean all that, Daddy. He's just upset."

Nick merely looked at her, saying nothing. She wasn't sure whether his cold expression stemmed from hurt or not.

"Come on, Cathy," Jonathan urged.

Reluctantly, she turned and followed the others out of the room, feeling sick. There had never been a fight like this in the family before and it had left her deeply shaken.

Giles and Margaret were waiting for them in the street below. "Let's get back to Holland Park." He looked tear-stained and deeply unhappy.

"Yes, OK, but we can't stay long," Elizabeth replied, not really wanting to go back to Giles's house but realizing he needed calming down.

"We've got to decide what happens now," Jonathan pointed out. "Personally, I think we should drop the whole bloody thing. It's all too damaging."

"I agree," said Cathy. "This has been the most horrible day of my life."

Back in Holland Park everyone automatically converged in the kitchen once more and Margaret put on the kettle to make tea.

"So you're going to sue Nick now, are you, Giles?" she asked hopefully.

"I don't see what else we can do," he replied wearily. The effects of too much wine and wrath had worn off, leaving him tired and dejected.

"If you're determined to pursue this, shouldn't your first priority be to get the full facts?" Laurence asked, seating himself at the table. "Maybe Sean exaggerated when he talked of large financial losses. Perhaps some investments did go down but as Nick said others made a profit. You must make sure you know what you're talking about. As for Wingfield Court, my feeling is, if it's gone, it's gone. Nothing's going to get it back."

"That's a totally defeatist attitude," Jonathan observed, helping himself to a can of beer from the fridge in spite of disapproving looks from Margaret. "I don't believe we should take Dad to court. Not because there's no point in fighting this situation but because I don't approve of suing a parent. It's as simple as that. We should do what we can to resolve this but in private."

"Quite right," Laurence agreed. "All of you, as directors, should convene a special Annual General Meeting with Nick and also summon Ernest Lomax, Norman Sheridan, and your stockbroker to attend. Lastly, and most importantly, an impartial, unbiased accountant to act as adviser."

"You're right," Jonathan agreed, "and the sooner the better."

They continued to discuss the situation, going round and round in circles, with Giles, egged on by Margaret, repeating his view that they should sue first and ask questions later.

Cathy was about to say she didn't agree with him when she noticed Elizabeth, who had been concentrating with fierce interest on what the others had to say, suddenly seem to lose the thread and become distraught. She kept looking around the room as if she expected someone else to arrive.

"What's the matter, Lizzie?"

But Elizabeth ignored her and turned to Laurence with a worried expression. "Can you phone home to make sure the children are OK?"

He looked mildly surprised. "What . . . now? They're with Herta and Gerhard, aren't they?"

"I know, but I'd like to check on them." She couldn't explain her sudden feelings of anxiety. Somehow she'd got it into her head, like a flashing image, that something had gone wrong at Willow Farm. What was worse, in the last few moments she'd become too apprehensive to make the call herself.

"Please, Laurence. I forgot to bring my mobile but Giles won't mind if you use his phone."

"My mother's there too, you know," he told her.

"What's up, Lizzie?" Cathy asked, while Giles, Margaret and Jonathan continued to talk among themselves.

Elizabeth's face was pale. "I've a terrible feeling that something's wrong with one of the children."

Laurence patted her shoulder. "It's all right. I'll ring home. Don't get so worried, Liz."

"The children aren't ill, are they?" Cathy asked as Laurence left the room.

Elizabeth shook her head. "No." She drew out the word uncertainly.

"Then why . . . ?"

"I don't know. They were fine when we left this morning but I just have this feeling . . ." Her voice drifted off and she looked confused, as if she didn't understand it herself. "Still, it doesn't do any harm to check up on them," she added, slipping her wedding ring on and off nervously.

When Laurence came back into the room she looked up at him anxiously. "Is everything all right?"

"I'm not sure." He too looked concerned now.

"What do you mean? Who did you talk to?"

"Herta."

"What did she say?"

He spoke slowly, as if trying to solve a puzzle. "One of the children has had a fall but they're all right, she said."

Elizabeth sprang to her feet, alarm etched in every line of her body. "Who? Which one?"

"She wouldn't say . . ."

"How do you mean, she wouldn't say?"

". . . but she insisted there's nothing to worry about." He was doing his best to sound reassuring but his own perturbation showed, increasing her feverish anxiety.

"That's not good enough," she exclaimed. "Oh, God! Ring her back at once, Laurence, find out exactly . . ." Her eyes were wide with fear. Cathy put an arm around her shoulders. "It'll be OK, Lizzie. You know how children tumble about — they're always having falls."

"Herta did say she'd called the doctor," Laurence pointed out, hoping that would calm Elizabeth but it had the opposite effect.

"You didn't tell me that," she gasped. "Then it must have been a bad fall. What did the doctor say?"

"Just that there was nothing to worry about," he repeated.

Elizabeth put her hand to her throat as if she had difficulty breathing. "I can't bear this. I know something dreadful has happened. What are they hiding from us, Laurence? You didn't speak to your mother, I suppose?"

"She's gone out apparently. She was invited to lunch and a bridge party by some friends . . ."

But Elizabeth was no longer listening. She'd raced into the hall and was dialling a number she knew by heart. Laurence followed her.

"What are you doing, Lizzie?" Cathy asked, following too.

"Phoning Dr Paige. Oh, dear God, if anything has happened to one of the children while we've been faffing about over bloody money . . ." Her voice broke and she ran her hand through her hair in a despairing gesture.

The others, realizing there was a crisis, had come into the hall, too, and were clustered around, trying to follow what was happening.

After a brief few words with their family doctor, she scribbled down another number and started dialling again.

Laurence leaned forward, speaking tersely "What did he say?"

Elizabeth looked distracted and her voice wobbled dangerously. "Nobody's called him from Willow Farm. He doesn't know anything about one of the children having a fall. Herta is either lying or she's called another doctor. Dr Paige suggested she might have rung . . . Hello? Can I speak to Dr Elkins? Please, it's very urgent."

There was a pause as Elizabeth waited to be put through and the others watched her sympathetically. She was shaking all over and when Laurence gently took the phone from her, she relinquished it almost gratefully.

"Hello, Dr Elkins? I believe you may have been called to Willow Farm just outside Thornby earlier today, to see a child who had fallen. Yes . . . I'd like to know exactly what happened and which child had this fall and . . . I beg your pardon?" Laurence looked startled. "What do you mean, what's it got to do with me?"

Elizabeth watched him, hanging on every word he said as if the rest of her life depended on it. But Laurence was listening to what the doctor had to say with an expression of mounting fury. Then he spoke firmly.

"Let me put you straight on one thing. That Austrian couple are *not* the children's parents. I am their father and my name is Laurence Vickers. They had no right to say they were the parents. Now will you kindly tell me which . . . ? Oh, it was Tamsin."

Elizabeth's hand flew to her mouth. Tamsin! Her beautiful little girl, all blonde and golden-skinned, with her lavender-blue eyes and tiny baby teeth that showed when she laughed. She was so bright, too, so funny and lovable.

Laurence was speaking again but Elizabeth only heard fragments of what he was saying. "Are the others all right?" "How long before we know?" "Yes, I'll call the agency as soon as we get home." When he finally thanked the doctor and hung up, Elizabeth rose awkwardly as if all her joints hurt.

"What happened?"

The others, clustering closer, strained to hear Laurence's reply, all thoughts of Nick and the family fortunes banished from their minds. This was about Tamsin. Something that really mattered.

Laurence's voice was low and shaky. "She's had a fall . . . quite a bad one . . . from a window."

Elizabeth gave a sharp little scream. "*How?* Which window?"

"The nursery."

Her eyes were pools of agony. "But that's on the first floor and it's always kept locked . . . always, always, always. How could it have been open? How could this have happened?" She swayed as if her legs were giving way and Laurence reached out to steady her.

Cathy put her arms around her sister, too, trying to comfort her although she felt deeply frightened herself. "But she's all right," she insisted. "Tamsin's all right, isn't she?"

"Jesus, that's a twenty-foot drop," Jonathan exclaimed, appalled.

"She landed on the grass," Laurence told them. "It might have been far, far worse. She might have landed on the stone steps under the window. Apparently she missed them by a couple of feet."

"But how is she?" Cathy asked again.

He took a quick deep breath as if to steady himself. "There are no bones broken, but she's very shocked and the doctor says she must stay in bed for a couple of days and have complete rest. We must watch out for her being sick or exceptionally sleepy."

"Oh, God." Elizabeth, her arms clasped around herself, rocked with anguish. "My baby . . . we've got to get home, Laurence. We've got to see how she is for ourselves. Tell me exactly what the doctor said? And *why* the hell didn't they call an ambulance or Dr Paige? She should be taken to hospital for a proper examination . . . X-rays, a brain-scan, everything."

"We'll do whatever has to be done," Laurence said, pulling her close while she sobbed into his shoulder. "Herta and Gerhard were obviously trying to cover up the whole thing in the hope we'd never find out. That must have been why they said they were the parents. Bastards!" he added ferociously.

"And as your mother was out they might have got away with it if you hadn't had that presentiment, Liz," Cathy told her. "Oh! It's the most awful thing I've ever heard. Poor little Tamsin. But I'm sure she'll be all right, love."

Elizabeth's anxiety and fear had turned to seething rage. At that moment she felt capable of killing anyone who had been responsible for hurting one of her children.

"Herta and Gerhard are going tonight," she stormed, "They must never be allowed to look after children again. We must tell the local authorities as well as the agency. Don't they realize they've done a terrible thing?"

Laurence, taking her hand and holding it tightly, spoke decisively. "Let's go. If we leave now we can be home in two hours."

"You'll let us know how she is, won't you, love?" Cathy said, hugging her. "And if there's anything we can do, just give us a call."

Elizabeth kissed them all goodbye, but briefly and silently as if she didn't trust herself to speak. And then she was gone.

By six o'clock, worried that Nick hadn't returned from his day in London, Philippa decided to phone Jonathan in his studio to ask if he knew where his father was. He was the one she got on with best.

Cathy, however, answered the phone.

"I'm staying with Jonno," she explained. "Have you heard how Tamsin is?" she added anxiously.

"Tamsin?"

"She's fallen out of a window . . ."

Philippa gripped the phone. "Oh, my God!" she gasped. "How terrible! Is she all right?"

"We think so, but she's shocked of course."

"When did this happen?" Philippa felt sick. Being pregnant had brought out strong maternal feelings in her and the thought of a small child having an accident affected her deeply.

"Earlier today, when Elizabeth and Laurence were up in town with us, having a meeting with Daddy . . ." Cathy's voice trailed off. "They're on their way home now, wondering what they're going to find when they get there."

"Oh, poor Elizabeth. She must be frantic. I know Nick will be horrified when he hears. I was actually wondering if you knew where he is? His mobile's switched off."

"He was at the flat the last time we saw him. I thought he'd have headed home by now."

"Maybe he's on his way. When you speak to Elizabeth, can you tell her how sorry I am?" Philippa asked. How she wished Nick's children had allowed her to become a part of their close-knit family, as she'd hoped. If things had been different, she'd have phoned Elizabeth herself.

"Of course," Cathy replied. "And could you ask Dad to phone me, please?"

CHAPTER ELEVEN

"Where have you been?" Philippa asked as soon as her husband arrived home. "I've been sick with worry, darling. I thought you were driving straight back after the meeting with your children . . ."

He looked at her in blank astonishment. "What's the matter, sweetheart? It's only . . ." he consulted his gold wrist watch ". . . half-past seven! I dropped in to see Ernest on my way home to discuss some business with him."

"But why did you switch off your mobile? What's the point of having a mobile if . . ."

"What *is* it, sweetheart? Has anything happened?" He'd never seen her so agitated before. She was standing in the middle of the hall, staring at him as if he'd done something awful.

She nodded vigorously. "I phoned Jonathan to ask him if he knew where you were, and Cathy told me there'd been an accident. Tamsin has fallen out of a window . . ."

"Oh, Christ!" Nick's confident expression was ripped from his face. "Is she all right?"

"Cathy did say she didn't think it was too bad. Elizabeth will be home again by now, and you could phone her."

"But how in God's name did it happen?" Now he understood why Philippa was in a state. She was such a tenderhearted girl, it would be like her to be desperately worried about someone else's child. "I'll phone her right away."

Elizabeth ran up the path that led to the farmhouse and burst into the hall. She paused for a second with Laurence close behind. Then, hearing voices, she charged into the kitchen where Herta was peeling potatoes and Gerhard scraping the mud off a very small pair of red wellington boots into the sink. They looked up, startled, as she threw open the door.

"You back early!" Herta exclaimed almost accusingly.

"Where's Tamsin?" Elizabeth asked grimly.

"She in bed, of course. It's after six. Dominic, he play a little longer . . ."

Elizabeth didn't wait to hear any more. "Come on," she urged Laurence. Taking the steep stairs two at a time they rushed up to Tamsin's little pink room under the eaves where she was lying in bed on her back. She was wide awake but there was something strangely still about her posture.

"How are you, my darling?" Elizabeth asked, dropping to her knees beside the bed.

"Aw 'right." Tamsin gazed up at her mother, her small face pale and unsmiling.

"Poor baby, does it hurt anywhere?" Laurence asked, going round to the other side of the bed and bending over her from his great height.

Tamsin looked at him and shook her head. "No."

"Let's have a look at you," Elizabeth said softly, hardly able to believe that this precious little scrap had actually fallen from an upstairs window. Very gently, she pulled back the bedclothes and started stroking the plump little arms and legs through her flannelette pyjamas. Then she placed her hands around Tamsin's waist, having no idea what she was looking for but believing maternal instinct would tell her if something was wrong.

"Does that hurt, darling? Does your head hurt?"

"No," Tamsin replied. "He said I was aw' right."

"Shall we get nice Dr Paige to check you over? Just to make sure you're not sore anywhere?"

"I saw 'nother doctor. He was nice."

"How did you fall, baby?" Laurence asked, gently.

Tamsin considered this for a moment, as if she wondered whether she was going to be scolded or not.

"Did you slip?" Elizabeth prompted.

"No, I wanted to get Eckit. She was on the lawn," Tamsin replied.

"You jumped?"

Laurence managed to keep his voice even. "At her age, it probably only looked like a little jump."

Tamsin nodded.

"And the window was open?" Elizabeth probed.

"Yes."

She leaned forward and kissed the soft little rounded cheek. "Try and go to sleep now, sweetheart. Mummy and Daddy are home again so just call us if you want anything."

For the first time Tamsin smiled then pulled her beloved doll, Eckit, into her arms.

"G'night," she whispered, rolling on to her side and cuddling down under her duvet in her normal sleeping position.

"She'll be all right," Laurence whispered as they made their way downstairs again, having looked in on Jasper.

"I'd still like Dr Paige to have a look at her."

"I agree, but I think she's more shocked than anything."

Elizabeth paused, closing her eyes for a moment. "When I think what might have happened."

He put his arm around her shoulders. "Don't, Liz." He kissed her tenderly and she clung to him in a way she hadn't done since they'd first been married.

"She might have been killed," Elizabeth murmured, weeping now.

"I know, Liz. I know." He held her in his arms, rocking her gently. "But she wasn't. She's going to be all right. Let's be thankful for that."

They could hear Dominic playing in the hall below. When he saw them coming down the stairs, he flung himself at Elizabeth as if he hadn't seen her for days.

"How's my boy?" she asked, picking him up and hugging him.

"Is Tamsin going to be OK?" He studied her face closely, his eyes anxious.

"I think she's going to be just fine," Elizabeth said. "Were you around when she fell?"

Dominic shook his head. "I was building a barricade at the bottom of the garden then I heard Gerhard yelling to Herta. I knew something was wrong."

Elizabeth caught Laurence's eye as she gently lowered Dominic to the ground. "Sweetheart," she told him, "you can go and watch fifteen minutes' television in the drawing room, if you're very good, and then I'll give you a bath. We might even put some nice bubbles in the water tonight."

"Where are you going?" he shot back suspiciously.

"Just to check on dinner with Herta," she said lightly.

Gerhard and Herta were still making an effort to appear hard at work in the kitchen. He was scrubbing the central table now and she was emptying the rubbish bin.

Elizabeth faced them, Laurence beside her.

"I want to know exactly what happened."

Herta shrugged in the way that always irritated Elizabeth. "I don't know. Tamsin play in the nursery. I haf a bath. Then Gerhard, he tells me Tamsin has fallen."

"But why was the window open? You *know*, everyone in the house knows, that all the upstairs windows have special locks so they can't be opened. The keys are kept hidden from the children. Only the adults know where they're kept, in case of fire. Who unlocked the nursery window?" Elizabeth asked. "And who left Tamsin alone in the nursery with the window open?"

"I haf to haf bath," Herta said sullenly.

"But for God's sake, why did you open the window in the first place?"

Herta suddenly came alive with indignation. "You British!" she spat. "You so unhygenic, how you say. You never air your rooms! Now, in Austria . . ."

"Well, you can go right back to Austria *now*. Tonight. Get out of this house, both of you! My husband is reporting you to the authorities and the agency and I will personally see to it you never look after children again. Tamsin could have been killed. Your behaviour was utterly irresponsible."

Gerhard, who had remained sheepishly silent, suddenly spoke. "It was not Herta's fault. Dominic, he push Tamsin out of the window. He jealous of her."

This was too much for Laurence. "That does it! My son said he was playing at the bottom of the garden, and he's no liar. Stop whatever you're doing and go and pack now. You'll get your wages until the end of this week and I'll drive you to the station. After that I never want to set eyes on you again."

"Just go. Go!" Elizabeth ordered, leaving the room without a backward glance.

Gerhard looked accusingly at Herta. Lawrence could only guess, in the flow of guttural Austrian that poured from his mouth, that he was blaming her for everything.

At that moment the phone rang. Laurence snatched it up, in no mood for social chit-chat. "Oh, Nick," he exclaimed, surprised when he realized who it was.

"Philippa has just told me about Tamsin. How is she? What happened?" He sounded concerned, and Laurence had to forget the fact that this was a man he didn't like and remember Tamsin was his granddaughter.

Briefly outlining what had happened, he assured Nick that Tamsin seemed to be all right.

"Thank God for that! By the way, Laurence," he continued, "to go back to what we were all discussing in London this afternoon, I hope you'll bring your influence to bear to stop Giles from making a complete ass of himself. He's barking up the wrong tree, you know, if he thinks he's got grounds for suing me. It's Margaret's fault, of course. She's always been ambitious. Never liked her. But tell Giles solicitors cost a fortune and there's no point in his wasting his money just because he's annoyed I'm selling this place."

There was a long pause which Laurence rather enjoyed. Let the bastard stew for a few moments, he thought. When he spoke it was coolly.

"The thing is, I've really nothing to do with any of this. I only married into your family. Decisions like that are up to Giles and the others. Now, if you'll excuse me, I must go and say goodnight to the children."

"By the way," Philippa said teasingly, when Nick had assured her there was no cause for worry over Tamsin. "I have a nice surprise for you. We've sold the house!"

"Sold . . . ?" His jaw dropped, and he turned to stare at her.

She nodded vigorously. "For more than the asking price."

He frowned suspiciously. "Who to? This isn't a wind-up, is it?"

"Ever heard of The Young Blades?"

"Never," he replied flatly.

"Number one pop group with a string of hits? Their lead singer is Matt Blade. He also writes the music."

"I'm not into the pop scene." Nick sounded dismissive. "So what's happened?"

Philippa told him all about the young star arriving by helicopter, falling in love with the house, and then going back to Rudd, Palmer and Wright to make a firm offer, for more than Nick was asking.

"He's not interested in buying the contents," she explained, "which is OK, isn't it? Because we'll want some of the stuff for Woodlands. But he does want to buy everything in the library: the leather sofas, the desk, and *all* the books. Isn't that perfect?"

Nick looked stunned. "Are you sure it wasn't just talk?"

"No, it's definite. The estate agent phoned to say Matt had already paid the deposit and wants to move in as quickly as he can. He's setting up his own recording company, you see, and wants to convert the dining room into a studio."

Nick downed his gin and tonic in one throat-scorching, stomach-churning gulp, and the room seemed to spin for a moment and the ground shake beneath his feet. It was as if his father was turning in his grave, rocking the foundations of the old house in retaliation for what Nick was doing.

Cathy was on the phone to Elizabeth early the next morning. "How's Tamsin?" she asked anxiously.

"Running around as bright as a button," her sister replied, surprise in her voice. "Aren't children extraordinary. Dr Paige has been to see her and says that apart from a few bruises she's fine. He doesn't even think she needs X-rays or anything, unless she suddenly seems unwell. God, it's been a nightmare. I feel I've aged twenty years since yesterday."

"Oh, Lizzie, poor you. I couldn't help wondering, in the night, about what might have happened. What about Herta and Gerhard?"

"They've gone. Laurence has been wonderful. He took complete control of the situation and phoned the police while they were packing. Imagine them telling the doctor they were Tamsin's parents! The Home Office has been informed and the agency is issuing a warning to other employment agencies . . ." Elizabeth still sounded stressed, her voice wobbling dangerously.

"Thank God you had a premonition something was wrong."

"Yes, and it certainly puts everything else into perspective, Cathy. To hell with the house and the money! There are more important things in life to worry about. We're not on this earth all that long, and I really hate not being friends with Dad. It's his life, too, and if he's happy, I should try and be happy for him."

"That's exactly what Jonno and I were saying," Cathy exclaimed. "Frankly, we've no intention of suing him and all that."

"Neither have we." Elizabeth sounded relieved. "Where does that leave Giles?"

"I don't know. Poor old Giles, he's no match for Dad, and Margaret isn't helping."

"Did she ever? Listen, love, I have to go. Tamsin's gone rushing off into the garden after Dominic and I don't want to let her out of my sight at the moment," she added hastily.

"I don't blame you. Take care. Talk to you soon."

As Cathy hung up, Jonathan came strolling out of his galley-size kitchen, still in his dressing gown and munching a piece of toast. "Everything all right?"

Cathy nodded. "Tamsin must have several guardian angels." She looked up from where she sat, cross-legged on the floor by the phone, and shook her head in disbelief. "It seems she's only got a few bruises."

Jonathan draped himself along his red living-room sofa and gave a huge sigh of relief. "Thank Christ for that."

"Elizabeth said she's no intention of taking Dad to court either."

"Quite right. I always thought it was a terrible idea. We must get Giles to change his mind."

"You'll be lucky. Margaret won't let him in a thousand years," Cathy said crisply. Then she looked sad. "I do feel upset about Wingfield Court, though."

"Didn't Dad say the place they're going to move to would be another family home?" Jonathan asked hopefully. The idea of not having a real family base depressed him deeply.

"We'll never have a family home again, Jonno," Cathy told him flatly. "Those days are over. I don't know what we'll all do at Christmas. Forget about Dad's new house being a home for us, too. It'll be for him and Philippa, and I bet they end up having at least two children." Leaning sideways, she rested her head on her arms on the seat of a nearby chair. "If only Mummy hadn't died," she said softly.

"We all felt so secure until then, didn't we?" Jonathan agreed.

Cathy raised her head. "Let's be honest, we all felt secure until Philippa came on the scene. Everything seems to have fallen apart in the strangest way since then, hasn't it?"

"You can always come and live here with me. Pip is thinking of working abroad permanently, did I tell you? He's hardly ever here anyway so you could make this your base. What do you say? It would be cool."

"You're a babe," Cathy said, grinning affectionately. She didn't mention that if she shared with anyone it would be with Jack. Instead she giggled and replied, "I'd rather cramp your style though, wouldn't I?"

"Not at all. You can have your lovers . . . and I'll have them, too!"

"Oh, there you are, darling," Nick exclaimed, coming into the bedroom where Philippa was resting on the chaise-longue by the open window. "I'm just off to see Norman, but I'll be back in time for dinner."

"You seem awfully busy these days, sweetheart. Is everything all right?" she asked, reaching for his hand.

"Everything's fine. I've spoken to the estate agents and we'll soon be exchanging contracts with Matt Blade. We should, with any luck, be able to move in six to eight weeks."

Philippa's face lit up. She stood and flung her arms around his neck. "Oh, Nick! That's marvellous." Then her brow puckered. "You're not having any more problems over the sale with Giles and the others, are you?"

His jaw tightened. "Nothing I can't handle."

She could tell from his expression that he was deeply angry but trying to hide it.

"You don't sound too sure. Are they still upset, darling? Oh, God, and I was the one who suggested we move." Distress filled her. "They'll never like me now, will they?" She stepped back and went and sat on the window seat, leaning forward to press her forehead against cool clear glass. "And I did so hope we could all be friends."

"They'll come round, sweetheart," he said with a bravado she'd never heard in his voice before. "Don't let it worry you. I want you to be happy. That's the main thing."

"I am happy but I can't help worrying about your relationship with your children. If you fall out over the sale of this place it will be a tragedy."

"It won't happen, I promise you. Now I must dash or I'll be late." His kiss was swift. "See you later, darling."

"Phone for you, Cathy," Jonathan called to her, just as she was getting out of the bath the next morning. "It's Jack." He kept his voice even and non-committal, determined to hold his emotions in check. Then, laying the receiver on the table, he went and busied himself in the kitchen so she could have some privacy. When he heard a cry of distress and then Cathy's exclamation of, "What do you *mean*?" he shot back into the living room and looked at her questioningly.

She was huddled in a corner of the sofa, the phone clutched in both hands, her face white.

"But *why*? How can you do this to me, Jack?" she was saying. And then: "Oh, come on, there's got to be an explanation. We were supposed to go to France in three days' time!"

Jonathan slipped out of the room again and went to the bedroom, shutting the door behind him. He knew that

Cathy had been trying to get hold of Jack for the past couple of days, and now it looked as if there might be a problem between them. God, he thought, I hope I'm not to blame. Why couldn't I have kept my big mouth shut instead of getting drunk and telling Jack how I felt? Suppose I've ruined everything for Cathy?

Cursing his own stupidity and moment of weakness, he waited until he heard her replace the receiver and then, just as he was about to leave the room, the door burst open and Cathy stood there, tears streaming down her cheeks.

"He's dumped me!" she sobbed. "Jack's dumped me, just like that."

Jonathan felt the blood drain from his own cheeks and his heart gave a lurch as he realized only too clearly what this would mean to his sister.

"I don't believe it," he gasped. "How can he possibly have dumped you? You've been together for over a year. He adores you, Cathy."

She shook her head, her dark hair falling over her face as she slumped onto the bed beside him. "Not any more it seems. I finally got out of him what's happened. It seems he's met someone else. And would you believe it? He met her on the train going back to Edinburgh, after he left us in London," she added, wiping her eyes on one end of her long silk scarf.

Jonathan, still filled with dread that he might be in some way to blame, asked, "Are you sure that's the real reason? You don't think I had anything to do with it?"

She shook her head and said with conviction, "No. He was cool about that. Sad for you, and very sorry, but cool. Oh, shit! I should have gone back to Edinburgh with him instead of staying on in London and making a song and dance about the sale of Wingfield and everything. How could I have been such a fool?"

Jonathan looked at his sister with concern as she covered her face with her slim brown hands, understanding her pain, empathizing with her suffering. Jack had been someone special, with his slanting aquamarine eyes and platinum-tipped hair. He'd been one of the best-looking young men Jonathan had ever seen. But more than that, he was kind and funny, intelligent and friendly, and very, very sexy. It wouldn't be easy to find someone else to equal him.

"Come here, love," he said, giving her a hug, trying to be positive. "You're not going to agree right now but maybe you're better off without him. After all, if he's capable of breaking off a love affair with someone he's been going out with for a year, just because he happens to meet a girl on a train, then he might do anything. He's not worth having."

Cathy rested her head on his shoulder, her breath still erupting into little sobs. "I suppose you're right. But I feel so . . . shocked, Jonno. In fact, I can't take it in. I keep thinking the phone will go again in a minute, and he'll say ha-ha-funny-joke-got-you-that-time-didn't-I?" She dried her cheeks with the palms of her hands and sat upright. "And to think I was wasting my time fussing over us losing Wingfield and some money when I could have been with Jack, fishing in Scotland!"

"Poor babe. God, we're a couple, aren't we?"

"And over the same man, too."

Jonathan gave a mirthless guffaw. "I wonder if he got a kick out of that?"

"Jack's kind, he wouldn't think it was funny."

"I suppose not." He stroked her back thoughtfully. At least she knew what it was like to have been loved by Jack.

Cathy rose, her shoulders hunched as if she was cold. "Shouldn't you be going to the studio?"

"And leave you here on your own?"

"Maybe it's something I ought to get used to," she remarked cynically. Yesterday . . . was it only yesterday? . . . Jonathan had offered to share his flat with her, and she'd thought to herself, How sweet, but of course I'll be getting a flat with Jack. Now . . . God, life could be so painful. In eighteen months she'd lost her mother, she was losing her old home, and her boyfriend had just dumped her for a girl he'd met on the 15.46 to Edinburgh.

As if he knew what she was thinking, Jonathan spoke.

"Remember the old saying? If one door shuts, another opens. Who knows? It may be fate. Something marvellous may be waiting for both of us, just around the corner."

She gave a watery smile. "Maybe. All this certainly makes me realize that what Jack once said is true — people are more important than possessions. Something like this proves that money isn't everything."

Jonathan looked thoughtful "Do you still want to go to France? I wouldn't mind getting away myself. We could go together, if you'd like?"

She looked at him as if he'd offered her a lifeline. "Oh, Jonno! It would be wonderful! What a brilliant idea."

The original plan had been to take her car over on Le Shuttle to Calais, and then she and Jack were to drive down in a leisurely way to the South of France, exploring as they went and spending the night where they felt like it until they reached the Mediterranean. It had been planned as a real break before she and Jack started their second year at university, but now she saw it as a way of helping her to get over her immediate heartache. The same thoughts were going through Jonathan's mind. He felt he needed new sights to give him fresh inspiration for his painting, staled at the moment by his own emotional turmoil. Getting away from everyone and everything was exactly what they needed.

Somehow they were both going to have to forget Jack.

CHAPTER TWELVE

Sean Chapman had introduced Giles to a solicitor in his firm who specialized in criminal law; he was a big burly-looking man who looked as if he'd been a boxer in a previous incarnation. His name was Barnard Alexander. Margaret thought he looked imposing and powerful. At her prompting, Giles instructed him to put together a case charging Nick with a variety of criminal misdemeanours, including the illegal purchase of Wingfield Court, and the squandering and mismanagement of the family trust fund.

"On the face of it," Barnard Alexander told them, after he'd gone through everything and made some inquiries of his own, "I believe your father was in financial trouble as far back as eight or ten years ago. He seems to have made some foolish investments and indulged in the stealing from Peter to pay Paul syndrome. In the past year his losses have escalated rapidly. He's also been spending money like water and, whatever the wishes of your step-mother sooner or later I think he would probably have been forced to sell Wingfield Court, not only to meet his current expenses but also to cover losses incurred in the stock market on shares owned by the trust. I have to say," Barnard continued, "the problem looks more like profligate spending rather than criminal activity, although we could probably bring a civil charge of criminal negligence."

Margaret, on hearing all this, did not waste a moment. It was essential she and Giles should have a working knowledge of the ins and outs of trust funds and company law so that they would understand exactly what their lawyer was talking about.

"'Forewarned is forearmed'," she quoted at Giles before stomping off to Kensington Public Library where she spent several hours a day, poring over heavy volumes and making copious notes. She felt quite bitter and martyred that Cathy and Jonathan were in France, saying they didn't want to have anything to do with taking their father to court, and that Elizabeth also refused to cooperate because she said, she had no intention of becoming embroiled in a squalid family feud.

"It's too bad," Margaret complained to Giles. "They're leaving everything to us. We're going to have to fight this case on our own although it will benefit them, too."

"If we win," he pointed out gloomily.

"Of course we'll win," his wife retorted sturdily. "We've got the law on our side."

"It's having sufficient evidence that matters."

"We'll get that." She was puffed up with confidence, ready for battle. Now when Giles returned from work each evening she was eager to tell him interesting snippets about trust funds from the books she'd been studying.

"Did you know there's something called Acts of Waste?" she said triumphantly one evening. "And your father is certainly guilty of that, buying Philippa that ridiculous engagement ring then having that big wedding . . . and just think whose money he was wasting all the time!"

Contracts had been exchanged on Wingfield Manor and now it was just a question of settling on a date for Nick and Philippa to pack up and leave. Matt Blade had been to look at the house again with an architect, an electrical engineer and a designer, and between them they'd formulated plans for a high-tech recording studio in the old dining room, and a modern office, fitted out with the latest technology, in the morning room. From here the business activities of the group, and all the arrangements for their world tours, would be conducted.

"It's going to be at least a couple of months before we can actually move in," Matt told Nick and Philippa, who felt bemused by the incongruity of such a modern set-up in a historic setting. "There's a lot to do before we can be operational so there's no immediate rush for you to leave. Providing you don't mind having some of the work going on around you?"

"Not at all, my dear chap," Nick replied. "We haven't exchanged contracts ourselves on the house we hope to move to, so a breathing space would suit us very well."

Philippa, standing beside him, felt her heart lurch. She turned to him, unable to hide the stricken expression in her eyes.

"It's going to be all right, isn't it? We won't lose Woodlands, will we?"

"The lawyer is just completing the searches," he replied lightly.

"But the baby's due in nine weeks, Nick," she said before she could stop herself. Then, because Matt was there, forced herself to add jokingly: "I don't want to find myself giving birth in a removals van!"

Matt smiled warmly and understandingly as if he sensed tension in the atmosphere. "I've still got all that to come."

Philippa smiled back. "What? Moving house or having a baby?"

"Both, actually, but as I don't even have a girlfriend at the moment, the baby bit will have to wait." His eyes twinkled delightfully, making Philippa feel less stressed. Nevertheless, why was it taking so long to secure Woodlands? Which they'd found before Matt Blade had even been to see Wingfield Court. Oh, God, let it be all right, she prayed inwardly. She felt the baby kicking as if in agreement.

"I'm going to love it here," she heard Matt telling Nick. "It'll be great having a swimming pool, too. I've never had my own pool before," he continued with boyish enthusiasm. "I expect you've had great parties here, haven't you, in the summer? With barbecues and midnight dips?"

"My children did that sort of thing . . . in the old days," Nick replied, a touch wistfully.

Philippa turned away, misery washing over her. Maybe she was getting paranoid but she could sense Nick was feeling definite traces of regret at having to leave. It wouldn't be surprising, she thought, considering he'd lived here for over thirty years.

A sudden sense of isolation made her eyes prick with unshed tears. Life seemed to have become so complicated in the past few months and yet, when she'd first fallen in love with Nick and agreed to marry him, it had seemed as if nothing could go wrong and everything was going to be perfect from then on.

Barnard Alexander phoned Giles a couple of days later to tell him his old home had been sold.

"There's nothing to stop us from suing for compensation for the loss of your inheritance, though," he continued. "And we've made sure there's no way your father can try and sell the thousand acres, the Home Farm and the cottages that still belong to the Wingland Estate. You can always build on that land at some future date," he added.

"Oh, Jesus." Giles felt sick. Wingfield Court had gone. And Margaret was going to be furious. She'd take it out on him, and say it was all his fault.

"Any further news about the trust fund?" he asked with fatalistic dread.

"Too soon to have all the details but I'll let you know as soon as I've gathered the evidence. Don't worry, it's all in hand. These things take time."

"Oh, well . . . thanks." Even handling the perfect 1840 Penny Black he'd been showing to a rich client and was about to return to the office safe did nothing to cheer Giles at that moment.

"A pop star?" Margaret shrieked. "He's sold it to a pop star?" She collapsed in a plump heap on their living-room sofa and burst into tears. "You know what this means, don't you?" she sobbed. "There'll be ghastly music blasting out twenty-four hours a day and they'll all be on drugs and having sex in every room and never washing . . . the place will become a dump."

"We don't know that," Giles said glumly.

"Don't be so stupid! You know what pop stars are like. I can tell you one thing, the whole village will be up in arms when they find out what your father's done. It's an absolute tragedy," she added dramatically.

"There's still the land. A thousand acres."

"Fat lot of good that is! It's mostly wooded and hilly, and I certainly wouldn't want to live anywhere near Wingfield Court now it's going to be inhabited by a bunch of degenerates."

Giles decided to go off to the kitchen to get himself a drink without answering. It seemed the easiest thing to do.

Brooding for a few minutes on her own, Margaret finally wiped her eyes, blew her nose, and seizing the phone, dialled the number of Wingfield Court.

"I'd like to speak to Mr Driver," she announced when Morton answered the phone.

"I'm afraid he's gone down to the village, madam. Would you like to speak to Mrs Driver?"

"Yes, please."

"Who shall I say is calling, madam?"

"Mrs Giles Driver."

There was a pause, and then to Margaret's great surprise Philippa came on the line.

"Hello, Margaret," she said cheerfully.

Margaret switched into top gear by taking a deep breath.

"I hear you've sold the house to a pop singer. Do you realize what this means? Have you any idea how upset Giles is? This is a criminal offence, you know. Nick had no right to sell Wingfield Court and Giles is going to take him to court where he will seek damages and compensation for the loss of his inheritance."

There was a long chilling silence before Philippa answered.

"I'm sorry if you and Giles are disappointed the house has been sold but I consider it an impertinence that you should challenge Nick's right to sell. And as for thinking of taking him to court, what possible grounds do you have for suing him?"

This took Margaret aback. Was it possible Philippa didn't know that Wingfield Manor had been the main asset of Wingland Estate Ltd? She spoke carefully and slowly as if addressing a rather stupid teenager.

"Wingland Estate is a limited company set up by Nick's father. It owns . . . or rather did . . . the house and its contents, the garden, and a thousand acres of surrounding land together with nineteen tenanted cottages and a dairy farm. Giles, Elizabeth, Jonathan and Cathy are all directors of the company, and Nick is chairman. Recently we discovered that he went behind all our backs and secretly purchased the house from the company for a knockdown price six years ago. I don't know how he expected to get away with it, but he managed to until you made him put it on the market. The house and contents were the main company asset so of course we have the right to sue. You don't seem to understand that Wingfield wasn't his to sell."

This time the pause was even longer. “I don’t believe this,” Philippa said in a shocked voice.

“Well, you’d better. Why don’t you ask Nick? And while you’re about it, you might also ask him what he’s done with several million pounds that appear to be missing from the family trust fund.” Margaret was on a roll. She had the upper hand now, a sense of power and the thrilling feeling of knowing she was in the right. She could even afford to feel rather sorry for Philippa, her one-time rival for Wingfield Court, who had just had her false sense of security utterly demolished.

So it was all true. Philippa sat curled up in one of the deep leather chairs in the library, looking at Nick and realizing she didn’t know him at all. Not that he’d admitted everything even now. As she’d repeated what Margaret had told her, she was met with a smoke screen of bluster and excuses and evasion. Everyone was to blame except him. It was Rosalind’s extravagance that had caused them to spend, spend, spend. Then it was inflation and the boom-and-bust period under Mrs Thatcher, the recession, the collapse of the yen and the rouble, interest rates, the strong pound . . . anything he could chuck at her in his obvious efforts to blind her with a veil of obfuscation.

Philippa watched him through tear-filled eyes, seeing the man she’d loved with all her heart transformed into a fool. Someone with no business sense at all; a man who had invested stupidly and spent recklessly in order to serve his own vanity. And, worse, a man prepared to gamble with his children’s inheritance.

"I don't believe it . . ." she kept repeating brokenly.

"I don't know why you're making such a fuss," Nick retorted. "The new investments I'm involved in will generate huge dividends in due course. As for the house, the bank were going to foreclose . . ."

"But you've let *me* take the blame. Your family think we're moving because I wanted to."

"And didn't you?"

"Yes, I did," she replied honestly, "but I wouldn't even have mentioned it if I'd known the house really belonged to them. My God! I'm not surprised they hate me."

"Listen, darling. This is just a hiccup in financial terms, nothing for Giles or anyone else to get so excited about. I'll be able to reimburse the trust when the docklands scheme is up and running. They're not going to lose out on anything in the long run," he coaxed, coming over to sit close to her, putting his arms around her and gazing deep into her eyes.

Philippa desperately wanted to believe him. He was her husband and she was still in love with him . . . wasn't she? Giles and Margaret were avaricious, wanting to inherit everything . . . weren't they? The stock market had been through a rocky period . . . hadn't it? But nothing he'd said had added up to the picture of a clever and successful man, conscious of the trust placed in him by his late father. How was she to condone what he'd done? His children might seem greedy to some people, but Nick had behaved in an utterly profligate way with money that their grandfather had said was to be theirs.

"I wanted you to have the best of everything," he was saying now. "Your engagement ring . . . the wedding and honeymoon . . . all the clothes you wanted."

"Stop it, Nick!" she cried, bursting into tears. "Don't you dare blame me for your extravagance. It seems your financial problems started years before you even met me. Why did you let me think you were a millionaire! I wouldn't have cared if you'd had nothing. It was *you* I fell in love with." Sobs racked her body and she was shaking all over.

"Please, sweetheart." He was on his knees beside her, wrapping his arms around her, trying to kiss her, but she turned her head away. "I love you, darling. I only wanted you to be happy. Please listen to me," he begged. "Everything's going to be all right, I promise. Trust me, darling."

But all Philippa could think was: This is it. The death of love. The moment when the truth is revealed and the bones of a relationship are laid bare. And for a terrifying moment she wondered if she was going to be able to cope.

"You bloody fool!" Giles shouted. "Why did you tell Philippa so much? Why did you tell her anything at all? Don't you realize she'll go and tell Dad what you said and now he'll be forearmed when we get to court? He and his lawyers have a chance to prepare their defence. Oh, God, what a fucking mess."

Margaret looked abashed. "She was bound to find out from someone if not from me."

"Yes, but not until it was too late for Dad to dream up answers for everything."

"But how can he cover up what he's done? If we have the evidence it won't matter whether Nick knows what we're suing him for or not. Don't you see?" she asked, flustered and with the dreadful feeling that maybe she had done the wrong thing.

Giles sighed. "You're so hot-headed. Dad *always* has the answers to everything. And now he'll go and get the best QC to represent him, and he'll have a wonderfully prepared case . . . I don't know how you could have been so stupid."

"Don't you talk to me like that," retorted Margaret, stung. "You seem to forget I'm doing all this for you. You're the one who's going to be the most affected by what your father's done. We've got to fight for what is rightfully yours."

"It's too bloody late for that," Giles shouted, banging out of the room.

In the days that followed, Philippa stood fast.

"Woodlands must be put in Giles's name," she insisted. "It's only fair, Nick. If your father wanted the family home to be handed down then we're just going to have to create a new family home."

"After the way he's behaved, I wouldn't put a chicken coop in his name," Nick retorted. "Norman has had a letter from Giles's solicitor, threatening to sue me! Have you ever heard anything as despicable as that? Taking your own father to court?"

"I agree, Nick, it is, but that doesn't alter the situation."

"How would you feel if, in years to come, our baby turned round and sued you?"

Philippa paused, considering the question, trying to imagine the situation.

"I'd be terribly hurt, of course," she replied slowly, "but I would ask myself what I'd done wrong in the first place to cause a child of mine to treat me like that. Your father wanted this house to remain in the family and it was only entrusted to you for your lifetime. You've actually broken that trust, Nick, so no wonder Giles is upset. And what sort of a father does that make you?"

They looked at each other, Philippa filled with anguish and disappointment, Nick angry at having been caught out, hating being in the wrong.

But she couldn't help feeling guilty, too. If she hadn't suggested they move, would this financial crisis have come to a head so soon? Was it possible Nick could have kept the bank satisfied until he got his docklands scheme going? And then Wingfield Court might have been safe.

Philippa had lain awake all night, going over and over what had happened. Trying to see things from Nick's point of view, trying to look for excuses but unable to come up with anything that justified what he'd done. If only he'd told her the truth from the beginning, she'd have handled things differently. For a start she wouldn't have bought so many clothes, the new furniture for their bedroom . . . she was struck by a sudden thought, a way of perhaps making some amends to his children for the loss of their old home.

"Matt Blade is only buying the contents of the library, isn't he?" Philippa asked the next morning as she and

Nick had breakfast on the terrace overlooking the pool. "He doesn't want anything else in the house?"

"Not that I know of. Why?"

She looked at him squarely. "You must invite Elizabeth, Giles, Cathy and Jonathan to come here and choose what they want from the rest of the contents. If it all belonged to Wingland Estate once, then they should have it now. Furniture, pictures, silver, china, the lot. Let them share everything four ways, Nick. It's only fair."

He looked at her as if he couldn't believe his ears.

"Whose side are you on?" he asked hoarsely.

"I hope I'm on the side of fair play. Half the stuff in this house won't even fit into Woodlands in any case," she pointed out. "And we don't need it. Let's get your family here for a weekend, as soon as possible, and let them choose what they want."

"When are Cathy and Jonno due back from France?" Elizabeth asked Giles on the phone the following day. "If we're all going to Wingfield Court to split up the furniture next weekend, they must be there, too."

"I think they're back on Monday or Tuesday."

"Good. And Giles . . ."

"Yes?"

"Let's make this a happy weekend. It'll be our last at Wingfield and, you know, Tamsin's accident made me realize the importance of family life. That's what's truly precious, not property or money. I don't want any unpleasantness and neither does Laurence. This is our father after all, and whether it's his fault or not, what's gone is gone."

"Maybe, but we have to try and get back what we've lost or at least make sure he doesn't squander what's left of the family trust," Giles retorted, reminded of a similar conversation he'd had with Philippa when she'd phoned him the previous day.

"I'd like you to promise to drop your case against your father," she'd said. "I know he's behaved stupidly and I feel it's partly my fault but he's genuinely sorry for what's happened. He's not a bad man and he does love you all very much, but . . . well, I think things got out of hand and he got himself into a mess."

Giles had praised her for her loyalty, her devotion and consideration, but hadn't promised to abandon his intention of suing his father. To Elizabeth he said: "I think we're beyond the point of no return."

He didn't add that Margaret would never agree to his making friends with his father again.

"Yes, Ma, they're all coming to stay at the weekend," Philippa told her mother when they met for lunch in London on the Wednesday. Now that she was coming up to town each week for a pre-natal examination with her gynaecologist in Harley Street, she'd got into the habit of persuading Honor to come up from Ashford so they could meet. It made an exciting outing for her and they both treasured these days when they could talk uninterrupted and catch up on what was happening. Philippa went out of her way to make them special by choosing a nice restaurant, something she'd never been able to afford to do before she married Nick, followed by a leisurely stroll looking at the shops in Bond Street or Knightsbridge.

Today she'd chosen Launceston Place where they could enjoy the exquisite food in a calm, unhurried atmosphere.

"Is Elizabeth staying as well?" Honor asked. "I thought Nick had kicked her out of the house?"

Philippa nodded. "He did, but I think he's forgotten that. Laurence and the three children are coming as well, which will be really nice. Then there's Cathy and Jonathan, who are back from France, and of course Giles and Margaret."

"Oh, darling." Honor looked at her anxiously, wishing she could bear some of the burden that had been heaped on her daughter's shoulders since what she considered to be this disastrous marriage to Nick Driver.

Philippa smiled. "Don't worry about me, Ma. The children are all over me now they realize I'm not to blame for everything. I think they actually feel sorry for me. Giles really hates his father, though. I'd no idea there was such an undercurrent of hostility between those two, and Margaret's attitude doesn't help. At least they're both slightly mollified at the thought of getting a quarter share of the contents."

"How are you going to arrange that?" Honor sipped the well-chilled champagne and looked with pleasure at the lobster and foie gras salad she'd ordered as a starter. "Won't there be blood on the walls by the end of the weekend?"

"I'm going to suggest that in order of age, which means Elizabeth starts, they each choose one thing and keep on doing that, item by item, until there's nothing left. I think it's the fairest way, and we won't allow

Margaret to choose just the valuable items. It's got to be done fairly."

Honor's eyes widened with approval. "Excellent, darling. Then, hopefully, everyone gets at least a few of the things they really want. And what are you and Nick going to do about furniture for your new house?"

"Buy some beds and tables and chairs at Peter Jones, I suppose," Philippa replied, shrugging. "Somehow I seem to have lost interest in home making. I expect I'll feel more like it after I've had the baby. I get so tired these days, I don't really want to do anything much."

"You and Nick are still happy though, aren't you, darling." Honor asked anxiously. "Remember, God never throws more at you than you can cope with."

"I'm sure we can get back to where we were once we've moved but it's all a bit tense at the moment," she replied. "I do love him, Ma. I know he's made a complete mess of things with his children but it'll sort itself out, I'm sure it will."

Honor smiled but merely said, "It's obvious he loves you, darling. Very, very much. I think he'd do anything for you."

"It's strange to be going back," Elizabeth observed as they drove to Malmesbury with Dominic, Tamsin and Jasper strapped in the back.

Laurence glanced at her profile then swiftly back at the road again, the steering wheel held lightly in his capable hands.

"You'll miss it, won't you?"

She paused, trying to find the right words. "I'll miss what it used to be like, but I've been missing that for a long time anyway."

"I used to feel you were comparing it with Willow Farm," he continued in a low voice so the children, singing "One man went to mow", wouldn't hear.

"I never thought of comparing them. I mean, how can you? One is a cosy farm house, the other grand mansion. I was so excited at having a home of my own, I suppose it never occurred to me to miss Wingfield Court in that sense. I'd have been happy if we'd gone to live in a semi-detached," she added, grinning.

He carefully took a sharp bend in the road before replying, "I was always afraid I couldn't offer you enough, you know."

Elizabeth reached out and laid one hand on his knee.

"I think you did all the offering and I did all the taking," she remarked. "I know I'm rather a bossy boots . . ."

"But am I enough for you, Liz?" She could still hear the pain in his voice, although they'd recently become much closer.

"Of course you are," she replied robustly. "We're a great team, you, me and the kids. Especially now you're going to work for the council, and I'm going to look after the children without dreaded au pairs cluttering up the place." It was true. Since the drama of Tamsin's fall from the window she and Laurence had found themselves pulling together instead of in opposite directions, and he no longer had time to tap away infuriatingly on the old typewriter or pick fault with everything.

"Are we nearly there?" Dominic shouted, above the din of Jasper banging two wooden blocks together.

"Not long now, darling," Elizabeth replied. Tamsin, she noticed, was rocking her beloved Eckit in her arms. She looked up, realizing she was being watched, and Elizabeth felt a wave of pure love fill her heart as she looked into the large blue eyes and smiling little face. How she would have survived if Tamsin's accident had been fatal, she had no idea. The very thought of it filled her with horror too deep to bear.

"Has Philippa had her baby?" Tamsin asked suddenly.

"Not yet, sweetheart."

"I've had mine," she said shyly, hugging her doll.

"But it's not the same," Dominic blustered, all macho arrogance. "They've got to come out of your tummy, like when Muffet had her puppies . . ."

"Ah, here's the turning for Malmesbury," Laurence interrupted in a loud voice. "Let's see who can spot the tall chimney pots of Grandpa's house first." He caught Elizabeth's eye and smiled and she smiled back. His intimate look had made her feel strong enough to get through the coming weekend, no matter what happened.

Margaret looked at the list, carefully written out on a pad of ruled A4 paper, and looked at Giles as he headed the car up the motorway to Swindon, before turning off for Malmesbury.

"I've put down the pieces of silver we want, and the red and gold dinner service, the Georgian wine glasses, the Waterford decanters, the big tapestry in the hall . . .”

“Where are we going to put the tapestry? It’s far too big for our house.”

“We’ll worry about that when we’ve got it. We should also go after the Persian rugs in the drawing room, the Dresden vases on the mantelpiece — I’ve always loved them — the Chippendale mirror in the dining room . . . Oh, how I wish we had room for the dining-room table but maybe we could get the chairs . . . Then there are the Louis XV commodes with the matching jardinière . . . that gilt clock I’ve always adored, studded with lapis lazuli . . . the Rockingham china parrots . . . the painting of Venice . . .”

Margaret’s voice prattled on excitedly, making Giles realize with a slight sense of shock that his wife knew a great deal more about the contents of his old home than he did. But where was it all going to go? Their house was already crammed with stuff. They’d received a lot of wedding presents and Margaret was a compulsive collector of anything pretty, showy, and usually utterly useless. He was rather worried about something else, too.

“You do understand we’re to take it in turns, each choosing one item starting with Elizabeth as she’s the eldest, then me, Jonathan and finally Cathy. You can’t just produce that list and say that’s what I want, you know.”

“I don’t intend to,” Margaret said crossly, “but it’s important to plan what we want so we know what to ask for. I bet the others have ear-marked certain things.”

"I doubt it. Elizabeth has never cared for what she calls geegaws, Cathy's only interested in something if she can wear it, and Jonathan's flat and studio are minimalist to the point of being positively spartan!" Giles retorted.

"I know," Margaret agreed in distress. "Have you ever heard of such a waste? I've thought this so-called method of being fair ridiculous from the beginning. You'd have got everything if you'd inherited so it's not right the stuff should be divided four ways now. Maybe we can do a deal with the others?"

"If you're thinking of buying them out, forget it. We haven't got that sort of money. And in a way this is a much fairer method."

Margaret looked at him as if he was mad. "But your father has done you out of everything! How can you sit there and say it's fair? There's not a damn' thing fair about it . . ." She started crying, angry tears spurting from her eyes, her hand clapped over her mouth. "It's so unfair."

Giles didn't answer. He was not looking forward to the weekend and wished he'd come on his own. No doubt Philippa was going to have another go at trying to persuade him not to sue his father, and Nick himself would be belittling everyone, acting as if he were doing them all a great favour.

"Giles, you will make sure you try and get the things I've listed, won't you?" Margaret implored. She looked at him with eyes sunk in lakes of watery mascara, her freckled face and red hair reminding him of a sad-looking clown.

"Of course I'll try," he replied wearily, "but if the others particularly want something and it's their turn to choose . . . well, there's nothing I can do about it."

Cathy wound down the side window of her red Golf and let the wind ripple through her hair.

"Hurray to be nearly home!" she exclaimed, gripping the steering wheel. She was browner than ever after their holiday in France, and in contrast the white of her eyes seemed to have taken on a delicate shade of pale blue.

Jonathan, elegant in oatmeal-coloured linen trousers and a pale blue shirt, was brown also, but a paler, more golden brown, the front of his hair ash blond as it flopped over his forehead.

"I rather wish we could have stayed in London for a few days, though," he commented, "instead of having to drive straight home."

"Yes, but it'll be nice seeing Lizzie and the children."

"You will be staying with me when we go back to London on Sunday, won't you?" He'd so enjoyed Cathy's company, he knew he was going to miss her when she returned to Edinburgh in September.

"Where else would I stay, Jonno?" she asked gaily. "Remember, I'm homeless now apart from my digs. Thank God I never shared a house with Jack. At least I've got Venetia and the others to go back to."

It was the first time Jack's name had been mentioned since they'd left for France and his name hung in the air above their heads like a banner, bloodied and torn from the pain he'd caused. When they'd set out, and as if by some unspoken agreement, they'd decided he belonged to the past and the best way to get over him was for them to move forward. They'd each thought about him, though, Cathy recalling in moments of silent anguish the happiness she'd shared with him, the love and the laughter, the companionship and the closeness; while Jonathan could only fantasize about what might have been if only Jack had been gay, too. Like twins they each knew what the other was thinking, but also like twins they knew that to talk about it would be rubbing salt into deep wounds and so they'd talked about everything else as they drove around France, while at the same time "eating for England" as Jonathan described it.

"I'm getting so fat!" Cathy wailed one day, her waist still a man's handspan, her limbs as delicate-looking as a fawn's as she tucked into a plateful of escargots, dunking her crusty bread into the garlic butter and licking her lips in ecstasy. "Oh, these are to die for!"

Jonathan drank deeply from his glass of white Burgundy before refilling it. "And I'm getting a paunch," he echoed, patting his flat stomach. "God, I think food and drink is better than sex."

Cathy burst out laughing. "Steady on, Jonno! I wouldn't go so far as to say that."

"Oh, I don't know . . . when does a *tarte tatin* with cream, or *pommes noisettes*, or even a bowl of *consomme Fedora*, let you down? You can trust food."

"Not if you have a bad oyster, you can't."

"You can have food when you want, not when someone else is in the mood," he continued almost dreamily. "And food doesn't turn on you and accuse you of being selfish or inadequate. It's far more satisfying than bad sex."

Cathy opened her mouth to say she'd never experienced bad sex and that Jack had been wonderful then stopped herself in time and said instead, with a wicked smile, "And there's a bigger menu to choose from, too."

When they reached Wingfield Court the others were having drinks on the terrace and Nick was filming Dominic and Tamsin on his camcorder as they chased a ball around the lawn. Philippa, billowing in a gauzy blue maternity dress came forward to greet them. Cathy instantly noticed the change in her. Gone was the assured, breezy young woman, all light-hearted smiles and without a care in the world. Chastened, Cathy thought, was the word that sprang to mind to describe her now; older, sadder, disillusioned, but very calm.

"Come and have a drink and tell us all about France," she said. "You're wonderfully brown, Cathy. So are you, Jonathan. Did you have a marvellous time?"

Then Nick greeted them as smoothly as if their last antagonistic meeting in London had never taken place. "Nice to see you," he said. "I must say, you're looking very fit."

Then the rest of family came forward and Cathy felt as if she was a spinning top, reeling from person to person as she turned this way and that, first flinging her arms around Elizabeth, then kissing Laurence, embracing Giles, pecking Margaret on the cheek, bending to hug Dominic and finally sweep Tamsin off her feet to cuddle her.

"I feel like we've been away for ages," she declared, setting her niece on her feet again and accepting a glass of Pimm's from Nick.

Dominic had got hold of the camcorder and was pointing it at Cathy. "You can say something . . . I can do the sound as well," he declared importantly.

"You are clever," she told him. "Is it switched on?"

"Yes, Grandpa showed me how. Go on, say something."

"What shall I say?" she giggled, suddenly feeling ridiculously self-conscious, but at that moment Dominic was distracted by the antics of the dogs and swung away from her to film them.

Philippa came up to her, subtly drawing her away from the others, obviously anxious to talk to her privately.

"I've already spoken to Elizabeth and Giles," she began, almost nervously, "but I want you, and of course Jonathan, to know that it was I who suggested we leave this house, not your father. I had absolutely no idea it belonged to all of you. What I'm really trying to say, I suppose, is I hope you won't be too hard on him."

Cathy immediately placed her hands on Philippa's shoulders and looked earnestly into the older woman's face.

"Listen, you're not to get upset about it. You're to concentrate on keeping well and having your baby. How were you to know everything was tied up in companies and trusts if no one told you? It's sad we're selling this place, but what's done's done and it certainly isn't your fault. And Jonno and I are not going to be suing anyone by the way." She glanced over at Nick, who was quaffing

Pimm's and chatting to Laurence. "Daddy doesn't seem too bothered."

Giles joined them, overhearing her remark. "Dad hasn't been too bothered for a long time," he said with a touch of bitterness. Philippa drifted away to join another group, so they could be alone.

"Things have moved on while you and Jonathan have been in France, Cathy," Giles continued. "Sean Chapman's put me on to another solicitor and he's been telling me there's been a gradual haemorrhage of the family fortune for the past six to eight years. Maybe longer. He's collecting all the evidence and when it comes to court Dad won't have a leg to stand on. We'll also be suing Norman Sheridan, Ernest Lomax and probably Andrew Kingsley as well. They're all guilty of negligence if nothing else."

Cathy frowned and looked round anxiously. "I don't think you should be talking like that, Giles. For one thing Daddy might overhear you and that would completely wreck what's already going to be a difficult weekend. For another I'd hoped you'd dropped this idea of suing him. Jonno and I don't want to have anything to do with it."

Giles shrugged. He'd had quite a few drinks since he'd arrived and was on the verge of being belligerent.

"The sooner he realizes he's lost the case before it's even begun, the better," he retorted.

"I thought we'd decided to let things be?" Elizabeth protested in a whisper as she joined them. "You can't take Dad to court, Giles."

"Watch me!"

"It'll only reflect badly on you," she warned.

"I don't give a fuck. He deserves to be publicly humiliated after what he's done."

Cathy, listening, could tell the words had been put into his mouth by Margaret. "For God's sake, Giles, shut up, will you?" she hissed, exchanging exasperated looks with Elizabeth.

Dominic came zooming past, still filming.

"Take care, darling," Elizabeth remonstrated. "Be careful not to drop that camera."

He lowered it and put it on a chair. "I've finished, anyway." Then he tore off to retrieve the ball which Tamsin had thrown into the middle of a flower bed. "Tamsin!" he yelled. "Don't do that. You'll break Grandpa's flowers."

Cathy watched him, an indulgent smile on her face. "He's growing up fast, isn't he?"

"Too fast in many ways. I've learned to appreciate every moment of their lives since Tamsin's accident. I hate the thought of them growing up, going away, leaving home."

"She's absolutely OK? No after-affects?"

"Fine, thank God. She must have a guardian angel to have escaped . . . Oh, Dominic!" Elizabeth exclaimed suddenly. She picked up her father's camcorder. "The little devil's left it switched on."

"Now Dad's going to have to watch hours of a close-up of my legs," Cathy laughed.

Laurence suggested to Giles they walk around the garden and Cathy watched as the two men strolled across the lawn, Laurence so tall and thin and dark, and Giles beginning to get tubby and with thinning fair hair. She noticed Margaret was also watching them as she cuddled Jasper on her lap.

Cathy nudged Elizabeth and indicated Margaret.

"I wonder why they haven't had a baby," she whispered. "She's obviously mad about children. Do you think perhaps she can't?"

"Maybe it's Giles's fault," Elizabeth pointed out intuitively.

At that moment Philippa joined them, a jug of Pimm's in her hand. "Can I top you up?"

There was a harmony between the three women that hadn't been there before. We could have become friends, Elizabeth reflected, if it hadn't been for Dad.

"Where are you actually having the baby?" Cathy asked, smiling.

Philippa gave a quick sigh as if bracing herself for an ordeal. "The London Clinic, I think. We'll probably go straight to live in the flat when we leave here, and as there isn't all that long to go . . ." Her voice drifted off and her expression remained enigmatic.

"Aren't you moving to the new house Dad's bought?" Cathy burst out in astonishment.

Philippa's expression was strained. "To be honest I've no idea what's happening. All I know is that Matt Blade wants to take possession in less than three weeks and I have this whole house to clear first. Hopefully," she added with a little smile, "the four of you will be taking the bulk of everything. I've ordered four large furniture vans to come on Tuesday, and providing each of you marks what you want with colour-coded labels it shouldn't be too difficult."

Elizabeth looked at her with renewed respect. "And you're supervising all this while you're seven months pregnant? God, when I was at your stage I looked like the side of a house and it was an effort to make a cup of tea!"

Philippa looked her straight in the eye and replied with devastating candour. "Well, I brought it all on myself, didn't I?"

A delicious dinner with plentiful wine managed to oil the wheels that night. Even Giles was polite as the result of a bit of friendly advice from Laurence. Jonathan was himself: flippant, funny, full of witty one-liners — and secretly wondering if he'd get the chance to ask for his mother's desk. From an early age he remembered her sitting at it, writing her letters and shopping lists, and he'd liked the way she kept the little pigeon holes so tidy. One for envelopes, one for postcards, another for receipts, and a fourth for all the letters and birthday cards her children had sent to her over the years.

He looked at the others around the long mahogany table, wondering what they were thinking, wondering what they all wanted. Giles and Margaret would go for the best stuff, of course, and Elizabeth would want the practical things, furniture that was strong and durable and able to withstand the onslaught of three children. Cathy? The only one without her own home now she'd go for Mummy's books of course, and the silver-topped jars from her dressing table, some of the smaller paintings perhaps, and what else . . . ? And then it suddenly hit him with heartbreaking force. This weekend really would be the last time they'd all be together under this roof. By tomorrow the contents would be divided up, by next week the house would be stripped bare, and within a month someone else would be living in their family home.

Laurence, purposely not wanting to get involved, suggested after breakfast the next morning that he look after the children while Elizabeth took turns with the others to choose what she wanted.

"Why don't you help me with Jasper, Margaret?" he suggested guilelessly. "It's the most wonderful day. We can take them into the garden and Jasper can lie on a rug while I play games with Dominic and Tamsin."

Margaret looked quite panic-stricken at the thought of missing out on the chance of picking the best goodies.

"Oh, I've promised to help Giles," she retorted, flustered. "You know how hopeless he is and I'm going to have to make a list for him and everything."

Giles, meanwhile, was venting his spleen against his father, as a result of Margaret's telling him to assert himself. His voice, shrill and hectoring, could be heard coming from the open doorway of the estate office where Nick was talking to Ernest Lomax.

"Cooking the books again, are you? Trying to cover up what you've done?" Giles challenged them.

To his surprise Nick rose to his feet, refusing to be drawn into an argument, and turning to Ernest, suggested they drive over to the latter's house to continue their discussion.

"Something to hide, haven't you? Frightened of the truth, is that it?" Giles persisted. "Well, don't think you're going to get away with it. I'll take you through every court in the land if I have to . . ."

But Nick ignored him, locked the office door, and swaggering out of the front door and into his car, followed by his embarrassed and sheepish-looking accountant.

"Where are they going?" Philippa asked anxiously, as she crossed the hall at that moment.

Jonathan, who had overheard everything, told her.

"To Ernest's house. I don't think Dad could stand another minute of Giles hassling him."

"Oh, fuck off," his brother snapped, heading for the drawing room.

"Let's get with it then," Philippa sighed, producing boxes of four different-coloured labels and stickers, pens and note pads.

It was a long and arduous business, with Elizabeth, Cathy and Jonathan trying not to step on each other's toes or appear grasping but fairly and carefully making their choices in turn, while Margaret, straining desperately on the leash of greed, eyes picking over everything with the avarice of a market dealer pricing the goods, grabbed what she could.

By lunchtime, when Nick returned, they'd only made their choices from the drawing room, morning room and hall. Jonathan had secured Rosalind's desk and was ecstatic. He'd had no idea that Cathy wanted it too, but seeing his expression when he looked at it, she chose instead a small armchair their mother used to sit in when she was doing her needlework.

At Philippa's suggestion, lunch was a picnic on the terrace by the swimming pool so they could get on with dividing up the dining-room furniture immediately afterwards. Philippa worked hard to make it a jolly occasion, and Elizabeth, wanting this last day at Wingfield Court to be a happy one, helped her. They handed round plates of sandwiches and legs of cold chicken. Wine was poured into unbreakable beakers and there were miniature hamburgers for the children. Morton had thought of everything and the informality of lounging around the pool lightened everyone's mood. With the exception of Giles. He studiously avoided being anywhere near his father or entering into the friendly banter as they laughed and teased each other. Margaret sat near him protectively, whispering the occasional remark.

But the others entered into the spirit of goodwill that Philippa had striven to create; even Laurence seemed light-hearted, and from time to time Cathy saw him and Elizabeth holding hands.

This is a day I shall always remember, Cathy thought, leaning back in her chair. It was a picture forever printed on her mind's eye, the sound of her family's laughter an echo she'd never forget. The warmth of the day hung over them like a comforting blanket, heavy with the scent of roses and jasmine.

Jonathan closed his eyes as he lay along the edge of the pool, fingers trailing in the water, listening to the chatter. Then quite suddenly he thought how much his mother would have enjoyed this picnic. She'd loved the garden. She was never happier than when she was out here, surrounded by her family on a lovely summer's day. Then he remembered Philippa's presence and wondered if, under different circumstances, Rosalind would have liked her.

"Hadn't we better get on?" he heard Margaret ask, and the spell was broken. Everyone was clambering to their feet and Morton and a maid were clearing away the food. Philippa announced she was going upstairs to rest and Elizabeth followed her, wanting to put Jasper in his cot for his afternoon nap. Then Laurence announced he'd take Dominic and Tamsin for a walk while the others continued to divide up the furniture.

Nick remained in the garden, enjoying another glass of wine, while the countryside shimmered and slumbered in the heat of the afternoon, and the air was still and languorous. The only sound was the faint buzzing of lazy bees as they hovered slowly from flower to flower.

After they'd all chosen things from the dining room they moved on to the monumental task of selecting items from the pantry where all the china and glass was kept. Jonathan, who had little idea what went on beyond the green baize door, stared in astonishment at the vast dinner services, tea and coffee sets, dishes and platters and hundreds of glasses of every shape and size.

"Jesus, what can we do with this lot?" he gasped, gazing up at the glass-fronted cabinets that reached to the ceiling.

"Let's start with the dinner services and count how many plates and dishes there are. Then divide it up four ways," Elizabeth said sensibly.

"But where am I going to put my share? Giving dinner parties is hardly my scene," he pointed out.

"Put it in storage with my stuff for the time being," Cathy suggested. "When you're a famous artist, you're bound to give soirees in your studio and then you'll need it all."

They started stacking plates in units of a dozen, with Giles handing them down from his perch on top of a ladder. Then they moved on to the exquisite Sèvres and Rockingham dessert plates and bowls.

Giles began huffing and puffing, his face red and sweating from the heat and the wine he'd had at lunch.

"I've got to have a breather, I'm bloody exhausted. Why don't you carry on, Margaret? I think I'll go and have a shower."

"OK," she replied amenably. "And why not have a bit of a rest, too?" She saw it as a godsend to have him out of the way for a while. Now she could choose what she wanted without referring to him and be much more ruthless with the others than he'd dare to be.

After he'd gone they continued counting, examining, selecting, listing and labelling, feeling as if they were stocktaking in somewhere like Harrods and that the day would never come to an end. At one point they worked out there was enough glass and china for each of them to give a dinner party of four courses for twenty people.

"Yeah! Around my kitchen table," Elizabeth remarked, laughing. Margaret was already silently planning her menus. Cathy and Jonathan were wondering how much it was going to cost to store the stuff.

Eventually Philippa wandered in, looking bleary-eyed after her sleep. "How's it going. I wondered if you'd like some tea? It's nearly four-thirty."

Elizabeth looked startled. "Is it really? My God, I must go and wake up Jasper or he'll never sleep tonight."

"Giles must be having a sleep, too," Margaret observed happily. "Let's not disturb him. He's got a lot on his mind."

"Any sign of Nick?" Philippa asked Cathy, who was putting blue stickers on the vegetable dishes she'd chosen. "I haven't seen him since lunchtime."

"He must be in the office. I'll go and ask if he'd like some tea." Philippa ambled off, full-blown and flushed and feeling very relaxed. There was no answer when she knocked on the estate office door so she looked in the library and the drawing room, and finally the morning room, though he hardly ever sat there. His car was still in the drive which meant he must still be in the garden. Philippa went out through the front door and stood on the steps, surveying the view. The afternoon was cooling now and the sky fading to a dusky blue. She breathed deeply and caught the first of the evening's elusive perfumes wafting from the honeysuckle that grew up the side of the house. Above the eaves a paper-thin moon already hung in the sky like a distant Japanese lantern.

Wingfield Court, she reflected peacefully, had shed its contents bit by bit today, making her feel as if she were also shedding, layer by layer, the stress and uneasiness of the past few months. She and Nick would be out of this place very soon now and she'd be able to leave all reminders of Rosalind behind. She hoped she'd made her peace with the children today. They'd seemed quite well disposed towards her though maybe that had been an act. Although it was their father they should really blame, she knew the fault would be forever laid at her door but that was something she was going to have to live with.

Wandering serenely along the path that led to the terrace by the pool, where they'd had lunch, she suddenly stopped, staring ahead, frozen with a horror that threatened to engulf her. Her legs gave way beneath her and she staggered, almost crashing to her knees. Then a great darkness started to envelop her, threatening to sweep her away. She struggled against it, feeling sick and faint, her heart hammering and her veins turning to rivers of ice.

She heard a voice screaming, "No! No! Oh, God, no!" and realized it was hers.

CHAPTER THIRTEEN

Jonathan got to the swimming pool first, kicking off his shoes and jumping in fully clothed. Cathy jumped in after him, helping to turn their father on to his back, knowing instantly it was too late. And all the while the air was filled with Philippa's sobs, and the running feet of Elizabeth, and Margaret shrieking to a distraught Morton: "Call an ambulance! For God's sake, ring for an ambulance."

Then Giles, roused by the commotion, peered down on them all from his bedroom window, shouting, "What's happened?"

A wispy trail of crimson in the water swirled around Nick's head as Jonathan gently towed his body to the side of the pool. With Elizabeth's and Cathy's help, he lifted it out and laid it on the stone surround. Philippa dropped to her knees beside Nick, laying her hands on his shirt front, and staring with disbelieving eyes as rivulets of water formed pools around his body. His face was turned towards her, bleached a ghastly white, eyes open and unseeing. Then they all saw the deep gash in the back of his head, forming its own dark pool of blood.

"Daddy! . . . Daddy!" Cathy sobbed, clinging to Jonathan. They crouched down, water pouring off their clothes and hair as they stared at the body of their father, unable to take in the enormity of what had happened.

"Oh, my God," Elizabeth moaned, too shocked to cry. "Where's Laurence? Don't let him bring the children here."

Morton came running back towards them. "The ambulance is on it's way."

Elizabeth turned to him. "Can you find my husband? Tell him to keep the children away,"

Jonathan, the water from his hair mingling with the tears that ran down his cheeks, said huskily, "How in God's name . . ."

Giles came dashing towards them, red in the face and breathless.

"What's happened? Why is . . . Oh, Christ!" He stood motionless, crushed by the sight of his father's body, lifeless and bleeding.

"He was face down in the water," Elizabeth said in a flat shocked voice. "And his head . . . the back of his head's bashed in."

"But . . . *how*?"

She shook her head. "I think he's been in the water for some time." Then she buried her face in her hands but still she could not cry.

Philippa was shaking violently, her face white, her mind reeling, aware that she was already missing Nick in these first few moments after his death. And then came the dreadful realization that these moments were just the beginning of forever.

Margaret put an arm around her shoulders. "I think we should get her indoors," she told the others urgently, but they weren't listening. Grouped around Nick, they were unable to take in the fact that he had gone. Whatever their feelings towards him had been and whatever he had done, he was their father, and there wasn't a single day in the whole of their lives when he hadn't been a large part of their existence.

The distant wail of an ambulance coming up the country lane, shattering the peace of the afternoon, brought a dreadful sense of reality to what for a few minutes had seemed just a nightmare.

"I can't bear it," Philippa burst out, clutching her head, gripping great handfuls of hair as if she was going to pull it out. "I want him back . . ." She couldn't find the words to say that in dying and leaving her behind, he had also taken all her tomorrows with him.

"Don't let them take him away," she sobbed. Her cries of anguish roused the others from their own self-absorption to her terrible grief Elizabeth rose abruptly and walked around her father's body to Philippa's side.

"Come along," she said gently. "Let's go into the house. You should lie down."

"Yes," agreed Margaret, taking her other arm. Then she looked at Elizabeth and mouthed, "We should get a doctor to give her something."

"He must have fallen into the pool," Giles was telling the others as the ambulance men came running across the lawn with a stretcher.

"But why?" everyone kept asking. Why should he have fallen?

After an initial examination the paramedics backed away, talked between themselves, made urgent phone calls, and Giles, Cathy and Jonathan heard words that were unbelievable and almost farcical to their ears. "Suspicious circumstances", "forensic evidence", and "post mortem" were being muttered in muted tones.

Bewildered, Nick Driver's children found themselves being escorted back inside the house by a concerned woman paramedic.

"You should sit down and have some strong sweet tea," she advised. "Shall I have a look at the pregnant lady?"

Cathy nodded. There were sounds of children's voices coming from the kitchen and Lawrence appeared, looking shaken. He'd come back with the children and Morton had waylaid him, telling him in an urgent whisper what had happened.

"Where's Lizzie?" he asked Cathy.

"She brought Philippa back into the house. Maybe they're upstairs. Liz is being marvellous. So brave." Her voice wobbled until it ended in a squeak. "Unlike me." She wiped her eyes furiously with the back of her hand.

Laurence embraced her swiftly, his gangling frame towering over her. "I'm so sorry," he said, before turning and racing up the stairs two at a time.

Elizabeth was on the landing, talking to the medic. Laurence went straight to her, and took her in his arms in silent sympathy.

"Where are the children?" she asked.

"Watching television in the kitchen."

"I must wake Jasper up. I was on my way to when . . ." Her voice broke.

"I'll do it, darling."

Elizabeth looked up into his face. The man she'd fallen in love with and married had come back to her. "Thank you," she whispered.

Jonathan and Giles, left in the hall with Margaret, looked at each other, not knowing what to do. This had been so sudden, unlike Rosalind's death for which they had been able to prepare themselves for months.

"We quarrelled," Giles said suddenly in a hollow voice.

"You mustn't think about it now," Margaret told him briskly.

"I'll never see him again and the last time I did we quarrelled." Giles looked stricken. "Oh, God, we quarrelled." He crumpled on to one of the carved chests, his hands covering his face.

Jonathan marched to the drinks cupboard. "I need a drink. Want one, Giles?"

"You should have a cup of tea instead," Margaret pointed out.

"There's only one way to get through this and that's to have a strong drink," Jonathan retorted.

Police cars were sweeping up the drive now and uniformed policemen were hurrying over to the pool area.

"Why are they bringing in the police?" Margaret asked.

"Didn't you hear what they said?" Jonathan took a swig of brandy and felt it's fiery essence burn his throat. "'Suspicious circumstances'. They obviously think someone killed Dad."

Margaret looked horrified. "How could they think that?"

He shrugged and refilled his glass. "When anyone dies in strange circumstances they have to have a post mortem. I think it's the blow on his head that's made them suspicious."

"But they can't really think he was murdered?"

Giles turned on her irritably. "For God's sake, Margaret, of course they don't. It's routine stuff."

"We'll all be questioned," Jonathan said gloomily.

"Oh, God . . . and then there'll be his will," Margaret groaned, dropping on to a chair. "What new ghastly shock will that hold?"

It was several hours later. The police had taken photographs and the forensic team had examined around the pool. Laurence overheard them saying that the area had been contaminated by so many people rushing on to the scene when they'd discovered the body that their findings were not as good as they could have been. Finally, they'd removed Nick's body. A post mortem had been ordered by the coroner's office because of the suspicious nature of his death and the wound he had suffered, and an inquest would be held as soon as possible.

Suddenly the family found themselves part of a great machine that had been set in motion and from which there was no escape. They were all questioned that evening, though not at great length. They were told, though, that they must remain at Wingfield Court, and that they would be required to make statements at the police station the following morning. The police wanted a minute by minute account of the day from everyone.

But everyone, it seemed, had slightly different memories, according to their different viewpoint.

Philippa, who had been sedated by the local doctor, spoke brokenly of a busy day spent without discord. She'd helped her step-children choose things from the house and then they'd had a picnic by the pool. In the afternoon she'd slept while her husband had stayed in the garden and all the others had gone back indoors to continue selecting the things they wanted, with the exception of Laurence Vickers who had taken his two elder children for a walk. Throughout she maintained there were no problems between Nick and herself, that they'd been very much in love. His state of mind had been excellent, and no, he'd not been depressed. It was true he and his children had fallen out over the sale of Wingfield Court, but they'd come to accept that what was done was done, and were all getting along very nicely again.

Elizabeth described a weekend that she'd thought would be strained, as they split up the contents of the house, but which had turned out better that she'd expected. She and her father had let bygones be bygones; a recent accident to her daughter had given her a new sense of perspective, taught her the true value of life. She and her siblings had no quarrel. They'd always been close. The police picked up on Tamsin's accident and wanted to know all the details including the names of the au pairs responsible and the doctors who had examined the child.

Cathy wept stormily at first, saying she'd been dreading the weekend because she'd feared a family contretemps but it had turned out better than she had hoped. Her father had been well and in good form and they'd all got along perfectly. She'd been with her siblings all that day. Lunch in the garden had been really good fun.

Jonathan's version of events was rather more vague. He did remember, though, that his father had left the house sometime after breakfast in the company of his accountant, Ernest Lomax, and hadn't returned until lunchtime.

"You saw him leave?" he was asked.

"That's right. I was in the hall."

"Were you alone? Did anyone else see your father go out?"

Here Jonathan's memory failed him but he thought he was probably alone. The others, he was sure, had already gathered in the drawing room to start choosing what they wanted.

"And in the afternoon . . . after lunch?"

"Stuck into counting a two hundred and fifty piece fucking dinner service," he retorted. "Then we had to divide up four hundred assorted glasses. You know, sherry, white wine, red wine, tumblers, port, brandy . . . I don't know why my father didn't turn the house into a hotel!" He stopped abruptly, bit his lip and had a hard time suppressing his emotions. "I'll miss the old bugger," he faltered.

Laurence's version of events was clear-cut and simple. He'd spent the morning in the garden with his three children, playing games and reading to them, and after a picnic lunch by the pool he'd taken the two eldest for a walk. They'd collected a bunch of wild flowers to give to their mother, he'd given them ice creams in the cafe in the village, and returned to the house just after Nick's body had been found.

Margaret spoke arrogantly and grandly of being "forced to choose" with the others some of the contents of Wingfield Court which rightfully belonged to her and her husband in the first place. It had taken all day and been absolutely hellish. Nick hadn't been friendly towards them and she couldn't understand why, since he and not they were in the wrong. Now she wondered if this post mortem would delay the funeral and the reading of his will, and what about probate on his assets?

Giles was the last member of the family to be questioned before the police moved on to Morton and the rest of the staff. He was even more evasive and vague than Jonathan had been. He said he'd been with the others all day . . . then he remembered he'd gone for a shower in the middle of the afternoon and fallen asleep afterwards, and only been awakened by the commotion by the pool, which was under his bedroom window, when his father's body had been discovered.

Had he not looked out of his window before his shower and seen his father? he was asked. No, he replied, he didn't think he had. Was he upset at losing his inheritance? Did he blame his father? Had they quarrelled over it?

Panic lit Giles's eyes like a lightning strike. He wasn't pleased by what had happened, he admitted. He and his father had certainly disagreed over the sale of the family home. That morning? That afternoon? He couldn't recall. Surely he must remember? His father had been found dead in the late afternoon. There was a strained atmosphere in the house, wasn't there? Had he seen his father leave with his accountant, Ernest Lomax, that morning? What did he know about Lomax? Was it possible *he* had a grudge against Nick Driver? How did his father seem at lunchtime, after he'd returned from Lomax's house?

On and on the questioning went, while Giles wriggled helplessly like a worm that had been dug up and was clinging to the spade.

"I don't *know*!" he finally burst out, eyes popping, face scarlet. The police decided to detain him in a cell overnight, pending further questioning. They still had the staff at Wingfield Court to question, and of course Ernest Lomax.

When Nick Driver's body had been taken away the previous afternoon, they'd also removed the items left strewn around the pool, for forensic examination. There hadn't been much because Morton, with the help of the kitchen staff, had cleared away all the lunch things. A tray of glasses and a jug of orange juice had remained on the white wrought-iron table, together with Nick's half-drunk glass of wine.

On the ground by the chair where he was last seen sitting a paperback thriller by a popular author lay open at page 212, beside his dark glasses. Over the back of another chair, Cathy had left a silk scarf she'd bought in France. Dominic and Tamsin had also abandoned a few things of no consequence; a baseball cap, a tee-shirt, a pair of tiny white trainers and the book their father had been reading to them.

Early the next morning, fuelled by nervous adrenaline and aware the coming week was going to put a lot of strain on the household with the whole family remaining at Wingfield Court, and no doubt the funeral to see to, Morton looked out of the kitchen window and tut-tutted under his breath. The police hadn't put the garden furniture back the way it was meant to be and he couldn't bear things not being in their right place.

Hurrying along the terrace — wondering if it was his imagination or did the water in the pool have a pinkish tinge this morning? — he put the white wrought-iron chairs neatly around the table again, straightened the lounging seats, plumped up the cushions and smoothed the canopy and skirt of the swing-couch, thanking the good Lord it hadn't rained in the night. How could he have been so stupid as to leave the cushions out? As he picked one up he was astonished to find the family camcorder wedged down the side of the garden seat.

That child! he cursed under his breath. Did no one control him? Dominic should never have been allowed to play with something so valuable as this as if it were a mere plastic toy. He examined it closely, unable to tell whether it was damaged or not. Then he shrugged. Maybe it wasn't such a bad thing after all if this family lost some of their money. They'd always had too much to appreciate the simple things in life and had taken for granted the luxury of staying in this house, surrounded by beautiful things. Now if *he'd* had all that money . . .

He placed the camcorder on the hall table and went back to the kitchen. There were six adults and three children expecting breakfast very shortly so he'd better get on.

Philippa came slowly down the stairs a few minutes later, having slept fitfully. Numbed by grief one minute, and inconsolably distraught the next, she had simply no idea how she was going to get through the day. The first thing she saw was the camcorder on the hall table and a fresh wave of sorrow swept through her because there would be pictures of Nick on it; laughing with his head thrown joyously back, smiling his gently teasing smile, walking, moving, turning, standing, using his broad hands expressively, his strong body so incredibly sexy, his lean face tanned and healthy-looking. But no more.

She grabbed the camcorder. Moving as fast as her bulk would allow, she went to the library and stuffed it in a drawer in the desk. Matt Blade had bought everything here, she'd remove it before he moved in, but meanwhile she'd try and put out of her mind images of Nick and her desperate desire to have him alive again.

Ernest Lomax had a perfect recollection of what had happened the previous morning when asked to make a statement to the police.

"Nick Driver phoned me before breakfast and asked me to come and see him. He was having problems with Giles, you know. Over money. That young man thinks the world owes him a living and Nick wanted my advice. We were busy discussing the tax situation when Giles knocked on the door and then burst into the estate office where we were sitting, and he was positively abusive, raving and ranting at his father and accusing him of cooking the books . . . Oh, it was dreadful."

"And then what happened?"

"Nick Driver suggested we continue our meeting at my house."

"Not your office?"

"No. Well, my house is nearer."

"So you left Wingfield Court together?"

"Yes." Lomax pursed his lips. "Giles kept harassing us as we were going, yelling at his father and calling him names . . . using terrible language, actually."

"Was anyone else around at the time?"

"Yes, Jonathan, Nick's youngest son, was there, and his wife Philippa. They were in the hall. She looked quite disturbed by it all."

"Are you prepared to make a statement to that effect? Confirming that you saw the two men quarrelling?"

"Yes."

"Thank you, Mr Lomax."

The post mortem on Nick Driver revealed he had suffered from a fractured skull, which had caused a fatal haematoma, consistent with receiving a heavy blow on the back of the head, causing him to become instantly unconscious and to topple into the swimming pool and drown. After twenty-four hours of questioning, Giles was held on suspicion of murder and told he would be charged at the local Assizes in two days' time.

Margaret, incandescent with rage at the suggestion that he was guilty, immediately launched a campaign to clear his name, summoning both Sean Chapman and Barnard Alexander to Wingfield Court and telling them they must get bail set at the hearing and find the best QC in the country to defend her husband.

So far as clearing Giles's name went she had the backing of the others. They heartily refuted any suggestion that he had been involved in Nick's death. Even Philippa, whose parents had arrived to be with her, thought there must be some other explanation, although of all her step-children Giles was the one with the greatest grudge against his father.

Ernest Lomax, however, aided by Norman Sheridan and his legal firm and also Andrew Kingsley who had been Nick's stockbroker for over twenty years, were definitely of the opinion that Giles was guilty and went to great lengths to inform the police of how troublesome he'd been in recent months.

They said he'd been about to sue his father, accusing him of dishonesty and misappropriation of trust funds. They also told of Giles's fury at the sale of Wingfield Court. It did not make for a pretty picture but having interviewed Giles Driver, and found him to be a truculent and self-absorbed man, the police were not surprised. Though the case against him was so far circumstantial he could, they argued, have seized the opportunity of going into the garden during the afternoon while saying he was going upstairs to have a shower. He also had a motive: revenge.

Meanwhile Philippa, unable to bear sleeping alone in the big double bed she had shared with Nick, moved to one of the spare rooms, weeping and dozing alternately, her world shattered. Her blood pressure had risen alarmingly and the doctor, fearing she'd give birth prematurely, ordered her to rest.

"Don't let her know what's going on," he added, referring to Giles's arrest. "Spare her the details. Keep her in bed. What she needs now is peace and quiet."

Archie and Honor Sykes took it in turns to sit with her and Honor slept on a sofa in the room at night. One of the things they did not tell her was that the estate agent had phoned to ask if Mr Driver intended to go ahead with the purchase of Woodlands as contracts had never been exchanged and he hadn't even paid a deposit on the house.

To the family's relief, the coroner released Nick's body for burial the following week so Laurence undertook to help Jonathan and Cathy make the funeral arrangements, by which time Margaret fervently hoped Giles would be out on bail. Elizabeth, still deathly calm and hardly talking, looked after the children, taking them out for walks or drives in the car; anything to get away from the house and the hideous memories conjured up by the pool area. Never before had Willow Farm seemed so appealing or so safe.

"Let's go home as soon as the funeral is over," she told Laurence. I want to get right away from this place. First Mummy's death and now Dad's — it's too much to bear."

He held her close, feeling as if she'd come back to him, though he was saddened by the realization that his gain had only been caused by her loss.

Margaret, on the other hand, devastated that Giles was suspected of killing Nick, was propelled by manic energy, getting involved in everything that was going on and phoning Barnard Alexander several times a day, demanding to know what he was doing to get her husband released and the charges quashed.

"What about the case we were bringing against Nick?" she asked one day. "Can we sue his estate now he's dead?"

Barnard was beginning to feel uneasy, finding her determined efforts to get what she could distinctly unattractive.

"I don't think that's advisable," he told her bluntly. "Nick's various dealings have, so far as the courts are concerned, been buried for the past few years beneath layers of obfuscation. He was undoubtedly a stupid man, apparently unlike his late father and grandfather, and it seems he lost a great deal of money investing in very dodgy schemes. He was also wildly profligate . . ."

Margaret pounced like a dog discovering a bone in its basket. She clutched the phone tightly. "Dodgy schemes?"

"When we've talked to his accountant and his solicitor, and also his stock broker, I'll have all the details before me. It may be possible, I suppose, to sue the estate of the late Nick Driver for gross negligence in the handling of the trust . . ."

"So we've got him now, haven't we?"

"No, the undertaker's got him, Mrs Driver."

Margaret had the grace to blush as she bade him goodbye and hung up.

Matt Blade phoned that night, asking hesitantly to speak to Philippa Driver.

Jonathan, who answered the phone, explained she wasn't taking any calls. "Can I help you? I'm Jonathan Driver."

"I just wanted to extend my deepest sympathy. I read in the newspapers what had happened. You must be Nick Driver's son?"

"Yes, I am. Thank you. It's a bad time for all of us. What can I do for you?"

"I was ringing to say that if you'd like me to postpone moving into your house for a few weeks, I'll quite understand. You must all be having a terrible time and I'm very sorry. Probably the last thing you need at the moment is to have to pack up and get out."

Jonathan was deeply touched by such consideration.

"That's most awfully good of you. I've lost track of time. When were you supposed to move in?"

"At the end of the month . . . that's less than two weeks away."

"Can I do a rain-check with everyone else? As you can imagine the whole family's here, my brother's being held by the police which is a nightmare, and my step-mother may give birth at any moment. I've no idea what we're all doing except that Dad's funeral is next Tuesday. After that . . ." Jonathan's voice trailed off.

"Listen, why don't you ring me back? The only reason I've got to know if you'd like to delay is because I've people standing by who are going to install the recording studio so I need to tell them what's happening."

"Cool," Jonathan agreed. "Give me your number and I'll let you know as quickly as I can."

A family conference was held that evening. Once Nick's funeral had taken place it seemed they were all anxious to go their separate ways. Philippa said she would leave Wingfield Court afterwards accompanied by her parents and would move into the London flat in readiness for the baby's arrival.

Margaret said she and Giles, who would hopefully be on bail by then, would also be returning to London to start preparing his defence.

That left Elizabeth and Laurence, who had already planned to return to Willow Farm after the funeral. And so it was agreed that Matt Blade could move in when he'd originally planned, so long as he didn't mind if Cathy and Jonathan stayed on for a few more days in order to tie up a lot of loose ends.

Morton and the staff, who would have to look for other jobs, also agreed to stay on to help them until the last moment.

Meanwhile the division of furniture between the four siblings had to be continued if they were to clear the house in time. By now they were working their way through the first-floor bedrooms.

"God, will it never end? I can't believe this is happening," Jonathan remarked, flopping across the foot of Cathy's bed after another long day of choosing and listing and labelling.

She leaned back against the pillows, wearing a long red T-shirt that doubled as a nightdress. "I can't stop thinking about Giles," she said, unwinding her hair which had been in a knot on the top of her head all day. "How are we going to get him out of this jam, Jonno? Ernest and the others are obviously trying to cover their own tracks. It suits them to say they think Giles killed Daddy."

"Do you think Ernest did it?" Jonathan asked suddenly. "Or Norman Sheridan? I mean, we were all so frantically busy that afternoon, one of them could easily have slipped into the garden, hit Dad over the head, then pushed him into the pool and scurried away without being seen. Maybe they were afraid he was going to incriminate them over the financial dealings of the trust."

"You mean, if Giles had gone ahead and sued Daddy, his defence would have been he'd had no idea what was happening and it had all been done by Ernest and Norman?"

"Exactly. But the police obviously want a conviction, and the trouble is I lied and so did Philippa. We were trying to hide the fact that Giles was having a go at Dad that morning."

"Yes, even Philippa was protecting Giles, though God knows why. She'd no need to. The police must think it very odd."

"I know. I suppose she didn't want to cause more trouble than there already was. God, I wish none of this had ever happened! I wish Giles had just let things be." He lay back and gazed up at the ceiling, arms supporting his head. "What's to become of us all, Cathy?"

"I can't believe Giles will be convicted, Jonno. It's ludicrous. What evidence have they got for a start? No murder weapon has been found; no witness has come forward. It's all circumstantial evidence and guesswork."

"It's terribly worrying though, isn't it? Poor old Giles, he must be feeling ghastly."

"I'm sure he'll be let out on bail tomorrow."

"I hope you're right. This family's really been through it in the past couple of years, hasn't it?"

"We'll survive," Cathy said sturdily. "I think it'll be better once Daddy's funeral's over. That's what I dread most."

"Me, too. I don't think I like being an orphan."

"Oh, Jonno . . ." She reached out and gently punched him on the shoulder. "Did I tell you Jack phoned today?"

He sat up abruptly and looked at her. "What did he want? Are you . . . ?"

"No way." She shook her head and a cascade of dark silky hair swirled around her shoulders, making Jonathan think he'd like to paint her like that, emerging bronzed and sensuous-looking from a snowy nest of white linen and lace.

"Do you think I'd go back to him after he dumped me for a girl he met on a train?" she continued. "He just wanted to offer his sympathy and say how sorry he was about Dad and everything. Quite nice of him, in fact."

Jonathan flopped on to his back again. "Yes, very," he said dryly.

Archie Sykes and Laurence Vickers had become surprisingly good friends over the past three days, and after everyone had gone to bed that night, with Honor still sleeping in Philippa's room, the two men found themselves settling down in the library with a bottle of Scotch. The conversation, inevitably, turned to Giles.

"Nick and he never really got on," Laurence explained to the older man. "Giles, being the eldest son, was in line to inherit the estate, and I think the burden of expectation placed on him undermined his self-confidence from the beginning. The more he tried to please Nick, the more inadequate Nick made him feel. Though I don't think he meant to," he added quickly.

"But you don't really think Giles pushed his father off the perch, do you?"

Laurence hesitated just long enough to cause Archie's bushy eyebrows to bristle and a gleam to come into his eyes.

"You've got to remember, Giles was about to lose everything he'd been promised," said Laurence carefully. "He'd even had to spend the morning watching the others choosing furniture, all of which was supposed to go to him with the house originally." He sighed, frowning and gazing into the depths of his glass. "He's a strange chap, old Giles."

"He's only twenty-eight, isn't he?" Archie remarked. "Yet he strikes me as being somewhat older."

Laurence nodded, his normally saturnine face relaxing into a smile. "He's actually fifteen going on fifty, in my opinion. Terribly jealous of his father, too."

"Whatever for?" Archie looked astonished.

"For being everything Giles isn't. You have to admit, whether you liked Nick or not, he had charm, good looks, intelligence, and appeared to be very successful. And, as if that wasn't enough, he married a delightful young woman and they were starting a new life together, even expecting a baby. It was almost too good to be true. And too much for Giles to compete with."

Archie sucked in his lower lip, chewing it thoughtfully.

"Between you and me, Honor never trusted Nick. When she heard Giles was going to sue him over money and property, she wasn't at all surprised."

"Elizabeth didn't approve of litigation, neither did Cathy and Jonathan. Actually, I'm not sure even Giles would have gone ahead if it hadn't been for Margaret," Laurence added, lowering his voice. "She's the one who really wanted it all."

"Pity they've had no children. That might calm her down."

Laurence gave Archie a knowing look. "I have a feeling the big hand's stuck at six o'clock."

"What's that? Oh! I see." He looked faintly embarrassed.

They sipped their drinks in silence.

"Elizabeth's not acquisitive like Margaret, is she?" Archie remarked approvingly a few minutes later. "You're a lucky man. I think she's a great girl."

"I know I'm lucky. She's quite bright, you know. More than I realized when we first got married. I only hope I don't bore her to death." He gave a self-deprecating smile.

"Nonsense, man!" Archie said briskly. "At least she's not one of those bloody women's-libbers. Can't stand all that rubbish."

On doctor's orders Philippa did not attend court the following morning when Giles was charged.

"Don't put yourself through anything you don't have to," he warned her as he took her blood pressure. "Apart from anything else, you've had a severe shock and need all the rest you can get, for the baby's sake."

So Philippa, with Honor for company, remained in bed while the others drove into Malmesbury, taking their places in the public gallery at the local courtroom and watching as Giles, white and shaking, was formally charged with the murder of his father. The only questions he was required to answer were to confirm his name and address. Bail was granted in a cut and dried manner and it was all over.

Out in the street a few minutes later, they all felt confused and bewildered by the speed with which it had happened, coupled with a sense of unreality that it had happened at all. The presence of photographers and TV crews added to their agitation.

"Get into my car quickly," Laurence instructed his bemused brother-in-law who was clinging to Margaret's arm looking utterly lost. Elizabeth had stayed at Wingfield Court with the children and so the three of them set off for home, followed by Archie and Jonathan who had been given a lift by Cathy.

"How are you feeling?" Margaret kept asking, looking at her husband worriedly. He seemed to have aged ten years in the past few days. His hands hung limply between his knees and his shoulders sagged dejectedly.

He didn't answer but instead stared ahead of him with unseeing eyes. My father's dead, he thought to himself, and yet the heavy burden of unhappiness he'd always borne hadn't gone away. It still weighed in his chest like a cold heavy stone and there was still a dark shadow lurking at his shoulder. Would he ever be free of the dominant, powerful, charismatic parent of whom he'd been in fear and awe ever since he could remember?

The funeral was on Tuesday. Maybe seeing the coffin lowered into the ground would finally be the end of his misery but somehow he doubted it. Nick Driver wasn't the sort of person to allow himself to be easily forgotten.

For the third time in nearly two years the village church was crowded with people attending a service for a member of the Driver family.

"Why did I say I'd do a reading?" said Jonathan, blowing his nose on a large white handkerchief as he and Cathy had a discreet gin and tonic before joining the others to go to St Mark's.

"Oh, God, Jonno!" she exclaimed, half crying, half giggling with nervous hysteria. "I'm going to be reminded of Mummy's funeral all over again and I don't think I can bear it."

"Me, too."

Cathy wailed, "I've got to have another drink. I'll never cope at this rate." Her colourful Bohemian chic style of dressing had been replaced today by long dark clothes and she wore a black chiffon scarf on her head, tied gypsy fashion, with her hair cascading down her back.

Jonathan refilled their glasses. "There you go. Oh, Christ. Can't someone else do the reading?" His mouth was trembling.

"Well, Giles can't, under the circumstances."

"I suppose not. Everyone's going to be looking at him as it is."

"And remembering Dad and Philippa's wedding . . . And Mummy's funeral."

"Stop it, Cathy!" Jonathan took a long swig of his drink. "You don't suppose this family's cursed, do you?"

"Of course not," she scolded and immediately hiccuped.

"Cathy!" They clung to each other, hysteria rising.

Jonathan was the first to recover. "Listen, we must pull ourselves together or everyone will know we're drunk."

She wiped her eyes, knowing if they looked at one other it would set them off again.

The family had gathered in the front drive, ready to walk the short distance to the church. Philippa, in a simple black maternity suit and with a length of black lace covering her blonde hair, stood with her parents. She looked composed but dazed, as if she didn't really know what was happening.

By contrast Elizabeth's face was blotchy and wretched, her eyes red-rimmed and hands shaking. The black dress she'd hurriedly bought in Malmesbury the previous day didn't suit her and she knew it. She was also worried about having to leave the children in the care of Morton and the cook although Lawrence had assured her they'd be perfectly all right.

When the church bells began to toll their melancholy message, echoing dismally across the fields, the family set off, slowly and reluctantly, aware that they were taking the very route, in reverse, that Nick and Philippa had taken less than a year ago, after their marriage.

Insulated from the immediate pain of the occasion by their intake of alcohol, Cathy and Jonathan brought up the rear, feeling as if they were floating and at moments almost forgetting why they were there at all.

It seemed unbelievable that the vibrant Nick Driver was dead and now lay, forever still, in an oak box covered in flowers. The congregation, consisting of people from the village, friends and business associates from London as well as family, all held their memories of the suave millionaire. To those nearest him he was a beloved father and husband, generous, kind, and a source of stability until recent months. In the business world he had a reputation for being reckless, stubborn, and lacking the acumen of his late father and grandfather. But there were others, mostly women, who remembered him with friendly indulgence, considering him an eternal adolescent propelled by a high-wattage charge of testosterone.

A minute at a time, Philippa thought fiercely. That was the only way she could keep going. To think any further ahead would be to plunge head first into a black ravine and be forever swallowed up by despair. But a minute at a time she could cope with. She felt the baby, Nick's baby, kick vigorously inside her, and the sorrow that filled her at that moment was for the child who would never know his father.

The choir was singing "I Vow To Thee My Country", but Giles's sobs could be heard throughout the church; the one who had hated Nick most overcome by grief . . . or, some thought, guilt. Margaret was gripping his arm as if willing him to pull himself together but Giles had abandoned himself to infantile distress and was beyond comforting.

At last it was over and Nick was lowered into the ground, earth scattered on his coffin by Philippa and his children. Earth to earth, ashes to ashes . . . a minute at a time.

Nick Driver had made a new will just before his marriage to Philippa. In it he stated he wished her to have everything that belonged to him personally, including his share of the family trust as well as Wingfield Court.

CHAPTER FOURTEEN

"I'm going to hate him," Cathy declared. "I know I am. He's going to fill the place with hi-tech stuff, there'll be lines of coke on the mantelpiece and heroin on the sideboard. Oh, I wish . . . how I wish, Jonno, we hadn't said we'd stay to clear up all the loose ends here."

"I wonder if he's gay?" her brother mused.

They were expecting Matt Blade to move in to Wingfield Court the following day.

"Who cares if he's straight, gay or prefers sheep? I know I'm being childish but I really hate the thought of this place being turned into some sort of headquarters for a rock band. Imagine . . . our beautiful dining room, a recording studio."

Jonathan nodded. "I bet he's bought this place because it'll make a good setting for photo opportunities. In no time we'll be seeing a six-page spread in *Hello!* of 'Matt Blade in his magnificent new home'."

"Yuk! And I bet he'll put in sunken baths, a jacuzzi, a sauna, and a chrome and mirror glass cocktail bar! And a gymnasium in the wine cellar so he can keep his revolting muscles bulging."

"Definitely not my cup of Lapsang Souchong," Jonathan agreed with a glimmer of his accustomed spark. "Cheer up, sweetheart. Only another three or four days and we'll be back in London."

The house had already been stripped, its furniture and artefacts taken away in four very large removal vans, one destined for Elizabeth, another for Giles, and the contents of the other two going into storage until Cathy found a place of her own and Jonathan decided what to do with his share.

As they moved around the desolate rooms which echoed emptily, they couldn't help recalling that their father had sat by that fireplace or gazed at the view out of that window. Then, experiencing the swings of mood that follow the death of someone close, they would blaspheme against God for allowing his death to happen. Almost as quickly Cathy would look at Jonathan and exclaim: "Oh, we shouldn't be talking like this. Mummy always said we should never take the Lord's name in vain. We'll be punished."

Then Jonathan's rage at the unfairness of it all would subside and he'd look crushed and say, "You're right, Cathy. But why did it have to happen? Why did we have to lose both our parents?"

"So this means Philippa wins," Margaret declared when she was told the contents of Nick's will. She glared at Barnard Alexander as if it was all his fault. "She gets Nick's share of the trust *and* the money from the sale of Wingfield Court. I think we should sue her."

Barnard, looking more like a retired pugilist than ever today, gave her a scathing glance. He leaned forward, elbows on his desk, massive shoulders hunched.

"By playing into the hands of the Crown Prosecution Service when Giles is tried for the murder of Nick Driver?" His voice rumbled in his chest. "If you sue Philippa Driver," he continued, "it will be tantamount to admitting Giles had a grudge against his father for secretly purchasing Wingfield Court and then selling it. That will be looked upon as adequate motive for murder."

He paused, ruddy face deadly serious. "Giles's defence must be that there was no quarrel between him and his father. He had no motive for murdering him. In fact, he was grateful to his father for letting him and his siblings share the contents of the house. That is the line we have to take. There must be no talk of suing anyone."

Giles sat in silence, resting his elbows on his spread knees and gazing down at the carpet in Barnard's office, as if he had no interest in what was happening. The fight had gone out of him and Margaret's frustration at losing out on the inheritance just made him want to get away somewhere peaceful where he'd never be nagged again.

"It would be better," Barnard pointed out, "if we looked for reasons why Giles wanted his father alive, rather than dead."

Margaret's expression was tight-lipped and stubborn. "Then can we sue Philippa after Giles has been acquitted?"

Giles raised his head suddenly. "Drop it. Margaret. We don't want any more trouble in the family. The poor woman's having a baby at any minute, she's lost her husband, and the least we can do is to leave her alone and let her get on with her life. If Dad's left his share of the trust to her and she gets the money from the sale of Wingfield Court, so be it."

"Well! I must say, you've changed your tune."

Barnard Alexander looked up sharply. Something in the way Margaret spoke sent a chill down his spine. He glanced at Giles but he'd gone back to studying the carpet again, his expression blank, his eyes lifeless.

"I strongly suggest," Barnard said heavily, "that you give up any notion of trying to lay claim to the house or anything else."

But Margaret was not going to give up without a fight. "Nick bought the house illegally," she protested.

The solicitor looked her straight in the eye, his voice deeper than ever. "I should warn you that if we're to secure an acquittal, you must allow yourself to be advised by me."

For a moment Margaret wondered if she'd been dreaming. She rolled on to her back. But the racking sobs were real, and they were coming from Giles. She switched on the light. He was curled up in a foetal position, turned away from her. His shoulders shook as he tried to jam his fist into his mouth.

"Giles?"

There was no answer but his weeping grew louder as if he felt no further need to hide his feelings.

"Giles . . . what is it?" she asked, alarmed. It was the first time he'd ever shown his emotions in front of her and Margaret felt shocked. She also had a slight sense of relief; if he could acknowledge his misery, grief, or whatever was causing him to be distraught at the moment, he might also be able to acknowledge his impotence and get something done about it.

"What's the matter, darling?"

Giles turned, lying flat on his back, and avoided looking at her. Instead, his swollen eyes gazed up at the pink ceiling, and his mouth trembled.

"I never got to say goodbye," he said hoarsely. "And I was so nasty to Dad that day. We parted in such anger and now . . ." A sob rose from his chest, he couldn't continue.

Margaret patted his shoulder sympathetically, her maternal instincts for this man-child aroused.

"You can't be blamed for wanting to defend what was rightfully yours. He stole from you, Giles."

"But he was my father. I-I loved him. And now he's gone . . . and-and I'll never get to say I'm sorry."

Margaret was at a loss for words. She couldn't believe what she was hearing but Giles's distress was so genuine, she hadn't the heart to tell him to stop being ridiculous. Sorry? Why should he be sorry when it was Nick who'd wounded them? All of them. His four children, herself and Laurence. He'd cut the ground from under their feet. Even now he seemed to be reaching out from beyond the grave to destroy Giles by having him accused of murder. Sorrow? Margaret took a deep breath and decided the strain of the pending trial was making her husband hysterical.

"It'll be all right, darling. You'll get off," she told him cheerily. "You'll see. The QC Barnard's got for you has a wonderful success rate. I know that for a fact, I've been asking around. He'll get you acquitted."

"I don't care about the trial," he said. "To hell with the trial! I just wish I could tell Dad I'm sorry." The tears were running down his cheeks from the outside edges of his eyes, wetting the pillow. "And now it's too late. My mother always said you should never let the sun go down on your anger, but I did. I did." He rocked his head from side to side in despair.

"Oh, Giles." Feeling ill-equipped to deal with this new side to her husband, she simply didn't know how to handle the situation. "Can I get you anything?" she asked. "A glass of water? Or a cup of tea, perhaps?"

"No . . . no . . . I just wish I could turn the clock back." He paused then added poignantly, "I wish my father had loved me."

"Of course he loved you," Margaret responded staunchly. "You were his son and heir."

"But he never thought I was good enough. He expected so much from me . . . and I know I never came up to expectation. He thought I was hopeless. And weak. And a failure. And then he died, thinking I was vindictive . . ."

"Now, come along, Giles. Stop wallowing in self-pity," she said briskly. "Your father behaved badly, you merely responded. In your shoes," she continued, "he'd have done exactly the same, so stop blaming yourself." She didn't want Giles blaming her either. Clambering out of bed, she announced she was going to make him some Ovaltine. "That always helps you get to sleep, doesn't it?" she added kindly.

Philippa, living now in the Eaton Square flat, found it comforting to be back in the familiarity of London. Her friends were all here, and her colleagues from Christie's, and in those moments of calm between the paroxysms of grief that overwhelmed her several times a day it was almost as if she'd never been away.

She'd begged Archie and Honor to stay with her in the comfortable three-bedroomed apartment, at least until she'd had the baby. They didn't need much persuasion.

"I suppose this is what you'd call modern minimalism," Archie remarked when they arrived, looking around the glittering white living room. "I can't say it's much to my taste."

Privately Honor agreed but she didn't want to upset Philippa. Instead she said diplomatically: "Will you be making this your permanent home now, darling?"

"No, Ma. It will do for the moment but can you imagine bringing up a toddler in a place like this?" She pointed to the white silk sofas and chairs.

"What I plan to do," she continued, drawing the wild silk curtains and switching on the lights, to shut out the melancholy twilight of a London evening, "is buy a house in the country. Not Woodlands, that's probably sold by now. I shall never understand why Nick didn't even put down a deposit on it. Malmesbury is too far away in any case, and I never had time to make friends or put down roots there. I thought I'd buy a nice medium-sized house in Kent and you could both move in with me. What do you say?"

Honor gave a little gasp and her hand flew to her mouth. Archie reached for his handkerchief and trumpeted on his nose, touched by her offer.

"You see," Philippa continued wistfully, "there isn't a financial problem any more. We can all live in comfort, thanks to Nick. No more housework, Ma, or washing and ironing. And Daddy needn't dig the garden or chop wood . . ."

"Keeps me fit," Archie growled.

"We couldn't, darling, we really couldn't," Honor protested gently. "It wouldn't be right. You have your own life to live, and please God, you won't be alone forever. The last thing you need is your ancient parents hanging around your neck like a millstone."

"Your mother's right, m'dear. Very sweet of you and all that but we couldn't possibly."

"But I need you both," Philippa pleaded. "I'm going to have to bring up this baby on my own, and it's going to be a long time before I want to get involved in another relationship. I loved Nick more than anything. . ." Her voice broke. She continued, when she could speak again, "If you won't actually live with me, will you consider sharing a house? Dividing a place so we each have our own quarters?"

Suddenly Archie beamed. Now the scheme seemed possible.

"That would be an idea," he conceded.

"A granny flat?" Honor asked, allowing herself a tiny window of hope because she'd like nothing better than to be with Philippa and her baby.

"A bit more than that, I'd want you to think of it as your home too."

Archie turned to Honor, "It will be like living in those nice army quarters we used to have."

For the first time since Nick's death, Philippa laughed.

"I tell you what, Dad, I think we'll keep Morton on. He's looking for a job and think what a great batman he'd make! He'd love it, too. And as he's getting on, it wouldn't be nearly such hard work as running Wingfield Court."

Cautiously, because it seemed too good to be true, Archie and Honor agreed it was a wonderful idea. They wouldn't intrude on her private life, they assured Philippa, and of course they'd always be on hand for baby sitting.

"It'll be a new start for us all," she said softly, trying to sound cheerful. There were moments when she actually did feel cheerful, those moments when her mind played funny tricks, making her forget Nick had gone. Something would happen and she'd think: Oh, I must tell Nick. Sometimes the sound of the key in the lock would make her heart leap and she'd think, Good, he's home. Worst of all was when she thought she saw him in the street or a shop and would rush forward, convinced it was Nick, only to be met with crushing disappointment when she saw it was a stranger she'd pursued.

Meanwhile none of them mentioned Giles. Philippa had tried to erase him from her mind; bring down a shutter and pretend he didn't exist, hadn't killed his father, didn't belong to the Driver family. Archie and

Honor entered into this charade for the time being, thanking God that if they couldn't forget or forgive what had happened, at least Philippa seemed to have blocked her step-son from her thoughts. Instead she was concentrating on the baby's arrival by turning the third bedroom into a nursery, filling it with hand-painted furniture, armfuls of soft toy animals and drawerfuls of clothes.

"But she can't refuse to acknowledge Giles's existence forever." Honor pointed out worriedly. "What happens if he gets off?"

"We'll cross that bridge when we get to it," Archie advised. "At the moment, nature is doing its work by shutting out the worst of the memories."

Cathy, clearing out a cupboard under the stairs, was suddenly aware of someone standing in the middle of the hall. She emerged, blinking from the semi-darkness, cobwebs in her hair and a pair of ancient tennis racquets in her hand.

"Can I help you?" she asked, seeing the tall figure of a man in jeans and Tee-shirt standing with his back to the light. "Have you come about the boiler? I don't know what's wrong with it but it would choose today of all days to go wrong."

"Oh, really?"

She looked closer. He was grinning and his eyes were dancing with amusement. "Oh, God! You must be Matt Blade," she groaned. "Trust me to open my mouth only to insert my feet. Yes, well, there's no hot water, I'm afraid, so it'll be a case of cold baths unless they come to fix it."

"That's OK." He stood with his hands in his pockets and looked around. "I'm going to have to buy a lot of furniture, aren't I? I'd no idea the rooms were so large."

"Didn't you have them measured?" She felt flustered that he'd sneaked up on them when they weren't expecting him until the afternoon. "Where's your helicopter?"

Matt laughed. "I only use one when I'm pushed for time. I drove up here today."

"Oh."

He strolled around the empty hall, hands in pockets, looking rather lost. "You've lived here all your life, I gather?" he asked conversationally.

"I was born here. We all were. The house has been in the family for over sixty years."

Matt looked at her intently. "You must be sad to leave," he asked, suddenly concerned. "What a tough time you're having. I was so sorry to hear about your father . . ." His voice trailed off, uncertain whether he should continue.

"Yes, and now my brother's been wrongly accused of killing him." Cathy shook her head. "It's devastating." Her eyes were over-bright as she turned back to the cupboard. "Make yourself at home. It *is* your home now," she added before disappearing into the darkness among the cobwebs again.

"Hi-ya," Jonathan called out, coming down the stairs at that moment.

Matt looked up, grinning in a friendly fashion. "Hi, you must be Jonathan Driver?"

"Correct." They shook hands. "Welcome to the old pile. I hope you'll be happy here."

"I'm sure I will, it's exactly what I was looking for. How's the clearing up going? I gather you and your sister have endless cupboards to empty."

"Tell me about it," Jonathan replied wearily. "I've just discovered my old toy box in the attic and thousands of copies of *Boys' Own*."

"Lucky you!" Matt laughed. "I don't have this problem because I'm moving from a small rented flat in Islington where I've hardly anything." He looked through the doors of the various empty rooms beyond. "I'm going to be rattling around in this place, aren't I?"

"Are you going to be living here on your own?"

"Yes, but the boys in the group will be staying from time to time while we try out new songs and record the latest album."

Cathy emerged from the cupboard again, carrying a pair of rusty skates and an old toboggan.

"Look what I've found," she exclaimed in delight. "Remember this, Jonno?" She held out the toboggan. "Remember how we slid down the hill when we were small? There was always snow when we were young, wasn't there? And now we haven't had a white Christmas for yonks."

"Selective memories," Matt remarked affably to no one in particular.

"Oh, I don't know," Cathy said. "I don't only remember

the good times. I remember all the bad times, too. Though there weren't many of them. We were a very happy family until recently."

He smiled. "I meant, childhood memories are much more vivid and idyllic than events that happened last week."

"You're right," Jonathan nodded in agreement. "Looking back, summers were always hot and sunny and Christmases were white. There were always hot buttered crumpets and chocolate biscuits for tea, and my mother always smelled of lavender. Whenever I smell lavender now I'm reminded of her."

"How strange. It always reminds me of my mother, too," Matt said thoughtfully.

In order to hide how emotional these memories made him feel, Jonathan rejoined; "Which of course is fine if you want to smell like a linen cupboard."

The rest of the Young Blades arrived a few minutes later in a convoy of assorted cars which they cheerfully abandoned all around the drive. Matt went out to greet them while Cathy and Jonathan hung around, not wanting to appear nosy yet curious to see what they looked like in real life as opposed to performing on television. They heard Matt laughingly welcoming them to "this stately pile", which was followed by much jesting when they spotted the family crest of the Earls of Drysdale over the front door.

"Hey, you're the lord of the manor now," one of the group teased Matt loudly. "Do we have to bow when we see you?"

"And call you sir?"

Amid more laughter and back-slapping Matt led them into the hall and introduced them to Cathy and Jonathan in his easy and relaxed way.

"This is Jimmy Smart, he's on keyboards, and Ozzie Howe, second guitarist. Travis Moore, our drummer and percussionist, and Richie Dent, bass player."

Laughing, Cathy asked. "So what do *you* do?"

"I write the music and play the guitar," Matt replied modestly, as if it was no big deal.

"He's also lead vocalist," added Travis, looking curiously at Cathy and Jonathan. He hadn't much use for what he called poncey aristocrats. Although Cathy was dressed like a tinker, she had an air of authority that annoyed him. "What do *you* do?" he added.

"I'm a student," she replied, smiling disarmingly. "and my brother's an artist."

"Come and look around," Matt invited the boys. "It's a great place."

They followed him from room to room, footsteps echoing on the bare polished floors.

"I'd like to keep this house much as it was when I first saw it," Cathy heard Matt explain. "Classic English furniture, and I like the soft colours of the decorations."

Cathy caught Jonathan's eye and signalled her approval.

"At least he's got good taste," she whispered, heading back to the cupboard under the stairs.

Later, Matt came back into the hall to find her. "The boys have brought a picnic lunch," he said. "I hope you and Jonathan will join us. We've got masses of food and drink."

"Cool," Jonathan declared, answering for both of them.

"As it's warm we could eat out doors."

"That would be soo-pah!" Jonathan replied, putting on his fake pompous accent, "Wouldn't it. Cathy?"

". . . and for God's sake," Matt murmured to the group when they went to fetch the picnic from their cars, "choose a part of the garden that's nowhere near the swimming pool."

"Are you all right, Philippa?" Honor asked anxiously. It was two o'clock in the morning and she'd been awakened by the sound of the kitchen door closing and then a loud groan.

Philippa was standing in the middle of the living room. She was sipping from a glass of water and one of her hands was pressed to the small of her back.

"I think the baby might be coming," she said, her face white. "But it's too soon. It's not due for another four weeks. Oh, Ma, I hope it's all right!"

Honor went and put her arm around Philippa's shoulders. "How often have you had pains, darling?"

"Every ten minutes or so." She bent forward, supporting herself on the back of a chair as she was seized by another deep pang. "Why are they in my back? They're really deep and sharp," she gasped. Her forehead gleamed with sweat and she looked scared. "Oh, Ma, it's bad."

"Come and lie down," Honor coaxed. "How long have you been having these pains?"

"A couple of hours, perhaps. I thought at first I'd been sleeping at a bad angle, but now I'm sure it's the baby."

Honor became cheerfully brisk and businesslike. "That's the baby all right," she said. "I think I'll ring your gynae, just to tell him you've started. As it's your first, he might like you to get to the hospital sooner rather than later."

Philippa submitted to her mother's ministrations, allowing herself to be guided back to bed where she lay on her side, bracing herself for the next pain.

It came sooner than she'd expected, ripping through her with savage ferocity. She clamped her hand over her mouth, willing herself to stay calm. It was going to be all right. It had to be. This was Nick's baby, and if she lost it she'd have nothing of him left. This was her last link with him, there'd never be another one. When the pain subsided, she called to Honor.

"Ma, tell Daddy I've got to get to the hospital now," she said breathlessly. "I can't risk waiting any longer. He can drive me."

"Your father's going to be far too excited to drive when he's about to become a grandfather," Honor protested. "I've had a word with Mr Snyder. He's arranging for an ambulance to pick you up right away and he'll meet you at the Portland Hospital."

Philippa looked alarmed. "You'll come with me, won't you? I don't have to go on my own?"

"Try keeping us away, darling," Honer replied spiritedly. "Your father's getting dressed and I'll be ready in a couple of jiffs. This baby's going to get the biggest welcome ever."

Another pain shot through Philippa, deeper and more wrenching than the last.

"They're coming faster . . ." she said in a frightened voice. She was crying now, not so much from the pain as from terror that she might be losing the baby. "Will it be all right?" she kept asking. "It's too soon." She was sweating profusely and her mother gripped her hand comfortingly.

"Babies have a habit of coming when they want to," Honor assured her sturdily. "It will be fine, you'll see. In a few hours you'll be cuddling your little one and will even have forgotten how much it hurt."

Within ten minutes an ambulance had arrived, and then they were on their way to the Portland. The pains were coming faster still and Archie looked at Honor in alarm.

"Will we get there in time?" he whispered, shaken as Philippa let out another scream. "It's not usually like this, is it?"

She patted his hand. "It's all right, Archie. You're of the generation when fathers didn't attend the birth, but this is quite normal."

"It is?" He looked appalled. "Was it like this with you?"

"Yes, dear. It was."

He sat in silence for the rest of the journey, watching Philippa with an anxious expression.

"Soon have you there," the paramedic assured her. "Just relax, do the breathing exercises you were taught and don't fight the contractions."

As soon as they arrived, she was whisked up to the maternity floor in a wheelchair, her parents following.

"It's all right, darling. You're in good hands now and Daddy and I will stay with you all the time, if you want us to." Honor assured her as she squeezed her hand.

Archie looked aghast at this last remark, but mumbled; "Of course. That's right."

Her room was small and neat and comfortable. Within minutes Philippa was lying on the bed, being examined by her gynaecologist, Mr Snyder, while her parents sat in the waiting area. The gynaecologist was an attractive man in his forties, who had a charmingly teasing way of treating his patients, all of whom adored him.

"Right, Philippa," he said, smiling. "You've been having a nice rest, now you're going to have to work. Can't have you lazing in bed, can we?"

She gave him a watery smile.

"You're nearly fully dilated," he continued, "so it won't be long. Then I want you to start pushing boulders."

She giggled feebly before another wave of agony rendered her speechless.

"Excellent," he said.

Honor came back into the room a few minutes later to find her daughter sobbing as if her heart would break.

"I want Nick," she wept, between the pains. "I want him here."

Honor stroked her forehead and took her hand. "I know, sweetheart, and I'm sure he is here, watching over you and the baby. You'll be all right, my darling."

The searing pangs were coming every minute now, taking her breath away, making her feel sick. Philippa closed her eyes, trying to pretend Nick was beside her and it was his hand she held. She couldn't fight the pain any more; she hadn't even the heart to try. She just let it wash over her, surrendering her racked body to the torture. Without Nick's loving support, she wasn't even sure if she cared whether she lived or died.

Elizabeth was giving Dominic, Tamsin and Jasper breakfast in the kitchen the next morning when the phone rang. It was Cathy.

"How's it going?" Elizabeth asked immediately. "Has Matt Blade or whatever he's called moved in yet?"

"Yes, he's here, rehearsing some new songs. He's camping out with the boys in the band as he's got practically no furniture." Cathy sounded bright and happy.

"Is he nice? How are you all getting on? It must be odd to have the house full of strangers."

"He's fine. They all are. As the weather's nice we're having picnics in the garden, and there's music all the time, and . . . well, it's great. Listen, Lizzie, I haven't phoned to tell you about the Young Blades — I want to know how you feel about having a new half-brother?"

"*What?* A new . . . you mean, Philippa's had the baby?"

"Yes. In the middle of the night and four weeks premature, but he's fine. Apparently he weighed nearly six pounds. She's OK, too."

"Did she phone you herself?"

"No. Dear old Sir Archie rang a few minutes ago. He'll probably ring you, too. He's so excited he said he doesn't know what to do with himself. Apparently the baby looks exactly like Philippa, though I don't know how you can tell — all babies look the same to me. He's to be called Andrew Nicholas."

Elizabeth absorbed all this in silent wonder. A half-brother to the rest of them yet eighteen months younger than Jasper.

"Did she have a bad time? It was very sudden, wasn't it?"

"I don't know about a bad time. Archie didn't go into the gory details but it was very quick apparently. That sounds all right, doesn't it? You're the expert, having had three."

There was a pause and Elizabeth chuckled. "Nearly four, but don't tell the whole world yet."

"Lizzie!" Cathy gave a shriek. "Truly? My God . . . What does Laurence say?"

"He's thrilled. Four sort of evens it up, especially if we have another little girl. Anyway, it's not due until next spring."

"I can tell Jonno, can't I?"

"Yes, of course. Listen, I must go. Dominic's just knocked over a packet of Cornflakes and the dogs are going mad. Thanks for calling. Talk to you soon, love. 'Bye." Elizabeth replaced the receiver and started shooing the dogs into the garden.

"Do be careful with those Coco Pops, Dominic," she chided, as he waved another carton of cereal about. "You'll have the rest on the floor in a minute."

"What were you talking about? Who's had a baby?" he asked.

"We have!" Tamsin gurgled happily, pointing to Jasper. "But he's a big baby, not a teensy-weensy one."

Dominic turned on her. "I know that, silly! But who *else* has had a baby?"

"Philippa had a baby boy last night," Elizabeth explained.

"Wow!" Dominic's eyes were wide. "He must be excited 'cos this is the first day of his life."

Her expression softened and she looked at him fondly. "I'm sure he's thrilled."

"Why can't we have a new baby? Jasper's so *old*."

Elizabeth laughed. "Poor Jasper! Pensioned off at one and a half!" She stooped to kiss the crown of her son's golden head. "You'd better have a word with Daddy then," she added lightly.

"What's he got to do with it?"

"Or we could always have new puppies," Tamsin suggested, helpfully.

When Laurence came home that evening, cheerful and filled with a new sense of purpose in life since he'd got a job, Elizabeth told him about Andrew Nicholas.

"Imagine Jasper having an uncle who's younger than he is," she laughed as they sat in the den having a drink before she dished up the dinner.

Laurence looked amused but spoke compassionately. "It's sad that he'll never know his father, though."

"I'll tell him all about Dad when he's older," Elizabeth said softly. "He was a wonderful father when we were small . . ." Her voice broke from the pain she still felt.

"Any news from Giles?"

Elizabeth shook her head. "Don't forget we've all got a meeting with Sean on Wednesday to hear about the exact state of the trust fund."

"I thought Barnard Alexander was in charge of the case?"

"He's defending Giles in the criminal court, but Sean's still enquiring into where the money's gone. We've got to know where we stand." She reached out and took her husband's hand. "You may find yourself having to support a penniless wife," she said, half jokingly. Then she pulled off the scrunchy that always held her fair hair in a ponytail and ran her hands through her hair, transforming herself from an overgrown schoolgirl into a seductive woman.

Laurence looked squarely at her. "Then I will," he said positively. "I can always get a better job with more pay."

"There'll be six of us when the new baby arrives," she reminded him, resting her head on his shoulder. "D'you think we'll manage?"

"Of course we will." He turned and kissed her firmly on the lips. "I love you, Liz. I haven't always been the greatest husband but I've never stopped loving you, you know."

Her face was radiant as she looked back at him. "I know, and I've been prickly, especially when Dad married Philippa. I felt so hurt . . . for Mummy's sake, more than my own. It was Tamsin's accident that made me realize how lucky we were to have each other and the children."

"I know." Laurence's voice was tender. "We're going to be all right now, though, aren't we? Money or no money?"

"We certainly are," she replied staunchly.

Barnard Alexander, preparing the file for the QC they'd appointed to defend Giles when his case was heard in the criminal courts, was finding it increasingly difficult to quash a nasty suspicion that in fact his client might be guilty.

The problem was, if there was no hard evidence to prove his guilt, there was equally no evidence whatsoever to prove his innocence.

Like a short-sighted bear, pawing the papers in front of him, Barnard went over the facts again and again, reading the statements provided by everyone who had been at Wingfield Court that fatal afternoon. One thing struck him forcibly.

Surely voices raised in anger, before Nick was brutally struck on the back of the head, would have been heard by someone in the house? Unless Nick had been caught by surprise it meant only one thing: whoever had killed him was known to him.

And why had Margaret made that remark to Giles in Barnard's office: "I must say, you've changed your tune"?

He leaned back in his chair, closing his eyes and folding his hands over his rotund stomach as he tried to concentrate on this point. Margaret couldn't have killed Nick because both Elizabeth Vickers and Cathy Driver had sworn she'd never left them while they counted the china together. But she could have persuaded Giles to. She was the dominant one. The ambitious one. The one who'd wanted Giles to sue his father. The one who'd seemed most angry at the disposal of Wingfield Court. He also got the impression the others didn't like her much. They were a strange couple, Giles and Margaret. He so weak and she so strong. But even at her bidding, would he have gone so far as to . . .

Of course they wouldn't have known the contents of Nick's will at that time. This brought Barnard to further intriguing speculation. If Nick hadn't sold the house, could it have remained in his widow's possession as he'd bought it illegally in the first place? Or would Giles have had a case against his step-mother? This was, of course, hypothetical now but such legal problems fascinated him.

Reaching for the phone, he decided he'd ring Giles to make an appointment to see him. He was at home these days, having taken a six-month sabbatical from Bartwell's. Barnard hoped Margaret wouldn't answer.

When he heard her sharp voice saying "Hello?" in typically abrupt manner, his heart sank.

"Good morning," he rumbled, leaning back in his chair again. "Barnard Alexander here. May I speak to Giles, please?"

"He's busy, can't I help?" she asked in a voice which brooked no denial.

"I have to talk to him personally about a few points that have arisen," the lawyer said firmly.

"He's very tied up at the moment." Her reluctance to allow him speak to Giles was obvious. "He's on the other phone. I can take a message."

"I need to speak to him myself, I'm afraid."

"Oh, all right," Margaret said ungraciously. She sounded, he thought, in an even more aggressive mood than usual.

It was several minutes before Giles came to the phone and when he did, he too sounded rattled.

"How are you doing?" Barnard asked.

Giles sighed gustily. "Philippa had a baby. A boy."

"And are they both OK?"

"Oh, yes." He sounded, Barnard thought, both weary and depressed. "You should send her flowers," he suggested.

"Flowers? Why? That woman's caused nothing but trouble since she came into the family."

"Think about it, Giles," Barnard grunted firmly. "You've got to appear friendly towards her. Showing hostility will go badly against you when you're in the witness box. And go to a proper florist — don't get them off a street seller. Keep the receipt. Write something nice on a card. Keep a copy of that, too. Remember, you were on *good* terms with both Philippa and your father when he died."

"I don't see that it matters." Giles sounded resigned.

"I'm telling you, it does. Trust me, I'm a lawyer."

When he'd finished talking to Giles, Barnard hauled himself to his surprisingly small feet and started lumbering around his office, realizing that this was going to be a challenging case for both himself and John Waddington-Cairns, QC. It was almost as if Giles Driver wanted to be found guilty of murder.

Philippa lay back in her hospital bed, nursing her baby, unable to take her eyes off his exquisite, small face. It was a revelation to her that this new little being would so completely fill her horizon and bring her such happiness. Nick would have been so proud, she reflected, stroking the tiny hands, searching for a likeness in the shape of the mouth or the colour of the eyes, but seeing only a reflection of herself.

"My baby," she whispered, holding him close, already loving him more than she'd thought possible.

The nurse came into her room with a large arrangement of roses in a basket.

"You could start a florist's shop!" she joked, placing the basket on the floor by the window and handing the card to Philippa. For the past two days, dozens of bouquets had arrived, from her parents, her and Nick's friends, Cathy and Jonathan, Elizabeth and Laurence, and her old colleagues at Christie's. Roses and phlox mingled with peonies and sweet peas. Every flat surface was crammed with vases and baskets. Now they were taking up floor space, too.

"Thank you," she said to the nurse. "I'm feeling very spoilt. People have been incredibly kind." Then she opened the card, recoiling as she recognized Giles's handwriting.

He'd written a brief. "Congratulations. Giles and Margaret".

"Please take these away," she said. "I don't want them. Send them back." She was tearing the card into little pieces. "Get them out of here."

Suddenly she was sobbing, wild with grief at the loss of her lover, her friend, her husband, the father of her baby.

The last thing she wanted was flowers from the man accused of his murder.

Elizabeth and Laurence arrived a few minutes later to find Philippa still crying, the baby clutched in her arms, his head tucked under her chin. She was rocking backwards and forwards, tears sliding down her cheeks and wetting Andrew's tiny head.

At that moment, any last vestiges of animosity Elizabeth had felt towards her step-mother drained away in a flood of pity for this young widow and her fatherless baby.

"Oh, Philippa." Elizabeth put her arms around them, and then tenderly stroked Andrew's back. "What a beautiful baby."

Laurence had moved round to the other side of the bed. With newfound confidence he took Philippa's hand, gripping it firmly in both of his.

"You'll be all right," he said comfortingly.

She looked at them both gratefully. "I was OK until I got some flowers and a card from Giles . . . how *could* he send me flowers under the circumstances?"

Elizabeth and Laurence exchanged looks.

"I can understand how you feel," he said gently, "but although the police have charged him, he hasn't been found guilty, has he?"

"And I really don't believe he killed Daddy," Elizabeth added earnestly. "But I do realize what a shock it must have been, hearing from him like that."

"How else did Nick die?" Philippa queried, wiping away her tears and looking at them with stricken eyes. "*Someone* killed him and Giles was the only one with a vendetta against him."

Elizabeth, reluctant to agree, said nothing. "You've been through so much," she remarked instead. "When are they going to allow you home?"

"I'm going back to the flat tomorrow." Philippa, calmer now, laid Andrew on her lap, wrapping his shawl around him. "Would you like to hold him?" she asked Elizabeth.

"May I?" She gathered the baby into her arms. "Precious little one," she crooned, rocking him gently. "Isn't he adorable?" She looked across Philippa's bed at Laurence and smiled at him. He smiled back, knowing what she was thinking.

Philippa intercepted the smile. "Getting broody?" she asked, teasingly.

"I *am* broody." Elizabeth grinned. "Having number four in the spring. They can be playmates," she added, kissing the top of Andrew's head.

They didn't stay much longer, sensing Philippa was tired and might find their presence a strain. They also had a meeting with Sean Chapman, which Giles and Margaret were attending too, to find out exactly where they all stood financially. But that was something they thought it better not to mention at this juncture.

Giles and Margaret had already arrived at Sean's office. Margaret was irritated because he'd insisted on waiting until Elizabeth arrived before he presented them with the details he'd assiduously researched during the previous weeks.

"I'm sorry Cathy and Jonathan can't be here today," Elizabeth apologized as she and Laurence took their seats facing Sean's desk, "but they're still doing a final clear-up at Wingfield Court."

Sean liked Elizabeth, approving of her sensible straightforward manner and lack of rancour. Addressing himself to her, he spoke briskly.

"No problem. I'll be sending a report of my findings in any case but I thought if we met today it would give you an opportunity to ask any questions that might arise."

"So what's the score?" Margaret asked tersely.

Ignoring her, Sean opened the thick file on his desk.

"First, I should explain that I've spent many hours talking to your father's accountant, Ernest Lomax. He's running scared because he knows he's heavily involved in the shenanigans that were going on between your father, Sheridan and Kingsley. All of them are liable to be charged with fraud and each is trying to blame the other while they're all blaming your father. But I believe I've been able to gather sufficient information to get a picture of exactly what's been going on."

"We've got a good case against them, then?" Margaret asked eagerly.

Giles glanced at her for a moment, looked down at the carpet again and said nothing. It was almost as if he had disengaged himself from what was going on and wanted no part of these proceedings.

"It seems that as long ago as twelve, even fifteen, years ago, your father became reckless. He was investing in frankly hare-brained schemes. Entrepreneurs obviously saw him coming. He put money into a plan to dig for emeralds in New Guinea which failed. Then he invested in a company that promised to make millions of pounds by buying a large section of ocean bed off the coast of Peru where they could harvest a type of seaweed that would allegedly cure certain types of cancer." Sean was shaking his head as he picked out random investments from a print out covering several pages. Then there was a company that persuaded him to invest in a scheme to build a hotel and sports complex, with landing strip, the lot, on an island near Madagascar. That turned out to be nothing but a swamp . . . and so on and so on."

He paused to take a deep breath. "These were gambles rather than sound investments. Andrew Kingsley continued to act as his stockbroker but he had nothing to do with these so-called deals. He also told me that your mother, Rosalind, had no idea what was going on. The trust was a discretionary one so your father was able to invest, on behalf of you all, in any way he liked. That was the fatal flaw in your grandfather's will.

"During these years he lost a great deal of money and the trust fund was becoming depleted. So that your mother wouldn't find out the family income was dwindling, your father started borrowing from the bank, starting about nine or ten years ago, to cover his losses. And this is when his stupidity — and I'm sorry to have to use that term — turned into something worse."

Elizabeth sat still and silent then reached for Laurence's hand. Margaret gave a sharp intake of breath and leaned forward.

"I'm afraid your father started on a downward spiral of trying to extricate himself, with the help of Lomax and Sheridan from the mess he was in. Fake Board meeting minutes were drawn up, false tax returns were completed, VAT that was due wasn't declared and the accounts were tampered with."

"Why?" Elizabeth asked, incredulously. "Why would Lomax and Sheridan do that? Weren't they risking their own reputations?"

Sean looked her squarely in the eye. "Shall we just say they were scared of your father? He was a powerful man in the neighbourhood. The lord of the manor, in fact. He could put good business their way . . . or not. I also believe he gave them backhanders. Your father continued to invest unwisely, though not on the grand scale of his previous fiascos, and there is no doubt he spent a lot on medical expenses during your mother's illness." Sean paused, as if even he, a tough, smart lawyer, found it difficult to talk about Nick Driver in these terms.

"When he met his present wife," he continued slowly, "he finally threw all caution to the winds and spent money like water. As you probably know."

"What we want to know is . . . what's left of the trust?" Margaret demanded.

"I'm coming to that," he said quietly. "The sale of Wingfield Court reduced his overdraft by 3.2 million."

"But . . . ?" Margaret's eyes were wide, her red-lipsticked mouth partly open.

"There is still over £400,000 outstanding. However," Sean continued swiftly, "the land, cottages and Home Farm still belonging to the Wingland Estate have a market value of roughly three point six million. This is owned by the four remaining directors: Elizabeth Vickers, Giles, Cathy and Jonathan Driver. A charge may be put on it by the bank if the loan remains outstanding. On that you must make up your own minds, having discussed it with your accountant. One of your options would be to see if the new owner of Wingfield Court wishes to buy the rest of the estate, should you decide to sell it."

"What about probate?" Laurence asked.

"That's another question and will have to be dealt with separately," Sean advised. "Meanwhile . . ."

"But how much is in the trust fund now?" Margaret persisted. "It's the interest from those investments that we live on." There was a note of rising panic in her voice.

Whether it was deliberately to keep her waiting, or merely a momentary slip-up in his filing system, it took Sean several moments to find the relevant figures. Meanwhile Giles had not said a single word during the whole of the meeting or even expressed any interest in what had been said. Elizabeth glanced at him from time in time in concern but he didn't acknowledge even her.

"Ah! Here we are at last," Sean exclaimed. "The trust Fund currently has a capital figure of four million pounds."

"It was originally ten!" gasped Margaret.

Elizabeth, her face pale, exchanged glances with Laurence. Her father had lost six million pounds in crazy investments, she reflected sadly. What sort of madness had made him gamble away their money? Had it been a genuine effort, originally, to make them even richer? Or had he been trying to show off? Compete with his own late father to appear a financial wizard? The answer was probably a bit of both.

Margaret was trembling, her hands shaking in her plump lap. "So . . . four million pounds, properly invested, will produce an income, split four ways, of . . . ?"

"Five," Sean corrected her.

"Five? Why five?"

"Nick Driver's widow will inherit his share," he told her quietly.

She fell back in her chair, aghast.

Sean continued, "You must appoint your own financial advisers who will tell you the best way of handling the trust fund in future. If it invested in something like gilt-edged, you'll only get between three to four per cent return on the money but if you go for high-yielding investments you could get six or even seven. Now that will produce an annual figure of around two hundred and forty thousand pounds which, split five ways," he made a quick calculation on a notepad, "is around forty-eight thousand each."

"Gross. Before tax," Laurence interjected calmly.

Sean nodded in agreement.

"Oh, no!" Margaret burst into tears, distraught. "Giles!" she sobbed, thumping him on the shoulder. "We're ruined! Even with your salary, we'll have nothing!"

"It depends what you regard as nothing," Laurence murmured drily, with an amused smile in Elizabeth's direction. "Don't worry, I'll get that better paid job," he leaned over to whisper.

"This is dreadful," Margaret was wailing. "There must be something we can do."

"I'm going to need your help, you know," Matt told Cathy. "How do I start furnishing this house? I don't know where to begin. I must have been mad to think I could recreate it the way it was when I first came to view. I've never had to furnish a house before in my life."

"What have you done then, lived with your parents?"

He sounded almost apologetic. "I've always rented furnished places. Should I get in an interior designer?"

"Couldn't you ask your mother to advise you?"

They were in the library, the only furnished and unchanged room in house. Cathy sat perched on the window seat with the sunlight streaming in, making her hair glisten like jet.

There was a pause before Matt answered "Like you, I don't have a mother."

"Oh! I'm sorry." She eyed him anxiously, wondering if it was a recent bereavement.

"She died when I was two," he continued. "I have a step-mother but we don't get on. She thinks I should have followed in my father's footsteps."

"What does he do?"

"He's a doctor." He grinned at her disarmingly. "Help me, Cathy, please. You don't have to go back to Edinburgh just yet, do you?"

She longed to stay more than anything but wasn't sure whether she should. In the last couple of days any lingering thoughts of Jack had vanished as she'd found herself enjoying Matt's company more and more. But dare she trust her feelings, so soon after being hurt by Jack? And surely pop stars were bad news? Weren't they supposed to be wildly promiscuous? Into drugs and all that? All her instincts told her to leave while she still could.

"I promised Jonathan I'd go back to London with him. We've nearly finished here. It'll only take another day or so to clear the last of the stuff and he won't want to be alone so soon after Daddy's death. I really think . . ." She stopped, realizing she was babbling.

"Couldn't he stay to help, too? He is an artist after all. Maybe I could buy a few of his paintings? Without those tapestries your father had, these hall walls look awfully bare. What do you say?" Matt was looking at her intently but she couldn't be sure what he was thinking. Did he really need them to advise him or was he being kind, allowing them to prolong their last days in their old home?

"I'll have to discuss it with Jonathan," Cathy said hurriedly, getting up, from the window seat. "I wonder where he's gone?"

Matt stood gazing out of the window. "I think he went for a walk along the river bank with Richie."

"Oh . . . OH!" she added, before she could stop herself. Richie Dent, the bass player, was the joker of the group. Like Jonathan, he laughed a lot and saw the funny side of life. He was very attractive in a rugged way and she'd never have guessed he was gay if she hadn't heard the rest of the group jokingly referring to him as "Dockyard Daphne."

Matt ignored her exclamation as if he hadn't heard it.

"I've got to think about getting people to look after this house, too," he continued, as if he was thinking aloud. “Do you think any of the staff here would be prepared to stay on?”

Cathy thought about the elderly cook and the maids who’d been young women when they’d first come to Wingfield Court.

“I’m afraid they’re all getting on a bit. They’re due to retire fairly soon, you know. And they’ve got old-fashioned ideas. You need much younger people to look after this place, who’ll fit in with your lifestyle.”

“Do I, Cathy?” He turned to look at her then, fixing his dark eyes on her face in a way she found disconcerting. It was the way he’d said her name that seemed particularly intimate.

“Well . . . yes. It’s a big house.”

Matt turned to leave the room as if he’d thought of something else. “I’ve got to make a phone call,” he remarked vaguely, fishing in his back pocket for his mobile. Then he wandered off as if he’d forgotten all about her.

When Jonathan returned from his walk with Richie, Cathy scrutinized his face closely.

“What is it?” he asked, frowning with embarrassment.

She shook her head, laughing, and looked away. “Matt wants us to stay on for a bit to advise him on furnishing the house. What do you think?”

Jonathan frowned. “I don’t know.”

“Why don’t you know?”

“Why should I? Why don’t *you* know what we should do?”

Cathy held herself very straight, as if trying to keep a grip on things. Then she sighed and her shoulders sagged. "Because I think I'm afraid."

"What of?" He looked at her sharply.

"Getting hurt again."

There was a long pause while Jonathan shuffled around, hands in pockets, gazing down at his feet. "Me, too," he said at last.

"Richie Dent?"

Jonathan stuck out his lower lip thoughtfully. "Yup. I can't make him out."

"But he's gay, isn't he?"

"Yes, but I don't know if he's for me. I suppose you're falling for Matt?"

"I don't know either," she wailed. "But God, Jonno, I don't want to."

"You're not still holding a candle for Jack?"

"No. Isn't that strange? I was so devastated when he said it was over. That makes me a very shallow person, doesn't it? Capable of falling in and out of love so quickly?"

"Not really, Cathy. Maybe, with Jack, you were in love with love. Is Matt interested in you?"

She looked forlorn. "I can't make out whether he is or not. He seems to blow hot and cold. That's why I think it's better if I leave."

"At least I've learned from Richie that Matt is fancy free at the moment. Apparently he hasn't had a girlfriend for a year or so. I'd go for it if I were you," Jonathan advised.

"And Richie?"

Her brother's tone was dry and cynical. "People like Richie are always fancy free and ready for action, sweetheart."

CHAPTER FIFTEEN

Although the date of the trial was still some months away, Barnard Alexander wanted to go through every single detail of the case with Giles, challenging him on every point in order to prepare notes for the barrister, and also coaching Giles how to deal with his coming ordeal in the witness box.

"Mr Alexander will see you in a few minutes and apologizes for keeping you waiting," Sarah Wells told Giles. From her seat behind her desk, she smiled at him sympathetically. How he'd changed in the short time she'd known him, she reflected. When he'd first come to their offices to consult Sean, he'd looked confident and had carried his expensive suits and shirts and silk ties with the air of a man who knew where he was going. Now he didn't even look as if he knew where he was coming from. Giles Driver, she realized, had been crushed by the accusation that he'd killed his father. All the life had gone out of him. He looked as if he just wanted to lie down and go to sleep, never to awaken again. Not that she believed he was guilty, not for a moment.

At twenty-seven, Sarah had been a legal secretary for seven years. In that time a wide variety of people had passed through the office and she reckoned she'd become a good judge of character. And Giles Driver was no killer, although she had to admit the case against him looked dicey at the moment.

Barnard came out of his office, massive hand outstretched to greet Giles who rose lethargically like an old man.

"Margaret couldn't come today. She's in bed with 'flu," he explained.

Shaking his hand, Barnard tried to hide his relief. "Nasty thing, 'flu. Lot of it about at the moment," he grunted. "Come along in." He led the way into his cluttered office, waving Giles to a chair.

"We have a date set for your trial," he said immediately. "It will take place at London's Central Criminal Court on 7 November."

Giles looked appalled. "The Old Bailey? Christ! This gets worse every day." He rubbed his face with his hands. "How long will I get if I go down?"

"What are you talking about?" Barnard admonished. "We're going to prove your innocence, remember? We've been through all this a dozen times, Giles. No murder weapon has been found. No witnesses have come forward. You didn't have a motive because you were grateful to your father for letting you choose furniture and artefacts from Wingfield Court. If you're asked during cross examination whether you were upset about the sale of the house you say yes, you were, but these things happen. You add you never wanted to live in the country anyway. You already have a perfectly good house of your own in London.

"You've got to remember Giles, you're innocent until proven guilty, and the crown has to *prove* you guilty . . . and they're not going to be able to."

"Haven't you heard about our meeting with Sean a couple of days ago? We're all practically wiped out financially. Dad lost six million pounds out of the trust as well as selling Wingfield Court. Don't you think a jury will consider that motive enough? Margaret does."

"Don't pay any attention to what your wife says," Barnard soothed, his voice deeper than ever. "You have a top QC and our defence is that you didn't know how bad the situation was until now. When your father died, you were under the illusion the family trust was worth ten million, and that when he sold Wingfield Court he'd be buying Woodlands, a house big enough for you all, and you presumed, as his son and heir that the property would be put in your name. So where's the motive then?"

Giles looked mildly astonished. "The law is very clever at twisting things and presenting them in totally different ways, isn't it? So who *did* kill my father?"

"We'll suggest it could have been a business colleague who wanted him out of the way because he knew too much or because they were jealous of him. We'll muddy the waters by mentioning he had a lot of debts that neither you nor your brother and sisters knew anything about. We can even suggest money lenders could have been involved. The thing is, Giles," Barnard continued robustly, leaning across his desk in confidential manner, "all we actually have to prove is that *you didn't do it*, no matter who did."

Giles sat looking at him with glazed eyes, unconvinced. "But how can we? I didn't see anyone after I left the others to go and have a shower. Then I fell asleep and didn't wake up until I heard a commotion under my bedroom window. The police know all this. I've told them everything."

"What did you have to drink at lunchtime?"

"Wine."

"A lot of wine?"

Giles shrugged. "Several glasses, I suppose."

Barnard sat back for a few moments, deep in thought. "Was there anyone at lunch who could have slipped something into your glass, in order to make you feel drowsy during the afternoon? Someone who wanted you to fall asleep in order to get you out of the way, so you wouldn't have an alibi around the time your father was killed?"

"No one. It was just a family gathering."

"Mmm." He gazed up at the ceiling as if clues might be embedded in the plaster. "And apart from Laurence Vickers, who took his children for a walk, your siblings say in their statements they all stayed together counting china dishes?"

"That's right."

"Had any members of your father's staff a grudge against him, do you think?"

"Not that I know of."

Barnard began to feel irritated. He leaned back, his chair creaking under his weight. "You don't seem to be very interested in putting up a defence, Giles. What's the matter? You're facing a very serious charge and at this rate you're going to let the prosecution walk all over you. At the moment their evidence is circumstantial, but it's not good enough just to throw up your hands and say 'I didn't do it'."

Giles turned away, face suddenly flushed and contorted, his shoulders shuddering as he started to cry. The lawyer sat in embarrassed silence for a minute or so, shuffling papers and pretending to be busy, but he couldn't continue to ignore his client's anguish indefinitely so he heaved himself to his feet and walked around his desk.

"Come on, old chap," he said sympathetically, giving Giles a pat on the shoulder. "I didn't mean to bully you, and of course John Waddington-Cairns and I will be conducting your defence and will get you off, we just need you to co-operate a bit. Throw us a few leads. They might well be red herrings, but there's nothing like confusing the enemy. That's all I'm trying to do."

"My father always hated me," Giles wept bitterly, "and I feel he's still getting at me, even though he's dead."

"I thought you got on quite well with him?" Barnard queried in genuine surprise. "That is, until he remarried and you found out about the house and that there was money missing from the trust fund?"

"He . . . he always despised me," Giles sobbed, breaking down completely. "I wasn't like him, you see. Clever and successful. He hated me for being the person I am."

"I'm sure he cared for you just as much as he did for his other children?"

Giles shook his head from side to side, rubbing his eyes with his fists like a small boy. "No, the girls were his favourites. Elizabeth's the eldest, I think he'd have liked her to have inherited everything. But grandfather's will stipulated otherwise. That's the only reason the house was going to be mine. My father never showed me any affection . . ."

Barnard stood over him like a great bear and looked down at him kindly. "He was probably a typical English father, undemonstrative and always hiding his true feelings."

"No. He was very loving to all the others, but he beat me when I was small . . . only my mother . . . she . . ." Giles doubled up in his chair in a paroxysm of emotion, unable to continue.

The lawyer turned away, hating to see a man of nearly thirty so brought down, so deeply damaged by his childhood that he no longer cared he was humiliating himself in front of someone else. Shuffling out of the office, he went to Sarah. She looked at him enquiringly. The walls were thin. She'd heard every word.

"Get a glass of water, will you, Sarah?"

She nodded, jumping from her chair and running down the corridor to the water dispenser. A minute later she was back with a paper cup brimming with water.

"Thanks." Back in his office, Barnard tapped Giles gently on the shoulder. "Have some water, old chap."

Giles sipped feebly then fumbled for his handkerchief and blew his nose and wiped his reddened eyes.

"I'm sorry," he faltered apologetically.

"That's all right. You're under a hell of a strain right now. But don't worry, things will sort themselves out and we'll put up a terrific defence. I know your family are backing you all the way so you've no worries on that score."

Giles buried his face in his hands. "I always thought it would be such a relief not to have my father around, but it's made no difference. I'm still not rid of him," he said in a muffled voice.

Barnard looked down at him and a terrible thought crossed his mind. Was Giles actually admitting his guilt? Had he killed Nick Driver and was now consumed by remorse? Was that what Margaret had meant when she'd said, "I must say, you've changed your tune"? If Giles had committed murder, should he plead not guilty, as had been the first obvious decision, or would it be safer to plead guilty to manslaughter while suffering from diminished responsibility brought on by years of emotional abuse at the hands of his father?

Against her better judgement, Cathy accepted Matt's invitation to stay on a little longer. She knew she was letting her heart rule her head but Jonathan had persuaded her. Anyway, she found she simply couldn't resist the attractions of Matt Blade. He was the most dazzling man she'd ever met: talented, witty, enthusiastic, and alive to the thrill of the moment. No one could ever be bored in his company. Each day was like an adventure in living. She'd never felt so energized, determined to capture every second of the prevailing excitement.

The atmosphere at Wingfield Court had changed, too. It was almost as if they were staying in another house, and to Cathy's surprise she preferred it the way it was now.

Nick had been a stickler for formality, emulating the lifestyle of the aristocracy. He'd enjoyed seeing himself as the lord of the manor from a bygone age. Cathy had accepted this because she'd known no other, except the way she and her friends lived in shared digs in Edinburgh, which didn't count because they were students. Now, however, she was aware she felt more carefree in her old home than when it had belonged to Nick. Etiquette and observance of form had been replaced by an air of casual comfort and convenience. The old servants, accustomed to outdated ways, had been handsomely paid off and replaced by a brilliant young chef from Ayrshire and three young women from Glasgow who would almost have worked for nothing for the honor of being on Matt's staff.

Music drifted on the air most of the time, coming from various rooms and even the garden, impromptu snatches of sparkling notes and seductive rhythms, usually followed by bursts of laughter and jokes between the members of the Young Blades, who were in the planning stages of their next album. It made Cathy want to dance and when she thought no one could see her, she'd sway to the melodies her gypsy shawls and ethnic sarongs floating gracefully around her slender body. If she was in love with Matt, she was almost equally enchanted by his music. The creative force he generated pervaded every inch of the old house and every hour of the day.

A clean fresh wind seemed to have blown through the place, taking with it some of the sadness and bitterness, replacing it with a kind of magic as if the air was filled with rainbows.

Cathy was falling in love with Wingfield Court all over again. And with its new owner.

Philippa sat on her bed for a long time, reading and re-reading the report that had arrived in this morning's mail from Sean Chapman. He had sent copies to the five beneficiaries of the family trust and in his covering letter had outlined that her late husband's estate still had an outstanding bank loan of four hundred thousand pounds, highlighting the reason why he'd never gone ahead and bought Woodlands. He ended with the hope that her share from the trust, if wisely invested, would bring her an annual income of around forty-eight thousand pounds.

Shock and disappointment were uppermost in her mind because she'd hoped to be able to give her parents a comfortable home for the rest of their lives. She'd even told Morton they'd want him to work for them. Next week they'd intended setting off in the car, with the baby, on a house-hunting expedition.

And now this. As she bathed and fed Andrew, her mind ran in crazy circles, wondering what to do. Who to talk to? If it had been only Andrew and herself, she could have got a small flat and gone back to work in due course. The worry was Honor and Archie; she simply couldn't disappoint them now they were so excited about all living together in the country. And then she was struck by a brilliant thought as she put Andrew into his cot for his morning's sleep.

Waiting until her parents had gone out to buy some groceries, she phoned Sean.

"What can I do for you?" he asked pleasantly, after he'd congratulated her on giving birth.

"I wanted to know if the apartment in Eaton Square belongs to me or to Nick's children?"

"Under the terms of his will, I believe it belongs to you."

"Can I sell it if I want to?"

"I see no reason why not, but it will be subject to probate. Why do you ask?"

Briefly she explained how his financial report affected her future plans.

"I don't want to seem greedy," she said diffidently, a catch in her voice as she remembered how Nick had wanted to give her and the baby a life of luxury, "but I think my late husband would have wanted our son to be provided for, if not me." Then she was struck by a terrible thought. "At least . . . that is . . . providing his children are not going to sue me as they'd planned to sue their father?" She wiped away her tears, thankful she was speaking on the phone and not face to face.

"My dear Mrs Driver," Sean said sympathetically, "it was only Giles and Margaret Driver who wanted to take your husband to court and I don't think they're in any position to do that now. Between you and me I'd strongly advise them against it."

"I see. What do you think I should do then?"

Sean said earnestly, "May I suggest that, as it would be difficult for me to represent you, you get yourself a good lawyer. And rest assured I will be happy to see your best interests are served and you get your fair share of the estate."

"That's very kind of you," said Philippa, relieved. "Is there going to be a lot of unpleasantness, d'you think?"

"I doubt it. I think all the anger and resentment are over and the family are too grief-stricken by this latest tragedy to start any in-fighting over a fortune that has largely vanished. There is Giles's trial, too."

When Philippa hung up, partly reassured, she determined to go ahead with her plans. The sale of the apartment in the best part of London, even after probate, would be enough to fund a house in the country, especially if she sold the jewels Nick had given her too. And if she got a job locally she'd still be able to employ Morton and give her parents the dream she'd promised them. It would be tough but somehow she'd manage.

As soon as Sean put down the receiver, he phoned Elizabeth at Willow Farm.

"Hello," she said, surprised. "Have you phoned about the report we got from you this morning?"

"In a way," he began cautiously. "I'm actually ringing you, instead of your brother, because I gathered from Barnard yesterday that Giles is in a very distressed state of mind. I also wanted to talk to you about your step-mother."

"Is she all right? I feel so sorry for her . . ." Elizabeth said immediately.

"I've advised her to get her own lawyer, because obviously I can't work for both your brother and Philippa. My idea is this, Elizabeth. You're all going to be taking a drop in income, so why don't you sell the farm and the land, and maybe the cottages to the tenants?

As I said, the estate could be worth as much as three point six million. You could share the capital amount five ways or add it to the remaining four million in the trust. Either way . . ."

Elizabeth, who was making pastry at that moment, rubbed the flour off her hands and made an instant decision.

"Good idea, Sean. We'll do it. Do you want me to persuade the others?"

He chuckled. "I knew you were the right one to speak to," he remarked. "So you'll talk to them?"

"I will," she promised. "And is there any way we can keep Margaret out of this?"

"I'll do my level best." Again he chuckled.

"We must look after Philippa," she continued. "Daddy would have wanted that."

"My own sentiments exactly."

Jonathan was getting along with Richie as if they'd known each other for years, and Cathy was only too aware that the next week or so could be crucial to their blossoming relationship. She longed for him to find someone with whom to share his life, and as she and Matt drew closer every day, her hopes for Jonathan's happiness increased.

"How much longer is Richie going to be here?" she asked, as they lay on the lawn, listening to an earlier tape made by the group. "His home is in Yorkshire, isn't it?"

Jonathan grinned. "Yes. Matt wants him here for another week or two though. They're deep into rehearsals."

"And he wants me here to advise him on creating a home," Cathy said with a slow smile.

"I notice you're choosing all the things you like best?" her brother remarked slyly.

She flushed. "Not at all. It just so happens we like the same things."

"I'll bet!" he laughed. Then he looked at her seriously. "You've fallen for him, haven't you? He's definitely fallen for you," he added, rolling on to his back and gazing at the expanse of tiny white clouds passing by overhead.

Her expression became a mixture of delight and apprehension. She sat up, clasping her hands nervously together. "No! Really. Oh, my God, what makes you say that?"

"Something Richie said."

"What? What did he say?" She was all eagerness now, eyes alight with excitement, silver bangles rattling on her wrists.

"His actual words were, 'I haven't seen Matt so taken with anyone for a long time'. It's obvious, Cathy. I can tell just by the way he looks at you. He's besotted."

"Then why hasn't he said anything? Jack told me within twenty-four hours of meeting me that he was in love with me. Matt hasn't even made a pass," she added wistfully, "but we are very close. Like soul mates."

"You've got to remember the age difference," Jonathan pointed out. "Jack had the impetuosity of a twenty year old. Matt is twenty-six and much more experienced. He's travelled all over, made himself a fortune, probably considers every step he takes before he makes a move. I'd guess he has a sense of responsibility towards others, too. He probably wants to see how things develop between you."

"He must have thousands of female fans throwing themselves at him," Cathy said thoughtfully. "Oh, I'm terrified I'll blow it! I mustn't look like a groupie, must I?"

Her brother grinned. "From the rude way you treated him the day he arrived, because you obviously didn't even recognize him, I doubt he thinks you're just another groupie."

"It means I must stay on for a while, doesn't it? And what about university?" she asked in sudden dismay. "I should be going back in three weeks' time, and I can't even think about it."

"If you stay, it means you might be able to live here forever," he told her solemnly. "Just think what that would mean."

"Is this yours, Cathy?" Matt came out of the library holding a camcorder. "I found it in one of the desk drawers."

She examined it. "Yes, it belonged to Daddy. I'd forgotten all about it."

"Do you know what's on it?"

"I've no idea . . . Oh, yes! There could be hours of just my legs," she laughed. "My nephew Dominic kept playing with it, and then putting it down and forgetting to switch it off. I think I was standing in front of it the last time that happened."

Matt shot her a warm intimate look. "This I have to see. Let's have a look."

He'd had a state-of-the-art television with video and CD player installed in a corner of the library. He connected the camera and put a fresh tape in the video so they could make a permanent recording.

"This isn't going to be too painful for you, is it?" he asked gently. "It was obviously taken when your father was still alive."

For a moment she looked doubtful but then she said, "Actually it might be quite comforting to see him again, even if it is only in film."

Matt sat down beside her on the leather sofa and the television screen sprang to life, showing the family grouped on the terrace when they'd arrived for that last weekend. There were Giles and Margaret, and then Elizabeth with Jasper in her arms. A close-up of Jonathan followed, making a silly face, and then a pregnant Philippa, talking and laughing as if she hadn't a care in the world. The camera had been trained on her for such a long time, Cathy was sure her father had done the filming. Then it was obvious Dominic had taken over because the picture wobbled wildly, swooping, turning, never trained for long enough on anything until it was suddenly in a fixed position and the screen was filled with a picture of someone from thigh to ankle in a wraparound batik skirt.

"That's me!" Cathy shrieked with laughter.

"Shame! I can't see your legs. I feel deprived!" Matt exclaimed, reaching out and laying his hand on her knee.

Cathy was aware he was looking at her, his eyes hot and searching. Her heart was thudding as she turned from the screen to look at him, and a moment later he had his arms around her and was kissing her as if it was the only thing he'd ever wanted to do.

They were still kissing some minutes later, barely aware of the soundtrack of the video in the background, when Cathy suddenly heard what sounded like a loud groan of pain. And then, unnervingly, her father's voice, as clear as if he'd been in the room. "Christ! Oh, Christ!"

She pulled away from Matt and looked at the screen. And in that moment knew exactly how her father had died.

"What's the matter with you, Giles?" Margaret said in angry despair. "You're not making any effort to put up a defence. Don't you realize you might have to serve a long sentence if you're found guilty? Why can't you get your act together?"

Giles was sitting slumped in a chair, his face pale and expressionless.

"What's the point?" he said at last. "No one's going to believe me. All the circumstantial evidence is against me." He sighed despairingly. "What have I got to live for anyway?"

"Don't let me hear you talk like that," she admonished. "Where's your fighting spirit? We have a good life, we go to a lot of very nice dinners and parties, we . . ."

He turned his bleary eyes on her. "Do you really think all that crap is important?"

Margaret became flustered. "Yes, I do think it's important. Life is all about meeting people, furthering your career through the right contacts, having a good lifestyle . . ."

Giles looked at her as if she was crazy. "You really believe that, don't you?"

"Why else would I devote my time and energy to getting to know the right people if I didn't think it was important."

He slumped once more, head buried in his hands. "You can't take any of this with you," he muttered.

"And what's that supposed to mean?"

"It means that when you die, it doesn't matter whether you're worth ten million pounds or ten million pence. It's all the same. You can't take it with you."

Margaret clicked her tongue in annoyance. "That's a stupid argument. If that were the case, people wouldn't bother to achieve anything."

"Achieving is one thing. Grabbing all the money or property you can lay your hands on is another," he said quietly.

She looked at him. "Are you all right, Giles? I think you're having a nervous breakdown. What's come over you? Ever since we've been married we've cultivated the right people, gone to everything we've been invited to and returned hospitality in the appropriate style. We always planned to retire to Wingfield Court, as soon as your father died . . . and now you're acting as if none of it matters. But it *does*."

"To you, perhaps."

"And you, too, Giles. For God's sake, brace up. You don't seem to understand the seriousness of your position. Just because you can't prove your innocence, doesn't mean you can't disprove the allegations against you."

Giles let his hands fall from his face. He gazed ahead with unseeing eyes, almost as if he were in a trance. "I can't see the point in going on. Whether I'm found guilty of killing Dad or not, it no longer matters. I'm finished."

For the first time Margaret looked genuinely concerned. "Then you are having a breakdown," she said tactlessly. "I'd better get the doctor to come and see you." If Giles threw in the sponge, gave up trying to prove his innocence and let himself drift along in a muddled state, she could see her own lifestyle falling apart, too.

"What good would that do?" he demanded. "I'm burned out, can't you understand that? All my life I've tried to be successful, like Dad, and now I'm tired of trying." He sounded immensely weary, as if he'd been trekking up a steep mountain and now knew he'd never reach the top. "Dad was cleverer than me, more successful, better looking and popular with everyone. He was also capable, at the age of fifty-eight, of fathering a child."

His voice was raw with pain and he kept his eyes averted, unable look at her during this, his first admission of his failure.

"Haven't I always said that could be fixed by a doctor?" Margaret told him robustly. "You could be given Viagra."

Giles rose slowly, like an old man, ignoring what she'd said. "I'm going out," he said quietly, as he walked across the hall to the front door.

Alarm pierced her like a shaft of ice. "Where are you going? What are you going to do?"

He shook his head, not answering, and a moment later the front door slammed behind him.

"Oh, my God! Oh, my God! Oh, my *God*!" Cathy yelled, tearing into the hall, leaving a mystified Matt running after her.

"JONNO! Come quickly!" she screamed.

Jonathan came racing down the stairs, his long legs taking two treads at a time, blue eyes wide with alarm. He looked at his sister and then Matt.

"What's wrong, Cathy? What's happened?"

She was shaking all over and the words came tumbling out.

"I've just seen a video that shows what happened to Dad. How he died." She grabbed his hand and dragged him back into the library. "Matt, can you wind the tape back?"

He pressed the rewind button on the remote control and then pressed play. The three of them crouched close together on the sofa, watching.

Suddenly the screen was filled with the last few seconds of the shot of Cathy's batik skirt. The next scene showed the family finishing their alfresco lunch by the swimming pool. Once again it was obvious by the quality of the video that someone who knew what they were doing was filming. Then Dominic came into shot. His voice could clearly be heard on the sound track.

"Can I have a go, Grandpa? Please."

Nick was heard saying, "All right, Dominic, but be careful."

Jonathan winced at the sound of his father's voice and Cathy clapped one hand over her mouth. Matt was holding her other hand in both of his. Mesmerized, they gazed at the screen.

From the jogging and swaying of the picture, it was obvious the camcorder was now being held by Dominic as he captured Tamsin tugging off her sun hat and Elizabeth giving Jasper a rusk. Then, suddenly, in a moment that made Cathy feel sick with grief, there was Nick, alive and well and pouring himself a drink. He was laughing as he turned to talk to Elizabeth, unaware that time was running out for him.

These scenes continued for several minutes, as ordinary family at play. Then lunch came to an end and Jonathan and Cathy left to go indoors, followed by Giles and Margaret with Philippa. Morton and two of the maids could be seen clearing away the remains of lunch and in the background was the unmistakable voice of Laurence.

"Come along, Dominic, we're going for a walk."

"Do I have to, Dad? I'm making a film."

"Yes, I'm taking you and Tamsin. Now, come along."

Cathy dug her fingers into Jonathan's arm. "Watch," she urged.

Suddenly the picture went all over the place. A patch of sky. The tree-tops. The stone terrace. And finally came to rest on Nick's easily recognizable backview as he sat by the pool. And there it stuck. Once again, Dominic had put the camcorder down and forgotten to switch it off.

The sound track continued to carry voices. Laurence saying, "Tamsin, put your sun hat on," and Elizabeth's voice speaking to Jasper, telling him it was time for his afternoon nap.

Gradually the voices and footsteps faded and the only sound was a faint chink as Nick rose and put his half-empty glass on the table.

Jonathan strained forward, watching the screen intently, wondering what on earth was going to happen next. His heart was pounding and he leaned closer to listen. Cathy burrowed her face into Matt's chest and he put his arms around her and held her close to his heart. The atmosphere was fraught with tension.

And then they saw what had happened.

Suddenly and for no apparent reason Nick clutched his head, reeling as if in agony, staggering dizzily a few steps forward. Then his last words could be heard.

"CHRIST! OH, CHRIST!"

A second later he stumbled and fell, hitting his head with a crack on the stone rim of the swimming pool. A moment later there was a great splash as his body tumbled into the water.

Jonathan clutched Cathy and let out a sharp cry as they watched the water spray over the chair Nick had been sitting on. Then everything went quiet.

Cathy burst into tears. "Isn't that horrible?" she wept, knowing that image of her father, reeling in pain before he collapsed into the water, would haunt her forever.

"What happened?" Jonathan asked, stunned.

Matt said gently, "I'd say it was a stroke. You must show this to the police immediately. It's obvious the death was accidental."

"Margaret, this is Jonathan. May I speak to Giles, please?"

"He isn't here," she explained. "He was behaving very strangely this morning, I think he's having a nervous breakdown. Anyway, he's gone out."

"Did he say when he'd be back?" Jonathan asked anxiously.

"No. He just slammed out of the house, saying he couldn't see any point in carrying on."

"What? My God, Margaret, where is he? How could you have let him go off in that state of mind?"

"This is all his father's fault, not mine," she retorted defensively.

"But you're his wife! You *must* find him. God, this is serious. Have you phoned around? Could he have gone to his office or to see a friend? We've got to find him, tell him we've just found a video which proves Dad's death was an accident. He fell and hit his head. This means Giles is in the clear!"

"Do the police know?"

"They're examining the video now. They admitted their forensic enquiry was far from perfect. There were so many of us around the pool, lifting Dad out of the water, they probably couldn't find evidence of him hitting his head on the edge, and that's why they thought his blood clot had been caused deliberately by someone wielding a blunt instrument. Oh, God, I'm so worried about Giles. Where the fuck could he have gone? You don't think he'd do anything foolish, do you?"

"I don't know." Margaret was wailing with agitation now. "I'll ring the police, shall I? But he's only been gone a few hours they're going to say it's too soon to list him as missing . . ."

"It doesn't matter what the hell they say, just do it," Jonathan snapped. "I'll ring round the London hospitals, see if they know anything."

Richie Dent came into the library at that moment, having heard from Matt what had happened. "Any news yet?" he asked anxiously.

Jonathan looked at him, grateful for his support. "I'm about to ring up the London hospitals to find out if anything's happened to my brother," he replied. "I can't believe my sister-in-law allowed him to go like that, when he's obviously at breaking point."

"He's probably just gone somewhere to be quiet," Richie suggested. "Can I get you anything? Coffee? A drink?"

"I wouldn't mind a cup of tea. I'd better keep a clear head until we've found out what's happening."

"At least he's in the clear so far as your father's death is concerned."

"Yup." Jonathan frowned miserably. "I just hope to Christ he's all right."

Giles was found later that day, wandering in Holland Park by a park keeper who thought he looked ill and seemed disorientated. He didn't seem to know who he was and had nothing on him by which he could be identified. In the end, worried about his condition, the park keeper had called an ambulance and Giles was taken to Westminster and Chelsea Hospital.

"I'll go and collect him right away," Margaret said, when Jonathan rang her to say a man matching Giles's description had been found. "I know he'll be thrilled to hear the news. How marvellous that you found that video."

She, however, was in for a shock when she arrived at the hospital. The doctor told her that her husband was seriously disturbed and it would be necessary to let him stay in their psychiatric ward for a few days, so his condition could be assessed.

"But I must talk to him!" she insisted. "He's been charged with killing his father and is on bail but today his sister found new evidence which puts him in the clear. As soon as he knows that he'll be all right," she added with conviction.

The doctor nodded. "No doubt pressure of that sort could have brought on his present condition. But right now, Mrs Driver, he's under sedation and asleep. I don't want him disturbed. I want to keep him here for several days. His mind needs time to heal from the trauma he's been through and his general physical condition is that of someone who hasn't been looking after himself. He's been drinking heavily, hasn't he? I want to do a general examination in a few days' time."

Margaret flushed angrily, bristling with indignation.

"But I insist on seeing him. I know he'll be as right as rain the minute he hears the news."

"I'm afraid it may not be as simple as that," the doctor said firmly. "You may see him for just a moment, but I insist that you do not try to wake him up. That could greatly retard his recovery."

It was six weeks before Giles was discharged from hospital, and when he was, he managed to give Margaret the slip. Taking a train to Northampton, and from there a taxi to Willow Farm, surprising Elizabeth and Laurence with his unexpected arrival, he announced he was never returning to his wife.

Elizabeth looked at him in silent astonishment. "You're actually going to leave her, Giles?" she asked. "Have you thought this through, love? After all, you've been ill . . ."

He looked up from where he was sitting at the kitchen table, eating one of her shortbread biscuits with his coffee, and she'd never seen him with such a positive expression on his face before.

"Yes, but I'm fully recovered now. I've had time, away from Margaret, to reassess my life, see where I've gone wrong. I've always let other people run my life, Lizzie, that's been the trouble. I've tried to live up to their expectations and not my own capabilities. That's all going to change now."

She sat down opposite him, feeling a great warmth well up inside her for this younger brother who, unlike her, had been burdened from birth with the knowledge he would one day become head of the family.

"Good for you, Giles," she said encouragingly. "So long as you're happy. Have you told Margaret?"

"Yes. I told her just before I left hospital." He grinned sheepishly.

"How did she take it?"

"She wasn't too happy," he replied with typical understatement.

"I bet she wasn't! What did she say?" Elizabeth leaned across the table, her face near his, feeling drawn into the delightful conspiracy like a naughty child.

"Not much in fact," he confided. "I think she was too stunned to say anything, which was good. She said she'd get a solicitor and I wasn't to think I could get away with giving her nothing."

"You're obviously going to have to give her an allowance, or a once-and-for-all lump sum," Elizabeth agreed.

"Sean says she'll probably want to keep the house, too. She'll want the social standing a nice town house gives her, I suppose."

Elizabeth leaned back, feeling an enormous sense of relief that Margaret was no longer part of the family. "So what are you going to do, love? You can stay with us as long as you like, you know."

Giles smiled. It felt good to be close to his own family again. "Thanks, Lizzie. I'm going back to Bartwell's in two weeks' time and thought I'd rent a small flat."

She nodded in approval. "Remember, you always have a second home here. When you want to get out of town at weekends, don't wait to be asked, just turn up."

"Like the old days at Wingfield Court, without the pressure. All I want is peace and quiet now. No hassle and no nagging." He stretched his arms above his head, more at home in the shambling but cosy disorder of Willow Farm than he'd ever been in the formal grandeur of their old home. Through the open kitchen door he could see Jasper playing in his sandpit, happily chucking the stuff all around, including over his own head. Beside him, Daisy, Tessa, Plum and Muffet snoozed in the sun, an occasional paw twitching as they lay dreaming.

"You've got it all, haven't you, Lizzie?" he said thoughtfully. "You always had your priorities right and knew what really mattered."

"I've been lucky," she said briefly. "Another baby is going to make us a bit of a crowd, but who cares? It's what we want. And if money gets too tight, we'll grow our own vegetables!" she added, laughing.

"When we've sold Wingland Estate there'll be more money coming in," he observed, showing no regret that the last of his inheritance was to be sold. Elizabeth nodded. "It would be nice if Matt Blade were interested, wouldn't it? I've spoken to Philippa, and I think she's going to put her share in trust for Andrew."

"Are Cathy and Jonno happy about the idea?"

He hadn't, Elizabeth noticed with relief, made any objection to Philippa's benefiting.

"They think it's a good idea," she replied. "Cathy has to get herself somewhere to live for a start."

"By the way. . ." His cheeks flushed as he spoke, making him look quite boyish for a moment. "I also told Sean that I wouldn't be suing Dad's estate. He says we have a very strong case against Ernest and Norman, but as they were acting on Dad's orders, it would involve him and what he did, too . . . so I'm dropping it. I've got enough guilt to carry around without washing all our dirty linen in public."

"You mustn't feel guilty, Giles. Dad's death had nothing to do with you."

"But his stroke must have been brought on by worry and stress to which I . . ."

She reached over and put her hand on his arm with a steadying gesture. "I doubt if you'd have done more than thrown a wobbly if Margaret hadn't wound you up. Our doctor explained to me that Daddy's stroke was as likely to have been caused by too much good living as anything else. He did what he wanted. You have nothing to feel guilty about."

"Except that we parted on such bad terms."

"I know. I know, love. But Daddy would have wanted you to get on with your life now. You've suffered enough, Giles, one way and another."

He smiled, as if accepting a blessing from her. "Onwards and upwards?"

"That's right, and we'll back you all the way."

CHAPTER SIXTEEN

"You're beautiful, d'you know that?" Matt whispered, after a long night of lovemaking. It was the beginning of December and Cathy was making one of her frequent weekend visits to Wingfield Court.

"Am I?" she asked uncertainly. She'd known him for six months now and he was everything she'd ever wanted in a man; clever, funny, kind, good-looking, and an exciting lover. He phoned her every day, and sometimes flew up to Edinburgh to see her. He'd sent her flowers and a fine silver necklace for her birthday, having found out from Jonathan when it was, but did he love her enough to make a commitment? What did the future hold?

Her flatmate, Venetia, had thought she was mad.

"Why do you want to tie yourself down. Cathy? You're only twenty. And how old is he?"

"Twenty-six. A perfect age for me," Cathy had sighed dreamily.

Matt interrupted her thoughts by turning on to his back and rolling her with him, so that she lay on top of him. He held her arms down by her sides, imprisoning her.

"Now I've got you," he teased, lifting his head to brush her lips with his.

Cathy lay passively for a moment, then with a quick playful movement freed herself and slid on to the mattress. "I don't know that you have," she whispered archly.

"Oh, but I do," he laughed.

She didn't reply but gazed up at the ceiling as if he hadn't spoken. Something about the way she lay, ignoring him, made him sit up, leaning on one elbow and with the other hand stroking her bare shoulder.

"What's up?"

"Nothing," she replied pleasantly.

"Yes, there is. I can tell."

"Everything's fine," she lied, afraid she was going to blow it. Weren't men supposed to run a mile if they thought they were about to be tied down?

"Listen, Cathy." He spoke tenderly, thrilling her with the way he said her name in his deep-timbred voice, making it sound so much more intimate than "darling" or "babe". "You know I want to be with you always, don't you?" He paused and she waited, still silent. "Every moment of every day and every night, I want to have you with me," he continued.

She turned her head to look at him and he stroked her cheek with his sensitive musician's fingers.

"I haven't said anything before," he continued softly, "because I was afraid you'd think you were too young or something. But I want to marry you, Cathy. More than anything in the world. And if it's not too soon for you then . . . let's get on with it."

She stared at him, her dark eyes widening with wonder as what he'd said sank in. Then she let out a shriek of joy.

"You mean it, Matt?"

His face lit up. "Is that a yes? Of course I mean it . . . but what about your degree?"

"Don't worry about that," she giggled. "I'll learn more by going on the road with you."

He hugged her tightly, wrapping his bare legs around hers. "We've got several big gigs coming up. Will you really want to come on tour?"

"Try stopping me. With all those fans throwing their knickers at you, I'm never going to let you out of my sight," she retorted, arms tight around his neck, her warm breath mingling with his as they lay facing each other.

"But we'll always come back here because this place will always be home."

Cathy nodded. "Home," she repeated. "What a beautiful word."

He looked pleased with himself. "Yup. The whole place, lock, stock and barrel. You didn't know that, did you?"

"Know what?"

"I've bought the whole estate. Giles and Elizabeth and Jonathan know all about it, but I wanted it to be a surprise for you and made up my mind I wouldn't tell you until we were about to get married."

"Matt! I don't believe it!"

She lay in his arms, happier than she'd ever been, unable to believe this was really happening to her. So Wingfield Court in its entirety now belonged to Matt . . . and to her.

"As someone once said . . . funny old world, isn't it?" he teased.

She nestled into the crook of his arm. "Do you know what I want to do now?"

"I can't wait to hear." His smile was delightfully wicked.

She sighed luxuriously. "I want to stay in bed with you all day, and lick caviar off your skin, and drink champagne from the palms of your hands . . ."

Matt silenced her by putting his mouth over hers and kissing her as he never wanted to stop.

A month later, Jonathan moved into a new and larger flat which he and Richie had bought together.

"At least I can never be accused of being one of those people who have to buy their own furniture," he quipped as he took delivery of his share of the contents of his old home.

"What do you mean by that?" Richie asked, laughing. "Surely everyone has to buy their own furniture?"

"Certain people inherit the stuff," Jonathan joked, putting on a grand voice. "And when they do, that means they're aristocrats."

Richie nearly fell off his chair with mirth. "Get along with you! Who do you think you are . . . royalty?"

Quick as a flash Jonathan replied, "Of course. I'm a queen, aren't I?"

It was shortly after this that Elizabeth, heavily pregnant and blooming with domestic contentment, phoned Cathy one morning.

"Have you heard about Giles?" she asked excitedly.

"What about him?" Cathy asked, filled with foreboding. They all worried about Giles, hoping he was looking after himself, hoping he was all right.

"He came down for the weekend," Elizabeth continued "and he brought Sarah Wells with him. D'you remember, Barnard Alexander's legal secretary? Anyway, they're living together and she's pregnant. Isn't that terrific? They're getting married after she's had the baby."

Cathy and Matt's wedding, held at St Mark's in spite of all the memories it held, was a magical and musical affair which dispelled the sadness of the past and set a new style of originality and non-conformity.

As was to be expected, Cathy looked unlike any bride who had been married there in living memory. Her dress was made from a silver and white sari, with a train of silver tissue, and her long dark hair was covered with stars which hung on silk threads from a silver crown made of bigger stars. Matt chose to follow tradition and wore a silver grey morning suit, but it was Dominic and Tamsin, with Matt's niece and nephew, who almost stole the show. Cathy had decided they should be dressed as white rabbits, in costumes she'd hired from a theatrical costumier. With blue satin bows round their necks and tall fluffy ears, they drew applause from the crowds watching outside the church as they linked hands and followed her up the aisle.

"This is a very healing occasion, isn't it?" Elizabeth whispered to Laurence during the service, as he held Jasper's hand and she cuddled her new baby daughter,

Melinda. He nodded, glancing at Giles with Sarah by his side, and at Jonathan and Richie who, as ushers, helped by the rest of the Young Blades, had been busy seating the cream of the pop world.

"Very joyous, too" Laurence agreed. "Unbelievable it's all worked out so well — bit like a fairy tale really. Fancy Cathy ending up with Wingfield Court. Who would have thought it?"

"Happy endings can happen," Elizabeth assured him, smiling up into his eyes.

The family quickly lost touch with Margaret. She'd grabbed everything she could in the divorce settlement, including the house, and when last heard of was fundraising for several high-profile charities, in the desperate hope of staying in the social swing.

One person who never returned to Wingfield Court was Philippa. There were too many painful memories and too many deep scars for her to bear the thought of going back. She hardly saw anything of her four step-children either, but that was her choice. Elizabeth frequently invited her to Willow Farm, and they all sent Christmas and birthday presents to Andrew, but Philippa had decided to start a new life for herself and her son, and that meant not looking back. It was the only way she was ever going to recover from what had happened. She'd bought a comfortable house in Hampshire, with a large garden which she loved, and she'd joined the silver department of a local auction house in Andover.

One day, she hoped, she'd meet someone else, start over again, and have more children. But meanwhile

Andrew had become the love of her life, a joy she shared with Archie and Honor, who were living with her.

For reasons they didn't understand themselves, when the family looked back, years later, to the moment when Philippa had been brought into their lives, they remembered her as a shadowy figure, a mere thread that had linked them together in a state of half-forgotten hostility. An unwitting catalyst whose presence had turned their lives upside down, setting blood against blood, and yet in the end it had all had very little to do with her. Nick had been the trouble all along. Their father who, far from being strong, had been the weakest of them all; too weak to admit his own mistakes, too weak to risk being honest.

Only with his death had the air cleared, causing Philippa to drift out of their lives again like a cloud on a summer breeze, leaving nothing behind but a sense of peace.

The publishers hope that this large print book has brought you pleasurable reading. Each title is designed to make the text as easy to read as possible.

For further information on backlist or forthcoming titles please write or telephone:

In the British Isles and its territories, customers should contact:

ISIS Publishing Ltd
7 Centremead
Osney Mead
Oxford OX2 0ES
England
Telephone: (01865) 250 333 Fax: (01865) 790 358

In Australia and New Zealand, customers should contact:

Bolinda Publishing Pty Ltd
17 Mohr Street
Tullamarine Victoria 3043
Australia
Telephone: (03) 9338 0666 Fax: (03) 9335 1903
Toll Free Telephone: 1800 335 364
Toll Free Fax: 1800 671 4111

In New Zealand:

Toll Free Telephone: 0800 44 5788
Toll Free Fax: 0800 44 5789